RIVER'S DESTINY

RIVER'S END SERIES, BOOK EIGHT

LEANNE DAVIS

LEANNE
DAVIS
Raw. Real. Emotional
Romance

This is a work of fiction. Names, characters, places, and incidents are either the product of the author's imagination or are used fictitiously, and any resemblance to actual events, locales, or persons, living or dead, is entirely coincidental.

River's Destiny

Contact Information: dvsleanne@gmail.com

Publishing History First Edition, 2018

ISBN: 9781941522585

River's End Series, Book Eight

Edited by Teri at The Editing Fairy (editingfairy@yahoo.com)

Copyediting: Jeannie Brooker

In memory of Tyler
So many summers of you and your family at the property.
So many years our friend.
You were taken far too soon, and far too unexpectedly.
We will miss you every single summer,
and especially on all those fishing and camping trips that you
should be part of.
But in our hearts, you will always be there still.
We will miss most those quiet, little "Tyler" statements that left us
laughing for hours.
I'm so sorry you are gone.
Fish on, dear friend.

CHAPTER 1

~YEAR 10 FROM START OF SERIES~

STARS SHONE OVER THEIR heads like a black blanket covered in silver dust. Cami Reed tilted her head back, staring up and up and up. The universe went on forever. Then she lost her balance and started to fall back... and back... She expected the jarring thud of her landing on the ground, but instead, she was suddenly upright after being caught by Charlie Rydell. His arms circled behind her and supported her. She giggled at his catch and tipped forward long enough to regain her balance. They stood there, staring at each other, gazing into each other's eyes before her giggle started to fade. Her huge grin started to dim.

What was this?

Charlie kept staring at her and she at him, but they weren't letting go of each other or blushing or stuttering at the suddenly odd and intense exchange. Rarely did things become awkward with them. They were best friends. They laughed and joked all the time. They made fun of their parents and all the people who worked at the ranch. They boldly mocked and ridiculed the people they saw at school.

They weren't very popular with the rest of the students and only had each other to make it through those awful years.

That's why, of course, they attended the Senior Prom together earlier tonight. And now, they were standing in a field up in the hills above Charlie's ranch. His family owned and operated a thousand-acre ranch that spanned most of the town of River's End, a tiny hamlet in eastern Washington State. It was mainly horses and farming, with plenty of orchards and alfalfa pastures.

Today, she allowed her stepmom, Kate, to do her hair and makeup since she rarely bothered. Braided tightly, her hair was swooped up in the back before cascading in a cushion of curls. Lots of hairspray and makeup were professionally done and perfected to appear like she wasn't wearing any makeup at all. Her black dress was long, and it dipped down her back. Being small-breasted, she wore no bra and her perky breasts were firm enough that they did not need the support. She wore heels, which pinched and hurt her feet, so she quickly ditched them about five minutes after they arrived at the dance.

All she had to show for the experience were some pretty pictures her dad and Kate, as well as Charlie's dad and step-mom, Erin, had taken. Proms made all the parents so happy. Far more than she felt going to one. It was the only dance she ever attended in high school.

She hated her years at high school. So did Charlie, but for different reasons. This was her senior year's last dance, so everyone wanted them to go, and so, here they were. Hanging around the dance for an hour, they took the more formal pictures and said hello to a few friends before they left, driving back towards the ranch.

They swiftly bypassed it and disappeared into the hills above it. A maze of endless dirt roads cut up and across the hills and mountains, connecting dozens of miles for residents who lived up that way.

There were only a few people. Charlie hadn't passed any other cars and only a random light here and there indicated any residences. They pulled over after going down a long, unused road and parked so they could look down on the Rydell River Valley. The twinkling stars far outnumbered the house lights they saw.

They got out, and Cami was barefoot so she kept tugging her dress up to keep the hem off the dry, packed dirt. They walked around to the front of the car, and she was clutching the bottle of Jack Daniels she'd stolen earlier that night from Kate.

They sat down on the tailgate of Charlie's truck and she uncapped the bottle and downed a long gulp, coughing and sputtering when it hit her taste buds. With a loud laugh, she almost spat it out. *Yes, this would help.*

She offered the bottle to Charlie who shook his head no, exactly as she expected. She knew Charlie better than just about anyone else. He didn't drink, smoke, swear, or have sex. Charlie had a 4.0 GPA and was off the charts with his SAT scores. After being accepted for freshman year at a half dozen colleges, he chose Stanford University in California. So far away. She dreaded him going because she had never been on the ranch without Charlie.

But he'd decided. He was extraordinary. Only five percent of applicants got into Stanford and Charlie from their little town was one of them. It was impossible not to be impressed while simultaneously intimidated by Charlie's intelligence. But it also meant he was hardworking and serious and he acted with purpose in everything he did.

She well knew that Charlie Rydell would shake his head politely and decline the bottle. She tilted it up again and let the burning nectar slide down her throat. He didn't frown on it or try to admonish her, and she liked that about him.

He wasn't judgmental and never tried to control, change, or monitor her behavior. Charlie was simply her friend. She was prone to drinking and breaking the rules so having Charlie around often helped her stay out of trouble. Although it didn't always work.

Sitting there, they stared out over the valley, content to be together. Charlie eventually turned his truck back on so the music could play. They talked some more, and she drank until she stared back at the stars.

Now however, Charlie just held her and wouldn't let her go. She had no idea what to make of it. He kept a tight hold on her. She became acutely aware of his hand on her bare back.

She was very short, but Charlie wasn't too tall, so their height difference was comfortable. Their bodies matched somehow. His hands slid down towards her waist and he stood nearer to her while bringing her closer to him. Middle-to-middle. Almost confused by his touch, Cami became completely immobile.

She recognized that move from other guys, but was shocked when Charlie did it. He didn't behave like typical guys. He wasn't like any other guy she knew. They all tried to cop a feel or kiss her, but not Charlie. He'd always been different.

Her breath hitched and through the haze of her buzz, she slid her hands around his shoulders. He held onto her, his hands pulling her more to his front. She could feel him, but it was gentle and tender. Nothing about Charlie was ever loud or demanding.

The music played an oldies song that was slow and reminded her of her mother. She was a woman hardly anyone had very good memories of, but Cami still had a few and her mother's love of oldies was one of them.

He held her tightly against him. Relaxing, she rested her head on his chest. It felt so nice. Charlie's chin was resting on top of her head as they swayed to the music. The song changed three different times before Cami finally lifted her head. His hands slid back up to the bare part of her back and felt clammy. Was it caused by nerves? Between Charlie and her? They had been hanging together for the past five years. What was going on?

"Charlie?" Her voice wavered, and she felt odd. How could they suddenly be exchanging confusing signals? They never did that. They were friends, the best of friends. They were...

"Yeah?" His tone was as soft as hers. She licked her lips. His hands were around her mid-back, touching her bare skin... and he didn't seem as friend-like as before. Nervous energy churned her insides. What was this? Did she want it? It was Charlie. They didn't touch like that. They didn't hold each other. They also didn't wear pretty clothes or go out like this either.

"What? I mean... maybe we should get back. Don't want to miss curfew. AJ threatened me if I did it again, he'd set me on the curbside with my bags packed."

"AJ wouldn't do that. Besides, he trusts me." Her dad didn't have custody of Cami until she was thirteen, after her mom died and the state managed to locate him. Although he'd been very good to her and she cared about him, as well as his wife, Kate, she had a hard time calling him *Dad*. Perhaps because that ship had already sailed. She and authority figures clashed quite often, which ended by creating dysfunctional relationships.

"AJ would so. He's determined to make me behave. I can't

be a screw-up." She giggled. "Although the half bottle of Jack Daniels probably isn't what he expected tonight."

"Like you ever did what he expected." It wasn't the words he said, but the way Charlie's mouth suddenly dropped down closer to her face. And his lips nearly grazed her skin.

She stared up at him, her throat burning dry. "You and he wish I would behave better, huh?" Her tone was flippant, but she fastened her eyes on his, which made it sound heavy, unsure, and confused.

He leaned closer. Her head felt light. What was he doing? Why? He was holding her. Touching her was a rare event to begin with, but so closely? And what about the odd timbre to his voice? She wasn't sure what to make of it. "I'm not your father. I don't wish anything like that."

"Wh—what are you doing?" she whispered as his mouth began hovering over hers.

"I'm kissing you, Cami."

She stared up at him, unsure if she should say something. Charlie was never like that. He was not a direct or take-charge kind of guy. He had zero experience with girls. Went on a few dates, but nothing more. Cami was sure he'd never done more than just kiss a girl. Two girls, to be exact.

But now he was telling her what he intended to do, and his words made her face heat up while her breath stalled. She had sex long before she ever met Charlie and with several partners. Well, at least more than two. But not Charlie.

He was her friend. Her *best friend*. She'd always been teased and harassed in school. She was never one to fit in with the River's End locals. Not even now. With only three more days left of school before graduation, she was so anxious to leave it, she could not wait.

But at the ranch, the Rydell River Ranch that was owned by Charlie's dad and his uncles, she was unconditionally accepted and cared for. No one said she was different or acted like she was anything but what she was. She was never bullied or made fun of. She was safe there.

And the key reason was Charlie, who had always been there for her. He took her under his wing the first summer when she showed up and the two of them had been inseparable ever since. He was quiet and reserved in school, with little interest in the animal care or working around the ranch. He was so unlike the rest of the men in his family. He felt destined for a future that was far more unordinary and interesting than this rural valley or farming.

But despite all of that, Cami and Charlie became friends. The best of *friends*. What was he doing now by saying he intended to kiss her? They never kissed before. *Never*. She didn't know how to kiss Charlie. It would have been awkward to say the least and…

His lips touched hers. She stood stock-still with her back rigidly upright and her eyes wide open. What was this? But all at once, it became different. He leaned over her and dipped down to fit his mouth better on hers. His hands cupped her face and her eyes fluttered shut when his lips moved over hers in the gentlest, softest kiss she could have imagined. His thumbs rubbed her skin in a soft caress.

Her arms crept up around his neck and she pressed herself closer to him, going up on her tippy-toes until her lips reached his. His hands let go of her face and he drew her closer as his mouth opened over hers. He seemed to sip on her lips and tongue in a soft and gentle swordplay with his.

She was shocked when a *zap!* of feelings and nerve endings suddenly rushed through all of her senses. She didn't expect to like it so much. She also didn't expect for Charlie to suddenly dip his head down and plunge his tongue fully inside her mouth. In response, she reciprocated with as much force as he used.

They silently moved around each other with their mouths

fused and their tongues melding together. Everything she thought she knew about being kissed fled, along with everything she thought she knew about Charlie.

She pulled back, breathing hard, her blood warming and her body turned on. She stared at him with her eyes wide in surprise. "Why did you do that?"

"Because I've wanted to do it for years."

"Years?" she pushed back from him. "Is that why you've been pretending to be my friend? You were just hoping to have sex with me eventually?"

"No. I was your friend because I like you. I wasn't planning to get anything from you. And somewhere along the line, I guess I fell in love with you. You were just usually too busy for me, dating someone else or trying to."

"So… why tonight?"

"We look so good together. School's ending. Maybe it felt like the time had finally arrived for us." His shoulders twitched. "But if not, then I guess I'll be gone to college soon anyway."

Her eyes grew huge and she completely extricated herself from his embrace. Staring out over the valley, she began rubbing her arms at the chill his last words caused in her. "What? Are you saying that if I don't like you back, we aren't friends anymore?"

"No. No, of course not. We'll always be friends. I just feel a lot more for you now and I guess, I just wanted you to know that. You have to decide what you want to do about it."

"Me? You think you feel…"

"I know you better than anyone else. It's not a matter of thinking, but of knowing."

"But…" she started to pace before she stopped. Her gaze found his. "But what if it doesn't work? It could ruin us too. I mean, I can't lose you, Charlie. I can't risk that. I have to have you in my life—"

"Why? Why do you have to have me, Cami?"

"Because..." her thoughts instantly scattered. There was no one reason why, but he couldn't leave. He was the one she always called when AJ or Kate pissed her off or tried to get too close to her. She found their efforts too hard to return. He was the one she always looked for after school when she needed to vent about the mean-girl treatment she received, or when she felt she had to get away from the ranch.

She always took him with her to go anywhere. Whether they hid up in the hills and partied with the other school kids or just to be alone. Charlie always made sure she was okay. And she liked to think she did the same for him. She could make him stop being serious and quiet. She knew how to drag him back into real life.

"Because I can't imagine spending even a single day without talking to you. Needing you. Laughing with you. You make me feel normal, and I've never felt normal before. No one else does that for me."

He reached forward, setting his hand on her arm and drawing her to him until their foreheads touched. "You do the same for me." His lips dropped down and pressed on hers again. Just a soft sliding of his lips over hers. "I love you. We're not kids anymore."

That sent a shudder through her spine. It was easier when they were kids because then, she could blame her bad judgment on their youth.

The thought of being eighteen and suddenly getting thrust into the category of adulthood didn't exactly thrill her. She wasn't ready for that yet. Adult decisions and the idea of graduating from high school were major events in her life. The one guy she always liked and relied on was Charlie.

But how could she not love Charlie? It seemed so obvious. After all these years, and all the days they spent together, which amounted to hundreds, they always sought each other out first, above everyone else, even their own parents. After the River's End fire when her house and belongings had burned, Charlie held and comforted her. AJ and Kate tried to offer their solace, but Charlie was the only one she trusted. She always trusted him.

Her stomach knotted, and heat flushed her neck and cheeks. She could hardly raise her eyes to meet his, since this was such a new phenomenon for them.

And that kiss. Her entire body was still tingling and her stomach fluttering. All at once, he even looked different to her. He was slender with a small frame and a shock of red hair that set off his bright blue eyes and countless freckles.

"Cami? Am I wrong? Did I read this all wrong?"

She sucked in a deep breath and tears filled her eyelids. She finally turned to him, and slowly nodded before her entire face blossomed like a flower when she smiled. "No. No, I don't think you are."

He stared at her, looking almost stunned, which would have made her smile if they were their normal selves. She would have teased him for saying one thing and being floored that she felt the same. She would normally tease him for making all the right moves and getting what he wanted before he froze up.

But they weren't that Charlie and Cami anymore. Not now. Maybe never again. They were both different. Yet the same. They were still friends. Yet Cami was feeling new things, like being turned-on, and other wonderful things she never felt before.

"You think, you might feel something back for me?" His tone was incredulous.

She pushed on his upper arm. "First you kiss me like that, and now you don't know how I feel?" Tears rolled down her cheeks and she brushed them away. "Come on, Charlie, you know me better than anyone else. You *know* me..."

His face suddenly burst into the biggest smile she'd ever seen. He grabbed her just as quickly and she held on, laughing and crying. At the same moment, her stomach fluttered with butterflies when Charlie spun her around.

He kissed her again, long and hard, using his tongue and lips until he set her back on her feet. His gentleness returned to his touch and he cupped her face, holding it up to his. After smooching her again, he whispered, "I didn't think you'd feel the same."

She nodded, gripping his hands with her own. "I think I always did. But if we went there, too soon or too young, we could have screwed it all up and I never wanted that. But we're graduating now. We're no longer kids. We can do this, Charlie. Us. You and me. Against the world."

He smiled, staring dreamily into her face. She knew her eyes were glistening with all the hope and love that was rapidly filling her. "You and me against the world. It's always been that way, and now it can be forever."

"Forever," she echoed as he hugged her. Burying her face against his chest, she noticed that even their breathing fell into sync. As compatible as their personalities and friendship were, why not their love? Why not have everything she always dreamed of? She'd yet to have any of it in her life, but maybe she was finally ready for it.

CHAPTER 2

$\mathcal{C}$HARLIE HELD CAMI'S HAND for a long moment
before he let go. It was minutes from her curfew
hour and he knew better than to violate it. Cami was noto-
rious for being late and unaccountable. She spent half her life
grounded for one minor offense or another. Most of them
were easily avoidable stunts, like being too late or not calling
home. She drank and smoked and sometimes added getting
high to the equation, although how often AJ and Kate realized it, Charlie wasn't sure.

Whenever Charlie was involved, she usually arrived
home on time, sober, or like tonight, pretending to be. They
trusted him to keep her on the straight and narrow path,
although no one could really manage to keep her from doing
anything.

Charlie couldn't understand Cami's insatiable need to
constantly test AJ and Kate. It was endless, all the time, every
week. Cami began living with AJ when she was thirteen. She
was just six months older than Charlie and in the same
grade. They slowly warmed up to each other that first
summer because there weren't any other kids their age so

they naturally formed an easy friendship. That was the same summer Charlie learned Kate was actually a long-lost sister of Charlie's dad and therefore, his aunt.

Kate was the only reason Cami stayed, although she ran away once. Kate was the one who figured out where Cami ran off to and went after her. Kate gave Cami the assurance that someone was actually capable of understanding her.

Cami was bullied at school quite often, owing to her style, her quiet reserve, her rebellious look, and general indifference toward everyone. She hated school. Charlie didn't love school too much either. He wasn't popular or well liked, not like his brother, Ben, was. He was quiet and studious, which failed to draw the right kind of attention. Their shared hatred of school was what first bonded Cami and Charlie.

They settled back into the truck he borrowed from his dad for tonight. It was a big, shiny, black truck, all cleaned up for the Senior Prom. She scooted in and adjusted her dress. He started the truck, his heart still hammering. They exchanged a smile as the dome light lit up before it dimmed after Cami slammed her door shut.

He couldn't believe what was finally happening. He made his move on Cami. How many sleepless nights had he dreamed of this, only to choke at the last minute? Now he finally did it. He imagined it happening in dozens of different ways. From super smooth pick-up lines and romantic opportunities to totally screwing it up.

But tonight, all dressed up under the stars, listening to loud music, it finally felt like the perfect moment. The perfect moment to tell Cami that his friendship and feelings for her went far deeper than he had ever revealed before.

"Do you think our families will be surprised?"

"In some ways, yes. On the other hand, they might wonder why it took us so long to admit it."

"I think... I think AJ will be happy."

13

"I hope so."

They pulled into her driveway after spending those heavenly minutes up on the mountain. AJ and Kate owned the land directly across the road from the ranch. In all the years Cami had been living at the ranch, she had not quite adjusted to the fact that she had both a home *and parents*. Parents who truly cared about her.

Charlie put his truck into park. Taking Cami's hand as she came around the front of the hood, he watched her lips tilt up before her gaze dropped in a surprisingly shy glance at him.

She wasn't used to him holding her hand.

He wasn't used to doing it either.

They walked up to her front porch. "This feels... kinda odd."

"It's going to take a little while to get used to the change," he agreed.

His headlights shone on them. He should have clicked them off, but hadn't thought of it, although now he knew he would remember in the future.

He stepped closer to her and her eyes widened as her head tilted back. With his hands around her waist, he tugged her closer as he leaned down and brushed his lips over hers in a quick and easy movement. So easy. He had to give Cami plenty of time to get used to this. She was so skittish with everything and suspicious of everyone. Even Charlie after all these years. He was the closest she came to trusting anyone. Her miserable childhood left a deep scar on her sense of safety.

Naturally shy and quiet with anyone she didn't know, she never could muster the necessary inner strength required to deal with all the upheaval that surrounded her. By the time she came to the ranch and finally had two *stable* parents, it was almost like Cami had PTSD. The lasting effects impeded her willingness to accept her new reality as it actually was.

After he lifted his head, she blinked, and a small smile lit up her face. She touched her lips with her fingers. "Charlie? What happens next? How do we do this?"

"I'll call you. Tomorrow."

"You always call me tomorrow." Her brow wrinkled.

He gave her a half smile. "Well, now I'll call you as your boyfriend." He took her hands in his and squeezed them. "We'll figure this out. Together. I don't have an answer yet, but I know I care about you *and* want to kiss you... so we'll just have to figure it out."

She nodded, but her gaze was apprehensive. "Okay."

"Okay." He smiled again, feeling the heat rushing over his cheeks.

"It was... magical tonight. I never expected to experience that. Not at the Senior Prom. I thought I didn't care about such things. But with you beside me, I did."

He leaned forward and touched her lips again with a soft kiss. "Me too." Pulling back, he peppered little kisses to her ear. "Just don't speak directly to your dad and Kate. They'll smell the booze."

She nodded. "Oh, yeah... right."

Then they could only grin at each other until they heard thumping on the other side of the front door. He immediately dropped her hands and she reflexively stepped back. When AJ opened the door, they stood like they normally did.

AJ was a massive guy. He was extra tall and about as wide, maybe not literally, but enough so that Charlie had a healthy respect for him. AJ worked as the foreman on his family's ranch. Technically, Charlie's dad employed him, but lately, AJ worked for himself. He had almost complete autonomy at the ranch to do whatever needed to be done on his own schedule. AJ was already considered part of their family, but it became a reality when he married Kate Morgan, Jack Rydell's half-sister.

"Right on time, as always. I love it when she's out with you." AJ beamed at Charlie, who fought to ignore the stab of guilt he felt. For the first time, he placed his hands on Cami in ways AJ didn't know about, nor would he want to know. But AJ would soon have to learn about it since Cami was eighteen, soon to be nineteen, and he had to realize they were very much ready for this relationship.

Several things about Cami were still childlike. She seemed lost and unsure with anything new or difficult, and AJ often felt the strong urge to shield her. Not only from being bullied by other kids her age, but even the people at the ranch.

But on the flip side, Cami expertly tried to shield AJ from knowing all the underage drinking she did, or how frequently she skipped school or broke the rules in general.

"I always try to be on time. I should get home now. Dad will be looking for me." AJ nodded and smiled at Charlie as he turned to leave.

"Call you tomorrow?"

"Okay," she said, her cheeks flushing, both from what she drank and the recent change in their relationship status. She wasn't known for keeping her cool, so it would be a matter of time before everyone in the valley knew about them. That is, if she didn't get grounded for drinking tonight.

Charlie left her place and pulled into his house about forty seconds later. Originally, Charlie was living with his brother, Ben, his dad, Jack, and his dad's three brothers. After Dad met and married Erin, they built the house on a piece of land closer to the river.

The house was an A-frame with two wings off each side. The front was all glass and the magnificent view spanned to include the pines, the river, and the mountains. The original farmstead possessed a more sweeping and majestic view, but that house had tragically burned up in the fire.

The fire. That was how anyone who lived through the fire of a few years ago remembered it. How they lived their lives today stemmed from that one single night of tragedy.

After the fire, his dad seemed to have completely lost his way. Disillusioned, his spirit was broken, and he appeared unable to handle much. He succumbed to a nearly debilitating depression for close to a year.

Charlie noticed the changes, of course. He grew quiet and stayed out of his dad's way. Charlie had always lost himself in books and schoolwork, but he did even more so during that time. He also chose to spend all of his spare time with Cami. He feared that after her mobile home had burned, she might just move away. However, AJ and Kate rebuilt their house and so his best friend in Cami didn't leave.

The fire also brought about the relationship of Hailey Starr with his dad's youngest brother, Joey. Significant to Charlie was that she had two kids, and that also provided Charlie and Cami with built-in friends: Brianna and Jacob Starr.

The Starrs lived permanently in the Puget Sound area, approximately four hours away from River's End, but spent a lot of vacations and summers on the ranch. In fact, they were due to return to the ranch next week to spend the entire summer there and everyone knew it would be awesome.

One last summer before their *real lives* began.

Erin turned at hearing Charlie enter, setting down the hardback book she was reading beside her. With an almost ridiculous reverence, she reluctantly set any books she was reading down. She read only hardbacks and never balked at the expense of any of her books because they were more valuable than gold to her.

Having been illiterate until she was thirty years old, she

only found out then that she suffered from an undiagnosed and untreated learning disability called dyslexia. Watching her read for pleasure was still surprising and uplifting to Charlie. "Hey, Charlie. How was it?"

He walked in and flopped down on the opposite end of the couch. "It was good."

"Really?" Erin's eyebrows rose in curiosity. She knew how much he didn't like school, more specifically, the people his age who attended it. Not to mention that the teachers often insulted his intelligence by dumbing down the material or treating the students like small children.

"Really. We stayed for an hour and went up in the hills. Staring out over the valley, listening to oldies."

Erin sighed. "An hour, huh? Not exactly worth the cost of the tux rental and dance fee. But you had fun?"

"We always do." He leaned back, crossing one leg over the other.

"Uh huh. And Cami? She behaved?"

"As much as Cami can manage to..."

"AJ's got his hands full with that girl." Erin muttered. "I'm always grateful I never have to monitor your comings and goings like they have to with her."

"Well... she's not that bad. You know, she's my best friend."

"Then, as you're always telling me, why does she violate the rules so damn often?"

"You're right. I do say that." He shook his head and Erin's gaze remained sharply focused on him.

"Why does your tone sound so different?" Erin sat up straighter. "Did something happen? With... with you two?"

Charlie cleared his throat. Erin entered his life when he was already eight years old. He couldn't remember his real mother and Erin had eventually assumed the role of his mother. He never called her that, however, although she and Ben were *friends.*

To Charlie, she was not classified as a friend. She was his parent, and the parent that he felt closest to. His dad and he occasionally clashed because they were very different. Ironically, he and Erin were very similar in their personalities.

Jack was all rancher, farmer, and horse trainer. He had to run the ranch entirely on his own until his brothers were old enough to help. He also was tasked with raising his family, and all on the back of constant physical labor.

But Charlie? He was studious and quiet from an early age and didn't like physical work. He helped out whenever he was assigned any chores, but he personally had no interest in ranch management or any of the animals. Having dozens of horses at his disposal, he rarely took advantage of his situation and barely noticed them except as pretty scenery in the landscape.

"Yeah. Something happened."

Her eyebrows shot up. "Um… what, exactly?"

"I asked her out."

"Like on a date?"

"Yeah." He didn't elaborate any further or try to describe all the feelings they shared, much less, his actions. That had to remain totally between Cami and him, at least for now.

"You and Cami? After all these years?"

"Well, I guess we finally felt ready."

"I used to wonder about it, but after so many years went by, nothing happened."

"Now it's happening." He ran a hand through his hair. "Why? Do you think it's a mistake? You seem hesitant."

"It's just Jack and Kate… My only concern is that if things don't work out, you were such good friends. And—"

"And what? You've started it, you have to finish what you were thinking."

"And it's Cami. She's... you know, so emotional. Impulsive. I trust you to know when you're ready but what if she isn't yet?"

"Okay, the Aunt Kate thing is pretty weird. But I can't help it if she came here and somehow managed to hook up with Cami's dad. That was before Cami even knew her dad or started to live here. Besides, we are the best of friends. So doesn't it kind of make sense?"

"You always make sense, Charlie."

He frowned at Erin. "Meaning, Cami doesn't?"

"Well," she shrugged, "that isn't totally off the mark."

He smiled. "No. I get her."

"And this is what you truly want?"

"Yeah, Erin, it is."

She got up and passed him, patting his head before she turned to go to bed. "You know, I only want you to have the best and live the life you deserve to enjoy. Ben had such a hard time over the last years. Your dad and I just hope you have an easier path and make better decisions."

He snorted. "As if that is hard to do," he scoffed. "To act smarter than Ben did?"

Erin shook her head. "You were always hardest on him. He is well aware of all the mistakes he made. And remember, you haven't dated that much. Sometimes unexpected things happen that cause you to do things you normally would not do. So before you get too critical, don't."

"Okay."

"And Charlie?"

"Yeah?"

"Be careful. We adore little Lillian, but we don't need another grandchild, or at least, not yet, not from you."

He shuddered. "Erin... Stop. Besides I'm not..."

She turned and left, sparing him any further words of warning. He glanced around the large, open room. His niece was just three and he doted on her, but it still threw him that his dad and Erin were freaking grandparents at the tender ages of forty-five and thirty-six. Erin had no kids of her own and was substantially younger than his dad, but still, it was hard to think of them as grandparents.

Throwing his tux back onto the rental bag, he sunk down on his bed. His room overlooked the flowing river. He reclined and stared up at the ceiling.

Had tonight really happened? Had it finally happened? He couldn't believe it was real. He half expected Cami to change her mind about him either tomorrow or the next day. What if she thought it could work out, but the reality was she realized they were nothing more than friends? That could happen. He rolled over, trying to ignore the loud voices and all the what-ifs in his head.

That's why he restrained himself from doing anything about his feelings toward her for so long. Now, all he could do was move forward and hope what she said tonight described how she truly felt. Sighing, he tried to force his eyes to remain closed, but they kept flipping open. Excitement? Uncertainty? All of it felt so surreal.

THE NEXT MORNING, Charlie slept in and only got up after reading a while in his most current fantasy story. After downing a whole box of cereal and drinking a huge glass of milk, he got dressed and walked out towards where his dad was working in the barn.

Charlie glanced further up the road at the gigantic, towering arena that was recently completed. It was designed and built according to Ben's idea and inspiration. Well beyond where their original house stood, it seemed so far from the homes and Charlie. He felt ambivalent towards it.

Sure, it was good for the family and provided jobs for them, along with members of the valley community. And it also supplied them with enough money to keep their operations running, including a multiple-acre, organic apple orchard, and a surfeit of horses they trained and boarded year-round. There was also the twenty-cabin resort, and the new restaurant, which was housed in the arena.

Uncle Shane had an auto body shop on the ranch where he restored anything mechanical and also built custom motorcycles. There was a little bit of everything now on their once exclusive horse ranch. Only a decade ago, it was so much smaller and simpler. For Charlie, that was how he preferred it. His dad felt the same way too.

His dad handed the reins of running the resort and arena to his brother, Ian, and his wife, Kailynn. That allowed his dad and Erin to begin working on something entirely separate, different, and totally theirs.

Just like it used to be.

That also seemed to bring his dad back to life, back to being the man Charlie always remembered. So much larger than life. Strong. Dominate. Capable. Yet his dad was also very kind and generous to a fault. He returned to the barn he originally used to train his horses. Along with Ben and several hired hands, AJ took care of the new stalls and the magnificent, new barn that was attached to the arena.

However, none of them dared to approach Jack's personal barn. It was a much smaller and simpler outdoor arena attached to his much smaller barn. Charlie found plenty of comfort in seeing his dad working like he used to during Charlie's early childhood. "Dad? Erin?" he yelled inside the gloomy interior.

"Hey, Charlie, over here."

He followed his dad's voice into the bowels of the building. His dad was currently setting up a new operation to occupy his time. He planned to take abused, neglected, and wild horses to train and rehabilitate for new homes. He hoped the operation would eventually pay for itself and perhaps provide some kind of profit for them as well.

He already made arrangements to rescue and adopt the horses rescued by the BLM (Bureau of Land Management), who captured wild horses for training until they could be re-homed. It paid a nominal amount, but if done in great volume, and being led by such a skilled trainer as Jack, it could theoretically support the cost of feeding and training the horses Jack intended to rehabilitate.

Hot horse breath filled the barn with humidity as they nickered and neighed when Charlie entered the barn. Charlie enjoyed inhaling the earthy scents and hearing the familiar sounds, which were the backdrop of his entire life. A lot had changed during the last decade, but seeing his dad smiling and whistling while he worked with his own horses again elated Charlie. It reminded him of elementary school and when Erin first showed up there.

"Well, look who finally rolled out of bed. Late night?" His dad's tone was warm and good-natured.

He rolled his eyes. "Been up for a while. Just reading. Eating. Why? Did you need me out here?"

"Nope. Erin and I got it already." He paused, rolling his shoulders back. "God, I love saying that. She and I tending our own horses. They are all actually ours, belonging strictly to her and me and no one else."

"Finally. An improvement that turned out to be good for you and what you always wanted."

"Finally." Jack's eyes gleamed as he leaned against the stall near them, peering at Augusta, his favorite horse. He trained her to do all kinds of tricks that were unnatural for any horse to accomplish. Augusta was nearly twenty now.

Jack leaned on the stall next to him, putting his head

through the slats to touch Georgie's neck. "You had fun then last night?"

"Yeah."

"I still can't believe you already attended your senior prom." His dad shook his head. "You ever see the picture of your mom and me from our senior prom? It's in that old photo album in my desk. Check out your mom's bangs. They were so thick and long, but definitely the hottest style at the time. Hard to believe it was almost thirty years ago now."

"I remember that picture," Charlie chuckled. "You looked just like Ben but wearing a bad suit. Seriously odd how much you two resembled each other. Just like identical twins when you and he were both eighteen."

"But you did have a good time?"

"Yes. But I won't miss anything from that useless school."

"Yeah. I'm sorry about that. The school experience around here was never right for you."

Charlie shrugged his bony shoulders. He was several inches shorter than his dad and skinny. His collarbone projected from his too white and very freckled skin. He had a shock of red hair, brighter than either his dad's or Ben's. And he had the most freckles. He looked like the bookworm and nerd he'd always been accused of being, although he wasn't a nerd and resented that classification. "I probably could have tried harder. I just didn't care too much. Didn't like most of the other students anyway. Luckily, I had Cami, Jacob, and Brianna right here. They were enough for me."

"I didn't need a lot of people for friends either. That's how I always was. I had my brothers and you guys, so I never bothered with any outsiders, but well, you see how I lost…" he waved towards the enclosed arena and made a face. "Anyway, Joe told me Jacob and Brianna will be arriving here in a few days. Right after you graduate. I still can't believe you're graduating."

His dad had begun many of those sentimental discussions throughout Charlie's senior year. Nostalgia seemed to hit Jack pretty hard. "I can't wait."

"Neither can I. I think your smarts are totally wasted around here. You, Charlie—you're going places. I can't tell you how proud I am of that. I mean I love you unconditionally, no matter what you decide to do in life. But with that huge brain and your work ethic? Yeah, I'm really proud of you."

Charlie rolled his eyes at the flattery, but the shot of pleasure that jolted through his system was real. No matter how hard he tried to pretend that he found his dad's pride in him utterly lame, he didn't. It meant everything to him. He knew his dad was severely disappointed in Ben's path in life and where it led.

After eloping with a girl that no one liked only a year after he graduated, Ben couldn't even give their dad the pleasure of witnessing it. Then, on the night of the fire, Ben cheated on her before he ran away. His wife, Marcy, died in the fire. But a baby was also conceived and eventually, Ben and long-time friend Jocelyn worked it out, and chose to stay together.

Now Ben had a child to raise and he still worked at the ranch. That was his sole future. No choices about it. No dreams to try to fulfill. No experimenting with other lifestyles. No acting out. Ben went from one immature relationship to another.

His dad had often expressed his hopes privately to Charlie, doing so many times over the last two years, begging him to be different. He told him to wait to get married and have kids. To experience the world first. But most of all, Jack wanted both of his sons to attend college, and take advantage of the freedom and independence he, himself, was never offered. It was something he could provide for Ben and Charlie.

Ben's subsequent rebellion in many ways was the reason why he was now stuck on the ranch and living the same life-style that Jack lived. Jack often explained that it was the best route for him, and he had no regrets, not even now, but he wanted his sons to have so much more. To experience something new and different.

His dad didn't actually say it, but Charlie understood that his hopes were now fully invested in Charlie.

That's why Charlie hesitated before he mentioned the change in his relationship with Cami. At least he wasn't getting married anytime soon, and definitely not having a baby. For those reasons alone, he hoped his dad would stay calm and sane about the change in their relationship status.

"So, did Erin mention what happened last night?"

"Not really. Why?"

Out with it. Be direct and act confident or his dad would assume he wasn't ready for a change in their relationship. "Cami and I just started dating."

His dad gripped the boards of the stall with both of his fists. "Huh? Oh. Wow. Okay. So you're like..."

"Do you want me to draw a picture for you?"

"No. It's just... I consider her my niece, you know—"

"Well, I never considered her my cousin. I didn't even meet her until I was twelve years old. And she's not blood-related."

His dad ran his hand through his hair. "Right. But what if something goes wrong? We still employ her dad and Kate is my sister. Charlie, it could have real and lasting conse-quences."

"I didn't choose to do it lightly."

"Do what?"

Charlie rolled his eyes. "No, I'm not sleeping with her. I

meant, I told her how I felt about her, and she told me she feels that way too."

"How do you feel? Can you describe it to me?"

"I'm not Ben. I know what I feel. I know what I'm doing. I don't let my emotions control me. But I do love her. I thought long and hard about when to tell her."

His dad visibly swallowed. "I know. You're solid as the earth and just as reliable. I just hate to risk the chance that your enduring friendship could become tarnished. And the relationship between AJ and Kate is also important to me and all of us, actually."

"That's why I waited so long to admit it. It's pretty important to me too. I didn't do this just because she was dressed up so pretty last night. I planned it. For close to a year. But I told her last night because I knew it would make it much more special for her. She hasn't had a lot of special things in her life, like taking center stage in someone else's life and being sincerely cared about."

"Well… I… Damn. Apparently, you've already put more thought into this than I did with Erin or Ben did with Jocelyn or even Marcy. I mean, we were—"

"Awful at it? Really, you both were. And it hurt Erin and Jocelyn. You both made them cry and not believe you guys when you said you loved them. Me? I tried to make it special. It was all about her. Exactly what I knew she would like."

His dad pressed his lips together to stop the bittersweet smile of obvious regret. "Okay, yeah, you got me. You way outdid me, and I was freaking thirty-five years old with Erin. I certainly didn't wait until she was dressed up all pretty and, we were in a nice, romantic spot—"

"So give me some credit. This isn't any fling, or a whim. It's also no mistake."

His dad straightened up and nodded. "You've always been light years ahead of most in your maturity at whatever age you were. I respect your decision because you've done it as an adult and you can handle your shit. I have to tell you though, I think that's what I'm most proud of."

Charlie nodded his response, eagerly accepting his dad's unending praise. "Let's hope AJ sees it like that, but I doubt he will. That's my next stop."

His dad patted him on the shoulder. "I was sorry Erin didn't have parents, for her I mean, although it made it hella easier for me. Good luck."

Erin came up on the tail end of their conversation and swatted him as Jack slung his arm over her shoulders with visible warmth and ease. "Listen to you two. Handling your awkward stuff with maturity and no yelling."

Jack nodded. "I finally grew up." He grinned, and she shook her head. "But you know you loved all the drama between us. Remember how exciting us finding each other was…"

"It was something, all right. Anyway, I'm glad you told him, Charlie."

"Let's hope AJ and Kate feel the same way."

"Do you think she told them yet?"

He stopped as he was about to open the door. "Cami? Actually confronting an issue with quiet words and mature conversation? If she's not rebelling, then she isn't confronting anything. I highly doubt it. She'll wait for me to say the word."

"At least you know her well."

"I so know her."

He exited the barn and could hear them kidding around as he left. A wave of relief washed over him because there was a year and a half when his dad and Erin weren't inter-acting like that. Charlie started to fear that they might not stay together, and he *needed* Erin. As his mom. Yeah. She was that. It was meant to be. They didn't have to make a big thing out of it. They didn't have to announce it and he didn't have to call her his mom; she just was.

Cami, however, was the polar opposite of Charlie.

Prone to erratic behavior and impulsive responses, she tried the hardest to hide who she really was from her dad. She struggled to remain as quiet and serene as she could manage around him. AJ was unusually quiet, strong, and placid.

Cami wasn't strong. But she wasn't placid either. Yet, she strove to be like that with AJ, trying to become the daughter she believed he wanted her to be. To this day, Charlie never believed that was what AJ wanted, but nothing he said could convince Cami.

Crossing River Road to her house, Charlie knocked and waited. He skipped any phone call or text and just decided to come straight there. Holding his hands in his pockets until the door opened, he saw Cami standing there. She was right back to herself today. Her long, dark hair looked ratty and the jeans she wore hung loosely on her small frame. She was petite, tiny, and nearly doll-like in her appearance. Charlie liked how he felt whenever he was near her. She had a huge smile that lit up her dark eyes and dimpled her cheeks. Her skin tinged in pink as she stared up at him.

"Hey," he said, keeping his warm gaze fastened steadily on her. Last night was taking their relationship to a never-before-experienced level. She wasn't comfortable with the change yet and probably wouldn't be for a while. That's just how she was. No doubt, she would follow his lead, and act the same way he did. Therefore, if he appeared shy, uncertain or odd, she would too. *No.* That wasn't how he wanted them to start out together. With a confident, easygoing, and generally flippant air, this was how they would have to be now.

"Hey," she repeated, her husky voice soft and breathy as she stepped out the door towards him. With his hands on her waist, he pulled her forward, leaning down and setting his lips on hers. It was easy at first and very quick. He pulled back to gauge her reaction and look into her eyes. She raised up on her tiptoes and pulled his head down to bring him closer again.

The energy and heat rose between them and his cool logic fled as her mouth opened against his. They started kissing in a long and passionate embrace on the porch of her house. In broad daylight. The spontaneity took him, and he sensed, her too, by complete surprise. So new. Wow, all of this was so new.

"Charlie? Cami?"

They froze. Lifting his head, Charlie immediately let go of her. They stared at each other for a brief moment and she pressed her lips together before her eyes flashed. She tightened her lips into a flat line and her neck looked strained, as if… *Crap.* They'd been caught.

It was AJ's voice, of course.

CHAPTER 3

*N*OT EXACTLY HOW HE planned for this to go, Charlie squeezed Cami's hand and then turned towards her dad. AJ's gaze drilled straight into them. Arms crossed over his chest, he demanded, "When did this start?"

"Last night," Charlie answered. "I came today with the purpose of telling you."

"But what? You got distracted?" AJ's eyebrows rose, and his tone was challenging.

Charlie smiled, holding AJ's gaze with a strong look of his own. "I'm afraid I did."

"What did you come here to tell me, Charlie?"

With Cami hiding behind him, Charlie reached back and put his hand out, palm up. Cami waited a moment but soon slipped her hand into his. "I came to tell you that I care very much about your daughter, and we've decided to start dating."

"When did you decide? Last night?"

"Yes, last night."

AJ's eyebrows rose higher and his expression was grim.

"Have you told *your aunt* yet, Charlie?" His scathing tone got his point across.

"AJ. We are not cousins," Cami protested, stepping around Charlie, her hand still clasped tightly in his.

AJ pinned his eyes on that. "No. Nope. I didn't say you were. But Kate is Charlie's aunt. By blood. That's true."

Charlie met AJ's cool gaze. "We know that. But is this really such a stretch?" His eyebrows rose up in a tacit challenge. "Or such terrible news? We are still solid friends. I rarely get into any kind of trouble and follow all of your rules. It's not like you don't know me well or my family or what I'm all about. Couldn't it be a lot worse if it wasn't me dating Cami?"

AJ sighed, his shoulders hunching. "It could be worse, I suppose. It's just that I don't really want to see any guy…"

Cami sighed, standing next to him and rolling her eyes while jutting her hip out. "Don't act so old and judgmental. Come on, AJ. I'm not a baby and you can't possibly think I'm not going to—"

Charlie put a hand over her mouth. When Cami got mad, anything could pop out.

AJ's gaze darted from Cami to Charlie and then narrowed in on his hand covering her mouth as she sputtered from behind it. AJ smiled finally. "Huh. Well, looks like you got this handled. Good luck then, Charlie. I just hope you two know exactly what you're doing because a lot of family already exists between us and whatever happens could have far-reaching consequences that could entail a lot more than just you two, right? I hope you see the source of my concerns."

"Yes, sir," Charlie said, nodding and withdrawing his hand from Cami's mouth as she shot him an irritated look. AJ turned and walked back towards his shop. Cami sputtered and shoved his hand away.

"What the hell? Don't ever stick your hand over my mouth to shut me up." Her hands dropped to her hips, punctuating her point.

"You were just about to fling sex into your father's face and only to prove your point. First, we haven't had sex and we aren't having it yet, and second, he's so big, he could squish me with his fingers. Call it self-preservation." Charlie's tone was calm and quiet in contrast to her heated vitriol that had her almost screaming.

Sex. The one word they had never discussed before. They stared at each other and Charlie noticed she was breathing hard. "He has no right to insist that I adhere to something so archaic as his daughter never having sex."

"*His daughter.* It's got to be hard for him to imagine you having sex. Why do you always have to antagonize him? If it isn't AJ, it's Kate or anyone who'll argue back with you and for no real reason."

"Well, I could ask you why you always have to play so nice. You're always a parent's wet dream of a perfectly behaved child who became my boyfriend. Why can't you ever act out? Rebel? Be outrageous and abrasive?"

"Like you?" Again, Charlie responded with quiet and calm. She could fling all the insults. And it wasn't the first time. Usually after she got angry, she eventually apologized for her statements and he already knew she didn't mean any of them. "You spend half your life getting into trouble or grounded or being yelled at. Why, exactly, do I need to do that? Besides, AJ had the same concerns that my dad did. He works for my dad. It's not something he takes lightly, and you already know that. And of course, since Kate and my dad are blood relatives, if we'd known that fact years before, you and I would have been raised as normal cousins—"

"But we weren't."

"No. We weren't. I'm just saying that's why other people are so worried about us becoming more than just friends."

"Maybe we didn't consider this long enough. I mean, if you think this…" Her anger depleted her confidence, and her shoulders hunched forward.

"I did consider this for a long time. For a year, to be exact. And I eventually concluded that I was fine with it. I worked it all out in my head. But it might take others a little while to get used to it, including you. At least, that's what I'm thinking."

Her gaze shot up. "A year? You've been thinking of me like, like *this* for that long?"

"At least that long, Cams."

Her gaze rose to his before it darted away. "I haven't thought of you like that, Charlie. I didn't think of you like that until you said something last night that shocked me before we kissed. And until that second, I never considered us—"

"I know. I feared you might just shut me down last night and we'd have to try and avoid each other for a while, if only out of the inevitable awkwardness. I also feared that we would never feel the same together again because this would drive a wedge between us. I like you, and I developed a crush on you and I worried that you could only see me as your super nice *friend.* Believe me, I thought through every possible outcome before I admitted my true feelings to you."

"And yet… you did it anyway? Why?"

He lifted a hand to touch her cheek, cupping it before letting his hand drop. "Because I believed there could be a chance that you felt the same or could eventually start to feel the same way. And I guess selfishly, I didn't want to be rele-gated as *your friend* for the rest of this summer, or the next year, or for the rest of our lives. I wanted you, Cams. So, I took the one chance."

Her chest rose and fell as if she were breathing heavily. "I —I had no idea you felt this strongly. Thinking about an 'us' or that you analyzed it so thoroughly and for so long. But it's just like you."

He shrugged and stuck his hands into his pockets. "Does it really surprise you? You know how logical I am. How slowly I do anything. How much I over-examine and scrutinize everything. It usually drives you nuts."

Her smile was small. "It does. I can't believe that a teenager could be that methodical. Or that thoughtful. But you are. And yet, I've often wished I could be half as confident and careful as you are. Did you really worry you were risking our friendship?"

"I knew I was."

Her eyebrows dropped. "You took a huge risk. That's new for you."

"After a whole year of consideration and mental debate. Not exactly a wild leap."

"Why last night?"

"Senior Prom? Why not last night?"

She sucked in a breath. "I couldn't sleep last night. I kept thinking about it. The entire night, I kept replaying what you said and the moment when we kissed... and I've never had another night like it."

"That was my intent."

"You're the only person our age who has ever done anything so meaningful and made it all about me."

"I know you feel that way."

Her smile was meek. "You always know what's real. You're confident in knowing all the facts and accepting reality. It's not fake modesty, since you have no ego about it either. I always loved that about you."

"But?"

"But this morning, I've been pacing around, so unsure of

35

what to do now. What do I say when I see you? How should I act? I don't know how to go from being Cami and Charlie, best friends, ranch residents, and inseparable companions to suddenly being, you know, *Cami and Charlie*."

"We can take it slowly. I already figured we would. Why do you think I left you alone this morning? I knew you'd have doubts and start second guessing all of it. You never seem to get that I totally know you. I usually manage to predict your behavior long before you show it."

"You know, going slowly doesn't sound like something I can do at all."

"I know it doesn't. But you were never with anyone who mattered so much to you before or knew you so well." He stepped closer to her, making her eyes widen as he stared into her face. "I watched you date and sleep with guys who shouldn't have been allowed to polish your shoes. I was the one you always ran to in tears, broken-hearted. I was the one you trusted for comfort and love."

She licked her lips. "And all that time you had feelings like this *for me*?"

"All during high school."

"You've never dated anyone else."

"No. Because I knew the one I wanted. You know me well enough or you should. I don't bother with anything or anyone unless it's genuine and real. I liked *you*, Cami, so how could I waste my time with anyone else? Not when you were it for me? Why would I settle for second best?"

She sucked in a breath and color flushed her cheeks. "Because it's a sad state if I'm what you consider *the best*."

"The best in my feelings towards you. It's not rocket science, Cams. There isn't some standard you have to meet before I accept you. It's simply the way you make me feel."

"There were a lot of guys you saw me through. How

could you stand it? I have to admit I never once considered you or your feelings."

"You like the stupid, rebellious, idiotic guys, who do nothing but get you into trouble and never give a crap that they did. You always, always, always pick the wrong guy. The one who doesn't know you or care about getting to know you."

"How could you keep being so nice to me? You should have hated me, not wanted me."

He smiled and set his hands on her waist, drawing her totally against him. "Because I know you. You hated yourself, but I never did. No matter what you manage to do, I could never hate you."

Her eyes dimmed, and her thick lashes shut over them as she dropped her chin down. Being so close, he could see it begin to quiver. "How can you say that? You don't know what I've done or what I might do. You know, there's no telling with me."

He tightened his arms around her. "I know what was done to you. *I know.* Just believe me when I say there is no way I could ever hate you."

Her throat vibrated, and her eyes filled with tears at the sincerity of his words. "You're saying no matter what I might do, I can trust you to stay with me no matter what happens?"

"No matter what. Forever. Yeah, I can promise you that."

"You know I can't promise that to you. I don't know how I could accomplish such a task. I don't know how to start." Her head shook. "I'm completely inadequate for this relationship. I don't deserve you. You are so together and whole and sure, and I'm... not. Charlie, you are grossly out of my league."

"And you still think too little of yourself, so you react by picking all the jerks who will reinforce that familiar image of yourself. Of course, you don't know what to do with the first guy who doesn't do that."

Her eyelids blinked until her wet eyes dried up. She sucked in a deep breath. "Anyone would underestimate how strong and confident you are. Are you sure this, I mean, me, are you sure that I am what you want? You know, I'm not always... okay."

"I think we can work it out together."

She took in a breath. "I am so scared."

"I'm not. We complement each other."

"Why aren't you feeling weird about this? Not at all? It's really odd and people are going to find it odd and—"

"Take a slow, deep breath, Cami." He pushed his hand into her hair and cupped the side of her face. "We'll proceed one moment at a time. We'll figure it out together. That is, if you want to. That's the only thing that matters in all of this. If you want to be with me in this way and you ask me inside your house, then maybe... what? We could watch TV for a while or walk down beside the river or... do anything. *Anything.* Don't you see how easy this can be?"

Her head shook against his hand and she licked her lips. The former panic in her gaze started to recede. "I do. I want you to come inside the house with me."

"See? It's not too hard. No need for alarm. It's nothing we haven't done before."

"Except... we can touch now?"

His lips twitched. "That's something I'd be interested in pursuing."

His wry tone made her giggle. "It makes me kinda nervous. With you. I don't mean to insult you."

"It doesn't insult me. It's just new."

"New. Right. Okay, then do you want to come in and... and..."

"Let's just go inside." He leaned down and kissed her lips before he added, "I could get used to that."

She smiled. "I could too."

They linked hands and entered the house where he already spotted his Aunt Kate. She'd been peeking out and watching them for at least half of the conversation. No doubt AJ either texted her the news or went around back and told her.

Kate, being far more diplomatic and progressive than AJ, chose not to interrupt them. She was in the kitchen when they finally entered. It was a small, two story house. Three bedrooms were located upstairs at the right of the entry. The living room flowed into the kitchen, but a wall separated them, so it wasn't totally open.

They entered the kitchen where Kate had her computer set up and a sea of papers surrounding her. She was obviously working. "Hey, Charlie. Cams. Wh—what're you guys up to?"

"Going upstairs," he said, grinning. Testing her.

"No." Kate screeched far too fast and loud. He raised his eyebrows at her reaction.

Cami glared in dismay. "You know."

"Your dad already texted me."

"We can go into my room. We always have before anyway. I'm nearly nineteen years old. I can legally do anything I want," Cami bristled.

Kate started to straighten up. "Well, you're right and you could. Except you live here, we still totally support you, and damn it, Cami, that comes with a set of rules you have to respect."

Charlie set a hand on Cami's shoulder. "You can trust me, Kate. You always have. If anything happened, it would be because we were ready. You know me well enough to recognize that."

Kate quit her staring contest with Cami to glare at him. Her lips compressed as she shook her head in frustration and discontent. "Damn it, nephew. You're always so logical and mature. I've always said that any woman and her parents would be more than lucky to have you date their daughter. I guess I should heed my own advice. It's just the whole me-being-your-aunt thing."

"You are. I'm also not a child anymore. So, I think we can handle that. Or whatever happens."

She nodded, throwing her hands up in the air. "How do I argue with totally sound reasoning? Fine, then go to her room. But be aware, please, that this is our house and we aren't comfortable knowing you two—"

"We just started this, Kate. We're not doing anything for you to be uncomfortable about." Charlie interrupted her.

Kate shrugged. "Okay, then. Just be aware."

"We are, and we do."

They entered her room. Charlie had been going up there ever since it was finished three years ago. Cami decorated the black walls with horror movie posters along with a few heavy metal bands. They were only added for a bit of diversity. It was kind of terrifying to any visitor. Adding to that was the bright red streak of her bed linens. Cami didn't do anything soft or feminine.

She was half-gothic and half-rock star. Her nails were usually painted black and she hid her small, pixie-like features beneath ebony eyeshadows and lipsticks. That was just how *she* was. Charlie didn't have any particular opinion either way about it. She knew that.

"What did you do this morning besides being so calm and put together about this?" she asked. Charlie knew she probably spent her morning pacing with nervous energy. She was anxiety-ridden and hyperactive, constantly moving and fretting, like a ball of raw nerves. And that was on one of her good days.

"I read *Return of the Creators*." She also knew he read hundreds of pages often in a single day. Being a sci-fi geek, Charlie nerded out over anything in fantasy. She detested all of that genre. Charlie always wore jeans and t-shirts, keeping his red hair cut short and his face smooth. He wasn't trendy. He was average, ordinary, and generally, forgettable. She liked that about him. That's just how *he* was.

"How many pages?"

"Two hundred."

"And then?"

"Then I told my dad about us and came over to tell yours. I knew he'd be a pain in the ass with it, and I figured Kate would trust us. I worried you'd either change your mind or threaten to do so when I got here. So," he shrugged, "yeah, the day passed just about how I expected it to."

She dropped her head and started to giggle. "How do you manage to predict it all?"

He stepped closer. "By knowing my girlfriend better than anyone else."

She jerked upright. "*Girlfriend.*" She said the word a few more times. "Wow, that sounds official and so… odd." She licked her lips and stepped towards him, setting her hands on his waist. "I wish you didn't know about my past with other guys."

He shrugged. "I don't care about it. I only care about right now."

"Have you ever had sex?"

"No. You know that."

"You know I have a lot of times." Her gaze reached his before she looked away.

"Yes." He reached towards her and set his hands on her shoulders.

"I want this… I want us to be different."

"Of course you do, because it is, and it will be."

"So that's okay then?"

"Everything is okay."

She shut her eyes and leaned her head against his chest. He put his arms around her. "It is now. I didn't know you were what I needed to make it so, but it feels like this is what I've always been searching for, even though I didn't know anything was missing. You've been right here with me for years."

"We weren't ready before now."

She lifted her face and their mouths were just inches apart. Big-eyed, she stared up at him. "And we're both ready now?"

"Yeah. We are."

She smiled, and he dipped his head down to kiss her lips. Soft and easily, their lips pressed together before long moments passed. She opened her mouth to him and his tongue embraced hers. Her tongue caressed his while her hand slid up and anchored around his neck. He stooped lower and she stepped back as he followed her. She sat and lay back with him coming over her. Their mouths never parted. On and on, they kissed. Their lips twisting and turning, tongues going in and out of each other's mouths, their hands moved with restless abandon over the other, bunching up their clothes or sliding through each other's hair. He rested against her and let her legs cradle him before growing fiercely hard and pushing gently against her core. She raised her hips in response while they kept kissing and exploring.

Finally, with a groan, he lifted his head and buried it into the thick mass of her unruly hair. He knew it would feel just like this. You can't desire someone for years, imagining times like this, fantasizing about it, whacking off to lurid thoughts of her like this without ensuring one explosive feeling.

What might have surprised him, however, was how much she seemed to be into it. As much as he was and just as turned on.

But it wasn't happening yet. And no time soon.

He lifted himself off her and sat up. She had a mirror opposite her bed and he could see his mussed-up hair and his shirt halfway off. He tugged on it as she lay for a moment longer, blinking as she scrambled to sit up. "You're really stopping now?"

He gently adjusted her shirt. He hadn't ventured inside it with his hand yet. Soon. He would. His hand, almost on its own volition, strained to cup one of her small, pert breasts, but he resisted the urge. He promised her to proceed slowly.

"Slowly. This is weird, remember?"

"Yes. But I temporarily forgot it. Don't you ever forget about it?"

"I do but then I remember I'm not going to screw this up. So, wanna play that?" He waved towards her video game console. She was crazy into gaming, something she'd gotten him addicted to. It wasn't something he cared too much about until he met her. Cami was still much more into it than he was and often played half her nights away. He preferred to read books and learn more about life.

She let out a slow breath. "But that's what we normally do."

"Yeah. Isn't that the point? But also, to avoid doing that?" He nodded toward her bed.

She smiled. "Okay, Charlie."

Later, as Charlie came down the stairs, Kate was in the kitchen and he stuck his head in. She turned and said his name. "You know what you're doing?" she inquired innocently.

"I know."

"She… she can be very difficult. She might not mean to be."

"I've been here too. It's not like she's a new acquaintance."

"Right. You're right."

"I know, Kate. I know what happened to her when she was twelve."

She sucked in a breath. "I didn't know if she ever told you or not."

"She did."

"Then you understand her, better than most people could."

"No. Not totally. But I understand what she thinks of herself. I understand the kind of war going on inside her, a war between the good her and the bad her. Sometimes the bad Cami wins."

Kate slid onto a bar stool. She stared down at the counter, looking contemplative. "She can be… oh, God, the sweetest girl. Fragile. Soft. So kind and so in need of love that she could break your heart. You want to scoop her up and protect her, fight for her, fill her with goodness and light to combat whatever darkness she's ever known and suffered from, you know? But then… I suspect you know what happens."

"Yes. I do."

"But there is that other side of her. You… you know that person too."

"When she gets mean and nasty and acts out? Yeah. I've gotten calls from her asking me to walk her home from random guys' houses and then having to stop every mile so she can throw up. Yeah, I know the two sides of Cami."

"Are you sure you're ready to take that on? I don't doubt that your feelings run deeper for her. I'm sure it's real, mature, and very sincere. But she isn't totally as… I don't know the word… as put together, not as well organized in her mind as you are. She still carries a lot of resentment left over from her formative years. It could turn out to be hard to deal with. You should not take it personally if you're involved like that."

"I considered all the obstacles. But I decided to do it anyway."

"How long have you felt like this?"

"Probably always. But definitely throughout high school."

She nodded. "You're unusually mature and thoughtful for an eighteen-year-old kid. First thing that impressed me when I met you. What were you then, like twelve? I remember thinking you might have been more mature and together than Ben was. You still might be." She grinned briefly and continued, her tone softening. "I'm surprised I didn't catch on at the time. I usually do with stuff like this. Anyway, I won't tell you not to care about her. I won't insult you by trying to change your mind. I'll just advise you both to go into this with your eyes wide open. A good relationship is a very welcome prospect from my perspective. But it won't fully eradicate the scarring and damage inside of her. And you could also get hurt."

"Yet, she hurts almost every day of her life. I decided to accept the risk."

"You really did think this out."

"I really did. Most people don't understand Cami. I do. You do. But AJ is still baffled by her sometimes. She needs you and I more than anyone else. I know that. So who better to love her, Kate, than me?"

"You think you're in love with her?"

"I know I am."

"Okay. Then I'll support you two. You knew that already though. It was just startling at first, and seeing you two kiss is... well, strange."

"She's eighteen going on thirteen sometimes. You and I know that. So it's startling and strange to her too."

"And you really can deal with that?"

"Yes."

"What do you get out of it? Do you like to take care of her?"

"I like being the person she relies on and comes to. But I hope as time goes by, she doesn't need me taking care of her as much as being beside her. You know the difference in her from age thirteen until now. She's come a long way, and all because of you, AJ, and…"

"You."

"Yes."

"Damn, kid. You are one-of-a-kind. In the best way possible."

"I feel the same way about her. She doesn't. Maybe with enough time, she will have more confidence in herself… and in me."

"I think she already does. About you, I mean."

"But until she does with herself, we both know it doesn't mean much."

"Yeah. Thank you, Charlie. For being so honest with me and AJ and most of all, with her."

"I'd better go now. Promised Erin I'd help her with some horse stuff. Plus, it's the last few days of school."

CAMI KNEW Charlie was downstairs talking to Kate. She could hear the low murmur of their voices as she stepped forward and then stopped. No. No, she should not eavesdrop on them. She should simply trust them. They were the two people in this world she could always trust.

Even if she never fully did.

She crept backwards towards her bedroom and shut the door. Those four walls were her safety and anchor. This unlit, black hole where she kept the shades pulled down until it looked claustrophobic with all the crap she had scattered around it.

She possessed nothing until she was thirteen and came to the ranch. She came there specifically to meet AJ with no more than a smelly backpack to separate her from the rest of the world.

And now she had Kate and AJ, Charlie, Brianna and Jacob, as well as Charlie's entire family. Now she had so much more. Love? Security? A steady place to live? To Cami, that was pure wealth. Decadence, even.

Yet none of her present wealth and comfort could squelch the anger that was still lodged in her gut. Sometimes, despite her best efforts to subdue the beast, it clawed its way through her chest, climbing up her throat and moving into her head and mouth. It could so easily engulf her heart and eclipse her ability to keep it separate from her healthy, healed parts.

It slowly retreated as the years with AJ and Kate passed, but it never left. Sometimes, it had to come out and reveal itself again.

They showered Cami with love, loyalty, security, and the basis for cultivating healthy relationships. She frustrated herself in asking why that wasn't enough for her to be better, do better, and act better. When the bad stuff popped out sometimes, she knew she was too old to let it happen.

She sat down on her bed.

Charlie.

It was all different now. There was something very fearful about being different. Different was never a good thing for her. This time, she knew it was supposed to be. Charlie was always a positive influence in her life. How could this be any different?

47

He who always approached everything, no matter what it was, with a calm stoicism, a quietness that was comforting to her. He was so placid and unsurprised by anything she did or said, that when she became volatile or explosive, his easygoing, understanding tone of voice, and calm answers to her questions, and even his tolerance of her anger, gave her a sense of calmness too.

He was always first to support her, no matter what it was. A tough day at school. Someone picking on her. Some guy dumping her or treating her lousy. She knew she had terrible taste in boyfriends. So Charlie was a game changer there.

But it felt so odd to touch and then... kiss. Wow, that was... good, but weird. She wasn't sure how to describe it.

He stopped. She'd never known any guy to do that. Slowing. Stopping. Remaining in control. She wasn't sure how she felt about that. Perhaps it was healthy. Normal. And age appropriate. Especially with her parents being in the house. No other guy was allowed upstairs with her alone.

But Cami never practiced self-restraint or healthy activities, let alone, tried to stop herself. She began to kind of like it. But then again, it gave her time to analyze it. To think about it. And notice exactly how it felt. She rarely paused for any of those things.

She spent the morning almost fraying a hole in her carpet by pacing. It was still odd for her to imagine Charlie and her. And how could she face him now?

When the moment finally arrived, she became tongue-tied, speechless, and immobilized in his presence.

And that kiss. Definitely not what she expected from Charlie. He was so good at it. With so little experience. She was slightly bewildered by the heat that brewed and boiled between them.

Heat. Charlie. She was blushing.

She first considered throwing him in AJ and Kate's face.

Why? Certainly not because they were terrible to her. No. They were understanding and kind to her. They talked to her and took care of her, prodding her gently when necessary. They were lenient and tolerant of her friends, especially Charlie.

She went downstairs and found Kate cooking dinner. "I was just going to call you for dinner," Kate said.

Kate and AJ alternated in cooking dinner every other night. Stranger still, the three of them usually sat down and ate it *together*. Kate strictly enforced that rule. She used to see AJ staring at her with a puzzled expression and looking exactly as Cami felt, but still, Kate insisted they do this nightly ritual. It turned out to be something that, if they skipped it, Cami would have actually cared.

AJ walked in just as Cami slipped into the dinner chair at the pre-set table. Kate set the table every night. Real dishes, silverware and napkins. She even poured the damn milk.

Milk. Cami loved milk. She drank two or more glasses per night. It was ice-cold and so refreshing and was another thing she lacked throughout her childhood. Now she loved to drink it by the gallon.

Kate served the spaghetti and garlic bread along with a Caesar salad before she sat down. AJ was washing his hands at the sink.

Kate used to have a high-powered, high-paying job in Seattle. Running her own consulting business, which she now ran remotely, she used to commute back and forth. However, a few years ago, when Cami was struggling particularly hard, Kate stopped commuting and stayed at home to work.

She chose River's End over Seattle.

Cami's cheeks burned with fire anytime she contemplated it. She knew Kate gave up her entire career but not for AJ. No. She married him because she clearly loved him, but

Cami was the real reason she chose to settle down in River's End. For Cami, she became a full-time mother too.

Cami was saved by Kate.

Cami loved Kate like... how could she describe it? Like a mother? Cami didn't know. She doubted she ever loved her real mother. Thinking about Parker now only made her chest tighten and hurt. All the memories that filtered in had nothing to do with love. No, Kate gave her real love.

Kate was clear-cut and logical. She told you exactly what she wanted and expected and then provided all the tools to perform and meet those goals. If you failed, she punished you. If you succeeded, however, she rewarded you.

They were more like "corrections" than punishments. Kate's definition of "punishment" was a joke to Cami. Receiving a lecture and being sent to her room. Having her phone taken away. All of her punishments were centered on trivial stuff that Cami laughed about.

Yeah. That wasn't real punishment.

A coat hanger striking your bare back was punishment. Or a hard fist in your gut. Being deprived of food and water. Those were epic punishments, the kind children don't forget. So, there was a distinct difference in the way Cami's biological mom, Parker, administered punishment and Kate's choices. Cami found it easy to accept Kate's castigations. There was no fear or dread with Kate.

AJ was so big, and unfortunately, his physical form resembled many of her mom's nasty boyfriends over the years. Obviously, her mom preferred a certain type of man and to Cami, they all resembled AJ, which was disconcerting.

It wasn't AJ's fault, and neither was it hers that she couldn't be as close or trusting with him as she believed AJ wanted. But she could be like that with Kate.

Kate was her precious lifeline. Her heroine. Her soft spot. Her champion. Her advocate. Her savior.

It was so complicated and yet, so simple.

AJ sat down at the dinner table and smiled at Cami. "No boyfriend tonight?" His tone was amiable.

It was still an odd sensation to her. Having a boyfriend. Her boyfriend, Charlie. "Are you okay with it? Why the pleasant tone all of a sudden?"

"Because Kate convinced me it's the best thing that could happen if you insist on dating. He's the best choice. So now I'm pro-Charlie." His smile faded. "Ah, hell, don't let that change your mind. Not just to spite me."

Yeah, Cami would do that too. Seeing how AJ already knew and predicted that made her laugh. "I won't this time. Erin wanted him to go home."

"So... you graduate this week. You excited?"

Excited? She had no idea what to do with the rest of her entire life. Despite her general abhorrence toward school, at least she knew she had to go there and what was expected from her. "I'm sort of excited. It'll be strange. I find it hard to realize that I won't go there ever again."

Something she hated. Cami didn't like school, no, but she disliked anything "new" far worse. She needed a routine and the concept of not having anything defined or "pre-set" was much harder for her to picture herself handling.

"Have you thought about what we discussed?"

"Yes. I was thinking about asking Joey if I could work for the resort. I wouldn't mind starting in housekeeping, you know, to show my worth, and not just get assigned a good job because I'm your daughter—"

"As well as the owner and boss's son's girlfriend..." AJ added, flashing her a smile.

"Cute. But I think I'd like to work there. Eventually, I'd be interested in covering the reception desk or activity center or the gift shop."

"You're sure you don't want to look into some kind of trade or specialized schooling?"

"I know it would please you both, but it's not really for me." That was mostly because she never, ever wanted to leave here. This place. The ranch. Her home. Sure, of course, she knew she'd leave their house eventually, but she hoped it would be to move close by. Super close. Like... well... who knew? Maybe someday, she'd live right across the street. Especially considering who her boyfriend was now.

"Well, then, as long as you find some kind of work. You have a few months." Cami nodded, knowing what AJ's lecture would be. They spent most of the last year discussing Cami's graduation and subsequent path in the world.

Adult age brought adult responsibility and all that it came with. It wasn't like they hadn't given her plenty of time to prepare for it. Brave, however, wasn't Cami's best trait and she immediately considered the different avenues of employment that lay right across the street at the Rydell River Resort.

First of all, the commute would be a dream, but the security of staying in a place where she felt safe and comfortable was her primary motivation.

The Rydells hired people for horse-related and farming jobs as well as mechanical maintenance. But now, they also had the giant, enclosed arena with a full-service restaurant inside it. Ben's wife, Jocelyn, ran it and she was a lot like Cami.

Cami had a home and since belonging here, she had no desire to leave it. She'd only lived in it for three years of her life, having occupied more than a dozen homes before she ever came to the ranch.

At least now she had a plan. Her brilliant idea, however, involved talking to Joey Rydell, the brother whom she usually avoided. At the age of thirteen, she snuck into his bed and got on top of him and kissed him. That was when she first arrived at the ranch, dropping like an anvil into AJ's life. That mistake was something she couldn't live down, not even in her own head. Naturally, Joey was also Charlie's uncle.

Sighing, she filed that item away in her mental to-do list for after graduation.

THE RYDELLS, all of them, as well as her parents, attended the ceremony to witness Charlie and her walking across the stage to receive their diplomas. A huge party was to be held afterwards inside the arena. One good thing of owning that damn arena was having the ability to close it down for the party-to-end-all-parties. Cami listened to all the speeches honoring Charlie, occasionally with her name tacked onto them. She understood why. She wasn't the smart, hard-working one. Charlie maintained a perfect GPA and took every single advanced class he could.

When the party finally ended, Charlie lifted Cami's hand and tugged on her, urging her to follow him. She smiled, still startled by their sudden appearance as a couple. He took her towards a stairway that led to the attic of the structure. Emerging from a trap-like door, they were on the roof. There was a flat section which covered the restaurant. They were very high up. It had to be the equivalent of three or four stories in order to accommodate the center peak above the horse arena.

They stared out over the ranch and the valley. Then they looked up at the stars overhead. Forever. Her mouth popped open. "Wow... this place. I can't believe it. The stars... there must be millions of them."

"Ben showed this place to me." Charlie's tone was near

her ear. He wasn't looking up like she was, but directly at her. She felt his gaze on her profile and a smile tugged on her cheeks. "You're staring at me."

"I was thinking how pretty you look. Better than millions of stars."

"That's such a cheesy line."

"It is," he agreed, his arms snaking out to grasp her waist and turn her to face him. His head bent down, and he hovered just over her lips. "Did it work? At all?"

"It did," she said, staring up at him as her heart skipped a beat and she felt breathless. He leaned down and kissed her, long and deep, stirring up as much emotion as the stars overhead. When he lifted his head, she blinked. "What was that for?"

"For how glad you made me at graduation today. Standing beside me, as my girlfriend. If this had happened without you, I'd be scared now, wondering where you and I would go from here. School was a guaranteed place for us to spend every day together. The future is open wide for us now and we get to go wherever we choose. All that stuff about your destiny and dreams... It's really cheesy, but kind of intimidating too. You know?"

"I was thinking that too. Like, what? From yesterday to today, we are suddenly expected to find a profound reason for being here and a definite plan for where we're going? We're supposed to determine what we want to *do* and *be* for the next forty years, or more?"

"Yeah. And it just made me glad I had you beside me. I don't want to lose you, Cami, not ever."

Her eyes surprisingly filled with tears. "Oh, Charlie, you won't. Never. Where would I go? Who else could I ever want to share my life with but you?"

He grinned as he clutched her hands in his. She couldn't

restrain her smile in response. "So, you're used to getting a kiss from me now?"

"I love getting a kiss from you."

"Do you think you could love more than just a kiss from me?"

"Fishing much?" she teased. Then her expression turned solemn. "Yes, I think I could."

Charlie pulled her hand and they went over towards a blanket.

"You planned this?" Cami clapped her hands together, utterly delighted with him.

"Uh huh." He grinned as he revealed a bottle of champagne, two glasses, and food. Chocolate, fruit, cheese and crackers. Her heart thumped hard against her rib cage. No previous guy she dated would have ever shown any consideration for her. Not like this. A rooftop picnic on their graduation night?

She sat beside him as the warm air swirled around them. "You don't even drink alcohol."

"I know, but you do." He sat down and poured it, lifting a glass towards her, and then pouring some out for himself. "And I will tonight. With you."

Her heart skipped another beat as she fell to her knees beside him and took the glass. He held his glass next to hers. "To our graduation. We finally did it."

"Some fared better than others," she answered, raising her eyebrows in a teasing tone. He grinned back. Then she added, "How about toasting to us?" she asked, softly clicking her glass against his as they shared a smile.

"To us? Even better." They drank, and Charlie made a face as he did so. The bubbly libation instantly hit her.

"Where did you get it?"

"From Ben."

"It's not like you."

"Maybe I need to learn some new things."

She set a hand on the side of his face and stared into his eyes. "Don't. Don't change. Don't become like everyone else."

"How's that?"

"Typical. Stupid. I like how responsible you are. And that my parents know you and trust you. I like knowing that I can trust you."

He closed his eyes and sucked in a breath as if her words touched his heart. "Thank you. You can't imagine what that means to me. "

"Why would it mean so much to you?"

He blinked several times. "Because I'm nothing like the guys you usually date. And, let's be honest, I'm not the kind of guy you normally desire. Maybe it's only because you know me, but based on my appearance? And how I act? The 4.0 studious nerd? We both know I wouldn't stand a chance with a girl like you if you hadn't known me from us being kids."

She burst out laughing. There was no dignified answer she could give him except to laugh. Setting her glass down, Cami scooted forward on her knees, taking his face in her hands. "You realize, I hope, that only you think I'm special. And pretty. Only you, Charlie. You have a slightly skewed vision of who and what I am. Thank you for that. But no one wants me. And I always considered myself lucky to have you as my best friend, but even more so, now."

He took her hands and held them tightly in his. "I love you, Cami. I love you so much."

She shut her eyes and a huge smile brightened her face. She leaned forward and touched her lips to his. Lifting her face just enough to speak, she said, "Then show me how people who love each other make love. Because I have no idea how to since I have never done that."

He jerked his mouth from hers. "That's not what I was trying to do."

She leaned forward, still kissing him. "I know that, Charlie. That's why I want to."

He let her kiss him for several long moments as they knelt on the blanket. Then he pushed her back. "What about... things? I don't want this to be like your other relationships. Or the stuff—"

"I didn't tell you all of that just so you could use it against me at a later date," she said softly. "Nor as an excuse why I can't ever be normal. I am normal, Charlie," she insisted with added emphasis to her voice.

He immediately took her hand. "I'm sorry. I didn't mean to treat you as if you weren't. But bad things happened to you..."

"Yes. And you know all about them. It doesn't mean I can't be with you. It didn't ruin me. And wanting to have sex is not some kind of call for help. Don't do that to me. Don't reduce me to some tired stereotype."

"We agreed to take it slowly." He pushed her back. She could see him nearly shuddering as he squeezed her hands, almost forcing himself to keep her at a distance. "I think we should stick to that and not make mistakes. I think we'll get there soon enough. I just want to be—"

"Sure I'm not acting out? Or being a slut? Or going too fast for you?" she retaliated. The wonderful, sweet, amazing, romantic gesture had suddenly completely soured for her.

"No." His reply was sharp and sure. "No, to make sure *I'm* ready. Maybe everything isn't always about you. I'm just not... ready yet. I'd like for it to be with you and when we do, I want it to be good."

She stilled, and her entire body straightened up. He let go of her hands as he spoke and turned his head from her. Oh, crap. She never anticipated that. *It was him.* She thought he had doubts about *her* prior history and poor judgment, having sex for all the wrong reasons. Yes, she had a history. Charlie knew it all. She thought he was coddling her and treating her as if she were damaged merchandise.

No. That wasn't it at all. Turned out, Charlie wasn't ready. Not quite yet. She suddenly grabbed him. He was sitting with his body turned from her, his head down, when she all but tackled him. Grabbing him around the torso, she pinned his arms under hers and pushed him so he fell back at an awkward angle onto the blanket. She peppered kisses all over his face. "You stupid idiot. I thought you were treating me as damaged and broken. If it's just about you wanting to wait, of course, I can understand why and I support that and yes. Yes, Charlie. We can wait and take it slowly."

He finally started to laugh under her crazy onslaught as he tried to ward off her barrage of kisses. Landing flat on his back with her straddling him, he grabbed her forearms to push her back far enough so he could breathe. She stopped laughing too and they fell quiet, breathing hard after the long laughing jag and exertion.

"If we're going to do this, you can't treat me as if I'm something special or broken. I'm not. I had my moments growing up. But you can't treat me like that. That's for Kate and AJ, right? My parents' role. Not my boyfriend's. Can you do that?"

"Probably not now, or today, but I promise I'll learn. It's kind of new for me. As odd as you considered us kissing, I had pictured it in my mind for years. But I also knew… things. And it affected how I consider your opinion of having sex with me."

"Remember, I was broken when I got here. For a few years at least. But I'm not that Cami anymore. If you want to be with me… *me*, Cami Reed, then you have to treat me as your equal partner."

His hand slipped over to her cheek. "I think I failed to give you enough credit."

She shrugged. "It's okay. It happens. Especially with me. But you need to know better."

"Okay, I already know better."

She leaned forward, and they kissed, their tongues entwining as she fell heavily against his chest. When they stopped, she moved to the side of him and they stared up at the stars overhead.

"Makes you feel like the very heart of the universe is offering itself to us, doesn't it?"

He turned his head to look at her. "Yeah, how's that?"

"Young. Healthy. Eighteen. The world is spreading itself open before us. Our future. Our dreams... and God, I hope it's with each other."

"I hope so too."

She sighed, and they held hands, staring upwards. They discussed a few small things. The day. The graduation. Family members and friends. They ate some more. They drank some more. But not enough to make her drunk. The breaking dawn made Cami blink in shock.

They talked all night. Just talked. They could have done anything all night, being up there. They could have had sex a dozen times or gotten really drunk and high. But they just talked. Of course, anyone would never think of that if they found them there. Cami felt closer to Charlie than anyone else she'd ever been with.

"Best night of my life," she whispered as the sun topped the mountain ridge and her eyes blinked some more, still gritty from lack of sleep.

He leaned over, kissing her again. Dozens of kisses and tongue-tangling and hands brushing and touching intimate places and hugging and holding each other tightly. They experienced an intimacy and closeness she never enjoyed with anyone, not even friend-Charlie.

Finally, with contented smiles, they rose up together and started quietly folding the blanket. They gathered the litter of wrappers and empty bottles together and went to the door that led down from the roof. They silently climbed down, peeking around cautiously for anyone. The place was deserted that early in the morning. They shoved their trash into the dumpster behind the building and laughed, holding hands, and grinning at each other. Sneaking off with a little bit of guilt like the teens they were, they proceeded to the ranch.

He walked her to the ranch gate and they embraced. He held her a long time. "AJ isn't going to like the overnight thing."

"We aren't kids anymore. They all have to start accepting that."

"We could tell them we didn't do anything."

"Or we could stop them in their tracks by reminding them that it isn't any of their business and they'll just have to trust us."

They separated after one last long kiss and Cami watched Charlie walk off. They were high school graduates finally. Free from high school and their peers, including the ones that judged them. Now they could *choose* the people who would continue playing a part of their lives. It really was like a do-over. A new start. A new sense of forever.

CHAPTER 4

*C*AMI GLANCED UP TO see a figure hurtling towards her. Luckily, she had a moment to dig her heels in to anchor herself for the sudden onslaught. In the next moment, Brianna Starr was embracing her with shrieks and screams as her brother, Jacob, looked on.

"Oh, my GOD. You and Charlie?" Brianna said as she hugged and squealed and laughed, seemingly all in one breath. Cami cringed and then laughed as she tried to stay upright while also supporting Brianna's tall, lithe body. Brianna shoved her backwards. "Mom told me on the way over here. When? How?"

Gripping Brianna just to stay upright in spite of her body-crushing hugs, Cami replied, "A week ago. Not that long, I swear." She laughed and pushed Brianna back. "Let me breathe."

Brianna had texted they were home and Cami ran down to Joey's house. Joey was Brianna and Jacob's stepdad. Brianna was Cami's age, and only a year ahead of her in school, so she'd already finished her first year of college. Jacob, at sixteen, was in his junior year of high school. He came to River's End for the summer vacation as well as many of their school holidays, and even some weekends, depending on their schedules. Their dad lived in Everett, the city where they were from and where they continued to attend school.

Brianna barely let Cami get into their driveway before she had her wrapped up tightly in her arms. Cami couldn't stop laughing because Brianna looked like she'd been overexerting herself in the gym. High in color and breathing hard, she stared, bright-eyed, at Cami. "So spill."

Cami and Brianna were the least likely girls to become friends. If they'd gone to the same school and encountered each other, they most likely would not have even spoken two words to each other. Cami was part of the anti-social, goth crowd with disdain towards everything and never content with *fitting in*. Cami was sure Brianna must have been the "it" girl at her school the moment she saw her long, shiny, rumpled, blonde hair, perfectly oval face, and sexy, supple body. She dressed in the latest fashions, investing lots of energy into her hair and makeup.

Brianna and Cami met on the ranch, having no one but Charlie and Jacob to hang out with. It was just so. And they accepted how it was. Out of necessity, they spoke to each other when they were thirteen. That was just after Cami moved there full time, and Brianna was only there part time. Spoiled, high-strung, excitable, even annoying in her incessant chatter sometimes, Brianna was also fun, exciting, loving, loyal and sweet. Under her façade of mean-girl, she was really a very caring teen who never intended to actually hurt anyone or anything. Cami appreciated Brianna because she could manage to get Cami out of her own head and shyness.

Brianna was also into things that were more *normal* for

their age. She accepted Cami just as Cami was, something which no other girl in Brianna's capacity would have done.

"Senior Prom night, he suddenly busted out and told me he always wanted to be with me. I was shocked. Like no-words-for-it shocked, and I said yes... and yeah..." Cami sounded blasé, but her eyes still sparked with excitement.

"I always wondered. You two have always hung together, spending hours on end together, trailing each other around this place ever since the first time I met you. I obviously thought so then, but you guys never admitted it. I finally had to assume it was just me. However, it wasn't. You guys have to be more than adorable. I can't wait. I'm so glad I'm back. This will be the best summer ever. I swear. I know it."

Cami followed the still gabbing Brianna while Jacob slouched on the porch. He straightened up and Cami stopped dead. "Jacob?"

His smile was loose and easy. "Hey, Cams." He'd... changed. More than any of them ever had in such a short amount of time. He hadn't been back there since winter vacation, and now, at age sixteen, Jacob was heading into his junior year after growing probably five inches. His frame had also filled out, and his hair had grown darker but the tips of it were still tinged in blond. She blinked. "You've changed."

He shrugged. "I hope I don't look like I'm thirteen anymore." His voice was deeper and his smile, slower, stretching over his face. She blinked and laughed again.

"You don't. Not to worry."

"Come on, Cams." Brianna called after her. She smiled at Jacob.

"She hasn't changed a bit, however."

He rolled his eyes. "No. Brianna is as annoying as ever."

"I heard that." Brianna reappeared in the doorway. "Did you hear about Jacob getting busted for pot last March? Got grounded for two months."

"No. That isn't how you used to be."

"Just holding it for a friend. Dad refused to believe me and of course had to call Mom for advice. Because, you know, he couldn't possibly figure out how to be the bad-cop parent. Still trying to convince us he's Disneyland Dad, like we're still ten and can't see him for what he really is. He's completely incapable of taking care of us or being faithful. Anyway…"

Cami touched his arm as she passed. "No changes there?"

Jacob shook his head, so she went first, and he followed her inside. Brett Starr, cheated on their mom years ago, and lately, Jacob kept harping on that. Why now? After so many years? No one seemed to know. There was little love lost between Brett and Jacob for reasons that went back several years. They were the source of an ever-expanding chip on Jacob's shoulder. Brianna turned a blind eye. She was fine. She was great. Their family was wonderful. Cami wondered what might happen if she ever stopped trying to convince herself into believing that.

"So, do you have access to it then?"

Brianna's eyes popped open as Cami addressed Jacob. "Cami. Not that shit again. I hate it when you do it."

Cami rolled her eyes. "Well, none of you all do. Last person I suspected was straight-A, straight-laced Jacob Starr."

"No more is he either of those," Brianna sighed as she flopped down, glaring at her little brother. "He's rebelling now and pretending its super cool. Never mind that it's all stupid and bound to mess up his future for no damn reason other than to prove Dad wrong."

"Dad's an asshole."

"He's also the only one we got."

Jacob ignored her and addressed Cami, "I might have access—"

"Here?"

His smile was small and secretive. "Maybe."

"Later... we'll have to explore that."

Jacob gave her a smirk. "I don't think your boyfriend's going to like that."

"Well, then, he doesn't have to do it, does he?"

"He doesn't have to do what?" said a voice that came up behind them.

Brianna squealed and began repeating her spastic hugging and enthusiastic hellos. All were directed towards Charlie now, who caught her when she launched herself against him. With a tolerant, ambivalent hug, he patted her skinny back. "Hey, there, Bri."

"You..." she smiled as she leaned back and grinned maniacally at him. "I can't believe you and Cami. You surprised me, Rydell. Props." She gave him a fist bump and he did it back, his expression becoming more amused.

"Thanks, Brianna. Glad to get your approval," Charlie said, casually strolling past her. He leaned forward and fist-bumped Jacob with a nod. No crazy smiles or squeals or bubbling giggles as she and Brianna shared. "Hey."

Jacob bumped him back. "Hey."

Jacob and Charlie were best friends. Charlie couldn't say that about any other guy. Charlie turned and kissed Cami briefly on the mouth before he plunked down beside her on the couch. Brianna sat opposite them. "You guys are so-o-o cute together."

Cami blushed. "Could you not talk to us like we're puppies that you expect to start performing tricks for you? We're just Cami and Charlie with you guys," She glanced at Charlie and he nodded his agreement. "So don't act any differently."

Jacob leaned forward, his elbows on his knees. "I

wondered if you two would act differently. Annoyingly, like I'd have to get high just to be around you."

"Nah," Charlie said easily, leaning back, his arms behind Cami. "And getting high? That's not new with you, huh, Cams?" He glanced at her and winked. "No, but it is you, huh, Jacob?"

Jacob leaned back, sprawled out like a spider over the couch with his long, spindly limbs. "Sometimes. Not that big of deal. Not like my parents try to make it out to be."

Brianna thumped the back of his head. "It's a drug, you idiot. No different from if they caught you drinking alcohol underage. Of course, your parents are getting down on you."

"Brianna doesn't approve." Jacob's tone was dry as he fluttered his eyebrows toward Cami and Charlie.

"No, she never did." Cami grinned at her friend, who stuck her tongue out in return. Brianna, despite all of her mean-girl talk and pranks, wasn't into partying at all. Ever. She and Charlie shared that. Apparently, Jacob and Cami shared the other.

"Well, you had plenty of sad reasons for using that stuff, what with all the shit that happened when you were young. Jacob? Please. His parents got divorced. Boo hoo. Oh, come on and join the ranks of every other teenager in America."

"This from the girl who almost seduced our stepfather in her rebellion against Mom? Like you managed to deal with it so normally."

Brianna shoved Jacob. "You are such a little dick. I told you to NEVER mention that again." She pinched her lips together tightly and then added, "And he wasn't my stepdad then for God's sake. Give me some credit."

Cami cracked up, enjoying the Starrs and having them back at the ranch. She and Charlie exchanged a look and a smile and all felt right in the world just then for her. Even with the change in Cami and Charlie's relationship status, the four of them still retained their unique bond.

Brianna chased after Joey Rydell hard during the summer they first met him. It was almost like bad karma when Joey ended up with Brianna's mom, and not Brianna.

"So… you guys staying the summer?"

Jacob nodded. "Yeah, Dad's being a dick. No reason to visit him. Gotta put up with him the rest of the year."

"What's going on with you two?" Charlie's eyes narrowed on Jacob. Jacob rarely talked about his family like that.

He shrugged and leaned back, putting his leg over his knee. "Hell, just don't see eye-to-eye. He tries to tell me who and what to be, and when I'm not, he lectures me about it. Who is he to do that with me? Especially after considering what he so miserably failed at."

Brianna shoved him and sat down on the couch arm. "Jacob's changed, not Dad. Of course he fights with you. You're rude and disrespectful. What else can he do? And you're not much better to Mom." Brianna smirked at him as she told Charlie and Cami, "But now while we're here, he won't abuse Mom because when Joey heard him do it, he just about hit Jacob he got so mad. He told him to get out. Mom got upset and they ended up fighting and she cried. He told her she couldn't let Jacob be like that or he wouldn't ever stop. I guess Joey used to be like that or whatever. And crazy enough, Mom listened. She put the hammer down on Jacob, he had to follow their rules, and use respectful language or else he had to get out. End of story. So Jacob's almost tolerable now."

Cami's gaze twisted up. "What changed for you, Jacob?"

He stood to answer. "Grew up. Parents are stupid. Now you all wanna go out and hit the new pool? I'll behave here, 'cause it's way better than a summer at home. Dad kept pushing me to get a job bagging groceries or something equally menial. So," he rubbed his hands together, "let's get to doing something fun."

Charlie stood also and nodded. "I'm glad I'm not your parent then. Yeah, let's go."

"I'm so glad you guys are here. I think... I think this is going to be the best summer ever." Cami said in a rare rush of mushy, sentimental feelings. She and her friends and Charlie being all together there and surrounding her and laughing and talking and BSing felt like sheer heaven. She and Charlie were still together but it wasn't odd with the four of them either. It hadn't ruined anything, which she feared might happen.

They hit the pool for two hours, playing, splashing, laughing, and soaking each other. When they separated, Charlie walked Cami home. Taking her hand, he waited until they escaped the scope of the outdoor lights before he kissed her senseless. He left her heart thumping, and she felt weird, breathless, and very girlish in the rush of feelings she didn't usually have. A happy sense of light and wonderment filled her. "I'm so glad nothing's changed. I thought it might be weird with us and them."

"Nah. It's just Jacob and Brianna and us. Right?"

She snuggled into his chest. "Always the calm logic. Someday, Charlie Rydell, I'll rattle that right out of you."

His arms tightened around her. "Yeah, when? The next time you and Jacob get high?"

"Maybe. Would you stop us?"

"No. I just won't join you. You know I don't like to do that."

She tilted her head back. "And you're really not going to discourage me? Set some kind of limits on me? Try to make me more like you?"

"No."

"And for that, Charlie, I kinda think you're great. Maybe I

don't need to do that with him. Maybe... maybe I could just be with you."

"Well, that would be my preferred course of action."

The summer only started then, after the Starrs returned to the ranch. Charlie had to work with his dad for half days in the mornings and Cami started helping Kate with her business. It involved data input and making routine phone calls. Tedious and brainless, it kept her busy enough to justify how she spent the summer.

The last summer when they could still enjoy acting like half-grown kids. That was even encouraged by Jack and Erin and Kate and AJ. So they did. They sunbathed, soaked in the cool, refreshing water, and played volleyball down at the Rydells' private beach. They also rode horses when it cooled down or hung out at the beach stoking a bonfire. They laughed all the time with Jacob and Brianna. After floating on the river nearly every single day, the four of them often ran into town for ice cream or just to wander around Pattinson.

The four of them were golden, together, and the best of friends.

Cami still pinched herself to believe she was an integral part of such a special group. Friends. A couple. All of it seemed surreal. How could she, Cami Reed, deserve such things? A place where she belonged with people her own age. Who would think any of them would like her? Or accept her? She wouldn't have dared to believe it five years ago. But she did now. She trusted them as her friends and confidants, and Charlie was her boyfriend.

But as the summer's heat faded, the mornings grew colder, hinting at the reality that September was already here and the Starrs had to go back home to attend school. It was the first year Hailey wasn't leaving to join them, now that she'd married Joey she would live permanently in River's

End. She cried with Cami as they all stood around the car, saying their tearful goodbyes to Jacob and Brianna.

Hailey hugged and kissed and reassured them. She told them to come back next weekend, and promised she'd come to them if they ever needed anything. Joey hung back, his face screwed up with indecision. Cami assumed it must have been tough on them. Their entire relationship was an endless commute between two places. Finally, it would not be, but Hailey didn't easily accept that advantage.

Still waving when Brianna took the driver's seat and Jacob slipped into the passenger seat, they watched him slide all the way back before he slouched down. Brianna put on her sunglasses and waved again. Cami curved into Charlie's arm as she cried, and Hailey turned away after they disappeared.

"They'll be back. They'll be okay," Joey said softly, soothing her as she cried.

"Maybe I should have stayed there for one more year…"

Cami peeked at Hailey who cried hysterically. She pictured Jacob's new, but fairly confident opinion of anyone over the age of twenty-five nowadays. "I think Jacob needs more space. I think you'll find it's probably better this way, at least for now," she told Hailey.

Hailey lifted her head off Joey's shoulder while he hugged her next to him. "You think so?"

"I know so. He needs more space. I think he'd rebel against you for any more mothering. You're going to have to let go a bit and maybe this way, you can. And Brianna's already nineteen. She's okay."

Joey let out a surprised laugh. He glanced down at Cami and then at Hailey as he tightened his arms around her and mouthed "Thank you" to Cami over Hailey's head. Then he said softly, "I think Cami's right. Jacob is more honest with them than with us. She would know more than anyone. He's not twelve anymore."

Hailey nodded and pushed away from Joey, wiping her eyes and walking inside their house without another word. Joey flinched. "This part has never been easy. She wants to be in two places at once."

Charlie nodded. "Jacob is hell-bent on rebelling, and better to do it from a distance, letting Brett take the brunt of it, since Hailey won't tell him no. So it's probably a good idea."

Joey punched him gently on the arm. "You, my nephew, are always the smart one in the room. I think I'll go back to the resort and let her decompress. See you guys."

They watched Joey walk down the road from the houses towards the main part of the ranch and then further on towards the resort.

Charlie turned to Cami, who wiped her eyes. "Next it will be you. I can't... this was hard enough. I can't imagine letting go of you." Charlie still had three weeks before he had to leave for his dorm and college. It seemed so remote as if it were a hazy, long-time-from-now event. Surreal too, like it couldn't actually happen. They'd been in such a golden, wonderful, happy bubble, it was hard to accept the end of summer, knowing it was the bitter end of all of it.

He wrapped his arms wrapped around her as he so easily and often did. "We'll make it work."

She looked up and the angle made her stare up at his chin. "Charlie, it won't be that easy. I'll be here, and I'll be the same and you'll be there... it's entirely different."

He squeezed her. "Yeah, but nothing has to change between us. It's what we make it. You're not considering backing out now, are you? I mean, I hate the thought of not being with you every day, but it's better to be together and do it this way than not to be together at all, isn't it? I mean, that's what I assumed."

She gave him a weak, soft smile. "Of course."

He leaned back so he could look down into her eyes. "Cami? Y—you mean that, don't you?"

No. She dropped her face down and began fiddling with the buttons on his shirt. How could she survive without him? She relied on him and loved seeing him. She never had to wonder where he was or what he was doing. There was no time for any doubt because he was always right there.

He frowned, pushing back from her. "It never even occurred to me to doubt you. I thought it was just a given that we'd be together no matter what."

She nodded, biting her lip and sucking in the snot that her tears created. "I want to," she whispered. "It's just... it's so far away and it scares me so much. I don't want to lose you."

His arms pulled her forward. "You won't. That's why we'll still be together. Just like we are now.

"Except it won't be just like we are now." Her hands were around his waist, tugging him closer, as if that would fend off the thought of not being close.

"But being together and dealing with distance is better than not at all, right? I'm not the only one who thinks that, am I?"

"No. You're not the only one." She meant that, but the heat and confidence in her tone were lacking and it sabotaged her. Her voice wavered. The thought of changing and being different scared her. It wasn't as easy to do as Charlie made it out to be. It sounded intimidating. And Charlie took it as stoically as he did everything. The thing was, she wasn't that way.

She lifted her head and he leaned down to kiss her. "It'll be okay, Cams. We got this."

He had this. Just as Charlie had everything. He didn't

waffle or doubt or screw up or ever make the wrong decision. So sure, he had this. But left all alone, Cami wasn't as certain that she did.

The ranch was quiet and desolate. She missed Brianna's crazy exclamations and eager enthusiasm. Her brash loudness never failed to make Cami more outgoing when she was with her. She missed Jacob's ribbing of Brianna and her, and Charlie and Jacob doing it to both of them. She loved the dynamics of the four of them together. It was the only time she'd ever felt popular or young in a way that was fun. So much fun.

Now, without the Starrs, Cami missed them. Their departure meant it was time to quit being young. To quit pretending it all hadn't changed. And time to find her own damn path on the road of life.

CHARLIE STARTED to gather what he thought he'd need for his dorm room. Buying a mini-fridge, desk chair, and bedding to fill it, he collected all of his clothes and personal items. It was sitting in a spare room when the time came to go. His dad gave him a new laptop with all the latest hardware and operating systems. He registered for his classes. He was raring to go. He wanted to go. He'd been waiting years for this, pretty much all of high school to get there.

He loved his family, but he was ready for something very different and new. He wanted to see the world and what existed beyond the valley. Ranch or farm work was not what he wanted to do. None of it. He didn't know yet what, exactly, he wanted, but he knew River's End didn't have it.

However, he didn't want to leave Cami, although to him, it was not that huge of a deal. He figured he'd go to school and they'd continue to date all the while. He'd be back again.

It wasn't like this would last forever. Holidays, vacations, and summer. It wasn't that impossible. He didn't see why she panicked so much while discussing it.

She didn't want to go to college. She'd been adamant about that. For the last two years while he scouted the campuses and selected the schools he intended to apply to, her parents encouraged her to do the same, but she refused. So it wasn't like she was jealous of him going to college or she wanted to do what he was doing.

Hell if he wanted to stay there. And do what? Start working with Ben? No. He refused to end up with a position in the family business. His dad, his two uncles and brother, his stepmother and aunt all had their own little niches there. Shane might have worked in a different industry, but he still worked on the land.

Charlie didn't intend to live there his entire life. In fact, he was quite sure he'd only be coming back to visit after this initial departure. Cami referred to school and the people of the valley with as much disdain and annoyance as he did. But she was always talking as if *this*, as in all that comprised the valley, was it. She graduated and now, here she was. Charlie couldn't even imagine this being the one place where he lived his whole life.

One night, while lying on the couch together, she was tucked in before him, and their heads touched on a pillow as they alternated between making out and watching TV. Holding her hands, he asked, "You don't want to stay here for good, do you?"

"What? Here in River's End?" She shrugged. "Sure. Why not? Maybe. Where else would I go? Kate is here."

Well, yeah. So were his dad and Erin. And Ben and his family. He loved them as much as any kid loved his family, but hell, they weren't twelve anymore. He didn't need his family around him all the time. He had no intention of spending his daily life with his entire family.

"Yeah, but wouldn't you like to go somewhere else?"

"What would I possibly do? No."

"Well, when I finish college, I'll get a job somewhere else, make enough money that you'll come with me, won't you?"

"Where? Doing what? And you aren't actually thinking about things like… like supporting me, are you?"

He was. Because he planned to be with her then. She wasn't exactly following a path that could lead to anything that could support them. In all honesty, she had no plans at all. Yeah, he didn't care about that, or judge her for it, even if he did wonder how she could not care. He could not wait to get out of there and do something different. Something new.

So yeah, he thought about what he'd like to do to support them. He couldn't decide exactly what he would major in, but he considered architecture or engineering. He liked computers, and in some function, he knew he couldn't go wrong there. He also looked at a degree in business or economics. Awash in possibilities, he found it hard to choose a major. But he knew it wouldn't be one that would make him stay there.

"I like to think about what I'll do, yeah. Why do you think I'm leaving for college? Tens of thousands of dollars just waiting to be spent? Getting a decent job that doesn't include scooping up horse poop or checking people into my family's resort?"

"There's a lot more going on here and nothing is wrong with any of it."

"Well, yeah, but it's not like that for me. There's a lot more to do out *there*. Out of this valley."

She suddenly pushed his hands away and sat up. He sighed and sat up too. She glanced at him. "You don't ever intend to come back here? After college or whatever?"

"Not whatever, I'll get my four-year degree. I'm not starting college without finishing, Cams. You should know that about me. I won't waste my dad's money. But no. I don't intend to come back and live here. You think I will?"

"I assumed so, of course, you would. Your entire family lives here. It's beautiful and amazing and you have free stuff everywhere... land and a resort and... where else would you go?"

"I can think of lots of places besides here."

"You dislike it that much?"

"Of course not. I just prefer not to be neighbors with my dad all my life. I don't want to stare at my brother every single day. I want some privacy and space. Something different. I want some independence and to live my own life. Don't you?"

"No. Where could I go? What could I do? I have only AJ and Kate, and I want to be near them." She shuddered. She was way more dependent on them, of course, than she was on him. He twisted his butt back and forth. *Maybe she was a little too clingy?*

No. He banished that thought. It wasn't her fault. She had her reasons for needing them and him and he wanted, no, he *welcomed* that. He leaned over and rubbed the back of her neck. "Wherever I end up, it'll be with you, Cams."

Her head turned to him and she stared at him for a long moment. "We have quite a few differences in our opinions."

He hesitated, then shook it off. "Nah. We just got a few things to figure out. We have all the time in the world. Come on, lie back down, and let's finish the movie."

"Yeah. You're right." But her tone wavered, and he frowned behind her as she tucked up into him again.

"I asked Joey for a job and he said I could start with working at the reception desk of the resort."

"Oh. That's great." He had to restrain a shudder. Didn't

she want more than that? They could go and do and be anything. Both of them were free and independent. She had as much financial backing as he did and yet she was content to sit at a desk across the street from her home? Uninspired. Boring. Menial.

Not for him, that was for sure. He held her small body against him, enjoying the warmth and feel of her skin and hugging her more tightly against him. Cami had the ambition of a kitten, and it was kind of shocking to him. He had to work to understand and support her decision to simply stay, *right here.*

He absolutely could not stay right here. Nor live his life on the coat tails of his dad, uncles, brother, or family. No. Nope. Hell to the no.

So even for Cami, there was no wavering on his plan. She'd just have to deal with it. Maybe grow up a little. It was one of her biggest faults. She tried to avoid dealing with life's obstacles.

Charlie loved the summer; it was fun and awesome to hang out, but, it couldn't last forever. The best was the summer after graduation. Now it was time for him to do something. He was growing bored and restless, and except for Cami, River's End had very little to offer him anymore.

Eventually, it was move-in week for the dorm and time for him to go. He envisioned her coming and him so he could show her where he was living, but in the end, he changed his mind. After her odd behavior, he preferred to have his dad take him. He didn't want any long goodbyes or big deals made of it. He'd be back in just a few months. It wasn't like this was a permanent situation or that he was totally gone.

Loading all of his stuff into the back of his dad's truck, he finished tying it off with ratcheted straps before he jumped down. There stood his entire family. He had to restrain the sigh and the urge to roll his eyes. They were all making way too big of a deal about this. He had a good four years at a minimum and would still be coming and going, yet they all gathered around the truck as if he were marching off to war.

There were tears in Erin's eyes. He tolerated the warm handshakes of his uncles and Ben when he gave him a hug. He hugged Allison, Kate, Kailynn, Hailey, and Jocelyn. He listened to everyone say, "Good luck," and "We're so proud of you," slapping his back and high-fiving to avoid becoming too emotional. He graciously accepted everybody's congratulations.

It could not be over soon enough. He stared up at the road, longing to be heading down it.

He had one last goodbye to give and that belonged, of course, to Cami. She stood beside her dad, all huddled up, her arms crossed over her chest in a pathetic hug. She kept her head down, letting her dark hair fall over her face. She didn't bother to raise her head when Charlie made the rounds. Her face was long, tragic, and sad. She truly grieved over this.

He stretched and wanted to understand, but he just didn't see the tragedy. They'd be texting all the time, and would talk tonight. It wasn't like they were relegated to being pen pals for the next four years. Lord, they would virtually be living together. There were endless contacts and apps for long-distance romances. And gee, let's not forget the old-fashioned road trip.

But Cami couldn't see past her nose. She couldn't imagine the next few weeks with him so far away. He'd be busy until then, so it wasn't like he'd have to dwell too long over it. Besides, he'd be coming back to see her. It wasn't like he wouldn't miss her. Of course, he would, but that's when he'd reach out.

He wished she'd find a way to be busier, and more fulfilled, without his presence. He loved being with her and spending time with her, but they couldn't be together twenty-four hours a day.

He started this while believing she might not respond or even like him, let alone, fall in love with him. In most of his scenarios, he was always the one chasing her. But as it turned out, she relied on him as much as a boyfriend as she had as a friend. So maybe he shouldn't have been surprised by it.

He walked forward and scooped her up in his arms, tugging her against him until her head was just under his chin. Ignoring his entire family and hers as they stared on, he wondered what was the point of being embarrassed? They all knew. They'd all seen them over the last few months, hugging, holding, and kissing. So this was a little more up-close and intimate, but she clearly needed it.

"I love you. I'll call you tonight. Promise," he whispered into her ear. Her head shook, and hot tears fell from her eyes. He nudged her back and leaned down to kiss her lips. It wasn't a fast smooch, but neither was it a very deep kiss. It was sweet and tender, and he hoped it stayed with her, so she'd remember what she had to know: that he did love her and would always be there for her. Just not twenty-four hours a day. That was weird, and they were eighteen and they were a long way away from being married.

She nodded against his chest, her head down. Miserable. He kept the sigh to himself. He hoped she'd smile and kiss him back. Instead, he released her, burdened with guilt and feeling bad. He never expected to feel so bad for going to college like he'd always planned and dreamed of.

"Cami?" he questioned one last time, holding just her hand now. "You'll be all right. It'll be okay." He said it again, willing her to freaking believe him. She pressed her lips together. AJ pulled her against him. Charlie sighed and stared at Cami.

She looked miserable. Way out of proportion with the

day's event. She left him feeling like he'd done something wrong, and she wasn't inclined to release him from that feeling anytime soon. He glanced at AJ, expecting to see a scowl for the kiss in his presence and for making her so miserable, but AJ just gave him a sympathetic smile. Charlie felt helpless staring at her, so he finally gave up and turned towards the truck.

There was a last round of goodbyes and indecipherable yells. He jumped in and slammed the door, sticking his arm out the window in a final wave.

"Ready?"

"Yeah. Go."

Cami leaned into AJ more as the truck revved up and pulled away. It was obvious that she sobbed against her dad as he pulled out. Charlie tried to harden his heart, remembering it wasn't that tragic or dramatic or even permanent. He faced forward.

They had a fifteen-hour trip ahead of them. Sure, there was a major amount of distance that separated them, but it wasn't insurmountable. He tried to convince Cami that the first time he left would hurt more because it was all new. They'd get used to it eventually. He would always be back. They'd figure this out.

And what was he supposed to do? Not go to freaking Stanford? It wasn't like everyone got accepted there. Yeah, he had a certain amount of pride and his identity was tied up in that fact. He worked hard to get there especially from the minuscule place he came from. You had to be the best of the best to get in and he managed to do it.

And how did Cami react to that? She cried and made him feel guilty. She didn't even try to be happy that he was finally achieving his dream of getting out of River's End and attending an impressive college. She was all tears when he was bursting with pride. He was out of there. At last.

CHAPTER 5

*J*ACK STAYED QUIET FOR miles. "You okay about leaving her?"

"Yeah. I just wish she didn't take it so hard."

"Doesn't make it any easier."

"No, Cami doesn't make much any easier."

His dad glanced at him. "That's what you first liked about her. You always dealt with her so well, better than anyone else, even her parents."

"I know. But this time it wasn't about her." Charlie glanced out the window, surprised he voiced exactly what he thought.

"A few years ago, I took a ride with your brother, about as many hours as this drive. I intended to bring him back home. To stay for good. He had a baby and I didn't know then, but also a soon-to-be wife that he had to face and come to terms with. It was one of the saddest days of my life. And I've had a few of those." Charlie glanced at his dad, surprised. He and his dad didn't often voice their private thoughts. Not unless Erin was also there with them.

"Yeah, I remember that time. You were the worst then.

You got so depressed. I think Erin worried for a bit there that you might leave her… *us*… and the ranch."

"That was my fault. I hope you know how much I regret the way I treated you both then."

"You've apologized. We're good." Charlie wasn't like Cami. He could easily forgive and move on.

"Yeah. I was disappointed in my life and how your brother was turning out. I couldn't accept that this was *it*. Ben was just like me."

"Some would find that flattering. You've led a good life."

"I just wanted you boys to choose your own path in life, whatever it is. How can you choose if you never see all the choices? You know what I mean?"

"Yeah, I know. I'm going to see them. But Dad, Ben's good with it. He's happy. I don't think it's fake."

"Yeah, it is a good life. Luckily. But it could have gone the opposite way, Charlie. Easily. He's lucky it all works and fits and that he fell in love with his child's mother. But understand this, I don't think you would be as happy. I know you better than anyone, Charlie. Better than even Erin or Cami. They might talk to you more often, but I know you better. You could never think of settling down on that ranch and following in my footsteps. You never did. Ben always did. So don't forget that."

He glanced at his dad. Jack kept driving, his attention facing forward. "You think I shouldn't be with Cami?"

"Not at all. I think you love her. I know she needs you. I won't tell you that love at your age doesn't matter or count. I know it does. I wished you hadn't started it yet. I guess I wanted you to do what I could never do. You were meant for this, Charlie. From the time you were young, you had an insatiable curiosity and deep hunger to learn. You soon outgrew my answers to your questions and found them in books. Endlessly absorbed, there were countless books that you read. Forgive me if I want to see you go far in this world and seek more than what you can find in River's End."

"So, don't mess it up, in other words?"

"I don't have to say that to you. I swear, you were born with this innate sense of yourself. You've never needed me to help you figure things out. You had the confidence to know already. I feel pretty sure you won't. And I hope I don't need to remind you to take care of those you leave behind. You've never been selfish, and you don't forget too many things."

"I wish Cami would believe that."

"She might not, and you'll probably have to forgive her for that insecurity. Anyone you choose to be with will have their faults. You have to live with them and love them despite any shortcomings, just like you have."

At least his dad didn't advise him to break up with her. "So, you're okay with my plan to stay with her?"

"I am. I just hope you'll be sure to examine all the choices that are opening up for you out there in real life. I don't necessarily mean for women. But things like good jobs, hobbies, places, meeting new people. I can't say, actually, Charlie, since I never did it. And perhaps I have no right to pressure you, but I'm very glad you're doing this."

"Thanks, Dad." Their conversation from there fell into much more casual topics that were less personal. When they pulled into the parking lot for his dorm, he was met with chaos. Hundreds of other students were also moving in with their gear. He and his dad made quick work of it and Charlie soon met his roommate, Rupport, where he learned there was floor mixer that night. At last, Charlie had become a college student.

His dad put his hand out. "I'll see you, Charlie."

Charlie appreciated the lack of fanfare, congrats, and so-proud-of-you comments again. "Yeah, Dad. See you on the flip side."

His dad smirked before he turned and left the dorm room.

Charlie flopped on his bed. The room was split into identical sides right down the center. His roommate was a big, beefy guy who also happened to be a football player, playing on the college team. He almost laughed at the irony. They were such opposites. Charlie didn't play any sports. Ever. So sure, why not get a football player for a roommate? But Rupport had so far acted nice and outgoing. He casually walked in and started talking to Charlie before he invited him to go to a party.

And that's how easy it was. Definitely not high school. There were several mixers and orientations that week, enough to make his freshman year welcoming, and Charlie was eager to know everyone. He went to some of the parties and skipped others.

A few nights later, while talking to Cami again, he mentioned, "I got invited to a party by a football player."

Cami laughed when he told her that. He was holding his phone over his head to stare at her. It was quite late and Rupport wasn't there.

She smiled at him. "I miss you already. But I bet you're too busy to miss me."

"What have you been doing?"

"Missing you. Feeling depressed. Got in trouble finally for it so I have to start doing something. It's just so fucking quiet here without you and Brianna and Jacob, but mostly you. I've never been here without you."

"No… you haven't."

"Do you need to be there, like all there? I mean, do you prefer not having to hear from the moping girlfriend at home who will constantly be holding you back, and not letting you experience everything?"

"Cami, I plan to still do all that. You won't be holding me back and all the while, I'll be loving the hell out of you."

"I'm such a downer."

"Yes. You are. You, Cami Reed, have always been, so that's not new or even a big deal. I'm here, sure, Cams, but I'm also with you. There is no one else for me."

"But I'm—"

"Insecure. Unsure. Acting out off and on. Uh huh. Color me shocked. I don't care. And it's not that alarming to me."

"You make me sound like a moaning, crying, sad, needy, despondent downer."

"Well, if the shoe fits—"

"If I were there, I'd punch you hard in the stomach."

"Ahh, there's my girl. Showing her feisty attitude and badass meanness."

She finally started to laugh. "You said all that on purpose."

"Uh huh. It worked, and I got you smiling and you know it's all true."

"I do," she said, her tone turning glum again, but a smile still on her face. He brought the phone closer, enjoying her smile. "I'm still your girl."

"Four days, Cams, doesn't change a single thing. You know four years won't change anything either. But I'll say it every single day to you if I have to."

"It's hard to be the one who got left behind. You have all the new stuff to do, while I'm just living exactly the same life."

"Please don't punish me for choosing this."

She nodded. "I swear, I will make it my mission not to."

"All right. I got classes first thing tomorrow and need to sleep now. Call you tomorrow."

"I'll find something to say to you by then."

He stared at her. His heart swelled and nearly burst at the face she made at him. "I can't wait to hear it," he said softly.

"Go cradle your football player. Maybe he'll keep you warm."

"That was new."

She smiled cheekily. "I just thought of it. Bye, Charlie. This wasn't so bad."

"It's not going to be so bad. Think how amazing it will be when we see each other."

"Thinking… imagining…."

He groaned. "I know that voice…"

"Well, you're alone and so am I. We could try things, you know, separate but together. I feel like we'll have to get pretty good at that."

He got up and locked the door. Flopping back down, he said, "What, exactly, were you thinking?"

COLLEGE CLASSES WERE WAY HARDER than high school and required Charlie to actually study a bit. The extra hours of study did the trick of keeping him busy for once although it was an adjustment to be living with other guys and sharing a big, ugly bathroom with them. It had its moments when he could only wonder why *dorm living* was often exalted and advertised as the great "college experience."

But other things were just as great as he imagined they would be. Having so much independence was perfect. He loved that part. Being able to come and go on his own terms was something he'd been craving for a long time. He also liked that he could walk everywhere he had to go and there were plenty of places to eat or congregate or just chill. He liked being able to engage other freshman and in no time at all, he started to know quite a few people.

"You got a girl?" Rupport asked in week two as he offhandedly mentioned her.

"Yeah. Why?"

"I don't know. Didn't see that."

Charlie flipped out a picture of Cami to him.

"Wow, she's hot. Not what I'd expect from you."

"Thanks," he said dryly. "Not a lot of selection where I come from."

He flashed a grin. "She's edgier than you'd think for a guy like you."

That she was. As roommates, they got along well enough. Rupport became especially fond of Charlie when he started to flunk and nearly begged Charlie for help. He even offered to pay Charlie to do his schoolwork, but Charlie refused. Rupport had to settle for Charlie's guidance and advice in helping him do his own work.

Lots of texts were exchanged between Charlie and Cami. Dozens a day. He and Cami also had plenty of phone calls and Facetime and messages. They might have been talking more now than when they were neighbors. But it also confirmed to Charlie that they would be fine. Their relationship would survive despite the long distance and maybe even grow stronger because of it.

WATCHING Charlie pull away with all of his stuff loaded in Jack's truck made Cami feel as if they were saying goodbye forever. It seemed that heavy. That overwhelming. Watching the entire family come out to say goodbye, each taking a private moment with him, depressed her and made her very sad. And yet, Charlie seemed so unruffled. He accepted it so easily and casually. Jumping down from the back of the truck, dressed in his usual nondescript clothes of jeans and a t-shirt, he tolerated all the family hugs, tears, smiles, and words of praise.

Not one to hem or haw, he boldly embraced her when he saw her. He never ignored her or seemed ashamed of her, no matter who was around. It didn't embarrass him to say goodbye with a dozen people staring at them, although it did embarrass her.

Her hot tears blinded her. Her heart felt like it had been ripped out whenever she thought of tomorrow on this ranch, this land, this valley, without Charlie being right there. He'd always been right there beside her, no matter what else was going on.

Charlie was *always* there.

Not any longer. It made the bitter few weeks that it took for her to grow used to it pass even slower. And Charlie wasn't as sentimental or home-bound as she was. He could so easily adjust to almost anything new: people, relationships, expectations, places, schools.

Cami wished Charlie expressed a few doubts or concerns about leaving home for the first time. Anything that might make him slightly insecure at some point. He usually wasn't that way. It was what made him so reliable. But it bothered her how easily he could leave her and accept her absence after spending the last five years seeing each other every single day. She knew she would miss him like this even if they never started a romantic relationship.

She moped a lot and grew depressed, often sitting in her room playing video games for hours. Eventually, she was ordered out. Go do something. It was way past time.

She worked the resort reception, which filled some of the day's hours and seemed to placate everyone else.

A few times, she bummed several beers out of Joey's or Ben's fridge.

Jocelyn caught her one time. "Cami, are you drinking again?"

"No. I just get bored sometimes."

"Missing Charlie?"

"Duh," she grumbled.

Jocelyn sat down. "You doing okay?"

"I'm doing fine. He chose to leave and now he's having a wonderful time. Busy. Meeting people. All kinds of wonderful, stimulating educational opportunities. A library full of books. Who wouldn't want that?"

Jocelyn stuck her tongue in her cheek in an obvious attempt not to laugh. "I take it you're just a tad bitter?"

"He chose that. Not me."

Jocelyn tilted her head. "You guys can make this last, if you want it to. But you'll have to be honest and communicate throughout the hard times and your feelings of insecurity."

"Sounds like super fun."

"No, but that's also part of a real relationship."

"Right." Cami turned and fled. She didn't need another lecture on how she should be. She already got plenty of those. But Charlie was the one who chose to do that to them. To her. To leave without her. When they'd always been practically joined at the hip.

Cami took out the bottle of booze she stuffed in her bag. Jocelyn missed that. She escaped and headed towards the Rydells' beach, scrambling over the trail and up to the Rydell River Rock. She went there just to stare at the river. Plopping down on the hard rock, she let her feet dangle and pulled her coat more tightly around her when the nippy November wind chilled her. Damn. It was cold. Freezing in the morning, and she knew the first snows would be coming soon.

Uncapping the alcohol, she swallowed a gulp, then shuddered and cringed, savoring the pull of it. It zinged straight into her bloodstream and seeped through the rest of her in a warm, lovely radiation. Ahh, that helped banish the cold and her thoughts. Her phone rang. *Charlie.* She pulled it out.

"Hey."

"Hey," he said, his tone soft and caressing, like he always greeted her. "What are you doing?"

Getting drunk on Rydell Rock all alone and huddling in the cold seemed a bit too lame and sad so she replied, "Jocelyn invited me to dinner. Going to hang with her."

"Yeah, so what else?"

They talked, sure. But it was disconnected, and she kept staring at things he couldn't see and vice versa. She hated it. The days dragged on miserably and she wished she were back in high school and things were how they used to be. She wanted to go places but not without Charlie. She wished for Charlie to come home.

And stay there. Of course, he'd come home but she knew he wouldn't stay.

Finally, his stupid Thanksgiving break arrived. He showed up late Wednesday evening. He caught an early flight and had a friend drop him at her house as a surprise. He wasn't supposed to come, and certainly not for such a short time. But he did.

Her stomach jumped when she heard his footsteps crossing their porch at a fast clip before she heard a knock. She opened the door.

"Charlie?" Her shock was reflected in her tone and gaze.

He grinned a massively huge smile as he opened his arms and she launched herself into him. He had to take a step back to catch her. Their mouths met, and they started kissing passionately. His hands gripped her face and held her there, just as frantic as she was for him. Finally, they smiled as they separated barely an inch. "Hi."

"Hey." He grinned. "We probably can't do this here. Where's AJ?"

"Don't know." She rose up to kiss his lips again.

"Come with me?" he asked gently, his tone hopeful, eyebrows raised up.

"Anywhere," she answered softly, her lips touching his. Grinning wildly at each other, they clasped hands and fled the porch.

The ground was crunchy from the frozen cold, but no snow had fallen yet, although tinges of it rimmed the mountains all around. They snuck away from the house like two thieves in the night. She couldn't have cared less if everyone at the ranch figured out what they were doing. She fully intended to do it.

They ran down the road until they came to the old trailer, one that had passed through several ranch hands and family members. It once left the ranch when it was bought by one of the workers before getting sold back and taken to its original spot. Charlie opened it with a key they kept hidden in the latch. He took her hand and pulled her inside. It was freezing. He set the heat on and turned on one of the lamps. It made a rosy glow and had a cocooning effect.

"Here?" he inquired, raising his eyebrows. He didn't need to explain what he meant. *Here*. She knew what that one word implied.

"Anywhere." She grinned, tugging her coat off. But then she stuck it back on when the icy cold hit her. "In a few minutes," she added cheekily.

He stepped towards her and slipped his arms inside her unzipped coat, wrapping them around her waist. "I haven't been home yet. They don't even know I'm here. I told them I was coming in tomorrow."

"What a coincidence. I thought the same thing." She grinned. "And wow, this friend from high school wants me to come over tonight."

His fingers flexed on her waist. "This almost makes the time we spent apart all worth it." His gaze kept scanning her as if he wanted to memorize everything about her. "God, you are so beautiful. I feel like I almost forgot how much so."

She shook her head in denial. "I'm just ordinary. But I was afraid we would feel weird or different. And that you'd changed and outgrown me."

"And?"

She rose up on her tiptoes, setting a kiss on his mouth. "And it feels better than ever."

He grinned and pulled her until they were torso-to-torso. "I haven't outgrown you. There is nothing more I want in the world than you. I told you I love you, Cami. That won't ever change for me," he whispered in her ear. His lips hovered over hers. The cold made his breath look like smoke and her heart swelled and tilted in response at the rich meaning of his words.

The propane heater finally started to blast away the lung-shattering cold from the air. She pressed her mouth on his as he hovered over hers. Her tongue came out, sliding over his lips and she licked his lower lip before pushing her tongue into his mouth. He slid her coat off and his hands came back to her waist. Getting restless now, he fidgeted with her shirt.

"We're ready for this now, aren't we?" she whispered as her tongue came out and touched his lips before slipping into his mouth again.

He pulled back to say, "We're definitely ready," and he leaned down to kiss her again. "You can't imagine how good you feel. I missed you so much."

His hands followed the line of her sweater and he pulled upwards slowly, watching the reveal of her small stomach, ribcage and black bra, then up to her collarbone. He carefully flipped the bulky top over her head and out of the way.

His gaze poured over her and his eyes sparked with untamed lust. The tone of his voice and the way his eyes devoured her convinced her he meant it.

Sometimes Charlie sounded way too fine about their long-distance separation. He would robotically list off all the assignments he needed to work on. There was an inherent busy-ness just living in the dorm, from getting his meals to showering. Time for him was flying by, and she well saw it. Yes, he missed her, but not like she missed him.

Eventually, she felt his need and appreciation for her and she knew Charlie well enough to know he wouldn't pretend or try to fake it. He only showed her his sincerest intentions. He didn't bother with fake comments or false reassurance.

His hands slid to the back of her bra and he unclasped the eyelet hooks and it opened. He grasped her slim shoulder to slip the delicate straps off and pull them down. His gaze was riveted on her as he felt her up. He'd seen her breasts before, but now they seemed more like two surprising, new objects he'd never beheld before. Small, round, and perky in his hands, he covered both of them and she sighed at the abrasion of his coarse palms over her rigid, pointy nipples. So pert and upright, it was almost a tug-of-war between pleasure and pain when his fingers began to pull on them. Twisting and turning, then kneading and rubbing. They sent shooting jabs straight into her core as his mouth pressed harder against hers.

She pushed down his jacket while their mouths were still connected. He had to let go of her to allow her to stand on her tiptoes in order to work his coat off. He wore a sweater that she had to tug over his head and a long-sleeved t-shirt underneath that she had to remove.

Frustrated, he finally started to laugh as he took the edge of it in his hands and yanked it upwards until they were facing each other, both naked from the waist up. He had a long, thin torso with skin tightly drawn over his subtle muscles. His skin was shiny white and pale.

His jeans were low, hanging off his slim hips and she slid her hands to his waist and tugged him closer before dipping down below his waistband. He returned the favor, holding her the same way as he bent down. Sliding his mouth from her chin, he moved further down her neck and finally found her nipple before his tongue came out to loop and twirl around her hard, pebbled, completely turned-on tip. Her head fell back, jutting her breast further into his mouth. Her hair, thick and dark, rested on her shoulders and tickled her as she leaned back.

Moments, long, endless, restless moments passed, and he kissed her. He slid his hands under her dark leggings, groaning when he found a half bare butt cheek to grab. His fingers hovered as he kneaded and pushed on her butt cheeks, making her groan at the delightful sensations. He pressed her against his crotch, holding her there as his lips and tongue aggressively worked on her breast.

The contact seemed to inflame him. His skin warmed to her touch and his mouth moved furiously over her. Her groans grew louder and came more often as her breathing increased with his movements.

Between her legs, she grew swollen and tender and wet. His fingers teased her, nearly making her scissor her legs in order to draw him closer. Inside her. On her. Something to ease the increasingly sharp ache burning inside her.

His hands and mouth pulled away all at once. Her eyes blinked open at the loss of contact. Taking her hand, he pulled her towards the bed at the front of the trailer. It was all neat and tidy. He wrapped her up in his arms, hugging her almost platonically for a long moment. "You always doubted me, but there is no one else in the world I would ever want like this."

"You say that because I'm shirtless and you've never had sex before." Her tone was light and her smile teasing.

His was not. He leaned forward, cupping the side of her chin in his hands. "No. I wouldn't. It's because it's you. I waited for you, always. That's why it's always so crazy to me when you doubt it."

A multitude of voices reared up, ready to spill out of her mouth to answer why she doubted him and them. The distance. The new life he was exploring. All the things she wasn't included in and didn't even know about or understand.

There were times when she called him or Facetimed him and she saw several strangers going in and out of his dorm room. They were always chatting with him about things that had nothing to do with her. She also observed a few attractive, young freshman girls who were exiting or entering Charlie's dorm, mostly thanks to his football-playing roommate, but also, she suspected, because of him.

Charlie was the type of guy high school girls couldn't appreciate, but she believed, the older he got, the more attractive he became, and his quiet sense of self-confidence would have surely drawn lots of women to him. She knew what it did for her.

Cami, however, didn't occupy a huge chunk of his life and would not anytime soon. For years. *Years.* That was the part that so frustrated her. How could she go on like this for years? It intimidated her *and* made her feel like an outcast. She suffered the pangs of anxiety all the time inside her chest whenever she thought about Charlie.

But not when they spoke or touched or smiled or gazed at each other.

Those times were sacred. The world melted away and nothing but Cami and Charlie mattered. She knew with unfamiliar certainty at those times that they were the real thing. Their feelings were deep, endless, and the same between them.

Having him standing before her right here and now thrilled her like nothing else could. If only they could make it until they were old enough to live together and Charlie didn't want to go away to prove himself or expand his horizons. She believed she'd have to accept waiting for him to find what she already had: a safe place to belong.

She found it there. Right there in River's End. She wanted Charlie to feel it there too. It was desperately important to her that he did. But he didn't. He needed to go away and find new things and opportunities. She needed to stay there.

So, she decided to wait as best she could. Biding her time until they could finally be together for good. It was a hard, excruciating sacrifice for her to make and so unnatural too. But she was determined to do it. Let him be whatever he needed to be now, as long as someday, he would be content to simply be with her.

She tilted her head and he glanced down to catch her eye before he smiled. She smiled back up at him as all the mental voices that often spoke to her stopped. They hushed and faded. Only his smile remained as the center of her life and thoughts and ideas. "I love you."

"I love you," he answered, bending down to kiss her and start warming her body, thoughts and skin all over again. He kissed and touched and rubbed and enticed. There was no hurrying or groping or any sense that Charlie hadn't done this before. No, it was controlled and generous and passionate and exciting.

He turned and gently touched her shoulders to indicate that she sit down. She did, and he followed her as she lay back on the bed, lying down beside her. He kissed her and pushed his hands into her hair and along her torso, gently rubbing her bare skin until goose bumps appeared. The sensations were so soft, she moved towards him in her need to have him. He was expertly strumming her to a slow, perfect build-up.

He used both of his hands to pull her waistband down

and slipped her leggings off her hips along with her under-wear. He slid them all the way down her legs and only paused at her feet. He had to tug her wool socks off before he could remove her leggings.

The air was no longer freezing but still wasn't warm. Her skin flushed at the sudden draft of cold air. His heated gaze drifted up her calves, her knees, and then her thighs, only stopping at her bare, naked pussy.

His breathing escalated, and he froze for a moment. She sat up and leaned towards him, putting her hands behind his neck and pulling him forward until their foreheads touched and she kissed him. "Now you're nervous?"

His head slowly shook.

"You never get nervous about anything."

"I am now. And..." He dipped his head to kiss her between his statements. She rose up on her knees and her hands dropped to his jeans again. Digging into his pocket, she pulled out the condom and dropped it beside them before she pulled on his pant's snap.

"And what?"

He sucked in a breath as she undid his zipper, brushing her knuckles along the hard length of him, straining to be freed and inside her. "You're blonde." The words seemed to burst out of his mouth.

She stopped what she was doing and glanced up at him, puzzled over what the big revelation could be. Then she glanced down. "You really didn't know that? Yeah, I should be a golden-haired, natural blonde."

His head shook as he pointed at her head. "You've always kept it so black. I had no idea."

"Carpets don't always match the drapes." She grinned at his surprise and started on his zipper again. His attention dropped back to what her hands were doing.

"Honestly, I really thought you were a natural brunette."

Releasing his pants at last, her hands slipped around the front, taking his hard, warm length in both of her hands. He gasped, and his eyes shut as his expression switched to ecstasy. "Don't fantasize too hard on it. I will never be blonde upstairs." She touched her head. Then she dropped her hand on him and put pressure in her fingertips as his hips jerked towards her.

"Never?" he gasped. Her mouth tilted up at the twinge of disappointment in his tone.

"Never."

He sighed and pulled her chest to his as his mouth slid into her hair and he kissed her. "I can fantasize about you with black hair, however, right?"

"Yes. Only black."

Her last word went breathless because his hand dropped down and he cupped her, pressing into the swollen, wet-hot heat he felt there.

They held each other and pressed their bodies together and their mutual sighs filled the room. The heat on their bodies nearly steamed off them. Their tongues meshed together in long, sloppy, hot, wet kisses that had them licking each other while their hands explored each other with an insatiable curiosity and thoroughness.

She groped around until she found the condom. After she opened it, she slid it over his straining, engorged penis. She tucked it over him with a loving, warm embrace. His breath increased as his gaze stayed riveted on her. She smiled, because it was the first time she felt more comfortable and capable in a situation than he did. She pushed him to sit down as she climbed towards him, her knees splaying over him before she used his shoulders for leverage and handles.

"Are you ready?" she asked softly, her eyes fastened on his. He clung to her as he nodded, for once at a loss for words.

Sliding her crease over him, she let him rub against her several times as she sucked in a breath. All the nerve endings inside her were waking up, being bathed in warm sensations that soon became white hot. She rubbed herself over him until her body filled with the wetness that she craved.

When she lowered her hips down on him, his breath caught as his eyes widened at all the new sensations filling him. She smiled and watched him, letting her body envelop him. He suddenly leaned forward, and his mouth took hers before he kissed her long and deep. She put her hands around his neck and held on, pushing down and pressing their joined bodies closer together, as much as nature would allow, and he gasped and groaned.

His eyes shut, and he gritted his teeth. Probably to keep himself from coming. She wouldn't have been surprised. She understood. Building up his stamina might take a few times. She was thrilled to see his pleasure and how much he enjoyed being inside her. It made her feel grown-up, beautiful, mature, and powerful.

She pulled herself upwards and slid down on him following several longer, slower pushes and pulls. Their bodies excited each other with excruciatingly erotic friction. He held her, and she pulled on his torso, leaning back to position him on top of her before she opened her legs wider.

He let out a gasp as the sensations changed with her movement. Leaning over her, he finally moved his hips. Once, then twice and each time, she gasped out warm sighs. He seemed to gain more confidence in himself as he started moving inside her more. Slowly at first, half in and half out, until it was further in and out, and much harder and lasting longer. When she lifted her hips to smack into his, the sensations were explosive. She egged him on until he was pounding into her and she felt the warming sensations start to turn hotter. He came inside her with a forceful shove before collapsing onto her with a long, deep groan.

She accepted him, although she wasn't there yet. He slipped out of her and quietly fell to the side. She reached down and took his hand, showing him where she wanted him to touch her. Always a quick study, he immediately moved his fingers deftly and she leaned back against the pillow, arching her back and hips towards him until the delightful wave finally engulfed her and she screamed out when she climaxed.

He leaned over her, his expression nothing less than stunned. Her eyelids eventually fluttered open only to find him staring at her. "Hey," she said softly.

He blinked, as if he were surprised she could speak. "That was…"

She smiled and stretched before tucking her arms around his neck and pulling him down to kiss his lips. "Yes. It was."

His gaze traveled over her. "Was it at all… even close for you?"

"So close. It's good, Charlie. We were great. Trust me."

"You're okay?" he seemed very concerned about how she rated his performance.

She touched his cheek and lifted her head, so she could peck a kiss on his cheek. "I'm okay, Charlie. I loved it. I love you."

His expression wavered. "It'll get better."

She shook her head. "Don't do that. Don't cheapen it as if you're a stud service or you think I would compare you to others. It was strictly about us. Now. Here. Forever."

His head dropped down to rest on her neck. "Forever."

"And always," she said as she hugged his body closer to her. She knew she would love him like this, how she felt at that moment, for the rest of her life.

CHAPTER 6

*C*HARLIE AND CAMI SPENT the night in the trailer and Cami snuck back to her home before dawn with the sheets of the bed in her arms. She intended to wash them and put them back on the bed when no one else was around. No one else ever used it, so she was sure they could get away with it. They tried it two more times and her body got so sore, it protested with aches and tenderness. It was lovely and sweet and hot and new. As Charlie walked her to her house, he stopped and kissed her half a dozen times. She had to laugh as she shooed him off.

Then the thought drifted through her mind that, from now on, he'd want sex from her, and perhaps, it would make it easier for her to keep him. She instantly shunned the thought; she didn't have to do *that* to keep Charlie. She also didn't have to be manipulative or nasty or jealous. He was as true as the North Star and would have been so if she could simply trust him. She knew that in theory.

Even though it was so hard for her to do in practice.

But lying in her bed as the morning dawned, her body gleaming with the heightened sensations of love's afterglow.

She flopped down, wondering, for the thousandth time why just being there with her couldn't be enough to satisfy Charlie?

They were so good together and so much in love. Their sex was better and more fulfilling and genuine than she'd ever had before. Why did he have to go somewhere else to find whatever he still sought? Why not stay and work there? With a ton of different choices, why couldn't he pick one? Why did he need to earn a stupid degree anyway? Just to return and do what he could be doing here now?

He was the owner's son and had all the choices in the world, yet he insisted on getting a college degree? It was mandatory, however, and non-negotiable with Charlie. She knew not to try to sway him, but it took considerable effort to keep her thoughts to herself forever.

She had to be supportive. Cami knew if she didn't support Charlie, she'd eventually lose him. When he left the first time for school, he wasn't sad at all, but guilty. He felt terrible for upsetting her, but she also knew, he wasn't broken up inside about it like her. No. Nope. Charlie was okay, he was fine being away from her. So, she had to be okay with that or she would have lost him. And the only thing she felt one hundred percent sure about was that she had to do anything in her power to keep him. She loved him way too much to risk losing him.

It was so easy to express her joy at seeing him home the next morning because she felt that way. So easily they hugged and spoke quietly to each other. Her parents exchanged smiles of appreciation of their sweet greeting to each other. Charlie grinned and winked at Cami. Yeah, they fooled everyone!

It was a lovely few days. Almost enough to make up for the long, lonely months. They had a huge Thanksgiving dinner at Jack and Erin's house and the entire family came, including every sibling of Jack's and their extended families. Kailynn's brothers and their significant others also attended the feast, as did Allison's parents.

Cami's heart always swelled with joy when she watched Baby Lillian run up on her chubby legs, squeezed into white tights beneath her little, pink dress.

"Uncle. Uncle. Take me see horses? Pwease?" she twinkled and grinned.

Charlie, who was speaking to AJ, stopped and leaned down to pick her up.

"Let me finish talking," he said as he kissed her. She tucked her head onto his shoulder while he continued talking to AJ.

He gave his full attention to his niece, who giggled when he pretended to nibble on her chin and neck, acting like the "Cookie Monster" from Sesame Street. He even mimicked the voice and chanted, "Me want cookie." Lillian erupted into peals of giggles as she threw her head back with unbridled glee.

He tilted his head towards her and Cami loved how often he did that. It signaled that he wanted her beside him and she assumed that whatever he was doing, she was included. She scrambled to her feet and grabbed her coat, taking Lillian's other hand as they walked her towards the barn. They let Lillian guide them towards the specific horses she wanted to see. She was already showing a huge love and respect for horses and seemed quite fearless around them already.

They laughed with her as she kept them chatting and exchanging heated, happy glances. Yes, sex really had changed everything. It made everything that much deeper and closer and surer between them.

The most ordinary conversations and comments became intimate interactions, communication laced with innuendo. They often stared at each other as the words that were spoken seemed less important than how they looked into each other's eyes.

Charlie was the celebrity of the day. Everyone was so impressed with him and they all wanted to know how his first quarter went. People asked what he was studying and every other conceivable detail about it.

Thanksgiving dinner was huge and delicious, and Cami was grateful for her life and her future but most of all, for Charlie.

They snuck away to her room. This time, it was an ethereal rush of grabbing each other in long, sloppy kisses as they pushed and prodded to remove the lower halves of their clothes. When they finally freed the necessary organs, they were grinning at each other like two little kids, sneaking off to gorge on a stolen dessert.

As soon as possible, they united their eager bodies and groaned at the familiar contact. Using a condom, as always, they moved as one, and were still standing before Charlie lifted her upright and held her tight. When they were finished, they fell as one onto her bed, laughing, giggling, hugging, and kissing some more. She loved that part. The joy and ease they always shared. The intimacy. The bond and the friendship. By the time AJ and Kate returned, they were already downstairs, redressed and properly sitting on the couch together, watching a movie as innocently as ever. They smiled their hello to her parents.

Their stolen times were one thing, but occasionally, they could indulge in longer, easier, and more relaxed couplings. Even when it was quick and secretive, it only made it surprisingly hotter.

After Charlie left for school, he missed her much more. She was sure of it, judging by the urgency of his calls. The body's longing for physical contact was a powerful tug for someone who had never known it before. She used it to her advantage. She believed they were just falling deeper and more madly in love. By the time it was winter vacation, they were almost depressed whenever they spoke because they became so anxious. He snuck home again early, and they met at the trailer. Without kind words or slow reassurance, they came together in a matter of minutes, enjoying mutually loud, screaming, satisfied orgasms. All of that happened before Charlie lifted himself off her to suddenly grin. "Hi, girlfriend."

She smiled back, pushing at his sweaty hairline. "Hi, boyfriend."

He shuffled back. "You know I missed you a lot and for more than just this, right?"

"I know," she said with a grin. "But you have to admit, it's at the top of the list."

He snuggled against her. "I don't know, this feels awfully nice. Especially with a foot of snow outside and the temperature hovering at two degrees. Nothing feels better than having you wrapped around me. Even when it's all so innocent."

She agreed, sleeping together was the best treat, the highlight of it all. They both understood that. Although some parents might have tolerated their teenage children sleeping together under the same roof, Cami and Charlie knew better than to ask their parents. So they didn't. No one else knew about it, and if anyone wondered, they didn't ask. Cami and Charlie were both very discreet.

It was a blissful winter break. All their time was spent together. The weather was freezing cold and they could do no more than run to each other's house before shivering for half an hour.

Their busiest season was always between Christmas and New Year's. People came for the snow. There were sleigh rides and ice skating and a tree lighting ceremony. One of the centrally located firs was all decked out in silver, white, red, and gold.

A glorious wonderland and festival of lights were combined all in one. The staff had increased to a sizable number, but they invariably had to hire seasonal help, which included Cami. She still had to work even while Charlie was back home, and it often irritated her, although she didn't dare voice it to AJ, Kate or most especially, Charlie. They were glad to see her working and succeeding without being so hung up on Charlie that she couldn't do anything else but miss him.

And that's exactly what she was: hung up on Charlie.

Cami wanted to live with Charlie and looked forward to spending each dinner and evening with him. She wanted both of them to work there on the ranch in some capacity. And to spend all of her spare time with him. Not the snippets they squeezed in during his stupid vacations. Especially when the whole resort was packed full for family fun, it was hard for Cami not to get caught up in it.

She saw families frolicking together and thought, *I'd like to have that.* She started to imagine it, and often fantasized about it. She'd never had anything like it before. No family. Or siblings. Or sense of security. She fondly imagined having a baby who had two parents who loved her and a place like this to grow up. She longed for it as she watched Charlie interacting with Lillian, wondering what he'd be like with their toddler, their baby. She began to think of it more frequently. Naturally, she knew now wasn't the right time or even on Charlie's radar yet.

Cami and Charlie spent most of their time with Ben and Jocelyn. Cami couldn't help envying their marriage and baby. They were also building a house together. Both were happily working and being together all the time. She witnessed their tough start, but also how it turned out. Best of all, they had Lillian.

There was nothing special Cami wanted to do in her life. Her feelings, excitement, and passion were all about relationships: with her parents, her boyfriend, and Charlie's family.

How could she feel excited and passionate about school or work or training for a job? Those were so insignificant compared to things like getting married to Charlie and someday having his child. Children were the only things she loved to dream about. All the things she never had meant everything to her now. A family. Perhaps that made her more prepared to start one than most her age.

The vacation was a beautiful, wonderful bubble of pretending and imagining what it might be like to live together. The rest of the family was happy to see how well they seemed together. Dinners with Jack and Erin or her dad and Kate were always something Cami looked forward to. She had plenty of fun with the horses and the snow and teasing each other. Most of all, she had fun with Charlie.

But January came, and Charlie went back to school. The ranch put away its Christmas shine until next year and returned to normal except for an endless blanket of pristine, white snow. The winter hit hard, leaving several feet of snow on the ground all the time while the temperatures dipped below zero at night. It was dark by four o'clock and Cami felt depressed and alone.

She was bored, especially after the constant companionship and fun she had with Charlie. He was home for most of December and the first week of January. Now it was just Cami again. Alone. In the darkness and cold. Depressing couldn't begin to cover it. She tried to stay busy but with only a few oddball guests still at the resort, business was almost dead. After the holiday rush, the ranch relied on a skeleton crew for very few guests.

Charlie was cramming for finals and had little time to talk to her. She hated being put off or ignored because of his stupid schoolwork. Gritting her teeth, which he didn't know, she kept silent and stayed smiling, supportive, and sympathetic, even if it made her want to scratch her eyes out.

THE NEXT THREE months were a continuation of that theme. Her boredom and loneliness could have eaten her up and all the while, Charlie blossomed. Making straight As and meeting plenty of friends, which he certainly never had before. And Cami detested it. She was so envious over them stealing such large chunks of Charlie's time, without her, and hearing him experiencing so many new things.

Eventually, she saved up enough money to visit Charlie. She took the time off from her job to do so. During the entire bus ride to his college, all she could do was think about seeing Charlie and her heart felt like it could explode. She was going to see Charlie again. Charlie was the huge reward at the other end of her tedious road trip. At last, she could see her first glimpse of the mysterious life he lived.

In her more honest moments, she had to admit she hated his college life. It stole him from her. Like a new mistress, it was Charlie's main focus and it kept him busily engaged. He was changing and none of it had anything to do with her. It relegated her to being no more than an afterthought, the anchor back home that kept him rooted in River's End, instead of being fully submerged in the school's social life and culture.

Now she could almost be with him and she was so excited, it ate away at her stomach lining.

Just before she left, Kate asked her, "Do you think... we should go see about birth control? I mean, just in case?"

Cami blushed to the roots of her hair and shrugged. Kate sighed. "I know about the trailer, Cami. I'm not like everyone else. I know. I also know how you two feel about each other. That's why I think we should be safe, not sorry."

So Cami nodded. They went to the doctor and Cami started on birth control pills. She knew it was the right thing. Her desire to rush forward with all the things she witnessed in Ben and Jocelyn's situation wasn't practical. She knew that. She really did. She knew they should have a place to live and work and probably live together before they decided to get married. And that wasn't now. Or anytime in the next several years. Of course, it was a good thing. The right thing.

But it still didn't change her desires. She adored Charlie. She wanted to be with him every single day. She could only think and dream about what it would be like to live together every single day and even went so far as to fantasize where that place might be.

Now they were apart for several months at a time. Surrounded by young peers of Charlie's age, Cami imagined that thousands of students were always right there beside him. Living with him and partying with him. He had every opportunity to fall for someone else. The statistics of young love and long distance were dismal at best.

And Cami's past was also dismal. It was far easier at times for her to expect the negative realities than believe they were somehow special and could beat the odds. Her early life was a testament of *not* beating the odds.

She took Kate's advice about the birth control pills and pretended she was grateful although she was mostly ambivalent, only using them because, yeah, duh, it was the right thing to do. The most responsible and decent thing to do.

It didn't mean she couldn't long for something very different.

And it also didn't change how eager she was. Her stomach

bubbled with excitement. Finally, she would be with Charlie again. She never considered that taking such a trip could be hard or that it might be difficult to see him so developed and involved and independent without her. But she felt ready to face their long, uncertain and separate future. And to do that, she had to first find a way to dispel her crippling insecurities.

CHAPTER 7

CHARLIE MET CAMI AS she stepped off the bus. He swept her up in his arms and she huddled against this chest, breathing in his familiar scent, treasuring the feel of him and closing her eyes at his sheer essence. He was like no one else in the world to her. He wrapped her in his arms with a kiss that nearly devoured her on sight.

Anyone watching them, be damned, because for once, it wasn't anyone they knew. They kissed and hugged, plunging their tongues deeply into each other's throat before they finally separated. With broad smiles, they hugged tenderly, but tightly. "That never gets old," Charlie said, nuzzling just below her ear. She knew that too. It was the only thing she had to offer him that college and studying and new experiences and friends couldn't: sex.

They finally separated and held hands. He tucked her against him and they headed towards the campus. "That's the science and technology building. Library's over there. My favorite coffee stand..." He kept up a running monologue like a tour guide, his eyes sparkling with excitement. He loved showing her the campus. Yes, he was genuinely happy to see her and have her beside him. She believed Charlie now and that his love for her was exactly as he said it was.

But Charlie also loved college, the experience, the other students, and what he was learning. The passion he felt for all of it often emerged in his voice as he spoke to her. He easily prattled on about it, telling her everything about his days and weeks spent there. She knew the names of most of his close friends, along with all the people in the classes he liked, disliked or was working with. He was candid and open and didn't hold back anything.

She was as much a part of his life there as she could possibly be from so many miles away. It wasn't like he gave off subtle signals of wanting to be free from her. There was nothing to justify her insecurity or her fear of him outgrowing her. Charlie didn't seem anchored by her in any sort of negative way. So, it clearly was her issue, even though she could not fully understand it.

They stopped at Charlie's favorite courtyard, an all brick area with quaint seating, coffee shops, and unusual places to dine.

"Rydell!"

They turned at hearing Charlie's name and up came a huge, burly guy and two others flanking him. Charlie fist-bumped him and said, "Hey, Dawson. This is my girlfriend, Cami. Cami, Dawson, and that's Cliff and the other guy is Tyrell."

Charlie had friends on the football team. All three wore jerseys with the university football team emblazoned on it. Their physical bearing and body builds gave them away. She blinked. High school Charlie was only identified as the son of a famous family. Here? Charlie was known strictly for being Charlie, a friend to the football players.

The big one named Dawson turned towards her and pretended to push Charlie out of his way before draping a large arm over her shoulders. "Daaaamn..." he drew out the word. "Little Charlie here wasn't lying about you. I used to wonder if he made you all up. Cami-the-girlfriend, it's very nice to meet you."

She glanced up towards Charlie who let her go and smiled, looking amused while rolling his eyes at Dawson. His hands casually slipped into his coat pockets.

"It's nice to meet you too," she finally said, her words fragmenting. All of a sudden, her nerves made her self-conscious and she was unable to speak normally. She glanced upwards. He towered over her.

"You are so fi-i-ine. I thought Charlie only dreamt you up. Tell me, why are you wasting your time with that skinny bean pole?" Dawson was kidding, ribbing Charlie, but Cami fidgeted all the same. She wasn't used to anything like it and she glanced at Charlie for help. He noticed her discomfort and grabbed her hand, pulling her forward.

"Because she has better taste than that."

Dawson laughed, liking his answer. "Well, promise me we'll see you two later, out and about. Got some good parties lined up this weekend."

"We'll be around," Charlie said with casual ease as he held Cami's hand. They spoke a few more moments about class and an upcoming quiz they had to study for. Then the trio wandered off. Charlie continued walking, but when he glanced down at her, he was startled at the look she stared up at him with.

"What?" he prompted in obvious confusion.

"When did you become so... so with it? So well-liked? You have football player friends?"

"They're friends of Rupport, you know, my roommate. So naturally, they're around the dorm a lot. They're not so bad." He wasn't the least bit smug or impressed with himself. Charlie always knew exactly who and what he was, regardless of whomever he was with. He didn't vacillate or change his opinions, his behavior, or even his tone of voice for anyone.

Finally, they came to the towering hall of his dorm. She glanced up at the concrete structure with large windows and he keyed in the code before they entered the building to take the elevator up. Her backpack was still on her back. Down the hall of doors, most of which were covered in posters, chalk or white boards, signs and flyers, Cami thought it looked like a collage of colorful wallpaper.

Charlie unlocked his door and swept his hand, indicating for her to go in first. She entered and was a little shocked when she saw how small the square room was. A window at the center, each side was identical with a bunk bed and desk unit built in underneath. The only luxury was the small love seat placed under the window. Football gear cluttered the floor of Rupport's side and Charlie's was much better, but probably on account of her showing up today. She set her backpack down.

"It's not much. I told Rupport you were coming, and he said he'll crash at his friend's house so…" Charlie was really telling her they had the space to themselves. Her heart leapt with joy. She walked to the window and stared out. Her view was of green grass peppered with students walking or milling about, and trees that hugged the trail towards the brick and cement of the quad further off.

Cami grew up with much worse places to live than the dorm. One-bedroom apartments and once, a cheap shack that someone converted into a one-room living space. She remembered once sleeping in an abandoned church.

So, when she arrived at the wealth and privilege of the Rydell River Ranch with the invitation of staying there for good, she felt like Cinderella, minus a charming prince and a pair of glass slippers.

Giving all of that up and moving into something as small and tiny as his dorm made Cami shudder. It stunk for one thing and it was ugly with concrete outer walls and cheap vinyl flooring. Residents even shared a crowded, giant bathroom.

Why would anyone live like that if they didn't have to? And they paid for the pleasure! It was hard to figure out why Charlie would go backwards in his lifestyle. Especially since he had a choice.

She felt intimidated with Charlie in that setting. He was doing something she couldn't compete with, nor understand how to. He had friends she didn't know, and she doubted they were the kind of friends she could ever make.

He came up behind her and set his hands on her waist, his arms surrounding her while his mouth touched the top of her head. "What are you thinking about?"

She smiled. "Why you choose to live like this. You even pay for the privilege. This is a lot like what I was always trying to avoid for most of my childhood."

He laughed and rested his chin on top of her head. Sighing contentedly, she relaxed, leaning back against his chest. "That's a point of view I've never considered."

"But I know you're getting smart and worldly and knowl-edgeable and pretty soon, you will be trained and all that."

"That's kind of the idea." She felt his warm breath on her scalp as he kissed her again. He was extraordinarily affec-tionate and kissed her often. Just a peck on her cheek, fore-head, head or lips as if to say he was thinking about her. Or he could not resist her.

He held her and hugged her all the time he was with her. He clasped her hand or simply wrapped an arm around her shoulder or waist. He constantly let his interest, care, and concern shine for her. Even more flattering, he simply wanted to touch her and connect with her all the time. Often that was why the subsequent loneliness when they parted surged even stronger and felt more suffocating.

She adored his constant presence and the feeling that he could never get enough of her. Being beside her. Near her. With her.

She leaned into him and sighed, setting her hands over his and interlacing their fingers.

"You know I'm glad you're here, don't you?" he said softly, muffling his voice as he spoke into her hair.

She smiled to herself and tilted her head backwards so she could look up at him. He glanced down and dropped a kiss on her mouth. "I don't know. I never know. No matter how much I tell myself to be strong and confident when it comes to you and me, I'm not. You know, I could go out and beat up a mean girl or find a drug dealer with more confidence than I have to accept all the good things you try to show me and feel with me and share with me. I can't ever fully believe you could want me as I am."

"But that doesn't change what is. And I am the one who decides what is for me. If I say it is enough, and I support it with enough love, do you think you'll ever believe it fully one day and without hesitation?"

"I want to. So desperately, I do. I want to. But..."

"The thing you have to remember when you doubt or question it is that I am already aware of your doubts and more importantly, why you have them."

"Yes, you are, aren't you?"

"Yes." She turned in his arms and slid her hands up to his neck, trying to pull him closer to her. She closed her eyes as his mouth descended. The first contact was soft, sweet, and reassuring as if to punctuate what they had just discussed. It quickly grew ravenous though as their mouths opened and their tongues tangled and collided, and their hands started to roam and wander.

His hands pushed upwards against her breasts and her nipples hardened with his fiddling and contact. Her hands tousled his hair and he pushed away her shirt and bra to slide his tongue and lips over her erect nipples. She stripped naked and sat on his bed as he quickly followed her.

Minutes later, after rolling over and over and discarding clothes, the sighs and moans filled the air. He pulled out a condom and she took it in her hand. "Kate knows all about the trailer and she took me to the doctor to get some birth control pills. She told me to have a full exam and I'm clear and healthy... so we don't have to use these anymore."

He glanced at her hand then back at her face. His eyes were so blue and intelligent. She always loved watching his brain work, observing how he evaluated the situation and used his calm, cool confidence and reasoning. But he was taking an awful long time to respond. What was he doing? Doubting her?

As he sat there silently, she grew resentful. "Charlie?"

The mood instantly dissipated at his hesitation. She pushed on him and he let her up. She sat up, placing her back to where he lay behind her.

"You don't trust me?"

"Is this a test?"

"No," she snapped. But yeah, maybe it kind of was. "I just didn't think you'd hesitate like that."

"Well, it seems like it could warrant an interesting conversation, but not right when we are about to do it."

"They're birth control pills, Charlie, what do you think they're for? Exactly this. This is what works."

"Are you sure they're effective? You'll take them religiously and never forget? I don't want to make any mistakes, Cami. I don't want to be like Ben. It means everything to me." He pushed himself up until he sat beside her and rested an arm around her as he leaned towards her. Was he trying to soften the harshness of his words?

"Believe me, I know that; everyone knows how you disapprove of Ben," she scoffed, crossing her arms over her chest, trying to hide her nakedness. He leaned back and tugged on a blanket to wrap over her shoulder. He was considerate, wonderful, kind, caring and sensitive as always.

"I did judge them. They made their lives so hard and impossible when they didn't have to be that way. It worked out, but only because they fell in love. What if they hadn't? It wouldn't have worked out half as well for them or Lillian. And of course, I don't wish there was no Lillian. I adore her, but I'd like to *decide* when to have kids. I want to be responsible for my life… and you… and us. I don't want an unexpected pregnancy, not until we are ready, in every single way."

"I know all that. That's why I took Kate up on her offer to get the birth control."

"Yes, but you didn't discuss it with me. Or let me just a have a second to get used to the idea. You always seem so relieved that I know you. Shouldn't you know me too? I need a second. I don't react to surprises that well. I just need a moment to process it. Why do you have to assume that I'm hurting you or I don't believe you? Why do you always cast me as the villain when you should well know by now I am not, and especially when it comes to you?"

Her gaze shot to his. He stood up and shuffled around until he found his pants and slipped them on, looking back at her. He rarely got upset with her. She had a quick temper and exploded with him sometimes, but usually, his patience with her was admirable.

Something in her chest panicked. January third was the last time they had sex, three months ago. How could he so easily stop and blow this off? He must have been really upset with her. When honestly, he truly never was that way before.

So why was she so mad at him? He had every right to question her. She should have discussed it over the phone and told him what was going on and asked him what he thought.

It seemed so clear to her *now*.

But did she know that until this exact moment? No. She threw out the information and expected what? That he'd just change the entire foundation of having sex with her? And go from having some sense of control in how he prevented the one thing he didn't want to putting all his trust in her, especially without any physical proof she was actually doing as she said?

She just threw it out there at him without any preamble. Impulsive and presumptuous. Of course, Charlie wouldn't have reacted well to that. He was too orderly, controlled, and organized. Even with sex. They waited six months to have it because he wasn't ready.

She took a breath to calm her buzzing, hot brain. He wasn't saying he didn't trust her, but that he needed her to communicate better with him. She knew that, didn't she? Yes. She knew clearly that Charlie would not instantly assume she was trying to trick him. She knew he needed more time to analyze things. How could she throw that at him and not allow him a moment to register it?

He stood at the window, his hands on his hips, and elbows out. His back was slim and shoulders wide and white. He had a spray of freckles over his shoulders and around his neck. She always teased him about them and kissed the little dots, finding them adorable. They were one of the few things that made Charlie self-conscious, so she always tried to emphasize how endearing she found them.

Her stomach knotted. Three months, and they were

fighting after just spending several hours together. Hours of being alone and yet they couldn't figure out whether or not to have sex or talk. No. Oh no. What did this mean? Were they done? Hopeless? Had they lost the fragile connection that linked them so tightly?

She knitted her fingers together.

"Charlie?" she whispered.

His shoulders bunched up. She swallowed her raw nerves and took a deep breath. "Can I start over? I know you need some time with anything new. And I'm impulsive and I don't communicate well and too often turn it into a test. I didn't mean to do that with this. I just… well, let me try again."

His face turned far enough to glance at her. He was interested. She captured his curiosity. Tapping her fingers on her leg, she explained, "I should have said, a month ago, when Kate figured out I was coming here, she asked me to go to the doctor and get a check-up and birth control. She knew we were having sex, and like you, didn't want anything unplanned to surprise us. I agreed. I've taken them for twenty-one days. My period was last week so this is my second pack." She leaned over and grabbed her phone, quickly typing in a link about her brand of contraceptive pill. "Here."

He turned over and took her phone, glancing at her. "It's an information website."

He started to read and scrolled through it until he sat on the couch. He scrolled the entire article before he glanced up at her. "It's pretty safe, but—"

"I have to take them every day. No accidents for us."

"Yes."

"I will, Charlie. I know how you feel."

"Do you feel the same way?" His eyebrows lowered, and his mouth twisted. Obviously, he'd never considered she might feel differently. The surprise in his tone of voice made her hesitate, and she momentarily feared being totally honest. "Of course. I don't want any accidents either."

He got up and came over and held her phone out towards her. She took it. He flopped down next to her. "Why do you always have to take the most combative way to simply ask me something? Or to say something?"

She shook her head. "I don't know why. But honestly? It annoys me when I have to show you an official report summarizing what I tell you. Like you can't trust me to understand and repeat information. Or to follow it."

"Well, in this case, I don't know anything about it. So I wanted to know more. Sure. The moment I'm ready for sex with you isn't exactly the best time for me to be articulate or coherent even."

"You're still angry at me."

"I'm annoyed. Yes." She stared downwards. He let out a laugh. "It doesn't mean I can't get over it. But this annoyed me. Lighten up, Cams. If you intend to stay with me as long as I intend to stay with you, it's gonna happen. You can't take every altercation, big or small, as the end of it."

"Then how do I take it?"

"As a fight. A disagreement, a step in our learning process of how to tolerate each other, I don't know. It's just going to happen because it's normal."

"Normal," she muttered it as if she didn't know what the word meant.

He finally glanced at her. "Cami?" he sighed as he leaned over to grab her arm and pull her to him. "You make me insane and you drive me nuts and you know how to make me so mad, and then..."

She stared at him, wearily. "Then what?"

"Then you break my heart. You don't know what I mean by terms like 'normal disagreements' and little fights and

121

conflicts because growing up, what you saw wasn't the same thing that I saw, was it?"

She shook her head. "I never saw any conflicts that ended well. I think that's why I hide from them at all costs."

"Listen to me, okay? I can get annoyed, mad, and even angry with you or at you. And yet it means nothing and bears no weight in us staying together long term. One isn't the other. We *are* going to stay together, but we will have to communicate about issues and argue and fight and disagree about them. It doesn't threaten our love or our relationship. Do you see what I'm saying?"

"To be real, we can't always be getting along."

"Yes."

"Makes sense. And I know that you forgive my moods far more often than I have to deal with yours."

He kissed her head. She knew then that he wasn't mad anymore. Or annoyed. "And yes, now that I know the birth control you are on and how it works, I think it's great and so much easier than condoms."

She tilted her head up. "You trust me, then?"

"I do. I trust you, Cami."

Her heart lifted and thumped with pleasure from hearing his words. "Really?"

He kissed her lips when they became available to him. "Yes. Really."

A huge smile lit up her face. "Then... could we try it?"

He smiled and replied, "We could try it... maybe even a few times..."

CHAPTER 8

$\mathcal{T}$HE NEXT MORNING, THEY ran to get breakfast at a coffee shop on campus. Something as simple as that felt amazing to Cami. They held hands between bites of muffin and sips of coffee, chatting and grinning like kids as they gazed at each other.

Sex without condoms made it really good, no, great, even phenomenal. They made love three times before she grew so tired, she dropped off into a deep sleep, only to be awakened by him the following morning. Not for sex, however, but for class. Charlie wanted her to eat breakfast with him before his nine o'clock Economics class.

She walked with him to his classroom and he slung his backpack over a shoulder. "Call me when you're done. I'm just going to walk around and look at stuff," Cami told him.

"Okay. Soon as I finish. Sorry, I'd skip it, but finals are coming up."

She shook her head. "I'd rather you pass now, than have to make it up later."

He pulled her against him and leaned down to smooch her. Would she ever grow used to it? Would she ever feel the casual ease with which he did it? How special he made her feel? They ended the kiss and he hugged her. Idly. Just because. That always made her grin.

"Hi, Charlie."

He lifted his head to see who greeted him. "Oh, hey, Rosalie," he spoke over her head. Cami had to push back to see whom he'd spoken to.

Rosalie was a tall, leggy blonde who wore big glasses that perched on her nose, and hair that was tightly pulled back into a ponytail. She wore conservative clothes, almost on the nerdy side, but her natural beauty shown underneath it all and she could have worn anything and made it look good, Cami suspected.

Charlie let her go as he nodded towards her. "Rosalie, this is my girlfriend, Cami. Cams, this is the girl I told you about, my partner in the project final."

Yes, he had told her all about Rosalie Mintz. Every detail about how they worked together, how much time it took, what he liked about her style, and what annoyed him. He never, however, mentioned she looked like *that*. Cami scoffed internally.

As if she had to worry about Charlie Rydell, of all guys, cheating on her. No matter who or what, Charlie was the truest person she'd ever met. To her, especially. Always.

Rosalie scanned Cami with a critical eye and withering judgment. Her pleasant facial expression stayed put, however, and she smiled... finally. "Hi, Cami. Do you also go here?"

"No."

Charlie nudged her, answering for her when she didn't expand on it. "She's visiting from my hometown."

"Ohh," Rosalie's expression grew big-eyed as she pursed her lips. "Did you forget that I'll be gone this weekend? We still have to finish up the project before then."

"I didn't forget. We're on for seven, right?" Charlie let Cami go as he adjusted his backpack. Nope, Charlie hadn't forgotten. He even told Cami he had to do that after dinner and possibly tomorrow as well. No helping it. Cami said it was no problem. Her clinginess and need to have him around her seemed to retreat whenever she was actually with him. She found it much easier to handle him doing things that didn't involve her when they were together. She also had no problem entertaining herself, doing things as simple as listening to music.

Rosalie glanced at her. "Okay. Good. Well, nice meeting you, Cami. We'd better go. Professor just walked in."

Charlie winked at Cami as he released her hand, turning and following Rosalie inside. Cami peeked in and saw them sit next to each other, still chatting. Rosalie even touched his arm as they sat. Cami glared at the girl but invisibly.

Charlie was his normal, casual self, speaking to her while taking things out of his backpack. He was just as Charlie-like as Cami could ever conjure up in her mind's eye. There were no subtle or intentional signals from Charlie to Rosalie. But Cami noticed definite signs coming from her to him. A small smile curved Cami's lips, and her wonderful, sweet, handsome, confident, boyfriend had no idea of it. None.

It could never occur to him that someone as traditionally beautiful as Rosalie might like him. And he wouldn't have responded anyway because of his loyalty to Cami. The green-eyed monster of jealousy had no place in her heart.

But neither did she like it. As she turned to walk the campus and let Charlie attend his class, he texted her. That afternoon, they spent together alternately talking, making out and having sex.

"You want to just come with me? Rosalie lives in a regular apartment with some roommates so there's a lot more room than there is here." Cami pondered the idea. How much of his life did she never know about or witness? Strange friends in apartments and all the ways their time could be spent. But he invited her. He never excluded any details about Rosalie and Cami never ran across anything she didn't already know about from Charlie's own mouth.

"If you're sure…"

He stopped gathering up his supplies and zipping his backpack to glance her way with a small smile tugging on his lips. "Of course I'm sure. Besides, Dawson wants us to meet up later. So, we can go from Rosalie's to the local hangout."

"Okay." She glanced down at her jeans. "Am I dressed all right?"

His gaze flipped up and predictably, briefly scanned over her. "Since when do you care?"

"Since you started to hang out with football players and leggy blondes."

"Who's the leggy blonde?" His expression was deadpan.

She grinned and punched him playfully on the arm. "Gee, I don't know… Rosalie?"

He shook his head. "You still don't get it, do you?"

"Get what?"

"You are hot. Okay. Far out of my league in just your looks. I could only remotely stand a chance with you because of how you know me, and my personality. All the shocked reactions when my friends first meet you is because half of them believed that I conjured you up. Many commented on how hot you were, saying *no way would a girl like you date a geek like me.*"

"What? No. Not… no way. I'm pretty weird looking."

"For River's End, maybe. And you're really not. You have your own mental image of yourself that's still stuck on who you were at thirteen and everyone's initial reaction to that Cami. But that was more your own version of yourself. You've always been lusted after, Cams. You just never cared.

Here? You're hot and edgy. Not the kind of girl anyone expects to find with preppy, geeky, freckled, and bespeckled me."

"Bespeckled?"

He shrugged and grinned. "It just rhymed with the point I was making. You're hot. I'm not."

She paused. "You don't really think that, do you?"

"Of course I do. You're always so worried about me staying interested in you, when everyone who sees us as a couple rightly assumes that you'll be the one who eventually grows tired or bored of me."

"That's all bullshit."

"Hot. You are hot. Small and compact with wild hair and dark, mysterious makeup and clothes. No, you really are."

"You never say stuff like that to me."

"Do you want me to more often?" He set his stuff down and walked towards her, looking down into her face while wrapping his arm around her. His jaw clenched.

"No... of course not, that would be weird. That's not how we interact. But I'm just saying, I didn't know you thought that."

"I do. And you are. It's just not one of the reasons why I'm with you."

"It's what's on the inside?" She bit her cheek, holding in a snarky laugh.

He rose up from finishing packing his bag. "Actually, yes. It's how you make me feel."

"Oh, Charlie, how can you ever doubt me with you? There is no one that comes close to being like you." She grabbed his face between her hands and gave him a huge, loud kiss. He grinned as he lifted his head up from her grasp. "I'll say more if you'll promise to react like this. I just didn't think it was very important to you."

"It's not. Obviously, I'm feeling superficially insecure

here, on top of my usual insecurities. I guess I like hearing that you feel that way about me."

"I do. So, let's go see my leggy blonde and football player *friends*. Right? They are all just people I know."

She let him tug her out of the dorm as he locked it and she said, "It's still a tiny bit weird you have all these friends." She didn't add that she preferred him in River's End when Cami was his *only* friend that mattered. She was his *best friend*. His entire world. And the focus of his life.

Now? Being his girlfriend while he was at college? She was only one of many factors influencing his life. And shamefully, she preferred to be the one who dominated his thoughts, time, attention, and interest.

And except for Jacob and Brianna, she was it. His entire social calendar. But here she was one of many. His world had grown, expanding to places she never dreamed it would. And that was where her jealousy lay. She didn't care about Rosalie liking Charlie or Dawson and the crew wanting to take him out. She no longer held the title as the sole influence and most special friend in his life. She enjoyed thinking of the two of them against the world. He obviously needed more than she did.

They walked to Rosalie's apartment. On the way, she leaned her head into his arm. "By the way, you have some insecurity to overcome too. You are no longer freckled and geeky. You are confident, self-assured, handsome, and interesting and just a little aloof and not always accessible. Believe me, you will do nothing but drive women crazy the older you get."

"Yeah, but you are the only woman I'll ever direct it towards. So, it only matters what you think of me."

They entered Rosalie's apartment. Rosalie's smile wavered and dimmed after her initial greeting toward Charlie when she caught Cami's eye behind him. Cami smiled, her nerves swelling her tongue and making her unwilling to speak. But Charlie, ever the confident one, took the lead. Dropping his stuff down, he chatted to Rosalie and her roommates. There were two of them and he obviously knew them well, judging by their greetings and odd looks at Cami as she stood stupidly stiff as a statue behind Charlie. As if she couldn't survive without his presence. Owing to her shyness, that was usually the case. But in River's End it didn't matter. It rarely ever came up, not like it did here.

"Who's this?"

Rosalie turned to look at the dark-haired visitor. "Oh, Charlie's girlfriend, Cami."

Charlie glanced at her with a secret, little smile of amusement. "Cams, that's Kendall and Heather. Why don't you sit with us?" He glanced at Rosalie, adding, "We're heading out to meet Dawson and the gang after this." At least he offered a reasonable explanation for why she was trailing Charlie like a baby duckling.

"Oh. Fun. Maybe I'll join you too. Do you guys mind?"

"I'm sure no one does."

No one except Cami. Her eyebrows shot upwards in surprise. Charlie pressed his lips in an obvious effort to restrain a smirk and not crack up because he knew exactly what she was thinking. She liked that part about them. Their intimacy allowed them to discuss things using only their looks and tacit exchanges. He squeezed her hand as she sat near him. Then he turned toward Rosalie and started to discuss their project, none of which Cami understood.

Meanwhile, Cami perused her phone, putting her headphones on to avoid making chit-chat with the roommates. It took a while before Charlie was tapping on her hand. She yanked the earphones out. "Done. You wanna grab some dinner now?"

She nodded, her eyes lighting up in her eagerness to

leave. But then, oh yeah... All three girls grabbed their coats and keys, surrounding Charlie and fully intent on joining them. For a moment, Rosalie even managed to bump Cami out of the way. Rosalie insisted on telling Charlie a cute anecdote about one of their professors. Cami could only glare at her tall back.

Once free of the apartment and on the sidewalk, Charlie stopped and waited for Cami to come. He held out his hand, still chatting to Rosalie. But his smile stayed warm and completely fastened on Cami. He knew. She stared up at him gratefully. He knew Rosalie was into him and he couldn't have cared less. He saw her casually trying to shove Cami out of the way. *He freaking knew!* Taking Cami's hand, he squeezed it with a quick eyebrow lift, and wink of his eye, he pulled her right between Rosalie and him, causing Rosalie to physically step aside. He leaned down and grazed his lips on her mouth in a quick short kiss before walking forward. Cami underestimated him and had to restrain a laugh. She wrapped herself up in his love and attention, draping it around her heart as if it were a scarf she could physically wear. And in many ways, yeah, it really was something she could wear proudly. He loved her.

Shoring up her resolve, she found the strength and gumption to face them all. She ignored all the distractions that drew Charlie's attention away from her.

They walked into a crowded restaurant that crawled with college students. It was so odd for her to see Charlie as part of a popular crowd. Stranger still when he seemed as much liked and sought after as anyone else there. The girls tagging along with them were certainly there because of him. They all squished into a large table that had a booth on one end before sliding two more tables together with the accompanying chairs next to it.

There were a few hasty introductions. Cami nodded and smiled in return.

There was some teasing about "ask Charlie" stuff. Obviously, everyone already knew how smart Charlie was and how much he could help them. He'd already helped many of the players and won their respect and friendship. Rosalie and her friends knew he was smart too. They ate their pizza and drank their sodas and Cami heard plenty of jokes from the lewd to the perverted.

When they all suggested going to Tyrell's apartment for a party, her eyebrows rose. Charlie went to college parties? He didn't ever mention that to Cami and was so straight-laced at home. She trailed him when they entered the apartment. Music played as they all milled about the sparse furnishings.

The talk of alcohol and pot could be heard, and she briefly glanced at Charlie when Dawson offered her some. Cami rarely did any drugs in front of Charlie. It had become something she used to do in the past. And not too often. Then someone handed Cami a beer. She drank it quickly, grateful that it helped ease her nerves and loosen her tongue. She smiled a few times, and even laughed at some of the easygoing banter.

"Do you mind?" she asked Charlie as she eyed the joint being passed to her.

He smiled and made a sweeping sign with his hand. "I don't care."

Dawson, who was already half-baked, grinned and said sluggishly. "Oh, our Charlie don't do that stuff."

"Well, I know that. I'm the one who usually tries to make him join me," Cami said, laughing at Dawson. She was far looser now than she was at the start of the evening. She took the joint and drew a hit, coughing as she exhaled and sighing in happy contentment.

Dawson put his arm around her shoulder and squeezed it

as he grinned at her as if he were a proud new father. "Look at Charlie's woman. Never would have guessed he'd have a catch like you."

She let the drug relax her nerves and glanced at Charlie from under Dawson's arm. But he wasn't mad or even jealous. He smiled with a look of appreciation that she felt more at ease. She punched Dawson's muscled arm. "Then you're a dick if you can't realize he's the greatest guy here."

Dawson laughed out loud. "I like her." He let Cami go and Charlie took her hand as he grinned at her.

"I do too," he said right to her face, but quieter so the rest of the loudly obnoxious guys didn't hear him. But she saw over his shoulder that his words made Rosalie scowl harder as she stared at the back of his head. Cami shifted her gaze to Charlie, shining with love as his mouth descended on hers and he kissed her long and deep.

But as the night wore on, Cami became much more a part of it. Relaxing after the chemical substances began working inside her, she even entered some of the conversations, laughing at the constant ribbing and banter. They were actually a pretty cool group, mean and crude at times, but in a totally kidding and fond way. It wasn't hurtful to anyone but all in fun. Charlie was at ease with them.

That was the shocking part.

Cami always did better at social events with some alcohol and occasionally, weed. By loosening her natural reserve, she tended to drop her guard and allow some of her personality to emerge to the forefront. She found it harder to fit in without the drugs or alcohol.

Tyrell pulled her out for a dance with a few others who were as inebriated as she was and merely wanted to have fun. She glanced at Charlie to see his reaction. Typical, solid Charlie just raised his glass up to her. She was already pretty buzzed and well on her way to being drunk and she didn't want to upset him. No rise from Charlie, who just lay back and smiled. He was as sober as the day he was born.

Laughter escaped her throat and too many smiles made her cheeks hurt, but everyone responded to her. Usually, her stony face and shyness made her seem standoffish. Even after her *hands-off* goth look ended, most people didn't care to get to know her better.

She started having fun and was not just tolerating it for Charlie. Later in the evening, she spotted Charlie holding Rosalie up by her biceps. She was laughing so hard, she undulated like a wet spaghetti noodle. Rosalie said something into Charlie's ear and she nodded towards the hallway. He helped her walk down it.

Cami followed and hung back to listen at the door.

"You weren't making her up."

"Making who up?" Charlie asked as he helped her down onto the bed.

"Cami. The girlfriend. I thought she was like... I don't know, the hometown girl you were stringing along. But you're really into her."

"Yeah. I'm really into her," Charlie said as he moved away from Rosalie.

"I was really into you," she muttered, slumping over.

"Well, okay. But I'm not going to apologize. I told you from the start about Cami."

"She's not what I expected with you."

"How so? Too good for me?" Cami almost let out a laugh at his dry tone and blunt words.

"No. She's short. And she has weird hair. She was smoking pot out there."

"You're drunk. How's that so different? And she's not weird at all, she's hot."

"She's just... different." Her words slurred, and her head bobbled forward.

Charlie stepped back from her. "Are you okay?"

"No. Maybe you shouldn't leave me alone. I was just feeling sick."

"You just admitted you were after me and didn't believe how serious I was about my girlfriend. I'm not staying here. I have to go get Cami."

Rosalie sat up straight. "Your girlfriend? Didn't you hear me?"

"I heard you." He spun around and started out the door only to run directly into Cami where she hovered in the hallway. His eyes widened, and his brows shot up. "Cami?"

She merely threw herself at him and he caught her of course. "I am short with weird hair and you told everyone about me anyway."

He glanced down at her. "Did you doubt I would? I'm not available. I certainly don't go around pretending I am or encouraging anyone."

She gripped his forearm and squeezed, a huge grin splitting her face. "I love you, and I love how you hightailed it out of there to find me and get away from the girl who was crushing on you. You don't even hang around to let anything stupid happen."

He shook his head. "I don't want anything stupid to happen. I wouldn't set myself up for it."

"I'll sit with her."

He swept her hair back from her forehead. "By the way, I like your weird hair." Cami always dyed it black. Always. Ever since she was eleven years old. Sometimes, she wore it long and free, while at other times, she wrapped it up around her head.

Cami entered the room and sat down near the catatonic girl. After a few moments, Rosalie said, "It didn't seem like you really existed."

Startled, Cami sharply turned her head. "Pardon?"

Rosalie waved her arm. "With Charlie, he always talked about you, and named you even but you never came here so we doubted he had a girlfriend."

Cami's mouth tightened. "Well, he does. I'm her."

"I see that now. He's really into you."

"Yeah, he really is. What exactly are you saying?" Cami stared at the girl next to her as she looked sad about Charlie.

"I liked him. I know you saw that. You were cooler than most girls. They wouldn't have let him work with me and all. But he's like, totally obsessed with you, isn't he?" She sighed heavily and nodded towards Charlie as she said *he*.

Cami glared until she finally shook her head before a laugh slipped out. "This is the oddest conversation. What do you want from me? Are you warning me that you're going after him or... what?"

Rosalie tipped the cup and let it slide down her throat before she gagged and wiped her mouth with her sleeve. "Nope. Just realizing he's totally unavailable. Sorry, I was going to make a play for him after our project finished up, but now I know he'd have only turned me down."

"He totally would have," Cami said without scratching the coed's eyes out. Perhaps she would have if she hadn't caught Charlie being so faithful already.

"You're so lucky. You have no idea."

Cami had every idea. She knew what it meant to feel unlucky and to dare to suggest she didn't understand the value of a guy like Charlie Rydell made Cami laugh out loud. "You mean because he's honest and loyal and true? He didn't encourage you because he's so true to me? Because he's intelligent without making others feel stupid for it? Believe me, Rosalie, I really do know exactly what I have in him."

She sighed. "Ahh, shit. So, of course, he has to have decent taste in girls. I'm going to freaking end up liking you too, which only makes this more bitter."

Cami pressed her lips together, unsure if she should smile and laugh or punch the girl in the nose. But she was totally honest. "Why should I be friends with a girl who is trying to steal my boyfriend under false pretenses by taking him in here?"

She giggled. "You knew that, and it's so damn nice he didn't know that. He helped me here just to help me. And went running off as soon as he realized my agenda. Sending you in. Best put-me-in-my-place move ever, and he did it without being a dick. Yes, Cami Reed, you are so lucky." Rosalie shook her head. "Why didn't you try to scratch my eyes out?"

"Because I didn't need to."

"Right, Charlie takes care of himself."

"Uh huh. Are you really in need of babysitting? Or are you just practicing your manipulation?"

"I've been caught. But Cami, I'm really sorry. I just liked him so much."

"So do I."

She flopped her head back. "Maybe someday you can forgive me. I really enjoy being his friend."

"I'm sure he'll still be yours. I won't try to stop it. As you already saw, I trust him."

She sighed. "Yes, and you're the luckiest woman I know."

She left the mumbling girl, feeling so lucky. Seeing that someone like Rosalie also appreciated that, wow. They were a long way from River's End High School, a place where no one saw something so damn obvious.

She came back out to the living room where his friends still danced or talked in small groups, or just hung around. Taking Charlie's hand, they eventually left for his dorm, and only hours later, she woke up sick as a dog, spewing and heaving her guts out off and on for hours.

Bending over the toilet of the dorm and wishing someone

could end her misery made her rethink why she ingested such poisonous substances. She'd never done them consistently. Only sporadically and usually in a group setting that was brought on by her need to socialize.

Girls came in and out of the community restroom in the mornings, to shower and pee and style their hair as she sat miserably in a stall, rethinking why she did those things to herself. Maybe it was time to socialize without the aid of poisons that made her feel as if her stomach could expel her guts.

Finally, she hoped everything would stay inside. With nothing left to expel, how could any more come out? She took a shower, trying to wash away the hangover and its residual queasiness and shakes. Her mouth, dry and burning, felt as bad her head ached. She dried off and dressed before stumbling back towards Charlie's room. He turned at her entrance, looking bright-eyed and obviously fine. Wonderful. He grinned at her. "Any better?"

"Barely." She curled up on his bed, pulling her legs up to her chest.

He sat near her, patting her legs. "Well, you made a distinct impression. Seems you improved my reputation."

"I should never touch that awful stuff again. If I do, please take it away from me."

He leaned back. "It never interested me. I get ribbed about it every weekend at a minimum around here."

"Well, I'm no glowing recommendation for it," she said swiping a hand down the front of her. "Honestly? I've always wondered why you didn't try to dissuade me more often. Given my history, and coming from a place where drugs were so prevalent and you being so against it—"

"You rarely do it except with new groups of people. Like you need it to function in a social environment. So, I guess I don't see that as a problem. If you did it all the time? No, I wouldn't be supportive of that."

"You must hate seeing me when I'm high or drunk."

"I don't love seeing you the morning after usually, but you're pretty loose and easygoing and you smile a lot. So that's a point in your favor, and maybe I like that."

"I can't believe there is a world where you and I are well-liked by a group of people. People like football players and pretty girls and hot guys. How could this be us?"

He laughed and leaned over, pulling her against him. "I know. I felt that way at first. It started with luck of the draw in getting Rupport as my roommate. We hung out just naturally due to close proximity. He and his friends needed some help here and there with some of the classes we shared and for some reason, they seemed to like me. Here, I guess I cared more. Wanted to make my experience here more exciting. Since I had to be away from you, I wanted something to show for it."

"And this does."

"Yeah. You should have come here sooner. You should come more often from now on."

"Honestly? I didn't think you wanted me to. I wondered if you preferred to keep me and all of this separate. I mean, I could understand that—"

"No. It wasn't that. I just didn't think you'd like it. You know, considering…"

She grinned despite being so tired as she snuggled down against him and let her eyes fall downwards. "Considering how I am. I get it. And you know what's even weirder? I like the people here. The ones that are our age at home I just never did. I even kind of like Rosalie. She, at least, was honest from the start."

"I figured you'd forbid me from seeing or working with her."

"No." She tilted her head up to peek at him. "It helps a lot by being here, experiencing it, and seeing you in this new world, with these people, and this new environment. It also reminded me that outside things don't change you. And it totally reinforces how much I trust you."

"You ever consider applying to some kind of schooling?"

"I could never get in a place like this."

"Not here. But there are vast choices for this. You could think about community college. Even one close to here."

"I thought you needed this for yourself. You know, to establish more space and independence and all that."

"I just needed to get out of River's End. And see something more and meet different people. It wasn't to leave you or to get away from you."

"Sorry, but I still have no desire to go to college."

He squeezed her. "I get it. It's not for everyone."

She hesitated to mention she'd come here but not as a student, if she could live and work and mostly be near him. But she knew that wasn't what Charlie meant. Or wanted.

The rest of the week was idyllic, and just as full of surprises and discoveries as the first few days. He continued with his classes but at every opportunity, Cami was beside him. He hung out with his friends more often and Rupport slept in the room with them even if it seemed odd. He tolerated her presence without any issues.

When the day arrived that she had to leave, her heart felt like a rock inside her chest. Every separation they experienced struck her so hard. For close to three months she would have to go without seeing him. But then it would be summer. She'd have him with her again for almost four months then.

She lived for that moment.

He kissed her lips several times, and she held on to the front of his sweatshirt, trying to keep her tears back. They embraced and exchanged words of love and longing, reiterating how much they'd miss each other. Cami believed Charlie would miss her, but not quite as much or as badly as she missed him.

Seeing how true he was to her while being away, despite his new and exciting life soothed a deep, needy fear inside her.

When the three months trudged by, Charlie announced he was bringing Dawson, Tyrell, and Rupport back with him for the whole summer. Cami dreaded any interruption to her reunion with Charlie, but she smiled and pretended it was great.

Fine. Wonderful.

One week past their one-year anniversary, Charlie returned home after his finals. Dawson had a car, so he drove them to the ranch. When they pulled in, Charlie stepped out of the car to greet Cami and she hung back, unsure if she should make a spectacle in front of his friends.

He swung his bag to the ground when he spotted her, and a huge grin broke out on his face as he opened his arms as if to say *come here.* She had to quit doubting him. He seemed to always want her, even in front of his friends. Be they new or old.

The football players were amazed by the ranch, just as much as Cami was at the college. Charlie took them to the beach and the stables and barns. Their mouths dropped open in disbelief at the number of the horses being boarded and trained, as well as the resort, the arena, and all of the outbuildings. "I had no idea you were like a... freaking land baron!" Dawson exclaimed, shaking his head in amazement.

"Yeah, you keep yourself pretty humble, Rydell. I had no idea either," Tyrell agreed.

"I told you I was from a horse ranch."

"Yeah, this isn't the impression you gave us though."

"Damn. This will be one fine-assed summer."

And it was. The guys stayed in the trailer to give a little privacy to Cami and Charlie. But any time they managed to sneak away was valuable and precious to both of them. They got so desperate to see each other more intimately that they drove his truck into the hills above the ranch late at night and make do inside the cab or on a blanket.

It didn't matter though, since everyone had fun. They were loud and obnoxious and funny and raunchy. They loved to ride the horses and the ATVs, as well as swimming in the river or floating down the rapids.

When Brianna and Jacob showed up, the boys spent their time competing with each other in order to grab Brianna's attention and woo her affections. It was Brianna's best summer. She confided to Cami that she slept with Dawson and later, made out with Tyrell. When they almost entered a fist fight over her, however, she finally stopped seeing both of them.

But summer ended and Charlie, of course, went back to school. It was no easier on her than last year. However, she was dry-eyed and smiling as she said goodbye to him. No guilt-tripping. No scenes. She just pretended she was adept at their separations and although they were hard, they were doable.

Even if they weren't for her. Cami actually felt worse with every subsequent parting. It averaged every three months or so. He didn't return until Thanksgiving and then again at Christmas. She visited him during the winter and he came home for spring break. She visited him one more time in May before he was supposed to be back for summer. But he called one day in June.

"I'm sorry, Cams, but if I intend to get out of here after four years, I need to take a full load this summer. Plus, now that I'm definitely majoring in international policy, I need to get some prerequisite classes out of the way before I can start."

She gripped her phone at hearing his words and his explanation of why he could only come home for a few weeks. Three to be exact. Then he had to return for summer school. He was eager to go ahead and move farther along as fast as possible. After all, it meant his degree.

For three weeks he came home and then, he was gone for eight weeks. He returned home for just about three-and-a-half weeks before the fall of his junior year began.

He moved out of the dorm to live in an apartment with Dawson, Tyrell, and Rupport. Sometime during the previous spring, Rosalie hooked up with Dawson, so she too was moving into the new apartment. Cami detested knowing that and at first, she objected to it.

But Charlie reassured her, and she eventually held her tongue and had to accept it.

Sure. Of course.

Didn't she always agree with Charlie? And suck down her objections? She had to go along with whatever he wanted, needed and of course, deserved. She knew that. But the past two years were both hard and happy for her. She loved the highs of their reunions. It was always a dramatic feeling. Falling together in a desperate kiss, they held each other and looked forward to making love.

It was glorious, wonderful and exciting. But that wonderful high was always followed by another long separation. Even if it were just three days, three weeks or three months together, the separation always followed. She refused to lay a guilt trip on him or to complain. She just gritted her teeth and tried to prepare for however long the next separation would be.

Meanwhile, she worked the reception counter at the resort full time, and she still lived with AJ and Kate. That's it.

The only time she had company her age or anyone she cared about was when Jacob, Brianna, or Charlie came home. Cami loved it when their breaks coincided and they descended on the ranch at the same time. Between those perfect times, she was alone a lot and the only young person around.

During junior year, Charlie declared his major was International Policy with a minor in German. He took German in high school, as well as both years at Stanford. He thought learning German went well with his international studies.

His classes naturally grew harder and sometimes, he didn't have any time to talk. Definitely not as much time as they had before. Corresponding was even more sporadic. His temporary silences managed to always send her self-esteem plummeting before she began questioning and doubting him. However, she didn't voice any of it to anyone, not even herself.

Charlie needed to go to summer school again if he wanted to graduate the following June. Cami didn't object or raise an eyebrow. Somehow, she anticipated that announcement and knew it was coming. For three weeks in June and three weeks in September he'd be home but gone for all of July and August.

Brianna decided to stay home and go to summer school too, so Jacob was the only one who came back to the ranch that summer. He stayed with his mom and Joey and brought a backpack full of weed, booze, and even some harder drugs.

He smiled when he opened the door to her. "Cami Reed. How are you?" he asked before he embraced her in a long, tight hug.

She hugged him and smiled when he set her back on her feet. "Fine. It's been pretty sucky around here though being all alone. It's always just me."

Jacob stepped back, and his gaze roamed over her. "Charlie's going to summer school, huh?"

Had to. Oh yeah, he just *had to*. Couldn't possibly have done anything different.

He also had to have known for a long time although he didn't bother to let her know until the last possible second. *Anything that could have benefited her,* she thought sarcastically. It was essential for his degrees and the experience. Oh, let's not forget the experience. Stanford, California. Wasn't Charlie the most amazing and accomplished person to be able to attend Stanford? Fuck Charlie and all his new, being-out-in-the-great-big-wonderful-world—experiences.

"Charlie doesn't really want to be with me right now. I'm a big, fat downer because I'm kinda sick of his school and him always being away and becoming so wonderful."

Jacob's face scrunched up as he assessed her. "Come off it, Cami. He's your boyfriend. Don't be such a bitch about his educational opportunities. I'd dump your ass if you tried to tell me what to do with myself. But knowing Charlie, I'll just bet he's all sympathetic and sad and sorry. Quit guilt-tripping the guy for wanting more out of life and trying to be something better than all of us could ever hope to be."

She glared hard at Jacob. He was such an in-your-face, mouthy ass. And so, the opposite of when they all first met him. He stood tall now, at six-foot-three, with blonde hair and brown eyes. He was undeniably hot and gorgeous to look at. Unusually so. But his attitude often stayed in the weeds. "Well, my ass would have never been yours, so..."

Jacob flashed his teeth and threw his head back. "Oh, the things I'd do with your ass if you allowed it."

She pushed him. "You're such a pig nowadays. What happened to sweet, shy Jacob Starr? I miss him."

He pulled out a pipe and crumbled a bud inside before lighting it and taking a long hit. "No, you don't, Cami Reed.

You wouldn't have this kind of fun with that old, nerdy loser. And you've had enough of behaving nicely with our straight-as-the-As-he-gets Charlie Rydell. You love me, and you know it. Enjoy," he said while raising his eyebrows up and down salaciously and grinning.

She rolled her eyes but grinned back. "You're such a dick. And I would never date you or sleep with you, but I will smoke with you."

"See? I. Am. Fun."

"You are mixed up and definitely on your way to juvenile hall. But you're not my idiot, so I guess we can have fun getting there."

So, Cami's summer was better than she expected. Without listening to Brianna and Charlie's constant chatter of how wonderful and together and accomplished they were, Cami found it much easier to cope than she expected. Brianna was in college and she earned As almost as often as Charlie. They were both doing so well and meeting bushels of friends between the two of them. Being so well-adjusted, they had become the pride of their families.

Jacob and Cami? They were simply tolerated and that summer they spent together was a huge relief for both of them to just be that. They lazed around and hung at the beach alone or together with an endless supply of alcohol and Jacob's drugs.

"Where the hell do you get all of this?" she asked Jacob one evening.

"I have a friend who sells it."

"Everyone needs one of those," she said, blowing smoke through her lips.

"Never seen you use as much as you have lately."

"Never felt like doing it as much as I have lately." She trailed her hand into the river. It was still very warm even though the dead of night surrounded them. "Anyway, what the hell kind of friends do you have?"

He grinned, leaning back and staring upwards. "Fun ones."

"Are you and Charlie still friends?"

"Sure. Of course. He's my best friend. But he doesn't have to know or approve of everything I do, correct?"

"Correct." She flashed a smile and took another drink from the flask Jacob provided. "He's always at me, telling me to find my calling. My passion. Something to keep me focused so I'm not longing for him when he's gone."

Jacob threw a handful of little, tiny rocks at her. Then he smiled when she glared at him as she brushed them from her hair. "Well, can you blame the guy? You sit around here mooning after him like it's the... hell, I don't even know... maybe the nineteen-fifties, and little ol' you is just missin' her man. It's weird. It's annoying. It's lame."

"I'm not weird, annoying, or lame."

"You are weird." Jacob raised his eyebrows. "You can't deny that. You can be annoying with your sad fragility, and you are totally lame to expect Charlie to complete you. Actually, that's ridiculously lame. Don't blame the guy for telling you to get a fucking life."

Jacob said things like that often. Rude and crude and mean and degrading. She should have hated him for it. But somehow, coming from Jacob, there was no sting in it. Jacob had known her as long as Charlie and their friendship came easy. They never asked or wanted the other to do or be something beyond what they already were. His honesty was tolerable, even when she didn't like it.

Plus, they were usually blitzed when they had those conversations and her acceptance of him was far more lenient. "So, you wouldn't put up with a girl wanting you to be her entire focus in life?"

"Lord, no. You want him to make up for the fucked up shit in your adolescent years. Imagine trying to do that for years. A mother lode of emotions I sure wouldn't sign up for."

"Then why are you sitting here with me if I'm so lame and horrible and annoying and... what else? Needy?"

Jacob propped himself up on his elbow, staring at her. Moonlight shone down, casting his face in a weird, white glow. "Because you're none of those things with me. You demand a little too much in the boyfriend requirements, Cami. You wanted Charlie to fucking settle here and marry you at age eighteen. I mean... dude. No. Things don't work like that."

"I never asked Charlie to marry me."

"You still pine for him. Even I know that."

"You don't know much else." She mumbled, and he grinned.

"Yeah, I'm a dick."

"No argument there."

He leaned over and wrapped his arm around her shoulders. "I'm just an equal opportunistic dick. I don't give a fuck what you do or don't do. I love you no matter what, you know? Like I do Charlie and even my annoying sister. I'm here strictly as your friend."

She leaned against his shoulder and realized that. He said mean things, but they were more of an observation than an effort to engage her or ask her to change. He would never judge her or try to determine the kind of person she was.

She tilted her head up towards him. "You still living with your dad in the fall? In Seattle?"

"Yeah. Back to school."

"Why are you there if you hate it so much?" Jacob intended to start classes at North Seattle Community College.

147

A shrug, then a sigh. "I talk a big game but it's bullshit. I really can't figure out what the hell to do. So I go to school. Dad likes it. Keeps me from working at some crappy job."

A short laugh escaped her. "So it's easier to go to college?"

"It's expected from me."

"Not for everyone."

"No. But it is for me." He shook his head. "I don't care what you do. I really just hate to see how mopey and sad you always get when I leave."

She smiled. Having no strings or huge emotional investment did have some serious plusses. He could be honest with her.

"But Cami?"

She glanced at him. He shook his head. "Charlie is solid as the earth. He does care about you and doesn't want you to be sad. So, don't forget that. He'll always be back. I really believe that."

She wished she felt as confident.

Once Charlie was back, she and Jacob oddly stopped hanging out. In an unspoken agreement, neither one revealed how they'd spent the summer. They didn't smoke weed or drink any booze now. Not with Charlie around. They also didn't talk or interact with the ease that being without Charlie seemed to foster. They didn't hug or wrap their arms around each other, like they did so freely without Charlie.

It made her pause. There was a distinct effort from both of them not to act the same way they did all summer. What did it mean? Did they share a valid reason to control their reactions to each other? Exploring what that reason might be was way too hard for either of them to delve into.

Cami had a fleeting thought of the reason it suddenly became so much easier to be around lazy, feckless, fun, easy-going, kind, smart, funny Jacob Starr. Much easier than being with the person who loved her most of all. She believed Charlie did love her. Sometimes, especially of late, she had to wonder why they couldn't find the same kind of closeness, and ease, and acceptance of one another that naturally sprang up with Jacob.

Jacob wasn't accomplished, ambitious, motivated or an overachiever. He was no role model or any other positive representation of his age group. He wasn't intimidating either, and that intrigued Cami. She found it intoxicating and it called to her more often than she ever suspected.

When Charlie came home before his senior year after summer school, Cami began to really feel the pressure of his amazing accomplishments and her ordinary, stale existence. He changed a lot during his junior year too. His shoulders were wider, and he'd also filled out, putting on a good thirty pounds. His once skinny frame had plenty of muscle and meat that were never there before. His voice also dropped even lower and the deep tone matched his solid confidence and achievements. He looked more like a man instead of the teen Cami remembered.

Sometimes when she was with him or listening to him talk, she did a double-take, finding it hard to believe he was her boyfriend. He could intimidate her now with his articulate speeches and handsome and confident physique. She felt like the total opposite of him, scraping out her life in tiny River's End in contrast to his sphere at college.

Had she become the burdensome hometown girl? Charlie never once said such a thing, but Cami observed the changes in him. And her insecurities began to drive her insane.

IN THE FALL of Charlie's senior year, Kate came to Cami. "Are you sure you won't consider it? I feel like it's time for you to pursue something more challenging than covering reception at the resort."

"I don't want to, Kate. I know that disappoints you, but I can't... I can't stand the thought of not living here."

She nodded and hugged Cami close to her. "I know."

Kate suggested that Cami move to Seattle and work for her company. Cami had no interest in doing that. She knew a real success awaited her, right at her fingertips, one that many would have killed for and yet, she really didn't want it.

They were only months away from Charlie finally being finished with college. *Months.* No longer *years.* She thought it would never end. But soon, in a matter of months, Charlie would be home for good. Hell no would she move to Seattle to work at Kate's firm. No. In a matter of months, she and Charlie could start their lives together for real, and it began with just freaking being together. She could not wait.

Until Charlie started hinting over the summer he might want to look into graduate school. And then talking seriously about applying. Then soon, he was *applying* to them and fully intended to go to one. Even further away than Stanford. Possibly on the east coast.

Her heart flatlined. No. She'd suffered enough already by supporting his BA degree from Stanford. As if that weren't impressive enough to get him a really good, decent-paying job almost anywhere. Especially if he brought his degree home. She knew of no one else with such an impressive degree under his belt.

But more schooling? No.

Cami couldn't wait for years. Not anymore. Not again. But of course, they weren't married. He didn't need her opinion or her permission. He explained his plans, ideas, dreams, and hopes to her.

What did she do? She smiled and cared and supported

him and listened. She didn't give voice to the scream that constantly rang in her head.

NO. No more. Just fucking come home.

She was tired of going back and forth. Of him being a student. Hanging with his friends. She wanted to be adults with Charlie now and move forward way past being in school. She wanted them both to get jobs and find a place to live and they should start doing just that: being adults together.

As a couple. For real.

But of course, she didn't express any of that. Still not the right time yet. She did not want to appear clingy and pathetic or needy to him.

So she kept silent as fall progressed. She sometimes wondered how he could not possibly know how she felt about that. But Charlie didn't always seem to know her as she was today, or how her feelings changed from when she was thirteen, fifteen, and eighteen.

He came home for Thanksgiving as usual. By now, their families weren't shocked by the fact that they were twenty-two and twenty-three years old and having sex. She was even allowed to stay at the Rydells' house. It was awkward at first. Coming out of Charlie's room to breakfast with Erin and Jack left her blushing and stumbling over her words, not to mention being unable to meet their eyes. But they treated her as they always had and eventually, she knew it was okay. AJ and Kate even allowed Charlie to stay with her.

Charlie came home for Christmas and as usual, that month was the highlight of her year. In fact, it was even better because Cami kept chanting in her head that this was the last time. Next year, he'd be home for good. Living with her. She truly believed that. She had to believe that.

⁓

"Cami? I have to tell you about something."

"What?" Her heart dipped. Did he do something wrong? No, she couldn't picture that, but an odd stabbing pierced her heart. She ignored it. No. She knew better than to doubt him.

"Well, there's a company based out of Hamburg, Germany and they have a graduate program here. They offer a scholarship opportunity every other year to one student. They will pay for my master's degree in economics from the University of Hamburg and also provide me with an internship the first year and a paid position in the second. It's a once-in-a-lifetime chance."

"You want to apply for this?"

He cleared his throat. "No, I already did, and I was chosen."

She shut her eyes as the pain and disappointment ripped through her. Two more years. Not just two years working on his master's degree but doing it from another country. His return meant so much to her. Charlie's news changed the entire forecast and direction of her life. She shook her head.

No. She didn't want that. Not at all. She had nothing left in her emotionally and she failed to be supportive. She could not be his cheerleader while she waited another two years right there. Holding her breath in River's End while Charlie followed his dreams until he had the desire to want to be exclusively with her.

Her heart banged into her rib cage. She should have been exclaiming her joy that he was chosen from all the other applicants. It sounded like a huge honor that few received and yet, Charlie did it. But her heart was so low now, she couldn't find the words to fake a happy answer.

"Charlie, that's very far away. And such a long time."

"It's only two years. This will firmly establish our future, Cams."

"It'll make our immediate future too far away."

"We'll be all of twenty-five. That's not exactly old."

Wilting onto her floor, Cami was glad they were on the phone and unable to see each other. Tears streamed from her eyes unchecked. She couldn't stop them. She wiped them and her nose but ignored the urge to sniffle.

She had to be silent. He couldn't know she was literally on her floor right then, weeping with sadness. Grief. Exhaustion. She simply could not do that for another two years.

"It was a long shot. I didn't think I would win, and that's why I didn't mention it or tell you about it. No sense in upsetting you because I truly never dreamed I'd be chosen. But now that I was, it's a huge honor and a chance of a lifetime. Getting my graduate school paid for and an internship and a job? This would open up my career and the sky would be the limit. I want this so much, Cami. Please… understand. It's not about leaving you, it's about adding something to my life, something I never thought I could."

But like always, Charlie wasn't asking for her permission. He was doing it regardless. She knew that, deep in her gut, he'd support her through anything and never cheat on her, but he would not let her interfere with his education. That was Charlie's line in the sand and she *knew* it so she didn't dare cross it.

But she wasn't willing to do it anymore. She could no longer fucking wait. And wait. And wait some more for Charlie Rydell.

What then, could she do? How could she stop herself from waiting? How could she force Charlie to quit making her wait?

Deep down, she knew that nothing could make Charlie reverse his decision. She was stuck and destined to be alone for two more years, unless she broke up with him.

That was her only choice.

And since there was no choice in that for her, as she would not break up with him... here she was back waiting.

So instead of doing as she wanted or even saying *anything* true to her feelings, to her heart, to her desires, to her wishes, instead all she said was, "I am so proud and happy for you. I believe you are one in a million and that's why you were chosen. See? That just proves it."

"I don't see how I can say no to this. I can't refuse such an opportunity."

She nodded, and more tears spilled. Luckily, he couldn't see her. "No, you can't say no," she agreed, even though Charlie Rydell once more was putting her off, failing to consult her, and breaking off another chunk of her heart. "Of course you can't. It's a once-in-a-lifetime opportunity."

It just had nothing to do with her, but it did have the effect of changing the course of her life, her destiny as much as it improved and fulfilled his.

She just wondered at what point she would matter to their destiny.

Would there ever be a time when her life didn't hinge on waiting out Charlie's plans? Plans she just didn't quite ever fit into.

CHAPTER 9

*C*HARLIE GLANCED UP WHEN a knock rapped on the apartment door. Pushing away from his desk where he was buried up to his neck in books while cramming for mid-terms and writing two papers that were due, he realized no one else was around. He opened the door and was floored to find Cami standing there.

"Cams?" Puzzled, he stared at her for a long moment.

She stood idly, shuffling her feet and staring down. He sighed. After three-and-a-half years, he still hadn't convinced her she had complete control of his heart and never should have felt shy, awkward, or wonder if she were disturbing him.

"Hey." She shrugged as she raised her hands up. "Surprise."

He leaned forward to take her hand and draw her to him, wrapping her up in a huge hug that lifted her off her feet. He kissed her mouth, long and hard, and her breath tasted like mint. She laughed when he raised his lips long enough to nibble on her lower lip and kiss her cheeks before moving over to her ear. "I don't know what you're doing here, but I can't think of a better surprise."

She giggled and shook her head. "I just wanted to see you, and I decided I could. Right? I mean, every once in a while, we cannot be held responsible and we have to break some rules, right? I don't usually take advantage of my job by just taking off and leaving it."

"Whatever you did to get here, I'm glad you did."

She beamed as she glanced around. "Where is everyone?"

"Taking a study break before getting themselves so blind drunk that they won't be able to study."

"And you, of course, intend to finish your studying first."

He beamed at her. Her tone was so dry as she easily summed up the situation. "Yep." He swung the door shut and pulled her into his room. She dropped her overnight bag on his bed.

"Do you have any tests tomorrow?"

"Just one and a paper that's due."

"I knew I should have called first." She bit her lip.

"It's okay, I'm almost done. Let me finish the paper and print it and then you can quiz me for the test and then I'll be done, okay? Maybe take an hour? Tops?"

She nodded, her gaze wavering. "I really shouldn't have done this."

"You really should have," he grinned. "Just give me an hour, and then I'm all yours."

He loved how she always respected whatever work he had to do. She understood deadlines and test days weren't things he could control but very necessary to his school career. Work had to be done even if it often interfered with their plans and phone calls.

"Okay. I'll get some dinner. Have you eaten in the last day?"

He pointed at a box. "Pizza. The college student's staple. You sure?"

"I'm sure." She left, and he quickly started scanning his paper, knowing he was blowing through it. He felt stupidly excited to see her. It had been almost two months, but it seemed so much longer this time. Probably because it was the middle of the damn winter and everything was dark and dull and boring.

Charlie fudged through enough that he was sure his perfect grade point average would not be tarnished, and Cami came back in. She was licking a frozen chocolate bar on a stick. She bit into it and the vanilla ice cream encased in the dark chocolate squished and dribbled down her chin and fell onto her shirt.

He got up, laughing at her as he touched the spot on her shirt and she glanced down, scowling at the stain. He leaned forward and sucked the ice cream off her chin. "You know, you're like twenty-three now, right? You're not supposed to look quite so adorable eating ice cream. And it's the middle of winter. Why are you eating ice cream?"

Her shoulders bumped up and down in her coat. She unzipped it and started to shrug out of it, one sleeve at a time. She took another bite and chewed the frozen dessert some more. "It sounded good," she mumbled. He kissed her again and she paused to let him, while long moments passed. When he finished, she leaned her head back. "Does this mean you're done?"

"It only means I'm not going to flunk. That's good enough for me."

She pushed him back. "My ice cream bar is melting." He let her go and she started licking and scooping up the dripping vanilla ice cream with her tongue. She stuck the last bite in her mouth and smacked her lips before she went into the bathroom to wash up. Coming back out, she dried her hands on her coat before taking it off. She sat on the bed and the mattress bounced when she bumped up and down gently.

He started to approach her, but she shook her head and put a hand up. "Wait... can we talk? Could you sit over there? I'm nervous and that'll make it easier for me."

"Okay, so this isn't just a happy surprise visit because you missed me?"

Her head shook again. "No. Not at all."

His eyebrows shot upwards. "What then? What's going on, Cami? Are you okay?"

"Not really," she said softly. Tears filled her eyes and she blinked several times. It was automatic for him to get up and go to her. She noticed he started to and she vigorously shook her head while putting up her hand as if to say, *stop.* He did and sat back down.

More serious now, he asked, "Cami? What is it?"

"You make it harder when you sound so concerned."

"Because I *am* concerned. What is it? You can tell me anything. Haven't you always?"

"Yes. That's why this is so hard."

"Tell me then."

She stared down at her hands, twisting her fingertips together, then apart, together, and apart. She swallowed and kept her eyes averted as she sucked in a breath. "I'm not sure how to say this."

His stomach started to knot up. There wasn't anything he could think of that might upset her so much or make her act afraid to speak to him. It seemed out of this world to consider she would have cheated on him. No, they loved each other too much and no, he wasn't naive or hoodwinked. He knew she would not cheat on him. What then?

"Just say it."

"I... I realized..." Breathe again. Her shoulders hunched forward.

"You realized what?" he prompted.

She jerked and closed her eyes as the words spilled out as fast as she could speak. "I realized last week that I'm pregnant."

He stared at her, waiting. For her to... what? Deny it? Make more sense to him? Say she was kidding? He blinked several times.

"Charlie?" she whispered his name and barely lifted her eyes high enough to catch his. "Charlie? Did you hear me?"

He swallowed and nodded. "I heard you say you... you think you're pregnant?"

"N-not *think*. I *know* I am. I'm pregnant." Her shoulders rounded again, and she hung her head. She had no confidence in what she was saying. "I'm so sorry."

He closed his eyes as the meaning of her words fully slammed into his brain. He leaned his chin forward until it fell on his chest. Arms crossed defiantly, he tried to let her life-changing words seep into him. He kept shaking his head all the while because his stomach was in knots and twisting with denial.

No. No.

That was the one thing he'd always been so careful of and so sure he didn't want. How could it now be happening? All those years ago, he was scared to give complete control of that issue over to Cami. The stupid birth control pills worried him. But as time went by and things were okay, he started to accept it. But now?

His breath released. No.

Just no.

His whole life flashed in his mind. Immediately, everything he ever worked for and wanted exploded in his face. All the things he'd accomplished and still wanted to achieve, along with his dreams and desires, were incinerated by a single sentence.

He lifted his head up, his eyes growing wide as his mouth dropped open in disbelief. This was obviously the last thing he ever expected to hear from her. He woke up this morning to study for a test, and now was he about to end the day by learning he was about to become a father?

"What… what should we do?"

"Charlie…" her voice drifted off. "You know…" her voice cracked as she tried again, "You know I can't…" She started trembling and tears flooded her eyelids. "I can't get rid of it."

He shook out of his reverie at hearing her pained voice. She looked sick and pale and terrified of him. This was happening to her too. He got up and sat down beside her, putting his arm around her slim, small shoulders. He knew this had to be much harder on her than it was for him. Pulling her against him, he kissed the side of her head. "I know. I know, honey. This has to bring up a lot of painful issues for you. Besides I would never ask you to do that. Not you."

Her shoulders shrugged under his touch. "Yes. I feel guilty, even if I didn't plan it or want it, it still happened. It was still the end result."

She had already told him about what happened when she was barely thirteen. One night, while she was drinking heavily, she told Charlie what occurred before she came to live with Kate and AJ. It was never reported in her medical records. Or anywhere else. She was tortured, and she suffered, but no one ever knew about it. No one except Charlie, at that point.

She had sex with a boy. He was just a kid her age who showed her kindness, attention, and care, so they had sex. When her mom found out she was pregnant, she drugged Cami. Cami didn't remember too much about it. Her mother brought in someone to perform an abortion on Cami. She'd awoken to bleeding and pain and was screaming with fear.

But she got no help. She was lucky she didn't die from an infection, which was perhaps a miracle. Her mom kept her locked up in her room for a week and fed her pain killers and antibiotics.

She returned to school and never told anyone. They moved shortly afterwards, and her mother was arrested again. Cami had to endure another abusive boyfriend of her mother's and she relapsed into silence. There was never anyone to tell of her unhappiness. Six months later, her mother, Parker, died of an overdose.

The day Cami told Charlie the entire story, she finished in tears, saying, "It was the happiest day of my life when my mother finally died."

"She could have killed you, you know."

"She could have. And perhaps that's why I didn't care when she died. And when I found out I had a dad out there somewhere, I hurt so much inside. Nothing sad or bad that happened to me ever really had any resolution. I just encountered more bad and sad things that got piled on top of the older stuff. I never expected when I came here, that everyone would show me a different way of life. Most of all, I never expected to be loved. I know I'm kinda fucked up, Charlie, but in so many ways you can't imagine, you, Kate and AJ even, have healed something inside me. Just knowing people like you guys existed helped me so much."

That was why Charlie was so hesitant to start having sex with her. He believed her previous high school hook-ups in River's End were not for the sake of having sex, but because she was still working through the damage her mother had inflicted on her. That she'd been sexually active at twelve years old and pregnant at thirteen threw him. They had such contrasting childhoods, you couldn't even compare them, as if they came from two different planets.

But now? She'd just said she was pregnant, right now.

Today. The words barely registered. The words made him shudder. "I'm sorry, it's hard to process... or believe. I mean, I thought the pills were nearly one hundred percent effective. I should have never stopped using condoms. God damn it. I'm so sorry to put you into a situation like this."

She sniffed. "Don't. Don't do that."

"What?"

"Don't apologize to me or be so kind and understanding."

He kissed the top of her head. "Again, I know what happened to you. Of course, I'm going to react kindly and with love."

"I was never sexually abused. You know that, right?"

"Yes."

"I wanted to have sex, but I had no idea it led to my mom forcing an abortion on me."

"You were a kid who had been neglected and abused in other ways. You were just looking for help or some kind of emotional connection or whatever you want to call it, and in all the wrong places. You see that, right? Your mother was... I don't even have words to explain her shortcomings. That's the most horrific thing I've ever heard a mother doing to her daughter."

Tears flowed down her cheeks and Cami sniffled. He wiped them away. His heart was heavy with disappointment and sadness for her... and for him too. "God damn. I just can't believe this. I should have been more responsible." He shook his head in self-recrimination.

"Don't..." Cami took in a shuddering breath. "Don't... please, it's... it's so hard when you insist on taking all the blame. I can't... I have to..."

"You don't have to do anything. We'll figure something out. I'm just sorry it came to this."

Silence filled the room as she huddled against him. When she finally pushed off him, she was shaking her head, crying harder, and saying, *"I'm not!"* and the words seemed to erupt from her. "I'm not sorry. I was careless... I didn't mean for this to happen... but I didn't exactly... well, I wasn't as careful as I should have been. We don't get to see each other for *months.*" She wailed out the last word. "And I hate it. I kind of forgot to take them sometimes, but I was not intending for anything to happen and then I started feeling so crummy and my period hasn't come—"

"You... you did this on purpose?"

"I—I don't know. I just... I—"

His breathing escalated, and he leaned forward, rubbing his hands over his face and shaking his head until he jumped to his feet. Unwilling to listen to her fumbling excuses and stuttering lies. Staring at her, he seemed disillusioned, shocked and rocked to his core. He inexplicably pushed her aside and walked out of the bedroom before slamming his apartment door shut and walking off.

CAMI'S BREATHING escalated after finally finding the courage to force the words out of her throat. She hadn't decided if she would admit the pregnancy wasn't exactly tragic or totally unwanted by her. But she never expected Charlie to start apologizing, somehow believing he were responsible for causing her trauma.

She flopped back onto his bed and stared at her feet as her stomach acid rushed up into her throat. She'd already had an abortion although she never wanted one. If it had been entirely up to her, she never would have considered having one, especially at the tender age of thirteen. Her mother forced it on her, and Cami never heard of anyone's mother doing that to her daughter. Imagine forcing your own child to undergo a dangerous medical procedure without anesthesia or even a real doctor.

A decade after her first pregnancy, now she believed she could handle it. After all, she was with a man she loved and adored, one whom she regarded as the highest caliber person she'd ever known. He embodied everything good and right in the world.

Years ago, after learning the gamut of cruel torture Cami endured at her mother's hands, Kate took Cami to the doctor for a complete work-up. Horrified to learn what happened to her, both the nurse and the doctor were extra gentle, tender, and kind. Cami underwent all the tests and exams, which thankfully, determined she had no diseases or permanent damage. Somehow, her mother hadn't managed to kill or sterilize her, although she easily could have.

Now... oh, God. What would Charlie do now? What if he dumped her? He'd have to. She betrayed him. She leaned forward, bending at the waist. That was why she couldn't reveal the whole truth. But she failed to keep it to herself for even an hour.

She'd surely lose him now. And be all alone. She'd have the baby alone, at Charlie's family home. It could only ruin his life. And hers. Definitely, their relationship. Somehow, she convinced herself it wasn't that bad, but now she knew it was. Oh, God. It was so negligent of her.

Numb and confused, she rose to her feet and stuck her arms in her jacket, zipping it up before she started to leave the apartment. She walked down the stairs and into the cold, clear night. Stars shone high overhead and her breath looked like smoke when it emerged from her mouth.

Cami walked and walked, stopping dead in her tracks when she spotted Charlie sitting on a bench. He was staring out towards the campus. She froze, wondering what to do.

But like a trooper, she steeled her heart and nerves. She deserved whatever his reaction might be.

She sat beside him on the bench. He didn't acknowledge her. The silence felt like a brick wall between them.

Finally, when her hands went numb, Charlie said, "I always feel sorry for you when I think of what happened when you were thirteen. Were you counting on that?"

"I don't know."

"That... *this* is the one thing I didn't want. You knew that. You always knew that. There was no secret about it. Yet, you risked it anyway."

"I didn't. I didn't mean to do it on purpose. I just didn't... I wasn't as conscientious as I had been in the past to make sure it did not happen."

"Semantics. A weak, stupid excuse for passively and irresponsibly and completely violating my trust. Of course you did it on purpose."

She hunched forward, rubbing her hands together. "Probably. Yes. It's probably exactly as you say."

He sighed as he rested his elbows on his knees, gazing down at his feet. "Why? Why did you do that? What did you think would happen?" His voice cracked when he asked her why.

"I was hoping for a baby," she said simply, quietly, and with a heavy, hardening heart. "I want one, Charlie. I want to have one now. I want to be a mom."

"Because you couldn't at age thirteen? Come off it, Cami. I'm not ignoring what you went through and all, but you shouldn't have been a mother then either. Your mother should have been locked up for what she did to you. But what did you do? Did you betray me in order to right that wrong?"

"Is it really that bad? *I betrayed* you?" Her voice was low and sad. She seemed lost.

"Yes, it really is that bad. But don't..." An edginess, like sharpened steel, tainted his words. "Don't you dare play contrite now or scared or sorry even. You knew it was a betrayal to me. You knew that, Cami. Don't you dare deny that."

Tears filled her eyes and she shuddered. "Charlie... are you... Oh, God, are you breaking up with me?"

"Why shouldn't I, Cami? You tricked me and betrayed me. Putting me in a position I explicitly said I never wanted to be caught in. You deliberately ignored our plan to prevent that. So please. Why don't you tell me, why I shouldn't break up with you?"

"Because I love you." Cami's statement sounded weak and hollow from her lips and immediately emphasized how useless her excuse really was.

"It doesn't feel like love right now."

That gutted her like a fish. She sniffled and hot tears rolled down her face and clogged her throat. Panicked now, she started speaking rapidly, "I didn't think you'd really break up with me. I'll... I'll... no. Please, don't break up with me, Charlie. If it's you or... or this, of course, I choose you. I will always choose you."

He sighed heavily, and the sound made her pause as she hugged her middle and cried.

"Stop it!" he snapped. "This isn't about you, not right this second. It's about me. So, stop crying and threatening to do something you know damn well you don't intend to do. You just want to coerce me into saying I want you to have it so you won't do that. Well, fuck, Cami, as a child, you were forced to have an abortion. What kind of monster would I be if I insisted you have another one?"

She sat back, utterly shocked at hearing him swear and the fierce tone of his voice. Her tears eventually stopped falling and she stared at him, bug-eyed.

"Yeah. So obviously, I'm not going to do that and you're not going to have one. So quit with the theatrics. Can't you just give me an hour or more to process this? I have to adjust to it. Can't I be the one who needs something from you for once?"

"Wh—what are you going to do?"

"What do you mean? What can I do? Apparently, I'm going to be a father. I am about to embark on the journey of parenthood."

She cringed at the cruel sarcasm in his voice. "You mean, you're not dumping me?"

"No. That didn't even occur to me. Judging by your desperation, however, maybe it should have crossed my mind. I'm so fucking pissed off at you right now. And you know what? This may astound you, but Cami, I have every right to be. So just for once, can you let me fucking be? Leave me be. I don't have the strength anymore to make *you* feel better. I can't fix you or help you or reassure you, not when it comes to something like this. Just please. Leave me alone." There was no yelling. Charlie's voice sounded tightly strung but mostly, sad.

Cami nearly dropped to her knees beside him in relief. She tried to hold herself together. She was suddenly aware of how bad she was in comparison to him. Obviously, there was an unhealthy balance and she needed him much more than he needed her. "I'll go. I'll go home and leave you… to…"

He sighed heavily, shutting his eyes. "Can you ever just try to be reasonable? It's eleven-thirty at night. I didn't mean for you to *go home*. I meant, just go back to my room."

"But where will you sleep?"

"In my room, when I'm good and ready."

"You can still stand to be near me?"

His jaw clenched in physical irritation. "I'm near you

right now, aren't I? Just go to bed, Cami. I'll come in when I'm ready."

"Charlie..."

"Look. *You* did this. We now have to do this *together*. But I can be mad too. I don't have to feel happy or relieved, do I? I don't have to feel anything right now. Not at this moment. And I don't. I'm numb. When I'm ready, we'll discuss what to do and how to do it, but that's not right now. Not tonight either. Give me that much time."

She scrambled to her feet. "Okay." She licked her lips. She had so much she still wanted to say, which included her pleading for his forgiveness. She also wanted more reassurance he really wouldn't dump her. She longed for a hug and what he normally did with her. But she knew that wasn't going to happen.

Still... he hadn't dumped her. Overwhelmed by fear, Cami all at once realized how betrayed Charlie felt and the revelation stabbed her in the gut. She couldn't lose him. She was awash with regret.

She stared back at Charlie's hunched figure in the cold, dark night. A light drizzle started to fall. She sniffled as she stared at him and fresh tears of sad longing fell down her cheeks. He was right, every single word he said. Her heart squeezed, wishing she could make him feel happy about it or even ambivalent. She'd gratefully have settled for that. But what did she really expect? That he'd be glad? He never kidded about not wanting to have a baby.

Duh. Of course he wasn't kidding. She shivered and pressed her arms tighter around her middle, feeling unsafe. She didn't like having Charlie so angry at her. It was unprecedented.

She entered the apartment as stealthily as a burglar and slipped off her coat and clothes. She put on her flannel pants and a shirt before climbing into his bed. At least, he didn't kick her out tonight although she deserved it. But Charlie was always Charlie, the best stand-up guy she knew. Of course, he wouldn't do anything that could hurt her. Or physically punish her. It wasn't how Charlie operated. It was also another reason why she needed and loved him so much. Perhaps too much.

Later, she felt his weight dipping the mattress down as he slid in beside her. His body was freezing and the cold emanated off his skin. Her eyelids popped open when his arms wrapped around her waist and he snuggled up behind her. She tilted her head up. His chin was above her head.

"I thought you'd never come near me again."

"I'm cold and you're warm."

"I didn't think you could stand to touch me again."

He sighed and set his mouth right at her ear. "I have loved you for almost a decade. When are you ever just going to believe that?"

She shut her eyes and blinked the tears that nearly fell back in. She nodded. "I didn't do it to trap you. I think it was more to try and heal myself."

"You have to understand, I'm not happy about this. It isn't a blessing to me or a wonderful surprise. But I had a hand in it too."

"You mean, because you trusted me with the birth control?"

"Yes. And realize this, clearly, you *chose* to break that trust. I won't forget that. Certainly not by tomorrow."

She tried to swallow the huge, emotional lump that was lodged in her throat. Tears fell down onto his arm, which he lay under her head. He sighed when he felt them. Cami tensed up and he nudged her leg.

"Stop it. There is plenty of shit here to deal with. And to do that, you first need to grow the hell up. We have to discuss some pretty hard things, and you can't break down and start

169

crying or ask me for my reassurance all the time. Things will be changing between us. And that's just what has to happen now."

"Oh, shit," she muttered softly. "How do you manage to articulate reality so fast?"

"It's just how I am. You know that. You always count on me to take care of everything, make it work. But no more. You're going to have to start doing some of that for yourself."

She nodded. "Okay…"

"Yeah, I know, it's overwhelming. Where do you start? I know. But here we are. I have three tests this week and I start a lab on Friday, so I can't come home right now. But you have to. So, you need to immediately tell AJ and Kate because—"

"I can't. They'll be—"

"Stop it. That's the kind of stuff I don't have time for now. Figure it out. Just tell them. Quit being such a child."

She snapped her mouth shut. Charlie so rarely chided her. She awoke to a different Charlie, and now only a matter of hours later, their previous interaction was gone, and he was already sounding changed. And she'd done it so she deserved it.

"Look, I have a huge test tomorrow, I need to sleep now. I'll let you sleep in, but I have to get up early. So go home and talk to AJ and Kate. I mean it. And I'll call you after my test."

"Okay." Cami barely whispered it. His hands clutched her waist and hooked together over her middle. Like he usually did. There was no special rub or intimate hold of her stomach. No. He didn't want that now.

But he intended to deal with it. That was something. That was *huge*.

With his steady breathing behind her, she let her tears fall. Only now did she realize that something very meaningful and precious was lost: Charlie's trust and respect.

She felt like she lost her boyfriend although she gained a baby daddy. It was only then, at that moment, when she fully understood what she'd done. The rush of regret that gripped her heart almost gave her a heart attack.

Cami's unwise mistake would change their destiny and their life together irrevocably.

LUCKILY, Charlie was blessed with a stellar memory and the ability to block out distractions. He had no problem trying to focus on the here and now. The test took two hours of which he was almost grateful.

But then right back to reality.

"Did you get home okay?" he asked after he called her. He wanted to avoid seeing her sad face, laced with an expression of too-late-to-regret on his phone screen.

"Yes," Cami answered quietly.

It sounded pathetic, she whispered as if she were *afraid* to speak out loud to him. He rolled his eyes. "Are you feeling okay?"

"Yes."

"Did you tell AJ and Kate?"

"I started to… and then AJ started talking about something and I didn't know how to…"

He sighed, closing his eyes and setting a fist to his forehead. *God. How could she be so incapable?*

"Charlie?"

"What?"

"Do you plan to tell everyone what I did? That it's all my fault and mine alone? And that you don't want the baby?"

He closed his eyes to the pounding headache. That's what she deserved to hear. He couldn't be blamed for it. They had a plan, a mutual pact they both agreed to. It was so easy and so effective, their plan to prevent this from happening and Cami broke the contract when she decided she'd simply not follow the plan.

But she was also the woman Charlie loved, and one day, the future mother of his child. Someday, his child would ask about how they met and came to be. No, he wouldn't besmirch Cami. "No. I don't. Your pregnancy surprised us, but we're still together in this."

She sucked in a breath. "Do you really mean that?"

"Yes, but not in the happy way you would like me to. I'm with you, and we're together on this, but only because it's my baby and we have no other choice. You saw to that."

"Charlie, how long—"

"Longer than just a day. I'll be angry and distrustful of you for longer than just a damn day, Cami," he interrupted her. Closing his eyes, he slowly began to suck in air while counting backwards from ten to calm himself. Her soft mutters told him she was crying again. He slumped forward. "Look. How about if I come home this weekend and we'll talk before we tell everyone? Okay?"

Exhaling a huge whoosh of air, Cami gushed, "Yes. Oh, yes. Thank you."

Seething inside, Charlie finished up his work for the week and made the long trip home early Saturday morning. He intended to repeat it the following morning so he could get back to school. But things were different now, and Cami took priority over whatever was going on at school, no matter what.

The moment she said *pregnant*, his life ceased to belong to him.

Now, it belonged to the baby and that realization would

have to sink in and grow in his mind just as her belly grew with the baby. With the snap of his fingers, he realized that he came in second now to whatever was right for the baby.

That was the whole reason he insisted on birth control, to make sure he didn't have a baby until he was ready for one. But now? That which he so valiantly strove to avoid was unavoidable.

Maliciously trying to trick him or not, Cami read all the information Charlie did, so she understood what was at stake, even if she chose not to take responsibility for it. Not the first time that Cami shirked her obligation, either. Never anything as serious as this, however, so he overlooked that fault in her.

Betraying him and making him look like a hypocrite since having a baby at his age was the very last thing he promised himself he would ever do.

Damn.

His heart sank with disappointment that the direction of his life so suddenly and abruptly plummeted. A baby at this point of his budding career was the last thing he wanted, not even a little bit. The years of responsibility. The money required. The limits on his freedom in every way. Maybe worst of all, it would tie him down to Cami and River's End.

First and foremost, he had to coach and encourage Cami to tell her damn parents. Cami easily became an emotional wreck whenever she had to face anything that threatened, worried, or bothered her.

His head was throbbing with a headache by the time he pulled into the ranch on a cold, snowy day in February. The last place he wanted to be. Or live. Or be bound or obligated to. He had no idea where he might eventually choose to be. He hoped that decision could be postponed for years. But here he was. *Home.* Sure, he liked to visit, being so close to his family and he didn't foresee that changing, but making it a weekly habit at this age? Hell no.

Cami came out of AJ and Kate's house. She wasn't running toward Charlie and she didn't seem too eager in greeting him. He was blank-faced, keeping his expression neutral as best he could. The façade strained him physically, centering mostly in his heart.

"Hi," she said, all but in a whisper. She didn't fail to see how upset he was. She could expertly play the scared, little girl whenever she was afraid to face him. She could beg him to make it all better for her. That wasn't how things would go now.

Not anymore.

"Hey." He leaned over by habit and kissed her mouth, grabbing an overnight bag from his truck.

"How was your last test?"

He raised his eyebrows at her. "Terrible, Cami. My entire week went pretty fucking terrible. Not to mention, I probably blew my perfect grade point average."

"Oh, no. No, Charlie. I'm... I'm so sorry."

He sighed and shut his eyes. Her distress and concern were real and true.

He stepped closer and took her arm in his hand, jiggling her as if to emphasize his point. "You can't cry every time I hurt your feelings by pointing out all the things you're supposed to do."

She nodded, blinking swiftly to dispel the tears. "What didn't I do?"

"How about telling your parents? Insisting that I come home this weekend to do it? Any of that ring a bell? I'm going to warn you, Cami, as often as I need to while this pregnancy progresses that once this baby is born, you will no longer be my first priority in life. Never again. The baby will be. You have to understand: this is a game changer. A real game changer."

"And it's all my fault."

"Yup. You arranged it. So don't even try to play the contrite martyr."

She avoided his gaze, darting her eyeballs all around with raw nerves and looking obviously upset.

Tightening his hand on the handle of his bag, he did not automatically touch her. First, he had to release his anger. Otherwise, it wouldn't be genuine. For once, he intended to be as honest as he could without backing off the truth in favor of protecting Cami. "Let's go talk to everyone. Might as well get it over with."

He went first, walking directly into the Reeds' house and setting his bag down. Kate walked out from the office where she'd been working. "Charlie. What a surprise," she exclaimed. "Everything okay?"

"No. Could we talk to you and AJ? I'd also like to ask my dad and Erin up here too." Kate's gaze wavered and flickered from him to Cami and back again. She kept her head down, her eyes totally downcast, interlacing her fingers before her. They were clear signs of her distress, but she didn't voice anything or try to explain.

"Sure. Yes. I'll text AJ. He's actually down at your place helping Jack with a side job. So I'll ask both of them to come over."

"Thanks." Turning, he picked up his bag and headed to Cami's bedroom as if he lived there. And why not? There was no hiding it now. Everyone would soon know everything that happened. Cami followed silently behind him.

She waited for him to drop his stuff before he went to her bathroom. When he entered her room again, he glanced around. Her previously gothic, austere room had undergone a complete transformation. "When did you dump the black and red?"

"During the last few weeks."

All white walls and a neutral bedspread replaced the rather hideous, but distinctly passionate blood red coverlet. "Why?"

"I got tired of it."

Maybe knowing she was pregnant, she decided to grow up? He sighed.

"How long do you intend to be so angry at me?" she finally asked when the ugly silence between them became intolerable.

"I have no idea."

"Are you going to keep treating me like this?"

"Like what?"

"So cold. As if you don't even know me or like me. You seem annoyed if you even have to look at me."

"I really don't think you see how serious this is to me. I don't want to be a father at twenty-two years old. I'm just a senior in college. Doesn't make me a monster. It makes me honest. I have always been totally honest with you. And all I asked was that you be honest back. If this had been an accident, I could not be mad. But you so carelessly ignored the risk without my knowledge. Yeah, Cami, it's going to be awhile."

"Are you staying with me now only because of it?"

He shook his head and shrugged his shoulders. "How should I know? I doubt it. I mean, I've loved you for nearly a decade. I doubt it can be so easily expunged, especially within a week. But am I nearly blind with rage? Yes, I am. Maybe next time, you won't forget to tell me when you decide you're ready to get pregnant."

Her face crumpled in distress the longer he spoke. "So, then I take it you obviously aren't going to marry me?"

His eyebrows jerked straight upright. "Are you serious? No. Someday? Yeah, I always hoped and planned to marry you someday. When we were old enough, and both ready. But now? No. For this reason? No."

"So, what do you think will happen?"

He almost laughed bitterly. She expected him to marry her and move home? Abandon his entire life's plans? Fuck. Only if he had no choice. Not yet. He'd be damned if he'd do it before he had to. "I still have to finish school. I don't know. Maybe you'll move there after the baby is born. But there is no reason for you to do it yet. You should keep working and save all your money. That shit is going to get real very soon. We'll need every penny of it. No one's going to take care of us. My dad and Erin have generously provided for my college and living expenses. But I doubt that includes my new family."

He saw her eyes rise and a glimpse of hope flared in her pupils at the words *my new family.* That's what Cami wanted most and hoped to get from the beginning. To start her own family and have a place of belonging. What she'd always been denied in her own childhood. He understood that. But it still wasn't okay for her to make that decision without him.

"Cami, what do you think is going to happen here? Do you expect me to support you while you become a stay-at-home mom and housewife to me?"

Her fingers started twisting again. *Oh, yeah,* that's what she secretly hoped for. He gentled his voice. "It's not going to be like that at all. You'll have to work so we can both support this baby. We have to do it together. I don't stand a chance of earning a decent living without finishing school. Then I'll have to find a job and work my way up to livable wages. Who knows how long that will be? What did you expect?"

"I don't know. I didn't think—"

"Exactly. You didn't think. And now look at us. Just look what you've done to us, Cami, and to our lives—"

She all but covered her ears as the tears leaked from her eyes. "Stop yelling at me."

"I'm not yelling," he stated in a cold tone, which was the antithesis of yelling. "I haven't raised my voice, not once. I'm discussing an issue and pointing out the factors involved. Telling you what I expect of you. Yes, I'm telling you that, which you may not like, but you don't get to change it just because you don't like it. Welcome to reality."

"Cami? Charlie?" Kate yelled, and Charlie sighed. His nerves were raw, and his heavy heart was rapidly sinking. He hated to disappoint his dad so much. The one thing he promised him was that he wouldn't do that, and now, here he was.

Her neck snapped back, and her face filled with terror. "I can't tell them. Not with you... not with us... like this. With you hating me."

"I don't hate you. I'm angry."

Her head tilted back. "What? You do still love me?"

"Exactly what I'm talking about. Your constant need to hear that. But yes, I still love you. I hate seeing you hurt. Yes, I'm really fucking angry. Imagine how confusing that is in my head. I never wanted to hurt you or see you hurt and now I'm the one who's lashing out at you."

"Cami? Did you hear me?" Kate yelled again.

Charlie pushed her off his chest. "Let's go do this."

She hiccupped and wiped her eyes, taking several deep breaths. "Okay," she whispered. Her face was streaked in pink shame.

"We'll say it was an accident. And we're together on this and determined to make it work. Okay?"

"Okay," she mumbled again.

He held her hand as they went downstairs. His dad and

Erin were sitting on the couch. AJ and Kate sat in chairs on opposite sides of the brick fireplace. A fire roared, creating what should have been a homey, warm setting in contrast to the falling snow drifting outside.

All eyes were predictably focused on them as they came down the stairs and the ensuing tension clung to them like unwanted poundage. Charlie nodded at his dad and smiled at Erin.

"We didn't know you were coming home." Erin's concerned gaze rested heavily on him.

"We needed to talk to all four of you at once."

"Uh huh. I see that. What's going on?" Kate asked, her gaze laser-focused on Cami before rising to him. Oh, yeah, she and Erin already knew exactly what was up. Their disappointment was visible in the grim set of their mouths.

Charlie sat down and Cami sat cross-legged on the floor near him. She kept her gaze downwards. His brain scanned his thoughts for something to say that could make this sound better than it was, but nothing came up and he had nothing to say.

"Oh, Charlie," Erin said in a tone full of disappointment and sorrow. "No…"

"What is it?" AJ asked next.

Charlie kept his face neutral and his jaw clamped. He fisted his hands, resenting this moment and the need to tell the adults this. Of all things, the one thing he promised all four of them would never happen with him and Cami.

And here he was. Breaking his word. Breaking their trust. Shattering their expectations, as well as his own.

All because of Cami.

No, it wasn't something he'd get over tomorrow. Or the next day. It gnawed at his stomach lining and he wondered if it would last his whole lifetime. Cami tricked him into becoming a father and for no good reason. It was totally preventable. Their relationship was vibrant and very secure, and there was no reason to compel her to do something like that in order to keep him or get him to commit. Why had she done that? Again, simply because she wanted a baby.

Taking a deep breath, he announced in a loud voice the one sentence he never hoped to say, "We're going to have a baby."

CHAPTER 10

AMI KEPT HER HEAD down, wishing she could bury her face in her hands. His words rolled like an errant rock off the top of a cliff, falling onto her parents and him. Stunned and shocked, the subsequent barrage of predictable questions soon followed.

"What about school?" Jack.

"Oh, Charlie, no," Erin sympathized.

Then AJ stood up without a word. His abrupt movement made Cami's gaze follow him. Clenching his jaw, he stared at her, his eyes turning hard and unforgiving before he simply walked past her and out the front door. He slammed the door hard enough to shake the door frame.

She immediately felt like curling up into a small ball and letting the tears fall without further restraint. But Charlie's words of admonition were still fresh, and right there in front of her. She had to stop being a child. Grow up. Find the strength within herself and stop relying on him to make her feel better.

No matter how bad AJ might have made her feel.

Charlie leaned down and dropped his hand to her shoulder, and Cami glanced up at him gratefully. "What are you going to do?" Jack repeated.

"We'll have the baby and figure out how to raise it and pay for everything while I finish school."

"Charlie, you don't know how hard what you're saying will be in practice."

He cleared his throat. "I have a pretty good idea."

"I mean, it's not like you're too young or anything... I just hoped you would have waited a bit longer," Erin added.

"Well, life doesn't happen like that."

Cami lifted her gaze finally and dared to look at Kate. Kate was strangely and uncharacteristically quiet and her face was wet with tears. Surprised, Cami stared at her, open-mouthed, and asked, "Why are you crying?" Her simmering anger laced her words. She wasn't eighteen or sixteen years old, and for goodness sakes, not thirteen either. She was twenty-three years old now. Their insistence on receiving it as such tragic news was their own choice. Lots of women had babies at her age. Why so much shock and dismay?

"I just wanted more for you."

"You wanted me to live your life." Cami snapped. She was sick and tired of people telling her how to feel and how wrong it was to have a baby now. There was so much *more* the world had to offer and *more* that she should want, but for Cami, this was so much *more*. Better than anything she could imagine herself wanting more. This was everything. This was a growing life. Safely developing inside of her.

"Are you two getting married then?"

"No," Charlie answered quickly. Way too quickly and sharply for Cami's preference. "No. We'll just continue exactly as we have been until the baby is born. Then we'll decide what to do."

Jack shook his head. "Okay. I guess there isn't much more I can say to that."

"Well, you'll have to go to the doctor soon. Find one you like. Get an appointment and figure out the payments. I'll have to see how well our insurance covers you. You're probably wise not to get married, for medical insurance reasons if nothing else. Mine is, no doubt, better than anything the two of you could buy," Kate said, wiping her eyes. At least, her voice was neutral and even.

Cami never considered medical insurance or how they would pay for the childbirth.

"I'll do it first thing Monday." Now that everyone knew her secret, Cami intended to do everything right. She would take very good care of herself and do whatever was advised to properly prepare for this baby.

Their baby. Her baby. Her very own child to raise.

Even Charlie could never totally belong to her.

A weird quiet descended on them and each seemed lost in their own special disappointment. Finally, Jack got to his feet. "I guess we'll go back home now."

"I'll walk you," Charlie said, rising to his feet. Cami gathered she wasn't invited on purpose. She supposed she should look for her own father.

Stupid AJ.

Why did he get so mad at her? What was he doing at twenty-three years old? Serving time in prison? Yes. Drinking and gambling and drugging. How dare he judge her?

They shuffled out the door together. "I'll be back later."

Cami nodded and found herself alone with Kate. The quiet lingered on uncomfortably. Finally, she got up and walked over to Kate to hug her. Kate was stiff at first. Cami hugged Kate's stout shoulders and stood beside her chair. "I'm not you. I want this baby."

"You did it on purpose. That's what I refused to say in front of them. And Charlie didn't know, did he?"

183

Stunned, Cami just stared at her.

"I'm your damn mother, child. How could you think I would miss that?"

"Charlie knows what I did. I told him the truth about everything."

"That was a crap thing to do to him. You knew he never wanted this to happen."

"No, he didn't. But I did." Cami shook her head. "I realize how heartless and selfish it sounds. I didn't just refuse to take the pills. I got a little careless about taking them. I kind of knew I was risking it but I pretended I wasn't. I already regret what I did. But now that I am carrying his baby, I find it more acceptable. That's why I'm not reacting the same as everyone else is."

Kate sighed and touched her face. "You suffered so much at such a young age. It still kills me to imagine it. But nothing can ever undo that, Cami, not even having your own baby. You alone must fill that void inside you. It's not Charlie's responsibility or mine or AJ's... not even this baby you conceived."

"Is that why you think I did it?"

"Maybe just a little bit. And you know I'm not wrong."

"You just hoped I'd be as independent and accomplished as you." Cami didn't like her stepmother's analysis and she snapped her reply.

"No. You're wrong. I believe a woman has the right to become anything she wants. I think you always missed that message about me. You have every right to get married at age eighteen and have a dozen kids, if that's what you truly want and need and desire. Or you could choose to be like me and live single and free, running your own business well into middle age. I think both are valid paths in life. As long as every woman makes her own choice, any extreme or some- where in between is acceptable. But this? I think you were doing what you wanted exclusively for you, without considering Charlie's opinion or your circumstances and I believe you were wrong."

"I was selfish, you mean?"

"Yes. You just want a full-time object you can love that will love you back."

"Yes. I do. Of course I want that. It doesn't make me a monster."

"No. But you deliberately deceived your boyfriend and limited his future. You're lucky he's the upstanding guy he is and that he is sticking by you, no matter what."

"He's so angry though."

"Well, yeah. And you have to start considering the consequences of your actions."

"He said something similar."

"I was thirty-six when I chose to bring you into my life. I took you and your dad on willingly. Out of my love and a desire for something more meaningful. I irrationally got angry at first, however, when you initially showed up. I almost blamed you for ruining all the fun I believed I was having with AJ. So things often manage to work themselves out. I just think you need to exert yourself more. How this started wasn't because of the finest motive or plan. So you'll have to make every effort to atone for that."

"I'm going to. I swear. Should I even try to talk to AJ?"

"Yes, Cami. You should definitely take care of that. Your relationship with your father hasn't ceased to exist."

Kate's warning was clear: start nurturing her relationships without expecting Kate or Charlie to do it for her.

JACK STOPPED to enjoy the view. Horses in the pastures made loud stomps and their nickers and neighs filled the air occasionally. Their hot breaths looked smoky in the cold, after-noon air. Snow fell, making the world silent and feel startlingly clean. Their voices softly muffled, they waited until Erin plodded ahead, giving them more privacy. Then they stepped into the barn.

"You didn't make a mistake. She got pregnant on purpose, didn't she?"

"How did you know that?"

"You're always too careful and you still have so many goals to achieve. Not to mention the thick tension I've never witnessed between you two before."

"Yeah, it's pretty hard to accept."

"But you didn't dump her?"

"No, of course not. I don't intend to either. She didn't do it maliciously or even on purpose, although she did it all the same."

He waited for his dad to reprimand him or lecture him. Instead, Jack stepped forward and set a hand on Charlie's shoulders. "I've never been prouder of you than I am right now."

Charlie tilted his head to the side. "How could you possibly say that?"

"You love her. You always have. You're so mature about it and able to see past your own anger. You also intend to stay with her and keep loving her. It's very easy to love someone in the beginning when it's fresh and new. It's not so easy when things gets hard."

"Well, I'm not exactly ecstatic about it. But I'll make it work."

"The thing about you, Charlie, is I know you will make it work."

"I'm sorry though. It's the one thing you begged me never to do. Repeat Ben's mistakes."

"It's different this time. I had no right to put that kind of constraint on you. Just because I had kids really young doesn't mean you or Ben can't have them early or late or whenever you choose to have them. You are now and always will be free to follow your own path in life."

"Except I'm not exactly free now. That's the reason why I wanted to wait."

"No, but at least you see that."

"I really thought you'd be angry with me. Or, at the very least, disappointed."

"No. And we'll help you. That's my official response."

"No. I gotta figure this out for myself. It's not like you aren't already helping me with school. So, no. This is strictly on us. And we have to start making it strictly about us."

He squeezed Charlie's shoulder. "You have built-in advantages you've never taken for granted. Of course, we intend to help you and you're going to need all the help we can give you. So just accept that and appreciate it."

"I won't." His heart felt heavy, and it would have been easier if his dad, known for his quick temper and opinions, wasn't so damn kind, considerate, and understanding. Not what Charlie expected at all.

Jack walked over to the stall where his horse, Augusta, was standing. He rubbed her head and stared at her for a long moment. Then he turned to Charlie. "Um... well, as long as we're confessing difficult announcements. I have one too."

"You have one?" Charlie blinked in surprise. "What?" He was wondering more, however, why his dad became so nervous. What was that about?

"It's going to make all of this even weirder. Believe me, I get that and I'm sorry too."

"What is it?"

"Ah... well you know how much Erin struggled with reading and her self-confidence..."

"Uh huh." It changed Charlie's whole perspective and gave him his first lesson in learning disabilities. He realized his own empathy when others failed to achieve the standard norms of education even if they appeared totally typical.

"Well, for the past decade, that was her main goal and what kept her from wanting... well, lots of things. And also you. She considers you her own child in so many ways..."

"Yeah. I know. What is this, Dad? I mean, Erin and I are good, so why are you defending her to me, of all people?"

Jack sucked in a breath and his gaze darted off... Was his dad embarrassed? Maybe, his complexion under the barn lights seemed to be turning red. "She's pregnant too."

He stared at his dad and his mouth dropped open.

Jack immediately started talking. "I know it's... it's a lot to take in. It must be kind of gross for you. I mean, you and Ben are grown men and I'm your dad... well, yeah. Even I ask myself what the hell am I doing starting over? Again? I can't even imagine it—"

"Was it an accident?" Charlie's initial shock wore off long enough for a few words to form on his tongue.

Jack hung his head, whipping his hat off and twirling it nervously in his hands. "No. No it wasn't any accident. She asked me two years ago, subsequent to my recovery and somewhat reclusive behavior after the fire—"

"Depression, Dad. You fell into a deep depression. It's nothing to be ashamed of," Charlie added quietly. His dad, ever the weathered, old cowboy, found it hard to admit any weakness. He temporarily lost control of his emotions and moods when the fire destroyed their property.

Nearly debilitated to everyone around him, it affected his marriage as well as his relationships with his brothers and sons. He could never apologize enough to Charlie for the two years it lasted. But Charlie had long ago forgiven him, and he credited that to Erin's influence, love, and guidance. In short, her mothering of him.

"I guess. Anyway, she asked me, and I said no at first. Really? Starting all over? I'm almost fifty freaking years old."

"But she's not that old and she's never really been a mother. Not from the start."

"No." His tone turned glum. "I realize that. I know how much it means for her to get where she feels ready and wants to do it. It was too hard for me to deny her that. Sometimes, I like the idea. Other times, I feel so odd and detached. I mean, I'm finally done with parenthood. Free. I can enjoy myself and do the things I never did and then... I think about starting over..."

He shook his head. "Dad, when have you ever wanted any free time? You only thrive when you have too much to do and too many people relying on you. That's what makes you, *you*."

Jack's face scrunched up. "I can't imagine my old man doing that to me when Lily and I were preparing to have Ben."

"It was different back then. And he wasn't married to Erin. She deserves this."

"I know. That's why I agreed. Until... it happened. I was going to tell you in a few weeks. And then to hear you make the same announcement. That was part of my reaction. Erin and I sat there clutching hands and our eyes grew huge. I knew exactly what she was thinking... How could we all be pregnant at the same time? It's weird. So damn weird. A grandchild that we are soon to have and now another child for us. I really don't do well in this kind of set-up or drama."

Charlie started to laugh. Hard. He laughed so hard, he had to bend over, and tears fell from his eyes. "Neither am I. But look at us. We were already a weird, blended family, with aunts and uncles and brothers and sisters all mixed up. Add in Cami's mom being my aunt and yeah. It all gets even weirder."

Jack first stared at him, looking puzzled and visibly upset. Then he too started to laugh. They laughed so long, they both were gasping for breath. Eventually, the wave of hysteria started to pass. "Well, talk about going through the same thing together..." Charlie finished.

"I feared that Jocelyn would pop up pregnant and Ben and I would be the new fathers. But I didn't think you and I—"

"No, no. It wasn't the reality I envisioned as late as last week." Charlie finally calmed down enough to act serious now. "You're happy though? You want to have a baby with Erin?"

His dad nodded. "I do. I have so much baggage with it. It embarrasses me a little bit, mostly with you boys, I mean, you grown men. To see your father like this, it can't be easy. But I'm happy, yeah. Erin started crying when she realized she was pregnant. Seeing her happy since she deserves only the best, makes me happy too. Her history wasn't very happy. So yeah, I am glad. It's just still news to me and something I have to get used to, but my excitement is definitely starting to percolate."

"You should be excited." Charlie answered.

His dad smiled and stared downwards. "Thank you, Charlie, you can't imagine how much your support means to me. Probably more than mine means to you."

"I wouldn't say that," Charlie said quietly. "At least, you gave me some news to tell Cami that I hope might break the block of ice between us."

"Don't be too hard on her. Considering her history, I'm surprised she didn't turn out more screwed up or broken than she already is."

"What do you know about it?"

"Most of it. Kate told us, years ago. She stole something from Erin and in the course of addressing that issue, other things came out. I honestly didn't think you even knew back then, although I assume now you must know."

"She isn't screwed up. A little confused or unsure and a little bit fragile. But it's not like... no, she's not screwed up."

"I know that, Charlie. I'm hoping you'll remember that. She misses you a lot when you're not here. She gets very lonely. And you'd planned to move across the world from her. That's no small thing. What she did wasn't right, but maybe she simply made a mistake."

I'll keep that in mind." He exhaled. "I'd better make nice with AJ."

"He'll come around too."

"Well, I guess we'd both best check on our pregnant significant others," Charlie said, raising his eyebrows for levity at the situation.

What else could his dad do but freaking laugh?

He exited the barn and they separated. Something struck Charlie: it never occurred to either of them that he'd stay home. He didn't reside with his dad and Erin anymore. He stayed with Cami. It was a slow switch and not spontaneous, but he now spent more time at her house than at theirs.

Walking the opposite way of his dad, Charlie knew he wasn't a teenager any longer. He wasn't the younger son of his dad and Erin anymore either. Their home wasn't his anymore. No. Cami's was. For good or bad. Anger or ecstasy. Annoyed or happy. He went to find Cami. He was all grown up, and soon to be a father. There was no choice and no getting around it. So, he might as well accept it and deal with it instead of trying to go against it.

But first, he wanted to see the one person who could best help him deal with his anger.

~

"Erin's pregnant. Can you believe it?" Charlie said the moment Ben opened their front door. They lived in a loft apartment that was added when Ben first married Marcy. Now, he and Jocelyn and Lillian lived there.

Ben's eyes widened into two round discs. "Are you for real? Are you sure?"

"Dad just told me while blushing and stammering like he was sixteen. He was so afraid how we'd react. It was pretty funny."

Ben opened the door wider, frowning. "What the hell are you doing here, anyway? I didn't know you were coming home."

"Cami's pregnant too." This time, Charlie didn't smile, and his tone was low and confidential. Ben's mouth became an "O," matching his round eyes.

"Come in. Jocelyn's at work and Lillian's at Shane and Allison's. You caught me alone, which is rare."

Charlie plopped onto the sofa and shook his head, letting his shoulders drop forward. Ben set a hand on his back as he sat down next to him. "You weren't kidding? About Erin or Cami?"

Miserable, and with little energy, his head shook as Charlie replied, "No."

"Accident, I presume. For you I mean. That is a lot to process. So, I'm going to be an uncle and a... a brother? And all within a few weeks' span?"

He nodded. "Appears so. Erin's pregnant. After all these years, what? Fourteen? She's finally ready and wants one. In my teens, I wondered if they would pop up with one and I usually resented the thought, you know, being young and selfish and all. I didn't like the idea of living with a baby. But they never did, and Erin was so adamant about not having one. I guess she changed her mind. Or decided she *could* have one. Dad's on board, but really freaked out because he's so old and we're so old."

"And he's got grandkids. Damn. That's oddly progressive for Dad. Blended family and now a second family. Wow. I feel a little weird about it."

"I'm sure it was a secret and he planned to tell you and me together or something. He just told me after Cami and I asked everyone to sit down so we could tell them about us. It's just... it was hard not to segue into that."

"Yeah, no kidding. So... you and Cami? For real? An accident, I assume?"

"I wish. It would make it easier. She didn't take her pills, after three solid years of loyal prevention. So, I'd say it was on purpose."

His eyebrows shot upwards. "I would not suspect Cami of doing that. Marcy did."

"Believe me, I've thought of that. I hated Marcy so much."

"So did I. She poked holes in my condoms. However, I used the same condoms to cheat on her, so karma's a bitch, huh?"

"Now, look at me. She didn't put holes in my rubbers, but her version was nearly as sneaky and manipulative. I didn't foresee it." Charlie shook his head and shuffled his feet as he leaned forward to push his hands into his hair with distress. "I'm struggling with that. Bad. You know how fragile she can be..." His words trailed off as his head shook. "She's not like Jocelyn. But she did this, and I don't know how to handle it. I pretended to be nice in front of all the parents. I supported her, and I keep trying to. But I'm so damn angry, Ben. If I could act exactly how I felt, I'd freaking yell until I was hoarse, and maybe break a few things."

"It was sort of the same for me. But I deserved it a lot more than you. I left here believing I was grieving Marcy's death and being with Jocelyn when I shouldn't have been, only to come back to a baby. Right here and now. It was the end of anything else I wanted or thought I wanted. It creates anger, Charlie. Everything changes so abruptly and so permanently. You're allowed a little time to let it register. One day your life is one way, and then bam. It's on another path entirely. You deserve some leeway for making adjustments."

"Except I can't with Cami. She really can't handle it."

"Are you sure you're not projecting the old Cami onto her? The one who first showed up here a decade ago? She's not like that anymore. She handled your relationship for three years despite it being a long-distance one. That's not easy. Maybe you got used to having her one way and missed it when she grew up to be another way."

He stiffened upright. "Maybe. Maybe you have a point. But how does that change what's happening right now? I feel trapped. I'm disappointed. I don't know how to reconcile it all."

Ben slapped his back. "I think you're expecting way too much from yourself and way too quickly. Go off. Be mad. Be angry. Be trapped and upset. Let it obsess you until you work it out. Stay with Cami. If you two love each other like you say you do, and not like fifteen-year-olds, but as adults, then shit comes up in life and you just face it and stick it out. That is my advice. You want everything wrapped up in a neat, tidy box, but Cami isn't like that and she will never fit into one. And honestly, most of us don't."

"Just me."

Ben pressed his lips together in a small smile. "Yeah, you do. And you are also accomplished and smart and ambitious, everything solid that most people strive to be. But flexibility is required in real life, which means life after school. Especially now that there's a baby involved."

He nodded. "Thanks, Ben. I probably don't deserve your good advice after what I said—"

"You're my little brother. Of course you do. You're just growing up like I did. It's hard. It sucks sometimes. It's also full of unexpected, unplanned situations. The lessons only get harder and your plans have to be ready to change into something you never imagined. Don't give up on you and Cami, but you can allow yourself to be mad. I mean, c'mon, be real."

Charlie left his brother with a fist bump and a promise to call more often. Trudging up the hill, he looked across the main road, staring at his future in-laws' house.

He turned and glanced out towards the snow-topped mountains, their slopes white from winter freezing and snow melt. This was not what he chose or where he wanted to be. Not right then, not today, nor in the future.

He sighed as he turned to head inside. He had to face his life. His unplanned, out-of-the-box, filled with surprises and unexpected circumstances, life. But the thing that still bothered Charlie the most was that it wasn't any accident.

"Erin's pregnant. Can you believe it?"

Crossing over the threshold of Cami's bedroom, Charlie entered it. She sat on the other side of the bed, still dressed, and numb. Her heart and mood were dipping low. She looked very down and only lifted her head up when Charlie's voice interrupted her dour thoughts.

"What?"

"Yeah." Charlie said, entering further. "He just told me while blushing beet red and trying to justify it. He's totally ashamed because he's so damn old, and too embarrassed to admit how happy he is to have a baby with Erin. However, he's already a grandfather at forty-nine years old and Ben and I are both grown up."

She bit her lip, staring up at him, growing stony-faced as he spoke. He sat down beside her.

"You must hate this then. Me and Erin pregnant at the same time?"

"No, I laughed."

"You what?"

"I just got hysterical and couldn't stop laughing. My dad and me? Sharing fatherhood? I mean, the guy's a grandfather and I'm still a college student."

She nodded, flipping her hair back. Charlie's hand fingerbrushed her hair and he wrapped it around her neck, pulling her gently towards him, until their foreheads touched. "How are we going to do this?"

Cami shut her eyes before her tears began to fall and soft sobs escaped her mouth. The need to apologize was lodged in her throat. But she contained it, trying to stay quiet. "I don't know."

"I know. Neither do I. Please don't ever make a life decision like this for us again unless we make it together. And you're sure it's what we both want. This? How you handled this situation was completely unfair."

She lowered her head and tucked it under his neck. "Charlie, don't you make most of your life decisions without me?"

His entire body jolted upright. "What are you talking about?"

"You always tell me what you're doing or planning to do without consulting me about it. You don't discuss it beforehand, or make sure we agree first. You *tell* me your life decisions. You *tell* me where you intend to go to college and when you are coming home or when you expect me to come to you. You *tell* me when your friends are coming with you or hanging out with us. You decided to attend summer school without even warning me and very little thought as to how it affects me. You also decided to go to *Germany* without preparing me. For two years you'll be gone. You don't *ask* me, you *tell* me about most everything in our life."

"I... I mean, school is my career right now. I have to make those decisions."

"Right. That's why I didn't argue. Ever. But don't even pretend that we make life's decisions together. We do not. I shouldn't have done what I did. Believe me, that lesson has been learned. This is not how something that's supposed to be happy should ever feel. But it's also shown me that it's not all on me. You don't live your life *with* me, you simply *include* me. And you say you're serious that you want to live *with me*. But your actions don't back up your words. That is part of my insecurity around you."

He pushed her off his chest and stared into her face. His gaze was confused but concerned. "You really think that?"

"Yes, I know it. So do you," she stated quietly.

His eyebrows lowered in concentration, then rose. His mouth started to open, then quickly shut. For once, he didn't know how to respond.

She shook her head. "It doesn't matter. I did the wrong thing, Charlie. I promise not to do it again. I don't like to hurt you or have you mad at me over something I caused. So I do promise you."

"Did you do this so I wouldn't go to Germany?"

"Possibly, yes." She winced. "I hate to believe I'm that spiteful, but I was always insecure over our separations and pretty sick and tired of it."

"You didn't ever object to it."

"What could I say? You won a prestigious scholarship and a free trip across the world. How could I tell you no? I was in an impossible situation."

"I should have said more, but I guess it's a non-issue now."

"I guess you can blame that on me."

"It's now *our* reality."

She shut her eyes. "I am sorry. I know it's hard to accept. If I had only stepped back and thought about it longer, I would never have purposely jeopardized your scholarship and educational future. I hope you will believe me. And forgive me for that."

"I know. I do. I will try, but it'll take a while."

"I'm terribly sorry."

He nodded and hooked his arm around her before they fell back on the bed together. He just had to move on from it and not think about it anymore. He had to concentrate on the here and now lest he lose his way again. "So Monday you'll see the doctor? We need to prepare for this, from your good health to all the supplies a baby needs and learning the due date and where you'll be at that time."

"Monday."

"You'll call me?"

"You want me to? I'm not trying to be a martyr, and I honestly understand when you said you deserved your space to be angry. I'm just not sure how that works."

"Just call me. We'll talk and try to be honest with each other. Right?"

"Yes. Right."

"There is no other way to move forward but to take it one step at a time. We'll just keep working at this, Cami."

His words were optimistic, but his tone was hollow and sad.

AJ WAS VERY quiet around Cami. He didn't say anything directly to Charlie or to her. He talked about other inconsequential things or mumbled questions and idle pleasantries to Charlie but never anything substantial. He disappeared the next day, and Cami assumed he went to work. She said goodbye to Charlie in a weird, hollow moment. All she could feel was Charlie's tangible relief to be leaving River's End... and her.

She walked towards the beach and spotted AJ. Surprised to find him staring at the ice-edged water in deep contemplation, Cami snuggled deeper into her coat before she approached him.

"AJ?"

He didn't turn towards her. She tried to swallow the lump of rejection in her throat and bit her lip. "What are you mad at me for? I didn't do this to you at age fourteen or sixteen. I'm twenty-three years old, AJ. What is your problem?"

"You do still live with Kate and me. You don't exactly support yourself yet, now do you? Not like some women your age. So don't pretend this doesn't concern me."

"Like you, perhaps? Weren't you doing time in prison at my age? I might have disappointed you but come on. I'm not in jail and being pregnant is not a crime. I'll move out, don't worry, so you won't have to take care of my baby. What is your attitude all about?"

His shoulders stiffened, and his head lowered. "I just wanted so much more for you."

"More than what? I already have more than I ever expected."

"I think you're only doing it to make up for what happened to you at a young age. I want you to have a chance to really live and be youthful in all the ways I never could. Not by drinking and partying or ending up in prison. Of course not. Or being responsible for a baby before you've even begun to live."

"But this is living to me."

"Because you did it on purpose." He stated it as fact, and as always for AJ, in a very quiet voice. She almost had to lean in to hear him speak.

"How did you…" she stopped herself, realizing what she was giving up. Everyone around her already knew. She might have miscalculated their hypersensitive awareness.

"I know you. I know Charlie. He was struggling so hard to remain neutral. He was trying a little too hard. That was a crappy thing to do to him. He's still in school. How could you take that away from him?"

Her mouth dropped open. "You're really upset with me, aren't you?"

"Yes. I really am, Cami."

"AJ…"

"Why won't you just call me *Dad*? Haven't I earned that? I've been right here for you for the past decade. Ten years. Almost as long as I wasn't around. Why can't I just be your dad?"

Her eyebrows scrunched up. What was his problem? He was all over the place in his emotions and so unlike himself. Then a thought occurred to her: did he think he failed at being a father because she was pregnant?

"Does my pregnancy somehow damage your parenting score?"

"I think if I'd been the father you needed, when you needed me most, you'd be calling me that. I doubt you would feel such a strong urge to become a parent yourself. Why? To do it better than me? Do it the way it's supposed to be done?"

"AJ? I mean, I don't know why but I just always called you AJ and I didn't know how to switch. It took me so long to trust you. I knew you were there for me but by then, we had already established our relationship and you guys were AJ and Kate. Besides, our names don't define us. You guys, both of you, are *my parents*. I know that. I feel it. All the time.

I never knew you wanted me to call you anything else but AJ."

"I always did. Well, maybe not at the very beginning, but in the last nine years? Yes."

She sucked in a breath and stepped closer to touch his arm. He turned at her contact. She stared up at him with big eyes and raw emotions, probably exacerbated by her pregnancy hormones, and still, she felt extremely vulnerable. "You never asked me to."

"You never seemed like you wanted to."

"I just assumed AJ was what you wanted me to call you."

He shrugged. "No. I hope you do consider me your dad, though."

She bit her lip and a wave of emotions filled her heart. "Oh, I do. I do. As much as I consider Kate my mom. Names don't mean much to me. Look, I called my biological mom that name for thirteen years and she never earned that title. Doesn't mean we had any kind of close relationship. Parker Sanchez never deserved my love and yet—"

"Yet you still called her *mom*."

Cami shook her head. The depth of his hurt truly upset her. She never knew. Not at all. He never mentioned how he felt or what he perceived or why she called him what she did. "Dad. I can call you Dad now, since I do consider you my dad. And I didn't get pregnant to hurt you or retaliate or... I don't know, somehow punish you for not being something more to me. You've been everything to me. You and Kate... What does she want me to call her?"

He shrugged. "It never bothered her so much. She said everything you just did: that names don't define our love or what we are. I just pictured you calling me AJ to your baby and having him or her call me AJ."

"Dad... I'd be honored to call you Dad and someday, Grandpa."

He peeked at her before he stared forward again. "Really?"

"Yes, really. But only if you'll quit being mad at me. Charlie, Jack, Erin and probably Ben, Shane, Ian… and the list goes on of everyone who is mad at me because of what I've done to Charlie's future. Can you just not be mad at me? Can you just be on *my side?* Right or wrong, I did it because I want to have a baby, *this baby,* more than I've ever wanted anything."

AJ nodded and turned towards her to hug her.

She leaned against him and he made her feel stronger and more accepted. "I really screwed up. Charlie is so mad at me."

"Charlie didn't have a child expelled from his body like you did when you were no more than a child. My child. And if I'd only known, none of that would have happened to you. I just don't want anything bad to happen to you ever again. Soon you'll understand how strong that emotion is for a parent. It makes your baby suddenly the most vulnerable person alive."

She leaned back so she could look up at his face. "It wasn't your fault. And good things are going to happen to me because I'm still alive and I have to seek my life's path. You have to let me." She squeezed his arm and smiled softly. "But you can be there for me when I do."

His grip tightened around her shoulders. "I will be there. I just didn't know how to handle this."

"No one does. I shocked everyone. Mostly, Charlie. I did it. But I didn't set out to do it. I was careless about my birth control. If I could undo what I did, I would. I hate having Charlie so upset with me. He thinks I've ruined his life. I didn't think he would take it that badly."

"You understand, I hope, that he has every right to feel that way."

"I do. But I can't undo this."

"But you also don't even want to." He held her. "Don't

worry, I'll be here for you. No matter what. Just like I always promised you."

"Thank you, Dad." It was the first time Cami called AJ that to his face, but now she had a reason.

∽

IT WAS SO FAR from what Charlie wanted but the reality was simply too big and important to ignore. Cami went to the doctor and learned she was seven weeks along and her due date was September eighteenth.

Charlie suppressed a groan of frustration when she told him over the phone. There would be no trip to Germany now or earning his master's degree. He withheld his instinctive reaction, trying to conceal and smash it.

It was just the start of a series of crushing disappointments, schedule conflicts and a shifting of his priorities until they were ruined. His entire future and the course of his life were suspended indefinitely.

Having accepted the scholarship, he had to formally withdraw from it. He hadn't done that yet and he wasn't sure why. What did he hope for? Some way to leave Cami and a new baby so he could go halfway across the world? Even his wildest longings and ambitions couldn't make him that coldhearted. So there would be no scholarship. But he couldn't force himself to withdraw it.

Not yet.

It was hard to concentrate. Even harder to talk to Cami or care about her pregnancy symptoms. It was hard to care about her, period. The distance between them had never felt so big.

He lost the connection he felt before. It went so wrong, at least from his viewpoint.

But frighteningly, it went so right from hers.

How could they ever unite again with such vastly different experiences to bear?

~

SORE BREASTS, vertigo, some morning sickness and lots of severe headaches, Cami was becoming increasingly tired and had to drag herself to work.

She told him all about it. The thing was? Charlie didn't really care. He was nice to her, always courteous, and conscious of her condition and how she felt. But the closeness they'd shared since they were kids was gone. It was the one thing that made nothing about them ordinary.

Now any interaction felt forced and kind of boring. They both sounded hollow where once, they were full. No, something very deep and integral had changed between them.

When he got back to school, Charlie felt a wave of unbridled relief, and a sense of guilt stabbed his heart. He didn't want to be happy as soon as he was away from Cami. And relieved to rejoin his friends and all that was fun and familiar at school.

And as for the formal acceptance that had him leaving for Germany on September fourteenth? He had yet to formally decline it. He'd done nothing to change it. Officially he was still going. He just needed more time to work up to letting the chance of a lifetime slip through his fingers.

All to stay home and do the most ordinary, mundane thing he could think of doing at this point in his life: having a baby. Like everyone else.

He didn't want to be ordinary. Never had wanted to be. But here he was. Exactly who he never wanted to be.

Destiny be damned.

CHAPTER 11

*I*RREVOCABLY, CAMI CHANGED THEIR former demeanor, as well as the natural ease and rapport that flowed between them. Her frequent headaches began to plague her. Fatigue gripped her. And a series of stomach aches stopped her from indulging in the foods she formerly liked.

The odd discourse and alienated feelings between them weren't because of Charlie. He didn't overtly say or do anything. He didn't withdraw, or mumble little digs or slurs. But something that was magical and intangible, something that always seemed to be "there" between them, had vanished.

Dragging herself out of bed one morning, Cami had to get to work. Charlie was very serious about what he wanted done before the birth of the baby and insisted they be ready for it.

Something that both intimidated and irritated her. But how could she fault him for that when she was the reason it happened? She ignored her incessant nausea and body aches in order to work and performed as best she could while trying to keep herself busy.

Groggy with the usual morning headache, the draining fatigue that consumed her made her stomach feel hollow and achy. Nothing unusual so she wandered into her bathroom to take a shower. Staring at her reflection, she stuck out her tongue. She stopped dying her hair because of her pregnancy, worrying the chemicals could bother the baby. She had no real reason for it, but it felt important to her. She hated her blonde hair. The only blonde hair she did not dye until now was her body hair.

As she sat down to pee, she suddenly froze, her mind going blank before she went numb. *What the hell?* Her underwear was wet and gooey, smeared with brownish colors. She stared at it without comprehending. No. No, see she didn't get her periods anymore. She couldn't. She felt a sudden cramp. Something that was happening off and on for several days. But that was from the pregnancy.

Except. She. Saw. Blood.

Whoa. Bleeding and spotting during pregnancy were conditions she'd heard of. It had to do with the fetus becoming implanted or something, so maybe it was just normal spotting. Nothing. Not… no. Her brain refused to say anymore.

She read about it in the prenatal book and a few different magazines she recently subscribed too. It was probably nothing. Yes. She was fine.

But she saw *blood*.

Her heart started pounding harder. She leaned forward and sucked in a breath of air to calm her increasingly climaxing anxiety. No. Oh, no. And Kate wasn't home, having gone to Seattle overnight for business.

What should she do? What could she do?

Cami rose to her feet and slid her panties back up along

with the loose, dark pants she wore. Shocked with alarm, she jerked the door open. "Dad! Dad!" she screamed his name.

Standing in the doorway of her bathroom, she gripped the knob tightly. She wasn't crying. Or doing anything. Just trembling. Her entire body shook as the primal fear of any mother-to-be filled her senses.

Then she *knew*.

She knew what happened. It wasn't spotting. Or her period. No, it was a baby. The remnants of a baby in her underwear.

AJ raced to the top of the staircase, still chewing on whatever he'd been eating for breakfast. He stopped dead and stared at her, his gaze drifting from her face to her hand as she gripped the knob so tightly as if it alone were holding her upright. Closing her eyes and shaking her head in denial over and over, she kept chanting a mantra in her mind.

No. Oh no.

It was a quiet plea in her heart.

Please, God, no. Don't.

Don't take this away from her.

So much of her life was taken away before she was allowed to bask in the salvation she found at River's End. Perhaps that was enough for anyone, but this was something she wanted more than anything else she'd ever dreamed about. She cared about having a baby more than absolutely everything.

Even Charlie. And her family. More than any dream she could possibly desire for her future. Still she raised up another silent prayer, *please God... just please, don't take her baby*.

Unlike her standard reaction, no tears came. No screams. No pleas for help or comfort. She stood there trembling but upright.

"Cami?" AJ said, his eyes darting around.

She shook her head again. "I think you'd better take me to the doctor."

"What? What's happening?"

Sucking in a breath, her heart sunk into a deep, watery pit before it drowned. "I'm losing the baby."

His eyes darted down. "Are you sure? How could you know?"

"Blood. There's too much blood. I haven't been feeling right either, but I thought it was just normal discomfort from pregnancy. But it's not. It's not, Dad." Her tone was cool and calm and even.

AJ's eyelids lifted, and his eyes sparkled with concern. "You can't be sure. You don't know. We'll go to the ER. They'll check you over and find out what's wrong. They'll know how to stop it and help you and… and save it. Now. Come on."

He spurred her into action, but Cami had to force her legs to move forward, slowly and steadily. Somewhere in her mind, she understood there was no hurry to get there. AJ rushed forward. "Let me help you. Take it easy."

She used his arm to lean on him. His giant arms held her and provided a tender touch. She knew he would. He'd always been gentle with her. The very first time he met her, he said to her simply, "I'm AJ." It was a terrible moment for her, coming to River's End, and AJ was a complete stranger.

Once more, Cami found herself at the mercy of adults and strangers. Once more, she feared what she'd find, and the extent of harm she'd have to endure. That's what she believed would happen after her first glimpse of the giant that turned out to be her father.

But that's not what happened. AJ was a quiet, solid, caring presence in her life. He never once put his hands on her in anger and never even raised his voice. And now she needed that even more than when she was thirteen.

He set her gently onto the seat of his truck. "I wish we had Kate's car. I'm sorry. This stupid, big thing." He dashed around to his side and jumped in. But he drove out with extra care and caution, making sure not to bump her on the rough, dirt road until they hit the pavement. Then he drove as fast as he could while using plenty of care on the curves of the valley road.

Cami stared out the window, dull and unseeing. AJ's jaw clenched but he respected her need to be quiet. When he pulled into the local hospital, he helped her out and they walked inside. AJ spoke quietly but quickly to the front reception. Cami was seen only minutes later. They rushed her inside to get examined. The nurse came in and took down all of her information as well as the details of what was going on.

Soon afterwards, now in a gown and on the exam table, Cami grimaced while they checked for the baby's heartbeat. As she already knew, they found none.

Her heart didn't dip or break upon the clarification and proof of what she already knew. Deep down in her gut, she sensed the baby no longer lived. Some brief expressions of their sincere condolences came from the doctor and nurses but at this point, they explained, her body could handle the natural processing of the miscarriage. No further medical intervention was necessary.

She got redressed and AJ stood up as soon as she walked into the waiting room. He took one look at her face and rushed forward, holding her body and hugging her against him.

She broke free and mumbled, "I just want to go home."

"Can we do that? Go home?" he questioned. Seeking a more official or dramatic release, AJ was not content to just quietly go home after that.

"Yes."

She stared out the window. He kept quiet. But when they got home, he quickly came around to her side of the truck and hugged her against him again. At his tender touch, Cami finally broke down and started to cry. She leaned quietly against his chest as he rubbed her back and patted her shoulders. "I wish Kate were here," she mumbled softly.

"She'll be home in probably less than three hours now. I called her. She left Seattle immediately."

"Thank you," Cami replied.

"I know I'm not what you need right now, but I love you, Cami, and I only wish there was something I could do for you."

"I know... Dad."

"I called Charlie too. From the waiting room."

"Oh? Oh, that's good. Thank you." Cami felt oddly disconnected from Charlie.

She *was* pregnant, but now had nothing to show for it. Now she looked and felt the same, and there was nothing for her to look forward to.

She let her dad turn her around and guide her inside before setting her gently on the couch and covering her with a knitted afghan from Kate's mother. Cami snuggled under it and used the pillow he tucked under head. He left her with a gentle pat on her head and she smiled up at him. He couldn't have handled her any better. "You were perfect, Dad. For this. For me. Always were. I was just scared to let you be. Scared you'd leave. Scared you'd abandon me. Scared I'd disappoint you and you'd leave. That's how Parker always was. She was never like you... Dad."

AJ was visibly choked up at her words. Then she turned her head and buried it into the pillow. "I just want to sleep now. Please." Of course, her dad respected her request and turned and left the room.

IT WAS STILL early April and Charlie was trying to listen to a lecture while his phone logged five calls in a row from AJ's number. Since it was completely unusual, Charlie walked out of his class, and into the hallway before dialing him back. "AJ? What's going on?"

"Cami's at the hospital. She's losing the baby, Charlie."

Charlie fell into stunned silence. "Oh, damn," he whispered to himself before replying, "I'll be there as soon as I can."

"I know you will." There was little else to say. They both hung on for a long moment before they finally hung up. The punch Charlie felt in his stomach nearly took his breath away.

He closed his eyes and his entire body sagged with defeat. *Damn. Just damn.*

He had no idea how to feel. It wasn't relief. And definitely not happiness. An overpowering indifference with an abject distance to it. He understood the words, but his feelings didn't follow if they were supposed to. As if it were happening to someone else while he listened in. He shook his head to undo the trance that overtook him. He had to go home. He had to get back to Cami, who would not like his reaction.

CAMI, of course, heard Kate's dramatically hurried and harried entrance. She ran in from the porch, slamming the door in her hastiness and dropping her bags and purse in the entry. AJ appeared from nowhere and was quietly… doing what? Cami had no idea. He'd been quiet as a mouse or an inanimate object while Cami simply kept her eyes tightly shut as she lay on the couch, lost to the world. But at least she was still in the world.

"She's resting. Shh. She has not moved since we got home."

"She's so quiet? Was she crying?"

"She cried just a little but only when we got home. Since then, she's been quiet," her dad said. His tone dropped so low, Cami had to shift her head until her left ear was free of the pillow to hear him speak to Kate.

"Cami always cries. What do you mean, she hasn't cried?"

"Nothing. A deadly, quiet calm. Even when we were at the hospital. She knew, Kate, right off. She stood outside the bathroom, shaking, pale as a sheet of paper and quiet. Then she said she'd lost the baby. I don't know... I didn't know what to do..." he repeated it several times. Cami sensed Kate probably took him in her arms by the sounds of their shuffling limbs and Kate's voice was a low murmur, like she was repeating something to him.

"Should I wake her?" Kate whispered.

"I think you should let her be until she decides to engage."

They turned and disappeared towards the kitchen. Cami lay there in the dark. She let it seep into her bones, her heart, and her empty stomach.

Finally, the crunching of tires on the gravel made her glance at her phone, and she saw it was past midnight. *Charlie.* Duh. Of course, he'd come home. He wasn't a monster. He might even feel sorry for her, but she sincerely doubted he felt the least bit sorry for himself.

And that perhaps would be the reason why she could not forgive him. But right then she succumbed to the heaviness of her body and limbs. Caught in a deep fog, she couldn't imagine working up the energy to express anything she thought. Let alone, anything that even resembled anger.

Charlie opened the door without knocking and stepped

inside before turning the entrance light on. He texted her several times over the last few hours and called her phone. She hadn't answered any of them and kept it on silent mode. Without stirring, she kept her head buried in her pillow and her body on her side, facing the couch back.

AJ and Kate came in and met Charlie at the entrance. There was more rustling, most likely an exchange of hugs and softly murmured words. She couldn't make them out. She didn't lift her head either, unlike before. Now she just didn't care. A bit louder, she heard Kate say, "I haven't even talked to her. She hasn't been up since I got home. I don't know exactly…"

"I'll talk to her. Why don't you guys go to bed?"

She sensed Kate's reluctance when she didn't answer at first but finally gave in with an, "I suppose we could." That was followed by shuffling, more footsteps, and a long silence. Charlie came in and stood over her. Cami could have turned over and acknowledged him or let him know that she was awake and aware that he was there. But she didn't.

He finally dropped down to kneel beside her. His hands caressed her shoulder and back in a gentle touch. "Cami?"

She didn't move or even acknowledge his presence. The soft tone of his voice seemed to spike her nerve endings, causing an uncontrollable and automatic response of tears. They began welling in her eyes and several slid free, leaving silent tracks on her face before pooling under her cheek.

"Cams? I know you're awake." He repeated her name and slid his hands around in small circles of soothing comfort. The heat radiated through her clothes. She finally turned a few inches until her body was half towards him and half towards the couch. She lifted her gaze up to his face. The only light came from the outside porch lights shining through the front window. With so few neighbors, they were rarely closed.

213

She stared at him and he stared back. A hand slid up to her face and cupped her chin as he looked down at her. "I'm sorry."

She nodded with an infinitesimal lift of her head up and down. He kept looking into her eyes, scanning her face and brushing her hair off her forehead. "Are you okay? I mean, are you in physical pain?"

She cleared her throat. "Not really."

He nodded, and relief flashed over him at hearing her words. He leaned over, still smoothing her hair back and he kissed her mouth with a soft press of his lips before holding her face. His head shook, and she gathered he was at a loss. He opened his mouth and closed it before finally saying, "I love you."

Cami's gaze was off in the distance, focused on nothing. She really didn't feel like talking or crying or identifying the emotions that were penetrating her brain and heart. She felt it despite her desire to ignore it. His words. His touch. His sympathy could so easily crack her. To avoid that, she turned her face towards the couch back and let her body follow.

Charlie didn't persist with her. Instead, he slipped in behind her, wrapping his arms around her middle. Taking one of her hands in his, he rubbed her fingers and fiddled with her hand idly. He stayed quiet and so did she. She didn't withdraw from him when he began touching her, nor did she lean into it. She closed her eyes and floated along, her thoughts drifting everywhere and nowhere.

She must have fallen asleep because she woke up and saw the daylight shining on the floor in squares of warm sunlight. She overheard the murmurs and mutters of a household waking up while attempting to be quiet for those who hadn't. The soft click and tap of cabinets opening and closing along with drawers and the familiar clinks and clanks of dishes on the table. She heard the coffee pot being set back on the machine and sighed as a heavy, gray fog enveloped her and she began to slowly suffocate.

She set her legs on the ground to sit up. The world felt new and different. Overnight, it had become a difficult place to live and only yesterday morning, everything seemed so normal and ordinary. She got up, messed around in her room, decided what to wear, wandered into the bathroom to brush her hair and teeth and then... she peed. That was when it all went wrong.

After rising from the couch, she walked on her bare feet into the kitchen, as quiet as a feather and equally unassuming. Charlie sat at the bar, talking softly to her parents. Kate noticed her appearance first and stared with big, wide and concerned eyes at her. Silence descended over the kitchen as they all took a long look at her. Their collective surprise at seeing her upright was reflected in their expressions.

"Oh, good morning, sweetie," Kate said in the kindest, gentlest voice. She rushed forward and scooped Cami up, pushing her against her busty chest. "I should have been here for you. I'm so sorry. I'm just so damn sorry," she crooned a few times. Cami didn't react or hug her back, but she did press herself into Kate's torso and let her nearly support her weight.

"You couldn't have known."

"Well, I'm here now, and I'm staying here. I promise you, Cami, you will be okay." She placed a finger under Cami's chin and raised her face up. In a serious tone, Kate insisted that Cami accept her promise as sincerely as she said it. She knew Kate wanted only the best for her.

Kate let Cami go, but still kept one arm around her shoulders and cuddled her against her tall frame. "You need to eat something, honey. Stay well and healthy despite how awful you feel. What would you like for breakfast?"

Cami slipped away from Kate's embrace and kept her

head down as she shuffled into a chair beside Charlie. He took her hand and held it. "Cereal," she finally replied. She knew better than to argue with Kate about food. She'd just keep offering things to her until she ate something. Kate quickly provided her a bowl, and the cereal and milk and spoon, which was prepared and ready to eat. Cami took it without smiling but she mumbled "Thanks." When she glanced up at them, she asked, "Can you guys stop watching me? It doesn't help."

They immediately reacted by turning away or shuffling their feet, pretending as if that automatically made them busy. She shook her head. "I'm not going to do anything irrational. You don't have to worry, and you can quit supervising me as if I'm planning to."

There was another silence. No one knew what to say to her. Kate just responded like she was wont to do. "Right. We just... oh, honey, we were so worried about you. Do you want to talk? Or do something to distract you? What can we do to help, sweetie?"

"I don't know. But staring at me probably isn't a good way to start," she said with the smallest tug upwards of her lips. Kate walked around her and messed up her hair as she kissed the top of her head.

"Ah, hell, kiddo, I don't know what to do either."

AJ walked towards her. Surprised, Cami lowered her spoon and stared up at him. He leaned over and hugged her. "If you want to hang out or maybe play video games... whatever, I'm your guy."

She knew that giving her comfort was awkward for AJ and his statement was somehow just right. "Maybe later," she replied.

AJ took Kate's hand and left the kitchen. Obviously, they were giving Charlie and her some privacy. She stared down at her cereal bowl and ate with intense concentration. She pretended it consumed all of her brain power. Charlie's gaze bored into her. But she resisted the urge to look at him. Sighing, he finally put his arm on the back of her chair and his other beside her on the table, essentially surrounding her.

"Cami?" His tone was curious, deep, and sincere. "What can I do?"

"Nothing." Setting her spoon down, Cami's hands fell onto her lap. She could only stare at the half-eaten, floating wheat squares in the milk. "You can't do anything."

"Can I at least be here for you?"

She swallowed and kept her gaze down. "Depends."

"On what?"

She rubbed her hands together, staring harder at them now. Something kept her from looking at Charlie. "Are you relieved? Are you happy? Do you only feel sorry for me?"

He leaned towards her. "How do you want me to answer those questions?"

"With the honest truth."

He took in a deep breath. "My only urgency was to get to you. My feelings are all tied up in you, Cami. So I'm not happy, although I might be slightly relieved. But I'm mostly just sorry for you."

She briefly spared him a glance. "So, you're not sorry for *us*."

"I don't know yet what I am. Can't it be enough for you to know how much I care about you? I'm not happy. I can't stand to see you in pain, full of hurt and grieving."

As he spoke, his voice dropped lower, almost into a gentle caress. His knee turned towards her leg and he gently nudged her. He leaned closer, touching his forehead to the side of her head. "I love you, Cami, don't turn this into a war between us. Right now, can't you just let me love you? Let me be here with you. Let me grieve with you and for you. Just for now, can't we let it be? Later, we can decide how I feel. I promise. But today, can't you just let me be here for you?"

Her eyes shut tightly as she tried to restrain the growing pressure of her tears. She slowly nodded her head and a few streams of moisture rolled down her cheeks. He set his hand up to the other side of her head and tucked her head against his shoulder, wrapping his arm around her. Her hands instinctively slid upwards and around him before she buried her forehead against his chest. "I was afraid you would be happy about it," she whispered.

He nodded. "I'm not happy."

Wrapping her up in his embrace, he buried his face against her shoulder as she hung onto his neck. His mouth touched her neck and he kissed the side of her face repeatedly. "Why aren't you crying?" he asked gently.

Her shoulders bumped up and down. "It hurts so much more than that."

His arms all but lifted her off the floor and she let him hold her. "Your calm is frightening."

"I know. I just don't know how to express what I feel."

"Can you try? This has to bring a lot of baggage up. What happened when you were with your mom?"

"You mean, Parker? Dad and I agreed to call her Parker and not Mom, and I'm calling him Dad now instead of AJ."

"When did that happen?"

"The weekend we told them about the baby. The night you left early."

"You didn't tell me about that."

"We haven't been talking to each other, Charlie." He let her go and slowly pushed her into the chair as he took his again. Facing her now, their knees were bumping together.

"We've been talking."

"We've been chatting. I could tell you the last detail about your schedule and classes, but I have no idea what you're thinking or how you feel about anything."

He nodded, his hands nervously fiddling with her fingers. Averting his gaze from hers, he stared at their joined hands. "Charlie," she said softly, but her tone was firm, "you know it's true."

"I guess. It's just… I wanted to work things out with you."

"But you left here six weeks ago. You *had to* stay with me because I was pregnant. And now? Do you think you still have to stay with me because I'm not?"

His head jerked up. "Cami!" he exclaimed. "What the hell are you talking about?"

Her tone was calm and even. She was neither angry nor snarky, but real. "I'm talking about reality."

"No. Damn it. I wasn't biding my time with you. I wasn't waiting around to leave you or dump you. I was working through everything that happened. You knew that. You knew what and why. But I never once intended to break up. Nor did I ever love you any less. I just needed more time to work it out."

"You were doubting everything about us and the future."

"I never once doubted my love or commitment to you. Not once. Ask Ben. Ask my dad. Ask your dad. Ask anyone. I never hinted that I was stuck with you. I was stuck with a baby. There is a huge difference there. I tried to be honest."

He scooted forward and took her face in his hands, holding it up so she had to look right at him. "You told me you loved me for close to four years now."

"Yes. I have."

He frowned. "Do you think we just became a habit? And started taking each other for granted?"

"I think you did. You left me here after starting a serious relationship with me that you said you wanted. But you went to school and lived as if you didn't have any relationship."

"So you're saying all this started because I neglected you?"

"No. I'm saying you neglected to even ask my opinions. You could've made some compromises," she snapped.

Sharply drawing in a breath, Charlie replied, "I guess... I really did that. It's gradually becoming more evident to me that I failed to see things from your point of view. But I never meant to hurt you."

She sighed, her gaze skittering off. "I know. That's why I couldn't confront you."

"You don't willingly confront anything. I didn't know you felt this way."

She chewed on her lower lip. "No, I don't suppose you did know that."

"We have to do better, Cami. We have to talk more and be more open and honest. You can't do things like lying about using birth control just because you want me to cut back on my schooling. That's not a fair fight."

"No. But I didn't know any other way to solve my problem."

He scratched his head. "What... what are you saying? This isn't what I expected from you today."

"I don't know." She withdrew her hands from his.

"Try to explain yourself. I think you do know, Cami. You just play like you don't. You are good at *not* saying what you really think and feel, but I know you know exactly how you feel."

"Okay. I wanted the baby. I live in fear that what Parker did to me permanently injured something inside me and now this happened. I've had a miscarriage. How can I find out if that's really the case? What if my uterus is scarred or ruptured and I might never carry a baby to term?"

He nodded. "I didn't know you worried about things like that."

"Yes. And now? I'm terrified I'll never be able to have a baby."

He took in a shuddered breath. "Oh, Cams…"

She lifted her face to his. "I know that's a stretch to you. But—"

"No, no." He leaned forward and pulled her to him. "I love you. We'll have a baby someday. And we'll do whatever we need to in order to make it happen."

"We?"

"It was always *we* in my mind, *just not now.* I still think that."

She titled her head to consider him. "Funny because now I'm so sure. Look, I'm tired, I'm going to go rest."

"Do want me to come with you?"

"No. I just want to sleep for a while."

He let her go there alone. She lay on her bed and held the pillow against her. The weight of it all sat heavily on her chest. Damn, she just hurt so much.

But for the first time, there was nothing anyone could do to reassure her that she was fine inside. What made her so sad, made Charlie glad. There was no getting around that and therefore, Charlie was the last person who could help her.

CHAPTER 12

THE FEW MONTHS FROM then to April were very quiet. Charlie went home for spring break and Cami was reserved and a little down. She lost a lot of weight and Charlie didn't like that. She blamed it on her grief and said she still didn't feel like eating. But she was surviving all the same.

Charlie, however, felt guilty.

At first, it was kind of nice to go back home. But Cami was so quiet. She didn't want to do much. Ridiculously skinny, he constantly urged her to eat. She did however drink quite a bit of alcohol and worse still, often smoked weed. He hated the smell of it on her, but he liked the way it mellowed her out. It seemed to help her forget her sadness and relaxed her strung-out nerves temporarily. Charlie felt a little guilty for preferring that Cami get high instead of grieving and sucking him dry emotionally.

When he returned to school, he was ashamed to feel so relieved to be back there, but he could not deny his gratitude for a little bit of freedom. He tried to talk to her over the phone, but it was stilted and awkward, and each time he hung up he felt a little bit more relieved each time. What was so wrong with them? Why could they not find their connection? The vibrant connection that had always bonded them, even as just friends, was gone.

But now it was formal, polite, uninspired, and worse still, boring. They were *so* boring in their conversations and discussions, even he almost fell asleep listening to them, because there was nothing about their interactions that was personal, emotional, or interesting. Biding their time together, that's what each and every interaction felt like.

The question he was too scared to pose was: what were they biding their time towards?

WHAT DIDN'T CHANGE, however, was that the deadline to withdraw from his master's program was fast approaching. He wanted to go, of course. Desperately. But they hadn't touched on the subject since the miscarriage and he didn't know what she expected from him. Did she want him to willingly give it up? Did she expect him to? Was it some kind of test for her to gauge his loyalty to her?

Though they rarely touched on any subject of importance in the last three months, he had no choice but to broach the subject. He couldn't keep tying up a scholarship if he wasn't going to take it. It wasn't fair to other applicants who could still be selected to go. However, the thought of letting it go rekindled the anger in his core.

No. He simply couldn't give it up.

But could he give up Cami? If she gave him the ultimatum of her or Germany? What would he do? He wasn't sure of the answer to that, and for the first time in four years, that scared him.

Finally, he had to bring it up. "What are your thoughts on Germany?"

She made an odd sound. "I never had any until you decided to go live there. Then I hated it."

"And now?"

"Now? I have no idea. You haven't mentioned it in months."

"I didn't know if I should or not. I'm trying to determine if it's worth our relationship?"

She snorted. "Is that what you think? Is that why you haven't mentioned it?"

"I hesitate to mention it, let alone go there, if I risk losing you."

"And you don't want that?"

He grunted. "Not even a smidgeon." Though... was he lying?

"Did you withdraw from it when I was still pregnant? When you believed you were forced to give it up?" she questioned.

He didn't "believe" he was forced to give it up. He *was* forced to give it up. By Cami. But he bit on his tongue to keep the sharp, sarcastic criticism to himself.

"No, I didn't," he admitted reluctantly.

"See? That's because you want to go."

"It's more than just wanting to go. It's hard to decline such an honor and a fantastic opportunity. But if it means I lose you, then... yeah, I won't go."

"You'd do that? Give this up?"

"If it meant the end of us? Yes." But... did he really mean that? Would he? He wasn't sure he could commit to that. He just hoped she wouldn't require it of him like some kind of litmus test of how he felt about her.

She was quiet before she sighed again. "But it's not what you should do. You should realize your potential. And the chance no one else I know could ever have. So you have to do it. It's your reality. Your reality and mine. I will grow up and deal with it. I'll find a better way to deal with it than what I did before."

Hard as it was for Charlie to admit out loud to, he said, "I hope so."

"I guess it's fair to say something interceded here, so I might as well take it as a divine sign that I should change some things. I can't be how I've been in the past. I have to improve. I am trying, Charlie. I really am. I've just been... so stalled. So unable to move forward. I agree not to have babies any time soon. And that's how it needs to be. I don't want us to end up hating each other."

"We never hated each other."

"No. But the resentment is something we almost haven't survived."

"Yes. And it's been on both sides. Don't forget that."

"It has," she agreed. "You have to go to Germany next fall and we'll have to figure out a way to stay together."

He fell silent. Then he said, "Thank you, Cami, for supporting me in my goal and realizing that."

"I finally do realize it."

They hung up and it was fine. The aching resentment of a few months ago was gone, but not the warmth and care and connection of a year ago.

So what was left? He wasn't sure he knew the right words for it. Hollowness? Emptiness? Going through the motions? A habit they didn't know how to break? His stomach twisted at the bitter thought they might have lost what they had spent so long trying to nurture.

All to fizzle out in the end when neither of them cared enough to even try to deny the obvious?

～

CHARLIE GRADUATED with his class the second week of June. Cami attended the graduation along with Charlie's parents, his brother, his sister-in-law, and his niece. It was a lovely weekend of celebration and joy.

Everyone clapped and cheered when Charlie walked across the stage to receive his diploma and shake hands with the top representatives of the school. Cami's heart rose and swelled with pride and she tried not to think about her lingering sadness and resentment at Stanford for taking Charlie away from her. Bursting with pride and amazement, she stared at the man Charlie had become during the last four years. He achieved all the goals he set for himself with near perfection.

Jack clapped and watched the ceremony with tears shining in his eyes. Cami began to understand how important it was to Jack, who was so overwhelmed that he wasn't sure he could contain all of his pride and joy at his son's foremost accomplishment.

The only hiccup in Charlie's otherwise sterling pedigree and promising future was Cami.

She truly believed her analysis. She was the only thing about Charlie that didn't fit him.

But Charlie held her in his arms when he wove his way through the crowd of graduates. He grabbed her and swished her all around with unmasked joy. He kissed her, and his face shone brightly while his family and Stanford friends looked on. It was hard to ignore Charlie.

It was also the first time in a very long time that they kissed or even hugged each other and maybe the first genuine smiles they had shared with each other in *months*.

But his joy and exuberance over accomplishing his childhood goal made him forget the discomfort that now defined how they interacted.

He was high on life, even her presence, in those moments.

That weekend was a good one and Cami stayed there with him. They went to a few end-of-the-year parties and spent a lot of time with his family. Cami went home with Charlie's family.

They left Charlie so he could spend a few weeks with his friends and close out his life in California, as well. Cami tried not to dwell on the fact that his post-college celebration trip was spent with Dawson, Tyrell, and Rupport going down to Mexico for a week. Her only consolation was that Rosalie didn't go with Dawson, either.

But still, it felt odd that after all these years of her waiting and supporting his college career, he chose to celebrate its ending with his friends.

They shared no more than that one kiss at his graduation. Other than that? She could have been his sister or friend for how they interacted. The fear that lingered in her after his graduation started to rise up from her gut up into her heart.

What was left of them?

In preparation for something she was sure was coming, Cami went home to try and make some sense of *her* life.

Before Charlie came home and ended their lives together.

The gnawing emptiness in her stomach told her he was about to come home and do just that.

JACOB SHOWED up at the ranch. He was spending his summer with his mom, as usual.

Cami grinned and ran to greet him upon her arrival. He swept her up in a huge hug. "Just returning from Charlie's graduation from Stanford? That guy... he's pretty amazing."

"He was and still is." Cami stepped back and let Jacob go.

"Well, my mom told me about the miscarriage. I was

going to call you, but I couldn't think of what to say. I'm really sorry though, Cams."

"Yeah, me too."

"What about Charlie?"

Cami shook her head to the negative, cringing. "You don't hem or haw about discussing sensitive subjects, do you? Charlie is very sorry for me, but relieved for himself. It's been... hard. And it gets pretty complicated."

"Well, can you blame the guy?" Jacob's eyebrows shot upwards. She gaped at him in astonishment, thinking he'd be on her side considering how close they were last summer.

"What do you mean?"

"You did get yourself knocked up without his consent."

She winced. "That sounds even worse when you say it like that."

"You did do something without asking his permission ahead of time. So... yeah, think about that. You should be sorry. And pretty grateful he didn't just dump your ass. I would have."

"So, you're saying I deserved the miscarriage?"

He shrugged. "Nobody deserves that, it just is. A sad fact of nature. Ten to twenty percent of pregnancies end that way."

"How the fuck do you know that?"

He shrugged. "I looked it up online when I heard about you."

"Why would you do that?" Her face scrunched up.

"You're my friend. I wanted to see what you were going through. You know how much I care about you."

"But you think I fucked over Charlie?"

"Well, he's my friend too. I can see both sides."

She dropped her head. "I know. I can see Charlie's side too. That's what makes it so hard. We can't go back to where we were before. I don't know how else to describe it."

"When you're old enough, you can do it right. With Charlie. And it'll be better because you'll have his consent and it will be a choice you both make. I think that'll happen, Cams."

She rolled her eyes. "Pretty scary when you start giving me such sound and decent advice on life."

"Well, it was pretty crazy you did that to him."

She smiled softly. "I didn't expect such sage advice from you."

"I'm a jerk, but I'm not stupid. I might not follow my good advice, but I know how to give it."

She shook her head. "I have to get my own shit together now. Do you think your dad and Trinity would let me stay with you guys this fall?"

"This fall? Why?"

"Charlie leaves for Germany then, and I shouldn't just hang out here, waiting like I have been for the last four years. I need to do something new and different so I don't regress into my past patterns for coping. I have to get out of here. Like everyone else keeps telling me."

"I think you should too. And sure you can," Jacob replied without hesitation. "Of course. But why? What's in Everett?"

"My plans."

"I didn't know you had any."

"No one does. I don't have specifics yet, but I figure a new town would be a good start."

"Wanna tell me all about it?"

"No. I just want to stay at your dad's place."

He shrugged. "Okay by me. Just hafta check with my asshole dad."

Cami called up Brett Starr, herself, to make sure Jacob's invitation complied with a higher authority. He offered her low rent, but she still needed the basics, like food, toiletries, and other incidentals. She saved some money after three years of working steadily at the resort with few expenses.

So, when the fall came around, she'd go to Everett. Away from River's End. Away from her dad and Kate and everyone else she loved. At last, she would embark on her own adventure and start doing something new. Training for a trade or learning new job skills suddenly appealed to her.

Just like everyone kept urging her.

Even if deep down, she just wanted to stay home.

But she intended to commit herself to something. She could no longer stay there alone.

She longed to tell someone. But she didn't, and why? She had no real reason. Maybe because she wanted them to be proud of her and believe in her. They had to now, no matter what, and she wanted to make them love her more.

A FEW WEEKS later at the start of July, Charlie Rydell came home for the last time from Stanford University and his wonderful adventure in California.

Cami's heart tugged, and she wished he wanted to stay home for good. She couldn't wait until they moved in together and started living and working. But she still wanted to be there.

In River's End. Together.

Just as she always dreamed. For years, she clung to her faith that if she'd just manage to hang onto Charlie through the four years it took to earn his bachelor's degree, she'd be home free. But as soon as he got it, he announced his next plan: going to school internationally. So much farther away. She got dizzy whenever she began to envision their next separation. It always seemed to get harder than the time before.

Charlie was tired when he first got home and he slept and slept. Then he rested and read. He was so quiet and withdrawn, he seemed to be having a hard time adjusting to having nothing to do. Four years of college with strictly timed breaks had left him both exhausted as well as depressed. Not because he was away from there but because those days were over.

Like he just climbed a mountain and when he got to the top, all he could do was stand there, wondering, *Now what?* A few pictures to commemorate the experience, but what did it mean?

Their first few weeks together were uncomfortable and Cami visibly struggled. Their wooden conversations bothered her the most. They often used Jacob as a go-between and Cami found herself grateful for his presence. He occasionally eased the awkwardness between Charlie and her.

Yet they never spoke of recent events, especially those of the last few months, and nothing meaningful seemed to occupy their minds. They were just there.

There was something so distinctly missing and yet, both of them were too afraid to say anything. Without Jacob between them, they had nothing to say to each other.

It started to seem like a game of unspoken chicken, the end winner of their game being: who was going to end their relationship first?

CHARLIE STARED out towards the river, thinking how hard it was to be home. Especially with Cami. It was a brand new lifestyle to him. He wondered how to penetrate the invisible wall that so efficiently kept them at a distance since her miscarriage.

That was not what Charlie ever wanted to happen. Depressed and dejected, he flopped down on a rock at the beach. The air helped him clear his scattered thoughts. "Hey."

He turned at the sound of Erin's voice. She lumbered towards him, her stomach round and very pregnant. "Hey." Erin sat down and nodded at him. "How's it going?"

"Could be better. Cami and I…"

He threw a rock as far as he could into the river. "I've noticed, you don't have to mention it, the awkwardness and tension. Ever since the miscarriage?"

"Yeah. We can't seem to get on the same page. What should I do? Lie and say I'm sorry too? I… I don't know if I really am. I'm so sorry Cami had to go through it, but the results of it were what I wanted all along. And she knows that."

"It's a son of a bitch. That's about all I know. It's a horribly unfair set of circumstances where you and Cami are both damned if you do and damned if you don't."

"We were so far apart on this before, how can we ever come together now?"

Erin waited a long moment and Charlie licked his lips. "Do you want to come together? Or is she no more than a habit? First loves are very potent things. Maybe you don't want the same things. You have differing goals and needs and timelines. You have to admit, she went to some pretty far extremes to change her life."

Charlie's breath stilled and stayed in his throat. His heart hammered. No. Erin's words struck him hard, but no, that wasn't it. He still had so much passion for Cami inside him. Confident of only one thing, he replied, "I still love her."

"You say that too fast. You say it too automatically. Don't you hear that?"

"She suggested that too. Well, in her way. Not in out and out words. We haven't come close to saying the truth out loud… at least not yet."

"Maybe you should."

"I'm scared to. I don't know if I'm ready for the answer. But I didn't want her to lose the baby, however."

"I don't think anyone suspects that. Especially Cami. She knows you too."

"She's pulling away from me already and insists that I've done nothing but pull away from her."

"Have you?"

"I did for a while. Yes. I was working out my shit. But dealing with what is real and working things out doesn't mean I wanted to leave her. I sometimes feel like I have to make up for all the bad things that happened to her when she was younger. I can't make up for any of those."

Erin reached out and squeezed his hand. "I think you need to tell her that, Charlie. But first, you must determine if your differing life paths still converge at any point."

"How do we compromise?"

"Maybe you don't always. Maybe you just have to find ways to live with it."

"If Dad refused to have a baby with you, what would you have done?"

She nodded, and her smile was small and tender. "I'd have found a way to live with it. It's just an never-ending balancing act of two people trying to work together."

"So, what do I do?"

"You have to be brutally honest."

"I don't even know what *my truth* is. So how can I tell her it? I didn't want her pregnant. Not even a little bit. How can I comfort her now that she isn't?"

Erin's face crumpled in sympathy. "Keep trying. Or break up. That's your reality."

He nodded before staring out at the water. Erin said, "I'm sorry to add this now, of all times, but I wanted you to hear it so you could tell Cami. Kailynn's pregnant now too. So, this has to be an even harder time for Cami to live here."

His eyebrows lifted. "I always wondered if they would have a kid. No, that's great news for them. See? They waited until they were ready."

"Some people don't see it as that big of a deal. It's just a difference in priorities and values, Charlie. She didn't consider what she did a betrayal to you, not as you did. So you have to keep trying or—"

"Break up." He closed his eyes with a deep breath. "I don't want to break up. I am sure about that."

"Then..."

His lips tilted. "Keep trying. I got it. Thanks, Erin. I don't say it often enough, but I'm so glad Dad married you."

She reached her arm around him, drawing him close for a hug before letting him go.

Rising to her feet, Erin left him to his thoughts. After a while, he got up and went back to Cami.

CAMI WAS SITTING on the porch, huddled in a sweatshirt with the hood pulled down. She kept her hands deep inside the pocket of the sweatshirt. Lifting her head up when she heard Charlie approaching, she stared at him as he walked closer. He stopped on the steps below her. He took in a deep breath and said, "We need to talk."

Cami stared hard at him and said, "Yes. We do. Or, maybe we should just break up."

How could she vocalize that so casually?

He sighed as he plodded up the stairs and dropped down beside her in a wicker rocking chair. Across the street, the pastures were peppered with horses that tossed their heads or stomped their hooves. Others were placid and calm, munching on grass or trotting through the fields.

"Do you want that?"

"Do you?" she challenged. Mouth set in a grim line.

In a hollow tone, Charlie's shoulders fell. He gave in first as his face crumpled with emotions. "No. I don't want to break up."

"We aren't the kids we once were. You in your jeans and flannel, always grabbing my hand to make sure I was okay and right beside you. Remember those wonderful times we had? They were so innocent and sweet. We were nothing if not adorable."

"We still are."

"We are not. We don't even look at each other anymore."

He nodded, conceding her point. "We could be then. We could still be them again."

"No." She shook her head. "We aren't that Cami and Charlie anymore. Too much has happened, even if it isn't anyone's fault. We've been separated a long time and now, and the things you want are opposite of what I want. Look how far I went to get what I wanted. But I was perfectly willing to do it. It shames me, even now. But I was willing. I don't want to be like that, Charlie. Doing all the wrong things to get what I want when our life's paths are so divergent from each other. Maybe it's time for us to realize we aren't right for each other."

He let her lethal words fall between them, like errant lead shot, scattering but with the potential of hitting and hurting. Instead of agreeing with her, Charlie turned and reached for her hand, tugging it free from her pocket. He took her fingers in his and squeezed. She let her hand stay limp. "I have to disagree with you. We *are* right for each other. We are just having a hard time right now. Because of the miscarriage and our opposing views on it. And you've been very sad. I've tried to respect that."

"Yes, you are always respectful of me. But maybe, respect

isn't enough. Maybe you've let respect mask that you are also indifferent to me now."

"No. I'm not. You are it for me, Cams. You always have been."

"You're also excessively loyal and short-sighted. Maybe you're too blind to see when two people have outgrown each other. It's not working anymore."

"We're just going through a rough patch. I clearly see and agree with that. But it isn't just loyalty and myopia. It's actually love. You are raw and hurting and so am I. But—"

"But what? We are suddenly going to feel the same about the baby and miscarriage?"

"No. And because we don't, we are going to have to work harder to fight this, not each other. We have to fight for each other. Even if it means we keep repeating this cycle of getting hurt and quarreling and making up, only to do it all over again. It can only keep on repeating until we figure it out. And I believe we will. This is real. This is love. This is worth fighting for."

"You seem to forget who I am sometimes." Her hand fluttered around, encompassing the land around them. "This place is everything I could ever want. No castle in Europe, or mountain top in South America, or glacier in Alaska could make me want to leave this place. Don't you see what I mean? Nothing that the world can offer me could ever be as perfect as what I have right here. And yet, you long to explore the very world I sought refuge from. For me, the outside world was a scary place where I was abused and neglected and hurt. Why would I want that? Your experience on the other hand, is practically the opposite of mine. So was your childhood. I know that. I understand your need to experience and learn more things you consider important. But you fail to realize that what I value is just as important to me. My top priority right now is being with my family. Being safe at home. All the things that were denied me have become the same things I can't pretend not to want."

Charlie's gaze penetrated hers. His eyes grew glassy with emotions, but he still opposed her logic. "All those things you're saying only make an argument for why we should *not* break up. It doesn't matter that we have very different backgrounds and motivations. I'm not denying that or the legitimacy of all the things that upset you. I even understood where the pregnancy came from, even if I didn't agree to it. But now I believe it's all the more reason for us to stay together. We have become each other's family, so we have to do whatever is required to make it work. We have to make sure we stay family. Lovers. Us."

"Again, just a string of pretty words." She snorted.

"You were lonely while you were waiting here for me, and unhappy for almost four years, right? That's what I heard you say?"

"Yes." She tugged her legs up to her chest and wrapped her arms around them. "I hate to just be waiting for you. Always waiting for my life to start again."

"I'm suggesting that you find something else besides the ranch or resort to do with your time. I don't want a baby any time soon. You'll have to accept that." He knelt before her, taking her hand in his and staring up at her. He cupped her cheek, lifting her face to see her dark-eyed gaze staring in pain at him. "I want you to choose to be with me. I'm asking you... No, I'm begging you to. But that means I can't have a baby yet."

"I know that." She shut her eyes.

"Cami? Do you want to have a baby with someone else? Do you want to break up, so you can find someone else to start a family with?"

Her eyes jammed open. "No!" she flung out the word with more feeling passion than he'd seen in five months. "No. Oh my God! No. It was never about having just anyone's baby. It's about having *your* baby."

"Then please, wait for me. Wait for me to be ready. Find something... anything that will keep you more fulfilled than the work you do on the resort. I think if you do, we can find a way to wait until we are both on the same timeline for wanting a family. Maybe we can make it easier to live with now. But the way I see it, we have two choices, break up and not have a baby or stay together and not have a baby. It honestly, doesn't make much sense to me to break up, when we both still love each other, right?"

"Yes. We do."

"Then what do you say?"

Her gaze was long and sad and her face solemn but serious. Finally, she nodded. "Okay."

"Okay?"

"Yes. I don't want... I can't stand the thought of losing you, so how could I want that? I'll find a way to wait. And do more than just bide my time. I will try to find a way to fill my life so full that I can't sabotage ours again."

He wilted, his head falling forward into her lap and startling her. She dropped her hands into his hair. He spoke on her jeans-clad leg. "I thought you might not choose this. Us."

Her hands stilled their stroking. "You really thought I would end it with you?"

He nodded, his lungs releasing the carbon dioxide as his racing heart started to slow down. "I really thought that." He tipped his head up to stare at her. "You have no idea how much I love you, do you? I wonder if you will ever see it and believe it and feel it. My temporary rejection of certain life benchmarks right now is no reflection of how I feel for you. My heart still belongs to you."

Her face crumpled up and tears, real ones, filled her eyes. For once, she started to cry very hard. Her sobs emerged from her mouth like a howl from a wolf. Natural, instinctive, and ridiculously chilling. "I'm so sad. And I don't know how to be that with you, but you are now and always the only one I want."

"Then be sad. Cry on me. I can handle it, Cami. I won't try to fix it or make it go away faster than you're ready, okay? I'll just be here for you."

He rose up and quickly took her in his arms, pulling her against his chest and hugging her to him. He was stroking her hair and letting her cry. She sobbed against him until her choking and shuddering grew more intermittent. It was a long while before she let go of him and wiped her wet eyes. "Round twenty?"

"Yeah," he said while brushing his thumbs across her wet cheeks. "And it might get to round one hundred too. But it's far better than zero rounds. That would mean we aren't even in the game anymore."

She held his hand. "So, we're still in the game."

"Yes. But I think it needs to change if we're going to make it to the final round."

Her face brightened with a smile. "Sports metaphors for the only two people in the world who never played a team sport."

Finally, he started to laugh, too, and they gripped each other in a warm, tight hug. It was the first genuine one they shared in a long time. She wasn't being comforted or having her sorrow soothed, and he wasn't mad or trying to deal with his anger.

Nothing was solved but the insistence on honesty changed everything. They started slowly. Going on a few dates and being alone, without Jacob as a buffer. They tried to reconnect. Their time together purposefully avoided the deeper, darker issues that plagued them. And it helped.

~

CUDDLING on her bed a few weeks later, Cami commented, "Your dad must be thrilled with your plans of being an international graduate student. From River's End to… where exactly are you going again? I'm sure I block it out on purpose as if it can protect me from you going."

"Hamburg, Northern Germany. It's about two hours from Berlin."

She whistled. "See? So continental. None of us can say the same."

"You know how much I worry about going. I made arrangements before…"

"Yes, I know. Before I miscarried." She smiled, being careful not to add that he did it without her knowledge or input. As usual, Charlie was planning his own future. She had no say in any of it even though he insisted he really wanted her in it. Always. Forever. She heard the words he said, and she believed that he believed them.

"I'm not running from you," he said, tugging his arms tighter around her middle. Nope. Charlie would never have considered running from her, but in the end? It was always the final result anyway.

"I'm going to Everett while you're gone."

He stilled his hands and stopped rubbing her. "What?"

She shrugged. "I found something interesting to fill my life with."

"You did? What is it?"

"I'll be staying with Jacob's dad in Everett. I got a job working the night shift in a place that provides housing for at-risk youth. I'm officially the night supervisor, receptionist, baby-sitter, and…"

He twisted her around and stared at her. "How long have you been planning this?"

"You're right, I need something to do. The only thing I know to do to force me to find something different, is to leave here."

"You never said a word."

She shrugged. "Just getting all my ducks in a row."

"Everett? For real?"

"Yeah."

"You've really arranged all this? I can't believe you didn't tell me." His tone was perplexed, neither angry nor upset, but obviously confused over why she hadn't said anything. She almost sneered, *like you tell me your plans before you make them?* No. That wasn't helpful. Even if it was the truth.

"Maybe I just wanted to make sure it would work out first. My track record for the last few years is pretty lackluster."

"Cams, you don't have to be successful or... or I don't know how to explain it, but you don't have to hurdle some kind of mental bar for me to love you and want to spend my life with you. You simply being you is the only thing I want to hear about."

Sure. Right. What did Cami want again? Safety. Security. Home. Family. A baby. No, Charlie didn't want to hear about that. Cami's needs had to be shelved again. They didn't fit in with Charlie's needs, or follow the path he wanted, so therefore, she had to change and grow up. At last, she was doing that.

"Well, at least I'll be busy too for once. Especially if I'm working the night shift."

He squeezed her. "You'll be amazing. Whatever you set your mind to."

"I'm kind of average, Charlie, not like you, so don't start pretending that I am something I'm not. I know what I am. Let me just do it."

He pressed his lips together. "Be average? Y—you think

you are average? Normal? Typical?" His tone of voice nearly erupted into a huge laugh.

Glaring at him, she hissed. "I am. What are you laughing at?"

"Imagining you thinking you're just average. Are you all sweetie-pie cute and nice too?" He laughed out loud then. "You're moody and totally exasperating, and difficult and mysterious and devilishly smart. So, don't even try throwing that average crap at me. You're incredible and you have kept me guessing and confused and hungering after you for nearly four-and-a-half years now."

Cami's heart melted and his kind words lulled her towards him. "You play dirty, with all your sweet talk."

"Yeah, because sweet-talking you is admitting how perplexing I find you."

"Uh huh." A secretive smile touched her lips. "It kind of is."

He roared out loud and twirled her around, hugging her body to him. "Ah, Cami, I freaking adore you."

Cami abandoned her anger, which was usually brewing, when he nuzzled her neck. "You're just trying to get lucky," she giggled, tilting her head back.

He froze, and his nuzzling stopped as he lifted his head off hers, meeting her gaze. Weariness suddenly overcame him, and his eyelids grew heavy. "Maybe."

They hadn't approached the subject of sex since she first got pregnant. The last time they had sex was probably when she conceived and that was sometime around last Christmas. It could have been forever for them. She froze and stared at him. What? What did she think of it? What did he think? He hadn't made any move or mention of sex in all that time.

And hell yes, it contributed to her problem with him and her general, overall anger.

His breathing escalated as he stared into her eyes, as

transfixed by her as she was by him. Their breathing seemed to stop and then start again in a long, profound moment. He pulled her closer and she straddled her legs over him as he sat on her bed. Facing each other, they stared some more. Color infused his cheeks. Was he turned on? Freaked out? Embarrassed? It seemed all three at once. His hands intertwined loosely at her back.

"Maybe I am, what do you think of that?" His tone was so soft and tender, even if his words were said in jest, they were challenging and flirtatious.

"I think it's been a long time. I think I've been scared and confused and angry and unsure of how to get past all those things and therefore, I was terrified to make the first move."

"Me too."

"I thought perhaps you didn't want to anymore."

"I thought perhaps," he flashed the barest of smiles and his hands kneaded her back. His fidgeting gave away his nervousness even if his expression appeared calm and confident. "You didn't want to."

"I didn't want to."

"I didn't either."

"I want to now." She smiled, staring right into his eyes.

"I do too." His smile was lopsided, and she leaned forward and touched her lips to his. He grinned too but when their lips touched, their smiles slipped away. Cami's eyes fluttered shut as she leaned closer and closed the gap between their torsos.

Their lips never parted from each other. They alternated ways of kissing and varied the pressure, which soon had her blood heating up and her insides trembling. His hands fell on her back, passing by the hem of her shirt and reaching up under it to touch the warm skin.

His palms were planted flat, covering the small area of her back. She sighed and heavenly feelings of desire and warmth flowed through her. Her mouth attacked his and she began brushing her tongue along the seam of his lips and plundering inside whenever he opened them.

Their tongues collided and intertwined. Tilting her head to the side, she deepened the kiss and pulled on Charlie's head, trying to get closer to him. On and on, their tongues and lips made out.

Her heart rate climbed, and her blood rushed, brightening her skin in a pink tinge that reflected her anticipation and energetic excitement. It had been so long. So much had happened and yet she could still feel good things.

The precious things she cherished from the hands of Charlie Rydell. A closeness and a sense of warmth filled her with joy and further celebrated and reaffirmed their love. She felt more like a woman. With Charlie, sex was always the most positive and wonderful experience. Before Charlie, however, it was lacking.

His hands moved up her back, passing over her bra strap and climbing up her neck and into her hair. Goose bumps broke out all over her skin wherever his hands roamed. The sensations were so tender and ripe. She pushed her tongue harder into his mouth to express the feelings that were bursting inside her.

She grabbed Charlie's face between her hands and pulled him closer. He kissed her more deeply and they separated for a moment, both of them breathing hard, almost panting, and staring at each other with huge grins. "That's been... sorely missed," Charlie said.

She scooched forward so their lower halves met, and he felt hard and warm through their clothes. That made her melt before she leaned into his mouth again. His hands held her head and their tongues slid and tangled together. She felt the beginnings of an orgasm right then, and from just that little bit of attention. It felt so good to her.

His hands unhooked her bra strap with the deft quickness of long practice. It loosened instantly, and his palm slid from her back to the side of her small breast. Placing his fingertips over her nipple, he pulled it towards him and Cami responded to the thrill of her nerves exploding with white-hot pleasure at the strong, yet gentle, touch. He pushed back, and her nipple went hard and beady. It became so tight, it was almost a pleasure-pain, making her groan into his mouth.

"Do that some more," she gasped before her mouth attacked his again. Sinking her tongue into his mouth deeply, she rose up onto her knees until she was higher than Charlie. He had to bend his neck backwards to reach her mouth. She ran her fingers through his hair while his hands manipulated, turned, and rubbed her pebbled nipples.

She grabbed her t-shirt and pulled it up and out of the way, tossing it aside before quickly tugging her bra straps down. His gaze stayed bright and hot on her dark red nipples. With gentle reverence, he caressed her breasts, slipping his fingers between them, tracing her rib cage before dipping down to her concave stomach.

She sighed, and her eyes half closed at the delightful sensations of his hands. Slipping her hands under his shirt, she pushed upwards over the silky warmth of his smooth skin. His stomach muscles contracted instantly at her touch and a shudder ran through his whole body. He disengaged himself from her long enough to shrug out of his shirt.

She ran her fingertips down his chest from his neck to his waistband. He mumbled something, and his lips searched her out again, his hands wrapping around her torso to imitate her strokes.

"Charlie?" she said, breaking apart to say his name before she kissed him again.

"Yeah?"

"I'm not using anything for birth control. Since... since... you know." He lifted his face off hers and she kept kissing the side of his mouth, cheek, chin and neck. He closed his eyes and let her kisses trail down his chest while his hand flexed and he held her.

"It's okay. I have a condom in my wallet. I mean... that is, if you want to do this."

"Why?" she lifted her head up. "Why do you still carry them even though we haven't had sex in seven months?"

He shrugged. "Well, I hoped someday we'd find our way here again."

She paused and separated briefly so she could look him in the eye. "Yet you never asked me. You didn't ever try to bring up the subject or even mention it."

"I believed, and I still do, that it had to come from you."

Her eyebrows furrowed together until she relaxed and said, "All lovers should be like you." She kissed his mouth. "Respectful. Kind. Intuitive. Caring. You make it so easy to fall in love with you and stay in love. In fact, I'm falling even deeper in love with you."

His mouth pressed into a flat, small smile and he wrapped his arms back around her. He pulled her against his bare chest and her eyes half closed at the sheer joy of having his skin touching hers. At last, they were together again. So special and unique, a connection Cami never felt with any other man. "You've always thought I was better than I really am."

"No." She leaned back and shook her head. "I hooked up with every wrong guy out there. Every loser and schemer and manipulator and sexual predator. I was so lucky to meet you. If not, I would never have learned how men and women are supposed to interact."

"I think your dad and Kate may have taught you something about that."

"Yes. They did. It's just lucky I didn't end up... you know, the opposite of where I am."

"Are you sure you want to do this, then?"

She smiled salaciously. "Oh, I want to. And I'm sure. Now strip down and find your 'just-in-case condom.'" Rising off her bed, Cami ditched the bottom half of her clothes and quickly went to check that her bedroom door was locked.

When she turned back, Charlie stood there as naked as she. There was no shyness, no awkwardness, and no discomfort. No. They both felt rejuvenated, refreshed, and refurbished again. They stared at each other for a long moment, far longer than they usually did.

When she approached him, he leaned forward to start kissing her again. His penis jutted between them impatiently and she slid her hand from around his waist to touch it.

It was very firm and warm, not to mention, long and hard as steel. He kissed her deeper when she played with his erection and he shut his eyes, moaning softly a few times in response to her bringing him pleasure. Taking his condom out, she gently rolled it down his eager shaft.

Without rushing, she kept looking and touching, making her body wet with desire and eager anticipation.

She pushed on his shoulder and encouraged him to sit down. He did, and she followed by straddling his lap again. His penis stood straight up in obvious demand for her. She held onto his shoulders and dipped her lower body over his, rubbing her hot, wet, swollen opening against him. Charlie could only sigh with joy at the singular, delicious sensation.

His hands rested on her waist and his fingers flexed and strained. She was sure his efforts were contrived to make him last longer. She let his penis gently massage her moistness before he slid inside her.

Finally, when she could wait no longer, she lowered her hips downwards, slowly and easily, taking him inside inch-by-inch, relishing the familiarity of him after so long, and so much pain and anger.

The connection and the peace of finding each other again were an aphrodisiac all its own. Their gazes were fastened on each other when she took him all the way inside her. Cami controlled the pace, since she was practically seated on his lap. She inhaled deeply and felt him in a new and sensuous way. Her eyes widened, and her breath stalled.

His eyes all but rolled back in his head when she moved herself gently over him. So gently while pulling his mouth onto hers and kissing him. They kissed as their bodies moved in tandem, rotating up and down together for several minutes. Cami was on fire and burning feverishly. Going so slow and mechanically only made her pleasure grow. Her eager anticipation pumped hot blood that seeped into every tiny capillary of her body.

Finally, Cami couldn't take it anymore. With a last push and prod of their joined bodies, she tilted her head back and bounced up and down, going faster as her nipples jiggled to the rhythm of their impassioned, excited, joined bodies. She climbed the crescendo of pleasure as high as her body could reach and her hands grabbed the back of his head.

She was anxious to bring his mouth over hers to keep her from screaming out loud. Her emotions were suddenly bright and wonderfully blissful as they flooded her entire body. Heart and soul on fire, Cami finally collapsed against Charlie's chest, clutching him tightly as he held her steady, ready to burst inside her with his own pulsating, hot orgasm.

No words could describe their joy. Warmth and heat. Skyrockets and flowers. All things beautiful. The wonderful joy fulfilled all of her senses. She lay against his chest for a long while, tilting her head up just enough to kiss his shoulder. At her contact, he turned, his lips searching for hers seeking instantaneous solace. When he finally lifted his head, he whispered. "Still love you, Cami, more than everything."

She smiled up at him and their hearts truly beat as one. "Still love you, Charlie, more than everything."

BUT SEX WAS ONLY a small part of life and it could not fix everything. Charlie still intended to go to Germany, and Cami was relocating to Everett. This separation would be the longest one yet. So, the next two months that they spent together were the most precious they had ever had together.

As they found a way to start connecting and acting like a couple again, Cami managed to shore up her resolve. They reasserted their commitment to each other, which both admitted they sincerely doubted at times during the last seven months.

After more than four years, Cami was exhausted from saying goodbye so many times.

But sex rekindled her interest in wanting to make them successful again. Having sex again and demonstrating their affection for each other, both in public and in private, reestablished their former intimacy.

All the love and care that was lacking since the news of the pregnancy and the subsequent miscarriage, manifested on both sides. And the promising words that they both claimed they still felt were greatly underscored by their physical expressions of love.

But as all good things must pass, theirs too had a time limit. An ending. So, Cami tried to focus on her faith that there was also a new beginning. Charlie spent many hours packing and preparing for his international adventure abroad. Much of it was spent figuring out his flying plans and other mundane details that were required. He had to know exactly where he was going and how he was getting there.

Soon they were engaging in another round of goodbyes, as they were preparing to leave the ranch, while the entire family gathered around him and Cami as they got into her car, and tears glistened in everyone's eyes.

This time, even Charlie had tears. He tried his best to hide them and shifted Cami's car into gear before they pulled out of the ranch driveway. Charlie stared at his dad in the rearview mirror, who was waving and holding onto Erin.

In her arms, she cradled their new daughter, Melanie, born just a week before. It was surreal. His dad had become a new father and he was leaving the continent.

"It feels somehow different this time," Charlie admitted to Cami. She, for once, was dry-eyed.

"That's because it is. You are no longer a young student in college, always coming and going. You're an adult man who is entering a whole new world. You won't ever want to come back to live here. You won't ever be the same."

He swallowed the lump that was lodged in his throat. "You're right. I won't. Are you... okay with that?"

"I'm okay with it now, because I've always known it in so many ways, Charlie. This is a big separation, so I want to make sure we both go into it being honest and open and loving and, most of all, trusting each other."

"Like grown-ups?"

She nodded. "Exactly."

Later, they pulled into Jacob's dad's house where they would spend a few days before Cami would take Charlie to the airport.

CHAPTER 13

"CAMI?"

"What?" she replied the night before the day Charlie was scheduled to leave. She was playing with the dusting of hairs on his chest. Nothing thick or carpet-like for Charlie. He had smooth skin with a peach-fuzz of blonde, almost like bee pollen, all over his arms, legs and chest.

"I was thinking about what you asked me a few weeks ago. Remember? If I'd ever have sex without a condom again? If you decide to go back on birth control pills, when I come back, we can just use that method."

She stilled. Each and every sexual act during the past few weeks relied heavily on prophylactic protection. Just as it had always been until she began taking the pill. Cami questioned him sarcastically about it one night, suggesting that he buy some stock in condoms, since there was no way he'd have sex without using a condom ever again. At least, not with her.

Her head jerked up. "You mean you'd trust me?"

"Of course I'd trust you. I doubt very much that you would do it again."

"I wouldn't do it again," Cami replied, and her gaze turned solemn and serious. She swallowed hard because an instantaneous lump of emotions climbed up her throat. "You don't know how much that means to me. It would prove—"

He nodded. "I realize that. That's my primary intent. And I intend to stick to it. If you do."

"I do. I will. By the time we next see each other, I'll be back on the pill."

Just as they were drifting off to sleep, Charlie said, "Promise me something."

"Anything." Cami didn't usually reply so willingly but after the amazing day they had, feeling so close and having so much fun, talking and laughing, she would have agreed to anything he suggested. The old, inside jokes that made her feel special and closer to him than any other person on the planet, kept resurfacing.

Cami found it hard to believe he was leaving this continent for more than a year. So did Charlie. Although it was happening the next day, neither one of them could really grasp the concept.

"Don't… don't try to convince yourself that Jacob's a better fit for you. I know it might appear like it. But he's not. He's got a lazy streak. An unkind streak… a fondness for trouble-making that you might erroneously think is like you, but it's not. He's not like you at all."

She literally sat upright. "Jacob? Are you suggesting… there's something between us?"

"I know about last summer, Cams."

"What? Nothing happened between us last summer!" she all but yelled in protest.

He sat up beside her. "No. Nothing happened. But I know how you two spent it."

"How did we?" she shrugged. "I mean, there's nothing to tell, but you weren't here."

"I know you. I know him. And I was gone. He hinted about what you guys did."

"He can be a total dick, Charlie. Don't listen to him. I wouldn't do anything with him."

He rubbed her shoulder. "I know. But you might find times when he's a lot easier to hang out with than me, but he isn't, and he doesn't bring out the best in you. You have so much good inside you. But he knows how to tap into your insecurities and he's just... he's not good enough for you."

She shook her head. "Do you honestly think I intend to stay here just so I can cheat on you? With Jacob?" Her voice rose higher, horrified he could ever think that of her.

"No. I don't believe you have any such intention. As for Jacob? Yes. Could it seem mutually attractive in six months? Maybe. That's all I'm saying. Be aware."

"You say this to me now, right before I prepare to live here in Everett with him?"

Charlie shrugged and flopped back on the pillow. "What could I say about it? You didn't ask my opinion. Just as I failed to ask yours regarding my school plans and where I intend to live. So, no, really, I couldn't and shouldn't say anything to dissuade you from your plan."

"So you really never wanted me to live here?"

"I wouldn't say that. I think your plan is a good one. No, it's a great one. I liked seeing how excited you got about it. I don't think you'd intend to do anything with Jacob. But he seems to have more in common with you than I do. I was just pointing it out, in my humble opinion, but I don't think you actually do have that much in common. For one, you're a far better person, and I just want you to remember that when I'm not here to remind you."

She stared at him for a long moment in cold silence. Then, to Charlie's surprise, a grin brightened her face. She turned over and flopped on top of Charlie, her body pinning his down and her head directly over his face. "You are the oddest man I've ever met."

"How do you figure that?"

"Because you're jealous. You, Charlie Rydell, are jealous. But you refuse to admit or believe it because you think you're above such a base emotion."

He made a choking sound and grumbled but eventually, he muttered, "Fine. Perhaps it makes me a little nuts whenever I picture you being with him here… alone. What can I do, Cami? I'm the one to blame. I'm the one who chose to go away to another country for school. My choice, so how can I dare to cut you off from your friends?" He shook his head as his mouth twisted up in disgust. "Fine. I'm just freaking jealous."

"So what is my sweet, kind, wonderful boyfriend's solution to such a base, ordinary, and normal feeling?" She leaned down and touched his lips with hers, then raised her head up. "Is it to gently warn me that I'm a lot better than him? I thought he was your best friend too?"

"He is. But over the last couple of years, he's not the same as he used to be," Charlie said, his tone no longer kidding. His inflection went from gentle to stern in one second flat. "He's not the same as he once was. Don't get me wrong. I'm glad you have him to talk to and that the Starrs are letting you stay here. I guess I just wanted you to be aware."

She set her forehead on his. "Okay. I'm aware. I promise not to have sex with Jacob."

He let out an annoyed huff and tickled her side. She giggled at his touch. "You are such a brat. You're not even taking me seriously."

"No. I'm not. I'm not going to cheat on you either, so I don't have to. But I can mess with you, can't I? And be a little bit glad to see you being as petty and insecure as the rest of us? Remember the first time I met Rosalie?"

He chuckled. "Yes. I remember."

"Well, I felt as petty and insecure as you do now. And clearly, you would not cheat. So…"

"Neither will you."

"Clearly." She smooched his lips and fell onto his chest and buried her face against it. "Oh, Charlie. I am so tired of long separations from you. I am going to miss you so much this time."

"I think it's because everything between us has been so good lately."

"It's exactly like it used to be." She agreed.

"No," he said.

She jerked her face up to his.

He smiled gently, brushing her wild hair off her forehead. "No, it's way better than before."

"Someday, you'll have to quit leaving me."

"It's not because I *want* to leave *you*. But because of the things I want to do that just can't be found here."

"Well, it totally sucks."

He nodded. "It totally sucks."

CAMI DROVE Charlie to the airport in her car. She had no experience in commuting around the area and zero navigational skills. She visited Everett before to see Brianna but they never drove anywhere. With tens of thousands more people in the immediate area than there were in the entire county of River's End, Cami doubted she could ever get used to it.

Their first airport goodbye was so final and poignant and sad, making it much bigger than any other parting. They hugged just before Charlie entered security, where a boarding pass was required. "San Francisco first, right?"

"Yeah, it's a three-hour layover and then I take a twelve-hour flight to Amsterdam, for another layover. Then I get on a small puddle jumper to Hamburg. A total of twenty-four hours before I'll be there with all the time changes and everything."

"Are you freaked out? Flying over the ocean, I mean?"

He shrugged and gave her a small smile. "If a plane falls from the sky, I guess it won't matter what's under it, huh? And you can die on a hundred-mile flight to Spokane, which is only a short distance away, right?"

"Always so pragmatic, aren't you?"

He shrugged and sighed before putting his chin on top of her head. Cuddling against his chest, Cami buried her face just below his clavicle. "Well, I won't cheat, and I won't fall in love with Jacob. But neither can you."

He chuckled. "I swear on my mother's grave I won't ever fall in love with Jacob."

She nearly swatted his arm. "Don't ever use your mother like that. You know what I meant."

"I know. I won't."

She sucked in a breath of air. Hot tears pricked her eyes. "Isn't this a little bit harder than usual?"

"This feels worse than all of them combined."

She let out her breath. "Thank God. I thought it was just me again, being overly dramatic and emotional and super-sensitive."

"Is that how I make you feel?"

She shrugged. "Sometimes."

He leaned her backwards so he could bend down and kiss her. "I never intend to make you feel like that again. We are in this together. We'll make this work."

"We always do."

He nodded, setting his forehead on hers and staring right into her eyes, long and deep. "Thank you."

"Why are you thanking me?"

"For staying with me while I've been in school. Thank you for standing by me while allowing me to pursue my dreams. Thank you for supporting me and pushing me to act better and be better. Thank you for being my heart and soul and for making me feel at home in us, wherever you are. Even when we're so far apart, I always find comfort in knowing I have us. Do you know what I mean?"

"I know exactly what you mean." Tears slid from her eyes as he gently rocked her. "You've never said anything like that to me before."

"Maturing," he replied with a smile, as if to lighten the moment, but for the very first time, Charlie had tears in his eyes too.

"We both have," she said softly, brushing the side of his eyes. He caught her wrist in his hand and pulled her closer.

"I love you."

"I love you."

He kissed her and finally let her go, shrugging on his backpack. "I'll call you when I get there. Don't worry, we'll make this work." His smile was reassuring.

"Yes, we will. We will make this work." A few stray tears slid down her cheek, but she wasn't sobbing anymore. In fact, Cami was half smiling when she watched Charlie back up a few steps before he stopped. With one last, long look and a sweet, genuine smile, he seemed to be forcing himself to turn and walk away to the boarding line.

She watched him give the attendant his boarding pass and identification before taking his place in the long, snaking security line. He waved at her and she waved back before he disappeared around the corridor. Now, she was all alone. Cami blinked at all the strangers around her, a slice of humanity in the process of following their travel plans.

She sucked in more air, trying not to sob. The lump in her

throat only grew larger and she wanted to cry. Scream. Sob. But she restrained the urge. She held herself together and even smiled for him despite the lead anchor in her heart that weighed her down.

Practice had already taught her, however, that the first moments after separation, and possibly the next hour or two would be the worst of it. It was best for her to go to bed early. Cami knew tomorrow would be a lot better.

Wandering out to the sky bridge, she walked across it, heading to the parking lot. Dejectedly, she found her car and flopped into it, leaning on the steering wheel and letting some more tears fall. She rationalized it was just sad to see someone you loved leaving on a plane.

However, now wasn't like it was four years ago. Suffering from such deep insecurity about herself, she constantly worried if Charlie would be faithful or continue bothering with her at all.

Straightening up, she threw her shoulders back and grabbed her seatbelt, clicking it into the latch. What was different? She certainly wasn't working on self-improvement, but somehow, despite that, she really had changed. She was acting like a grown-up. She found some strength inside herself.

Having become inured to their separate, yet together relationship, she actually honed her skills in perseverance and trust and communication. Things she once thought were all Charlie's domain. But no. She was just as responsible for their success to date as he was.

Regardless of her betrayal and subsequent miscarriage, they found a way to stay together. She wasn't the same way now because she'd grown up and succeeded in positive ways.

Now that they had to face another, much longer, separation with far more distance between them, an ocean even, she was not having a meltdown. She sighed, starting her car and using the GPS from her phone to guide her back to the freeway so she could head back to Jacob's house in Everett.

His name made her smile as she pictured Charlie being jealous. After a decade-long friendship. That showed how well Charlie knew her. She experienced the same things he listed over the summer she spent with Jacob. Those thoughts did flash through her mind, but she never surrendered to them or cheated. She never even considered it because she didn't want to.

No, her heart was always so full of Charlie, for as long as she could remember. There was no room for her to indulge romantic thoughts of someone else. Never. No. No. She started laughing when a song she loved came over the radio.

Turning it up to an ear-splitting level, she sang along, crying and smiling simultaneously. The reasons to smile came as she thought about Charlie's surprisingly emotional goodbye. Then she remembered the night before. She finally seemed to "get" the confidence he felt about them. It took her longer (years, in fact) to develop. Something she never experienced until now.

Glancing up, she saw a Boeing 747 directly overhead. It was loud and low and crazy close as it roared free of Sea-Tac, starting its climb up into the sky to carry people somewhere else.

Somewhere different. Perhaps tropical. Or utilitarian. Or extraordinary.

People who were vacationing or conducting business or visiting family or returning home. She doubted that Charlie was seated on the plane, but she decided to pretend he was. She stared up for a few brief moments and accelerated her car as the radio blared and her heart began to burst, but she wasn't crying. No, she was actually laughing as she pretended to fly away with the plane.

But she didn't fly away. She had no desire to leave. She

was too busy navigating through the multitude of cars surrounding her. Vacillating between two and four lanes, depending on the roadway or freeway onramp, Cami merged into the traffic that was already a sea of red tail-lights. It seemed as if all the commuters decided to go home at once and now, they were all stopped. Cami began to slowly work her way home in what mostly resembled a parking lot.

She could wait. She could also survive the year without Charlie, now living across the world. Until then, she had her best friends and a new job to start training for. She was very excited about it, more than she ever expected to be, actually.

This wouldn't last forever. She knew that now. It was just another separation. For the first time, it might even be okay.

For the first time, she had a whole lot of stuff to do too.

CHARLIE'S PLANE landed in the bustling city of Hamburg. From the sky, the city was fascinating to look down on. Lots of red-tiled roofs and white stucco walls as far as the eye could see. It also seemed brighter to Charlie. All the primary colors seemed to shine in comparison to San Francisco.

He flew out of there while staring down from the plane's window. The flight was long. Dull and tedious.

He met another student, a Japanese girl, who was traveling to Germany to meet her boyfriend's family. They met at graduate school in California and were now shuttling between Germany and Japan. They made the problems between Cami and him seem much easier to solve. Charlie eagerly showed her a picture of Cami and she reciprocated with one of her boyfriend.

Conversation helped pass the flight. Although Charlie found the Japanese girl fascinating, it only made him miss

Cami all the more. He tried to sleep but was too wired up to do so.

This was the first flight longer than three hours that Charlie had ever flown on. He found it exhausting and nerve-wracking. The ocean seemed so far below and the occasional, gigantic white caps, along with the frequent bouts of turbulence, concerned him as the sun finally set and the night fell. He remembered what Cami said and decided it *did matter* that the ocean below was hundreds of miles deep and thousands of miles wide. It seemed to go on forever.

By the time he landed for the last time, Charlie was grateful to be on solid ground. Hamburg was a grand city with a large port on the river Elbe. There were colorful flowers hanging from many of the window boxes and beneath the streetlights. The town was vast and beautiful, sprawling with so much charm and character, unlike any city he'd ever been to in America, that is, on the West Coast.

His room was very small and very old. Smelling a bit like musty, old socks, the furnishings were cheap, a badly done remodel that used clashing modern fixtures and styles. It was cold, ugly, and utilitarian. Setting his suitcase down with a sigh, Charlie looked out the one lone window and saw the wall of the neighboring building. Not much of a view.

But he was now officially an international student and ready for all that entailed. Naturally, it meant lots of work, but the excitement of living in a world that was foreign in so many small ways, not to mention, speaking a language he wasn't too proficient in, Charlie was buzzing inside. His instinct to speak in his native tongue was a struggle to restrain, but the biggest shock to his system was how very different everything was from both home and Stanford.

Suddenly overwhelmed at the extreme distance from River's End and Everett, he felt very much alone. Out of the loop. Missing Cami. He immediately called Cami.

"How is it?"

"Ugly room. I'm hung over from the jet lag, so honestly? Terrible at this moment. I don't know, but that's how I feel right now."

"It feels kind of the same on my end. I'm miserable on the days when you leave. I try to stay busy and go to bed early because tomorrow is always better. Try it. It really does work. Although, being at the Starrs' I tend to be a little more social and less depressed than I'm allowed to be at home. Dad and Kate give me all the space I need."

He stared at his phone. "I freaking miss you."

"Charlie, it's been one day."

"It feels so different this time. I didn't know it would be like this. The ocean between us is huge. You have no idea. We who come from central Washington can't possibly fathom how long it takes to fly over it. And I feel the distance between us this time, where before, I could always put it into perspective."

"It's probably because you feel like an alien: strange land, language, customs, city and you're on a whole different continent. But Charlie, it's totally you. You thrive when you're thrust into the unknown. I have no doubt you'll do amazing once you start your internship and school. You'll be so busy, you won't even realize how fast the time passes by."

"Promise?"

"I know you. So yes, I do. You always do better than just well. It's why you are destined for so much more than what River's End can offer. Who else do we know who could do anything even remotely similar to what you're doing? No one. Though it pains me to say this, you belong there, Charlie." Her tone was soft and sweet and quiet. There wasn't a trace of poutiness or doom.

"That's not what you said about college."

"Things change. People grow up. Who knew I was capable of handling it?"

"Me," he said instantly. "I knew you were."

"Well, let's see how I look and feel in a month."

He sighed. "I'm more tired than I thought. The distance between us is gnawing at me."

"Nah. We just had a good spell before you finally got laid again. You'll get your head on straight again and be back in the game."

He laughed. Before he began talking to her, he didn't feel the least bit humorous. "Thank you, Cami."

"For what? For being the girlfriend you always hoped for? Or for being so beautiful?"

He shook his head even though she couldn't see him. "No. For making me feel better. Especially when you didn't have to, since I'm the reason we're always separated like this."

"Think how it'll be someday when we're in the same city or... or only a few short miles away from each other. Think how easy things will be."

"Sometimes... I think I cannot wait." His voice was very soft. Cami sensed a tone of longing and yearning he so rarely, maybe never, used.

"Charlie... you *need* to do this. I see now what we almost lost. We don't have to lose anything this time, not if we do this—*us*—right. I want you to do it right since it's a major part of your ambition in life. Ambition runs in your blood and you can't hold it back. As we all know, I don't share that ambition in any capacity—"

"That's because for half your life you didn't have a reliable roof over your head. So, having a home *was* your main ambition. For good reason too. I don't think I gave you enough credit for that."

"True. I had other reasons. But the point I'm trying to

make is that you and I deserve the right to be the real people that we are."

"I'm so tired of all the obstacles that keep you from me."

"Me too. But in the end? Someday, probably whenever we finally get together and end all the distances between us, those will be our best times yet. It'll be a dream come true and the most wonderful joy knowing it will last forever. Just like you always told me to believe in. I didn't. Now, I want to. And I'm beginning to believe it."

"Why are you sounding like I used to?"

"Maybe I turned some kind of corner."

Charlie didn't grumble any reply although he wanted to. His complete exhaustion and jet lag were speaking. The strangest part was that he felt as if he were missing something. Always before, their separation was more like an escape. He didn't miss any of the things that went on at the ranch, not even most of the people there. He missed his family and Cami of course, but he could put it away in his pocket and be content. He was always satisfied and living in the present no matter where he was physically located. "Maybe I turned backward while you turned forward."

She laughed outright. "Go to sleep now, Charlie. Trust me, it'll all be much better tomorrow."

Lying down, he stared up at a ceiling that sloped downwards. It was comprised of dark planks of wood. He hoped she was right and that this wasn't a mistake. One that cost a ridiculous amount of money for him to learn. Maybe his ambition finally exceeded his capabilities.

WHILE CHARLIE WAS PACKING to leave for Germany, Cami had visited Everett and interviewed for several jobs. She hadn't told a soul what she was doing at that point. As far as everyone from home had known, she was visiting Brianna.

But in reality, she was meeting with prospective employers.

Kianna Goodman, the director of a place called Shield Shelter, held out her hand to Cami. "So why did you apply for this job?"

It had three locations: one in Seattle, one in Everett, and one up north in Bellingham. Most of the children who found refuge in the Shield Shelter system were homeless or runaways. Many suffered from sexual and physical abuse or were molestation victims. Some were on drugs. Some were starving. Some were pregnant. It provided short- and long-term housing for at-risk children and young adults.

Cami licked her lips. "I have somewhat limited experience. But I did work for my family's ranch resort and that included doing everything from housekeeping to food prep and waitressing. I also worked the front reception desk and shopped the inventory. I realize obviously, that the resort clientele is nothing like the young people here who are only coming to a shelter for help."

Cami knew she was stretching her luck, but she held her breath and added. "I once was homeless. I had to live in a car sometimes or in condemned, abandoned buildings because my mom was high or drunk. I was surrendered to foster care more than once and later returned to my mother's custody. So, although I can't counsel anyone, I fully understand and empathize with them after walking in their shoes myself. Maybe there's something I *can* give to them, something no one else can, not even you."

Kianna raised her eyebrows. "And what would that be?"

"Hope. I can prove to them that hope for change is always possible. Their lives can be different. And successful. I can show them there is more to life than all the factors that made them homeless or categorized them as 'at-risk youth.' Being chronically unsafe and unfed makes anyone distrustful. People are out to hurt you or abuse you or just use you. I think by seeing someone like me, still pretty young and close to their own ages, who suffered from their same circumstances, could help them. Just by my presence."

To Cami's happy surprise, she got the job. She was the house's nighttime navigator.

Navigator was kind of a fancy name for babysitter, although it was much more than that. Cami considered the position noble and worthy. She was helping new and existing clients of the shelter receive all the services they and/or their families needed most. Cami accepted the night shift without hesitation despite the hours and pay, which made it undesirable to people with more advanced training.

Cami could not counsel anyone, but merely help them slog through the necessary red tape to find the appropriate help they needed. She was also assigned to contact the people who could provide psychological or counseling services.

Housing was the highest priority in their program. There were numerous subsidiaries that the Shield Shelter cultivated, employing the area churches and other nonprofit organizations. The goal was always finding affordable, safe housing for all the applicants.

Her first day arrived and her heart pounded while her sweaty palms kept her nervously wiping them off. Kianna met her in the foyer of the Everett house to take her on a long, thorough tour of the whole house and all the facilities. She met the people who lived there and received a huge, in-depth overview as to how it was started and the reasons why certain rules and policies were firmly in place.

She saw the front desk where she would technically be in command, but when they entered the main living room, she felt like her presence there would be more appreciated.

Supervising, joining in their activities, and being there to monitor any problems, concerns or threats actually appealed to her.

Cami spent the first week training with Kianna, doing the job with her before another subordinate took over for the second half of her training. The required tasks shared many similarities to her job at the resort. Any time there are a lot of people staying in one area, basic human needs are the same.

Meeting the kids who were staying or living there was the best part to Cami. Most of them were teens between the ages of twelve and seventeen. There was one boy who was twenty-one, but he kept to himself.

"Well, how is it?" Jacob asked as she did a face-plant on the couch at the end of her first week. The hours of the graveyard shift screwed up her circadian rhythm and she was all jacked up from lack of sleep, causing her nerves to fill her with anxiety.

"It's terrible..."

"Then why are you doing it?"

"I don't mean terrible for me. I mean it's terrible knowing how many at-risk kids are out there. Did you know that thirty percent of the city's homeless are kids? Teens? Some are young adults, but all of them are as ill-equipped as you or me trying to live on our own. Yeah, sure. We'd do well. You can't even do your own laundry, Jacob."

"True. But then again, we aren't addicted to alcohol or opioids."

"Yet," she mumbled, thinking of his increasingly often recreational use. She sneered at him. "You're such a child," she snapped, rolling her eyes and walking away.

She knew she could not even begin to explain it. Jacob led a charmed life if only by having the same parents raise him. His only real trauma was his parents' divorce. However, when each parent found a new place to live, they were barely five miles apart. That was the only time Jacob ever had to lift a finger to move anything.

His entire life, he had food, shelter, clothing, medical care and without even a single thought about where it came from or if it would continue. From there, his life was all about what he *wanted,* and he got plenty of that. Sure, it's easy to criticize and judge homeless teens when you had no idea about their struggles.

Cami would have told Jacob all about it if he had the slightest curiosity in listening to her. She longed to at least educate him, but so far, Jacob hadn't shown the smallest amount of empathy or caring for anyone outside of himself.

While manning the desk of the house at about midnight, Cami looked up and saw a girl descending the stairs. She was perhaps fourteen or so and she flopped down on the sofa and flipped the TV on. Cami made a few benign attempts at small talk, but the girl failed to respond.

After a week of no interaction, the girl flipped the TV off and sat up. Out of nowhere, she asked Cami, "Why are you here?"

"They pay me," Cami replied dryly without taking the bait. Her only reaction was to flip the page on the paperwork she was reading. Cami read all the handbooks and materials provided by Kianna. Several were how-to-react manuals that used different scenarios she might encounter to explain how to cope and help others through them.

Since starting work, Cami provided numerous odds and ends to the kids, mostly to answer their physical needs, but also special things like new pajamas, hair products, and makeup. She sadly remembered all the things she longed for and never received during her stints in foster care.

She directed one young girl who believed she was pregnant to a safe doctor. Free health care for the residents was also provided by Shield Shelters. Another older guy, nearly twenty, was struggling with alcohol and drugs so Cami told him about all the local AA groups and rehab options that were available.

All of them had contracts with Shield Shelter to provide services at little to no cost as long as the participants were serious and attended classes and lectures regularly.

The longer Cami manned the desk, the more often the inhabitants stopped by to visit. Most came because she kept a bowl of candy out. Not those gross, cheap, hard candies that sit until they are moldy, like the kind that you find in doctors' offices.

No. Cami only offered good candy of all varieties. That instantly drew many of the shelter residents to her desk. After a few initial comments or questions, some of them stayed—they were obviously lonely—and many would sit down and talk to Cami. Most were fascinated to listen to her experiences of her life on a real farm and horse ranch.

Their collective loneliness just about broke her heart. Kids all alone without a family, or if they had a family, for whatever reason, they weren't currently living with them. No one understands how lonely, forgotten, and hopeless a child without a family feels.

It's a different kind of lonely. It's a constant gnawing, chewing-up-your-insides kind of pain that stays with you all the time. Cami could never explain how it felt, not even to Charlie. The horrible sense of not belonging to anyone, no one to protect or care for you, or provide the very basics.

The girl then said one night, "You must be really stupid if this is the only job you could get."

Cami didn't even lift her head up. "No. I'm not stupid."

"Dolly Do-gooder then? Trying to make yourself feel good by helping all the sad, little, poor kids."

"Yup, you got it." Cami flipped the next page.

LEANNE DAVIS

"You're wasting your time, you know. You can't really do any good for anyone."

"Then you won't mind if I continue reading this in peace," Cami replied, keeping her tone pleasant and her face down as if she were still reading without even giving the girl a blink.

Annoyed, the girl flounced off. Cami learned the girl's name was Samantha. She went by *Sammy* and had no family. Working as a prostitute for drugs, someone found her and brought her to the shelter where she was now a permanent resident and had been for a year.

Sammy became a frequent visitor, verbally accosting Cami in one way or another. Cami didn't react to her bait, not even once. It became a dance that Cami started to almost look forward to. It was so routine that after a few weeks, it was part of her day. Towards the end of the third month, Sammy suddenly announced, "I'm going to have a baby."

Cami made sure to have a magazine with her to read during the hour she figured Sammy would come to seek her company and interaction. "Oh, yeah? That's nice. What are you going to name it?"

"Aren't you shocked? I'm only fourteen."

She yawned. "Well, I was twelve when I got pregnant, so no, not at all."

"Twelve. You had a baby at age twelve?"

"No." Calmly taking a sip of the soft drink next to her, Cami explained, "I was twelve when I got pregnant. I was thirteen when my mother drugged me and while I was passed out, she had someone perform an abortion on me. But at least it wasn't a dirty, back street abortionist. That's why I didn't die or get an infection or anything."

Sammy's eyes were as big as quarters by the end of her speech. Cami lifted her head and smiled politely before she continued reading her magazine.

"You… you kind of get this stuff?"

"What? This shelter? Yes. I wish I had access to it until I was thirteen. I was lucky when my mother died. Best thing that ever happened to me…"

Cami started to tell Sammy about her life with AJ and Kate, the Rydells, the ranch and resort, and Charlie. Over the next several months, she wove lots of adventures into her story for Sammy and in exchange, Sammy slowly opened up to her.

"What's the horseback riding like? I've never done anything like that."

Cami smiled and told her. She described the land that rolled so far in so many directions, you couldn't see the end of it. At night, the land is so quiet and rural, you could count the few lights you see on one hand. Cami learned that Sammy wasn't really pregnant either. She just liked to tell a good story and grab the attention for a while.

Cami also realized, to her astonishment, she was the one Sammy wanted to impress the most. She was the one Sammy longed to get the attention from. It was a pivotal moment for Cami.

She could help someone else. She could inspire someone else to become different and better, showing them a small glimmer of hope despite wherever they were now. Cami recalled how insignificant she felt when she was all alone and powerless. With no adults around to protect or go to combat for her, she understood how easy it was to fall down and make negative choices because there was no reason or motivation not to.

For once, Cami just might have been the one to provide that motivation. To make that difference. To rekindle that hope.

Life was changing for Cami Reed and for those around her too.

CHAPTER 14

*C*AMI WENT HOME EVERY few weeks, whenever she had two days off in a row. The employee vacation days were on a rotation basis. One time, while visiting, Cami approached the barns where she found Jack working with a horse.

The poor animal seemed to be very upset and was bucking and rearing up alternatively. Its dangerous forelegs were pedaling furiously, like a windmill. Finally, both the horse and Jack seemed too worn out to continue and they took a breather at the same time.

"Why is that horse so crazy?" Cami asked Jack.

"You would be too if you were trapped for months on end in a barn."

"Oh, is that one of your rescue horses? What happened to it?"

"Some remnant of grisly human waste decided to keep the horse in a dark barn without food or exercise. His hooves went untrimmed and unused for so long, he couldn't even walk, and they still need more trimming. The condition of this horse was simply disgusting. I can't even fathom how anyone could do that to such a beautiful animal."

Cami grimaced. "It sounds almost as bad as the stories of some of the kids I work with..." Cami replied before she started talking about Sammy, Julio, and Janine. When she finally finished, she smiled at Jack apologetically with a shrug. "Sorry, they just—"

"Awoke something in you?"

"Yes."

"It's so great to see you, Cami, and to hear you doing so well. We all worried about you and how you struggled after..."

She shrugged. "Yes, well, ironically, my former history gave me a lot of street cred with these kids. I relate to them and I might not have been able to without experiencing it myself. And since I'm barely older than most of the kids there, I think they consider me one of them. I don't know, but I have a new appreciation for how I ended up."

"You ever consider bringing some of the kids over here?"

"Here?" Frowning, Cami stared with confusion at Jack.

"Yeah. Here. We could reserve some of the cabins and you could bring some of those kids here for a... I don't know, a summer camp or the equivalent. They could learn how to ride the horses, and work with the ones in need... you know, just to get out of the city. Lots of city kids have never experienced nature and probably couldn't imagine anything like this place. It might give them a new perspective, a spark of hope, a chance to see a new way of life. And you always refer to them as *your* kids so why not?"

Cami all but launched herself at Jack in her haste to hug him. "Yes. Yes, oh, my God. Yes."

Jack stepped back and smiled, a pale reflection of Cami's heart-soaring jubilation. "You like my idea then?"

"That's exactly what I was thinking about when Sammy

and some of the others asked me to tell them more stories about this place. They love my stories, even if they are more like fairy tales for them. They can't take vacations or go to new places and for most of them, the concept never even crossed their minds. I certainly never knew a place like this existed, not until I found my dad. So the offer and generosity of providing that for these teens is nothing less than inspiring. Oh, Jack. I'm sure the shelter will help defray the costs involved and—"

"Maybe we could help raise the funds here. Set up some kind of 'stay at our resort' or 'take a horse ride with us' and reserve a portion of the profits for the camp... *our camp,* Cami. But we'll have to work hard and fast if we expect to make something happen *this* summer."

"I want to more than anything, Jack."

"Me too," he grinned. A bright sparkle made his eyes shine with excitement. Something Cami hadn't seen in a while.

"I have no idea where to start."

"Lucky for you, I do. But I'll need a lot of help."

Jack put his hand out to shake hers and they shook with a nod and a smile. "You got it, Jack."

"Let me put Thunder away before we sit down and make a list. We have to figure out the logistics: what we need, and the best way to start.... I don't know, let's dream big and see what we come up with."

"Shall I meet you at your house?"

"All right. See you in a few."

They met at Jack's house and discussed all the activities and necessary sleeping arrangements. The huge list seemed to go on and on. Half of it was either unfeasible or too complicated to be scheduled so quickly in the near future, but it was a good start.

"This will enrich these kids' lives. Expanding their horizons in so many ways and experiences they might not have otherwise. I've never had anything to offer them."

Jack paused and looked at her as they were finishing up. Cami flushed and dropped her head. "You sound an awful lot like my wife when she used to talk about herself."

"Erin? Because of her learning disability?"

"Yes. Different root causes, but the same lack of self-confidence and pride."

She nodded. "Yes, that rings pretty true."

"Well, you should know this then: Cami, just your being here has been a blessing to all of us. I can only imagine how miserable my son would be without you in his life."

Cami flushed and smiled. "Yes, but you're mostly proud of what he's accomplished and where he's at right now."

"Yes, I won't deny that. But I'm also very proud of the relationship you two share. I've seen how much you both care about each other. That's richer than anything you can buy. But I know what you mean. I always wanted to do something... something more than I have done. Aside from giving money to charity, which we all do, I've wanted to do something more fulfilling. Rescuing the abused and injured horses has finally provided that for me. But doing what you're suggesting could be so uplifting for all who might be involved."

They shared a smile. "We'll do it."

When Cami left Jack, her heart was bursting with excitement as she rushed over to her parents' house.

"You'll never guess what I'm going to help organize."

A sense of accomplishment and pride elated her. She loved what she was doing and being. For once, she wasn't just waiting around for Charlie to return so she could restart her life. Being so busy with her night hours at the Shield Shelter, she never could get enough sleep.

The plans for a future camp were a full-time job, too.

There was much to arrange, including acquiring official permission and getting a list of the state's requirements for such a venture.

Everything had to be legal, too, and required a certain type of insurance as well as other unexpected costs, should anything go terribly wrong. Their first step was meeting with a lawyer. Cami quickly learned how valuable the Rydell support was, since there was no way this could have ever happened otherwise. It was a staggering investment compared to her hourly wage.

"Are you okay with that?" she asked Jack. She was stunned by the high costs involved after their first meeting with the lawyer.

"You'll gradually get more comfortable with the numbers. You have any idea what the enterprise that your dad runs costs?"

"What do you mean?" Cami scrunched her face up in puzzlement.

"The orchards he manages and the fields he looks after? They represent a substantial asset and expense. Really big numbers. All of it is totally under your dad's supervision. Just pointing it out. You'll eventually get much more comfortable as you become used to it."

And Cami did get better at it. She created spreadsheets to keep track of all the expected, as well as the unexpected, expenditures along with the set-up costs, and the insurance, taxes, and licensing.

The maze of red tape seemed endless. But the more Cami managed to accomplish, the more confident she became. She finally presented the proposal she and Jack devised to Kianna. Kianna nearly fell off her chair, she was so thrilled and astonished to hear what Cami suggested.

"This…" Kianna could not finish her sentence. "I had a feeling about you, Cami Reed, but this is so far over and above and beyond. It would be the most thrilling and amazing adventure. I can't begin to imagine the smiles on all their faces, being able to experience something so amazing and positive and nurturing to the soul. Thank you. For…"

"Whoa. We haven't pulled it off yet. Hold off with your thanks until the day when we are ready to open the camp, okay?"

Kianna nodded, pressing her lips together and shaking Cami's hand. "Agreed. Now what can I do to help?"

"Probably lots more than I can. I know how to coordinate with the necessary agencies and non-profit groups, but you have a lot more experience with the whole system and the players. So, I don't know how to ask this, but have you got any rich donors?"

"Some. And I also know a few successful fundraisers."

"I think we'll need them all." They exchanged happy grins before sitting down and starting a new list. Weekly meetings soon became necessary to discuss the numbers involved, as well as the more mundane tasks of how much food to buy, and all the other items that were needed. They also needed a way to transport all the kids there. The logistics were doable.

It wasn't long before Kianna visited the ranch. She couldn't wait to see it and meet Jack. Her eyes grew huge as she stood at the gate, staring over the long, wide pastures of grazing horses and white fencing, alfalfa fields, and picturesque outbuildings. Even Cami paused to take it in. She was used to it but could never take it for granted.

"You call this slice of paradise your home?"

"Yes."

"And the owners are really offering us this place at no cost at all? I imagine they could charge a rather hefty price, whatever they chose, really, if they wanted to."

"No. The only costs are as we discussed: food and incidentals, but the rooms, the grounds and most of the activities, including the horses, are being provided by the Rydells. Jack offered use of the horses and a chance to care for them on the ranch's dime, but looking after all the needs of the kids requires the assistance of Shield Shelter. However, I think we can work things out."

Kianna shook her head. "This is incredible. I can't wait to tell the children and foster parents."

Cami smiled, staring out. "Neither can I. Come on, let me show you around, including all the new facilities and food prep areas. Plus, I know you're dying to meet Jack and the horses. You'll never forget them."

Together Cami and Kianna went, adding items to their lists and exploring the entire ranch and resort inside and out. They tried to include every possible hidden cost to work it into the budget they needed to formulate.

Then they would put together a proposal for any potential backers. They also had to prepare a formal presentation for business ventures in the local area of the shelter and all around River's End.

Kianna had a diverse background. Community organizing was a major part of it. She earned two degrees: a bachelor's in psychology and a master's in social services. She knew countless contacts in the community, after seeking their services and recruiting volunteers, including businesses and organizations who were inspired to help in a more philanthropic way.

Kianna was a key player in making it all happen, while Cami was the intermediary, linking her to Jack. The work to prepare for the camp occupied many hours and Cami could only do it on the side.

It was like working at another full-time job. After clocking out from the graveyard shift, Cami slept in until the early afternoon. Then she dealt with any issues regarding the camp, working all afternoon and into the evening.

The level of leadership, responsibility and decision-making that were required became a challenge at times. It was a fast learning curve and she received little to no mentoring. Kianna helped with some of her questions, but almost everything Cami had to do was new to her and there was no advice manual for it.

The rest of her time was mostly spent bonding with the teens and other residents in the house. Cami had to maintain a relationship while keeping some professional distance, an artful skill which compelled her to seek advice from Kianna. Kianna was a trained counselor and she often helped Cami find her own solutions to best assist the teens and at-risk youth she wanted to help.

She wasn't all cuddly or sorry for them. A strict sense of guidance and boundaries, as well as rules and accountability were stressed more than not. It was exhausting at times, and Cami doubted just about every single interaction she had.

She would often discuss them with Kianna to analyze what she did right and wrong, learning a bit from each situation, which prepared her and gave her more confidence for the next encounter.

Often in the course of their discussions, Cami revealed memories of her childhood. They started to come out slowly, bit by small bit, and Cami gradually opened up and talked to Kianna about it.

First, as an employee to her employer, but later, she considered Kianna more of a mentor than her employer. Eventually, she became more of a counselor and Cami became more of a patient. Cami never considered what counseling could do for her, but after observing how much the teens benefited from it, she started to realize how valuable it was.

The only difference between the homeless residents of the house and her was her good luck. That was the game-

LEANNE DAVIS

changer. Lucky for Cami that AJ Reed was her biological father and her stepmother was Kate.

All the other factors faded since it was really just the luck of the draw. That was all that separated her from the minimal existences of the many she tried to help. Some were so troubled and lost, suffering from neglect, disease, and substance abuse, fleeing abusive relationships, addicted to drugs and unwanted pregnancy. The list of screw-ups and problems just went on and on.

But now, Cami was part of the solution.

The sacrifice for Cami, however, was her time. She barely had enough of it to speak to Charlie and even that was made difficult with the time difference of ten hours. When Charlie was up in the morning, Cami was leaving for work, and vice versa. They tried to connect, but more often than not, Cami was interrupted by urgent calls she had to take. When she found the time to contact him, her time frame clashed with Charlie's again. Usually, it just didn't happen.

The few spare hours she had were usually spent with Jacob and his wide swath of friends. Jacob knew people from Everett all the way down to Seattle. He partied hard. And even outdid her.

At one such party, Cami had to hold her hand over her glass to keep Jacob from refilling it. "No. I'm good."

"Ah, Cami. It's never good." Jacob nearly fell over as he tried to stumble his way back towards the kitchen. He had no trouble hooking up with drugs: anything from pot to pills, and every once in a while, hard street drugs.

The first few times Cami realized he was using something far more serious and having a much steeper high, she was really shocked. She remembered the days with her mother who was always under the influence of something. Seeing Jacob like that seemed almost a joke.

The well-dressed, suburban, upper middle-class, young

man named Jacob Starr got so high and sloppy, he often disgusted her.

"I don't know, Charlie. Jacob takes partying to a level I can't even describe. He's going to be on probation after this quarter, I really doubt he'll stay in school much longer," she told Charlie in February.

"I wish you didn't have to live there. Just be careful, Cams. Don't get caught up in Jacob's mistakes. You know I've never judged you for the dabbling here and there, but please don't go any further."

"Dabbling? Jacob's a regular consumer. I swear, I think sometimes he must be selling it, but he denies it anytime I corner him."

"At least he isn't living there *all* the time. How's Brett and Trinity towards you?"

"They are very nice. Besides, I pay the rent on time even if I'm so rarely here, and that has to help. Brianna is around a lot. Hanging out with her is fun. Plus, I'm mostly quiet and I never bring any guys home. Honestly? I'm so rarely here, they hardly see me."

He sighed. "You think Brett knows what Jacob's up to?"

"Probably not the full extent. He's seen how his son parties and I think he tells himself it's just the lifestyle at college and all that, but Jacob parties like there's no tomorrow. He drinks more alcohol and uses more kinds of drugs than anyone I've ever done them with. His benders are pretty epic and the sheer volume of them makes me wonder how far he can take it."

"Just don't get too involved."

"He's still our friend. If I think he's going too far, shouldn't I get involved?"

"He's got two parents, so you should stay out of it."

"Charlie, that's not very friend-like. You sound more like a jealous boyfriend."

Charlie sighed heavily. "I am that."

"Don't be. I want nothing to do with Jacob. Besides, the snobby prick criticizes the kids who live at Shield Shelter and he lives far worse than most of them despite having all the greatest opportunities and two loving parents to constantly prop him up. What does he do? He squanders it all and then dares to look down his nose on the homeless youth? Ha. I have no time for such hypocrisy."

"I can't say I'm disappointed to hear you talk that way about him. Besides, I was thinking…"

"What?" Her tone was a half groan. Usually at this time year, Charlie added extra time to their separations, blaming it on some new thing he needed to do or conquer or some new place he wanted to see.

She gripped her phone, steadying her breath and preparing herself. Whatever it was, she felt she could handle it. She'd handled everything he asked of her, or *threw* at her to date, so whatever this was, she would simply add it to the list.

Who knew what he might come up with? Sailing solo around the world? Taking a photo safari through Africa? Backpacking in the outback of Australia? Whatever it was, Cami knew it would include a long time and a great distance, because that seemed to be Charlie's way.

"Well, could you come here? Maybe for a vacation this summer? After you finish your camp activities? Fly here and stay for ten days or so? I can't wait to show you around. It would be so much better than touring or sightseeing all by myself."

"Charlie. Me? Vacation in freaking Europe? Are you nuts? I can't afford anything like that."

"My dad can and said he will. Don't object. He already agreed to it. I really want to see you. This has been… really hard."

To Cami, it just seemed *normal*. She bit her lip and did not give voice to the thought. Okay, maybe it was taking a little longer than normal. But still, it was very much the norm for Cami over the last five years. This time was so much better and easier for her, because she'd been so busy.

"Just imagine it. When will you have another chance? Think of the experience. It will be amazing. Please, Cami?"

She blinked, trying to remember the last time Charlie begged her to visit him. Then she realized he never begged her for anything.

Charlie also never seriously missed her like this before, exactly what she longed to have happen. She recalled all the years and the first time when he was a freshman starting college.

Now, an international student with a master's degree and an internship, he should have been more focused on that. Like he usually was. What was so different?

"I want to come, I'm just busy here and it's not easy to find someone to cover the night shift at Shield Shelter. Kianna always ends up doing it and she also works all day. It's irresponsible, Charlie. I can't just leave her in the lurch for an entire week to go freaking jet-setting."

He snorted. "Jet-setting? Ha. Wait until you see the one-room dive I have to stay in."

"Well, we'll go see the sights and visit the museums to see old stuff, right?

"Yeah. We will. Sure. I just wish you sounded happier about it."

Cami nearly screeched. "I'm not unhappy. I'm busy. I have serious obligations and I don't intend to totally space out or flake on them. That would harm Kianna and the kids. I wouldn't risk that after they've been so amazing to me in offering me the job opportunity and letting me grow into it.

They also approve of my work and my presence, which is important."

"I'm sorry." His tone was apologetic. "It's just... I miss you so much here. Maybe because everything's so different and—"

"I'll try to get away. I swear. It'll be my next goal. And I'll thank Jack for agreeing to it."

"You don't have to. He says all the work you've done on the camp rises far above and beyond what they'd have to pay anybody else. I could hear the joy in his voice when he spoke about you. You should be very proud of yourself, Cams." Dropping his tone, he said it with candid sincerity and she felt it all across the miles. "I am. I really am so proud of you with the work you're doing, the difference you're making, and just who you are in general."

She smiled. That was nice to hear. The rush of pleasure nearly burst her heart, but better still, it was nice to get the compliment from Charlie. Years ago, it might have triggered a crazy deep reaction of gratitude to hear those words, but it would have soothed her crippling insecurity. She wasn't crippled anymore. Neither by her own insecurities, nor Charlie's frequent absences. She stiffened her back.

Damn, that was nice.

They said their goodbyes. Cami couldn't count how many of those she said over the years. It was amazing what one could get used to.

CAMI WAS ASSIGNED by Kianna to be the camp coordinator. That meant she could move back home for the duration of the camp to coordinate with Jack and Joey. They were her main contacts.

Jack, naturally, because he ran the horse barn and Joey

secured all the lodging and food. They used the arena's grill to feed the campers and the resort to house them.

For many of the kids, it would turn out to be the nicest place they ever stayed. The generosity and kindness of the Rydells by shutting down the resort to the other vacationers and all the money they would have earned from people during the prime summer weeks amazed both Cami and Kianna. A multitude of teens and young adults that they supervised wanted to go to camp so they rented a bus to take them all to the Rydell River Ranch and Resort.

"Is this place for real?" Sammy asked as her head swung back and forth in awe when she first glimpsed it.

"It's for real and it's for all of you to enjoy for the next two weeks," Cami said. She couldn't stop grinning as she helped throw their bags and backpacks out of the cargo area, reuniting them with their owners. A total of forty kids, some of whom were staying at the many Shield Shelter locations or their affiliates, arrived. All of them were foster kids that signed up for the camp.

The first rule of order was assigning all the rooms. Then they allowed a few hours for the kids to get acclimated. They agreed to meet at four o'clock to discuss the rules, policies and procedures, as well as the times for meals.

Horseback riding and all the other planned activities were listed. There was also swimming, beach days, and full use of the resort pool. The basketball and tennis courts were open and available, along with indoor gaming rooms that were recently added to the resort. The schedule for all the different activities and events was posted and the kids rushed to sign up for them as well as the various levels of horseback riding lessons.

It was organized chaos. Cami took note of several things to change or do differently next year, but overall, they accomplished quite a decent job between the planning and the funding for this many kids to attend the camp.

Providing an extended stay with no blueprint to do so was truly a feat. Kids ran everywhere on the ranch and swam and enjoyed the river and the beach. Some of them had never played in real sand on a beach, just the sandboxes at parks. They built bonfires at night and many of the kids made s'mores for the first time in their lives.

The older ones rolled their eyes at the occasional sing-a-longs, but most of them joined in eventually, Cami noted. The brutal sun was tempered by the excessive application of lotion and sunscreen to combat and soothe any sunburns.

Maintaining constant supervision of the younger teens, as well as the older ones, Cami had to make sure no underage drinking or sex games went on. Cami knew exactly what those games were and where they'd sneak off to play them. She was revered as the "Queen of Prevention" on the ranch. No one dared to trick her or hide from her or try to get away with anything.

"Who knew all those years that I tested the limits would have so much value later on?" she quipped to Charlie on the phone. He laughed and added he was glad she could finally take advantage of it.

All the Rydells took turns getting involved with the kids. Erin and Jack, with Ben and Jocelyn's help, handled the horses and riding. But Ian, Kailynn, Joey, Hailey, Shane, Allison, Kate and AJ all took turns showing them how to saddle the horses, as well as helping out in general.

They all enjoyed pitching in with the supervision duties. Many hands were required to make everything safe and sane, yet fun and functional for the large group. They even hired additional help to assist in the meal preparations three times a day.

Her dad wrapped his arm around Cami's shoulders,

squeezing her. "You did something amazing here, Cami. I am so proud of you. It's... like you know how these kids feel. The experience of this has also filled me with hope and shown me a whole different way of life and a new way to live."

Cami beamed. "That's exactly what I hoped would happen, and if it changes only one person's life and attitude, I would be satisfied."

"It'll be more than one, I guarantee it. They will never forget this experience or the unconditional love and care shown by so many, when so few have done anything nice for them. These kinds of kids, as you know..."

She nodded. "Yeah, they need it the most. They haven't been on the receiving end of too many good things."

"Exactly. I'm so proud of you for giving back. I can't say I ever did, even though I hated foster care and I feel sorry for any kid stuck there. I never tried to help another or pay it forward. I just got out. Maybe I should have done more."

"It's never too late." Cami grinned. "You could always foster another kid. Especially with me being gone..."

AJ stared at her, his mouth dropping open. "I never considered that... I guess we could. I mean, we have no other kids to raise and plenty of money... wow..."

Cami barely contained her amazement when she realized how much she inspired others. She stirred up the imaginations of these kids as well as her own father and even Jack.

"Cami, this is exactly what I have been dreaming of doing my entire adult life. I just didn't know how to make it happen. It's like something so much bigger than us orchestrated everything and put you at Shield Shelter after you connected here."

"That's a really beautiful thought, Jack."

"It is a beautiful thing..." Jack swept his hand to incorporate the view before them, and several kids who were riding in the arena. Other kids laughed and joked as they ran through the pastures and played to their hearts' content. Some were getting snacks in the café and watching the kids ride the horses. "We always had so much, I always wondered how to give back. This is it. I want to keep doing this and expanding this."

"I think we could. Now that we have a model to build from. There would be all kinds of ways to raise the public's awareness, as well as the funds."

"I haven't felt so excited about the ranch and my work here in more than a decade. Yes, let's plan on it." His eyes glowed with delight and his grin was huge.

Cami felt high, unlike she ever expected. The kids were all smiling and laughing, joking and playing, and she remembered how she and Charlie, Jacob, and Brianna enjoyed the ranch together during the summers. It warmed her heart to see and made her nostalgic for all those wonderful summers. But this would be better. She had given the kids something to cling to as happy and fun as what she always enjoyed. It gave them a break, a vacation, a chance to rest and relax and just be kids. To see something new that also provided a source of hope.

"It's a pretty powerful feeling," Cami told Charlie on the very last day. She helped everyone pack and they loaded up the bus before they drove across the state to Shield Shelter, at the Seattle campus. That was where many of the foster parents met them to pick up the kids and take them back to their homes. Some stayed at that campus house and others went with Cami and Kianna to Everett. A little further north was the last house and drop-off point.

"I wish I could see it. Next year maybe, when we'll both be there. We'll make it a date."

"Yes. We will. I have so many great ideas for this."

"I love hearing your excitement and I am so proud of you.

Nothing but rave reviews about you from Dad, Erin, Ben, and Jocelyn, well, from all my aunts and uncles actually, and especially my Aunt Kate," he teased. She gripped the phone and tilted her head down.

"I am pretty proud of me, I'll admit. It was even better than I hoped for or could have dreamed of. You know what else?"

"What?"

"It reminded me of all those things you said over the last few years, remember? Talking about how young we are and all the things you'd still like to do and you were right. There are so many things I might want to do now and the dumb part is I don't know exactly what they are. I can't articulate it. But I see now that the older I get, the younger I feel. Isn't that backasswards? I shouldn't have a baby so young, and I don't think I want to anymore. I mean, definitely not now. I feel even younger today than I was at twenty. I feel there is so much I have to see and do. I didn't know I could do this, but it feels better than anything else I've ever done. What if there is something more?"

He sighed over the phone. "There is so much more. That's exactly how I always felt and what I was trying to explain to you. It wasn't about not loving you or not wanting to be with you or even having a baby with you."

"You weren't ready yet. You had too many things left to do, even if you don't know exactly what or when. You just want to explore and see."

"That's exactly it."

She shut her eyes and smiled with contentment. "I think we stumbled over the same timeline. We're not faking it. We can do it now without giving other things up. And without being disingenuous."

"I must say I never expected us to agree on this."

"It feels pretty wonderful too, not only for what I just did, but because I'm coming to see you. A week from now. Then we'll be together."

His tone over the phone sounded almost reverent. "I can't wait. You have no idea. More than ever before, Cams. I can't wait to see you."

"All right. I have to go unpack and chill with Sammy and the others for a while. I also have some more goodbyes to make. They are pissed at me for leaving, but overjoyed with me for starting the camp. You should listen to them talk. They constantly reminisce and kid each other. They took lots of pictures and are planning to fill a scrapbook and Jack asked Kailynn to figure out how to do a website. It's just the beginning, Charlie."

"For them and us. I feel like this is a new start for us too."

"It's always a start or an end because we have to separate. But that's okay now. I think I finally get it all."

"I finally get how it was for you too, that's the funny part." He said softly. "I'm sorry. I didn't know how you felt about me and I'm so sorry for not getting that sooner."

"I'm not. We became the people we are because our relationship progressed slowly, and in a way, we both grew stronger and better for it. Something I never saw at the start. I had a lot of growing up to do and soul-searching before I could find myself. The oddest part is that I only now realize what I want to do. I have tons of work still. But I finally see what I want to do."

"Well, I'll be waiting here for you. One week. Don't leave me hanging."

She grinned into the phone. "Never. One week."

Hanging up, she nearly laughed. It all felt different. So much better. A lot like the wave of collective hope she seemed to spread throughout the camp.

CAMI RECEIVED the necessary permission and she worked hard to find skilled replacements before she could take her trip. She made sure every "i" was dotted and every "t" was crossed before finally leaving. Kianna had to shoo her out of the office at Shield Shelter. "Go. See the freaking world, Cami. Think how many kids here would leap at the opportunity. You deserve to experience it."

When Cami frowned, Kianna shook her head. "That's not my version of a guilt trip. It's intended to make you appreciate this wonderful chance and for you to be grateful for such a gift. After organizing this camp and facilitating the management, your karmic reward is this trip to Germany. It was intended for you. You earned it. Now go."

Cami grinned and finally left.

Days later, Jacob just stared at Cami, and his eyes were red-rimmed. She asked him to drive her to the airport. "Are you okay? Are you high?" she questioned him.

"No."

"But obviously, you were quite recently. You look awful, Jacob." She leaned forward and sniffed. "You smell horrible too."

He grimaced. "Yeah, perhaps I hit it a little too hard this weekend," he mumbled as he hefted her duffel bag and put it into the trunk.

She held her small backpack and flopped onto the driver's seat. "I'll drive us there, and just be careful when you drive home alone. Maybe go to your dad's house for a few days… if only to shower and eat. You need to drink more water and stay off all of that shit for a few days."

He nodded, running his hands through his hair but his expression was glum. "Yeah, yeah, sure. Maybe you're right."

"I'm always right. Clean up, Jacob. You're turning this into a problem. I'll be totally on your case if you don't slow down right now and start living in reality a little more. Go to your classes. See your dad and Brianna. She's always calling me because she's worried about you—"

"Don't be my sister. You've never been judgmental with me. Don't start now."

"Okay." She sighed. "Still, you're making me worry."

"I'm just blowing off steam. And no, I'm not going home. I don't need to see that asswipe."

"Still mad at your dad. Why? He's so nice to me, I just don't get it."

Jacob's jaw clenched, and he turned to stare out the window. "Stuff."

She sighed. *Yeah, that explains it.* She rolled her eyes as she steered the car onto the freeway, restraining her urge to lecture Jacob about how lucky he was to have a dad, food, and shelter. She could have compared it to her upbringing and all the kids at Shield Shelter.

But Jacob was too narcissistic to listen to other people's problems. He didn't get it at all. His response was to detail all of *his* problems. Nothing he could say could compare to what she was talking about. But she reminded herself once again that their idea of a "problem" was very different from hers. The baselines were different. Having a privileged upbringing, like Charlie, they were even more privileged than most.

Eventually, Cami found a parking spot and they trudged towards the entrance, so Cami could check in. When they approached security, Jacob handed her backpack to her. She hugged him. "Thanks for driving."

"Yeah, of course. You're one of the few people I would always do anything for. You know how special you are to me." His arms were tightly wrapped around her. He was super tall now and Cami's face was buried against his side, near his armpit.

Her eyebrows jutted up in surprise. She didn't expect him to give her so poignant a sendoff, much less, his emotional message. He rarely said anything like that. Alarmed, but determined to remain natural and friendly as they had always been, she patted his back.

"Well, be careful. I'll only be gone for ten days."

"I won't forget you. I'll be here at the airport to pick you up. July first, at eight o'clock."

"Thank you." When she left him, a swarm of butterflies took off inside her stomach. Excitement that seemed to have eluded her until that exact moment suddenly overwhelmed her. She was going to freaking Germany.

Abroad in Europe.

Traveling across the world from River's End, and even Seattle. Cami Reed was becoming continental, an international traveler. AJ very subtly let his chest swell as he nodded when she told him where she was going. But his eyes were sparkling with unmasked pride. He joked with her, but Cami knew he really meant it.

"My daughter, savior of children and international jet-setter, who could have guessed? I still can't believe you came from me."

Cami hugged him especially hard. "Oh, Dad, you are the whole reason I became anything, and don't feign modesty, because you know it's the truth."

Since her miscarriage, Cami and AJ managed to breach the last wall that had separated them for so long. Cami's residual fear of his massive form and the flashbacks from her childhood that led to her distrust of older men vanished. Cami had accepted AJ and become his daughter.

Sitting on the plane, Cami stared out the tiny window as the pilot started to line up for take-off from Sea-Tac's runway. She couldn't stop smiling and her heart swelled with excitement as high and as fast as the plane rose.

When they left the ground, Cami could hardly contain her exhilaration. She was becoming an international commuter. Her first ride on an airplane was a trip to Europe. Best of all, she had no fear, just curious enthusiasm. She loved the speed and altitude while staring out the airplane window. Seattle slowly faded and blue water and sky replaced it. The plane turned around over the Pacific Ocean before flying to Minneapolis.

From there, Cami would catch a connecting flight into Hamburg. Charlie was waiting there. She realized how long it had been. At ten months, it was the longest separation yet. They'd been apart for three quarters of a year and yet, Cami was so busy, she never realized it.

She spent no time ruminating over it, having been too tired during her free moments, which were rare between working and managing the camp. Now that Cami could relax, she enjoyed the idea of flying to see him. She finally had a few hours to herself to think. Letting the music play in her ears, Cami could not wait to see Charlie.

Germany. Deutschland. The polar opposite of River's End. And a complete change in her life. If she'd stayed with her mother, and her mother had lived, Cami doubted she'd ever find herself on an airplane, much less flying to Europe.

In the last few months, she felt very different, like she'd finally grown up. She was discovering herself, and no longer identified as just Charlie's girlfriend or AJ and Kate's needy daughter. Maybe she wasn't so fragile anymore. She could also be helpful, capable and strong.

She could now fly across the whole country and see another continent. She smiled smugly to herself, imagining herself only three years ago. She could never have comprehended doing this. No way could the insecure, mousey, scared Cami do something like this.

After the initial excitement of take-off, the long hours of sitting grew tedious as they passed several time zones. It was kinda boring, actually.

Cami leaned back and smiled again. Life was full of lessons, and she knew the thing you were most scared of usually turned out to be half as scary as you imagined.

Yes, Cami had definitely turned some kind of corner and she was well on her way now.

CHAPTER 15

CHARLIE STOOD BEHIND SECURITY at Hamburg International Airport. Holding a single red rose, his red hair was a bit longer on top than normal and it fell forward over his forehead. His eyes were bright and his smile huge as he patiently waited for Cami. He wore a suit.

Cami paused for a long moment when she spotted Charlie dressed in a suit. He looked much older. More grown-up, more like someone who went to an office every day and bossed people around. He looked mature. The confidence surrounding him belonged to a man, not a boy.

It was also new for Charlie. And here they were, old enough to arrange for a tryst at an international airport. Cami had a typical case of jet lag and fatigue, but she exploded with surprise when she caught sight of him.

He saw her, and her smile mirrored the giant one on his face. She tried to fluff her hair a bit, and look a little less bedraggled, but her makeup was faded and all but gone. Her hair was flat and tangled, refusing to unkink after hours of leaning against the airplane headrest.

None of that mattered.

Cami had to restrain her instantaneous urge to shove her way through the throng of people that were disembarking the plane with her.

She longed to scream out from pure frustration, *move.* After waiting so long to see Charlie and feeling relatively content with herself and life in general up until then, now she wasn't. Her anxiety to see him overtook her mind and nearly made her hysterical.

When they were finally within a few steps of each other and no one blocked them, she let her bag slide off her shoulders to put her arms out and he did the same, catching her and holding her against his chest at the exact moment she stepped towards him.

They just stood there together, embracing. Sharing a long, tight hug, she closed her eyes to relish the feel of him, all of him, pressed against her finally. She leaned back, and her eyes were full of happy tears as she grinned up at him. "Hi, boyfriend."

He grinned and blinked back his tears as well. The pools of moisture in his eyes nearly fell but Charlie managed to hold them back. "Hi, girlfriend," he replied in his deep, calm voice. Despite being able to hear him and see him during the separation, Cami missed the in-person encounters when she could observe his facial muscles and expressions and mannerisms.

Damn.

There was no substitute. Nothing could replace live communication and being together in-person. Charlie leaned down, and his lips touched hers as she moved her hands. She was clinging to his neck as they kissed long and deep. When they stopped, they could only grin at each other and their eyes said it all.

"I missed you," he said softly.

"I'm really glad to be here."

He nodded. "Yes, you are finally here. Now that you are, I'm not letting you go," he teased as he clutched her even closer to him. She shook her head and separated far enough to scan down his body.

"Wow. Look at you. You leave me as a college grad and now I get to meet an international business man of mystery."

He rolled his eyes. "Hardly. I'm like the tenth in line on the intern list. But everyone who works in the offices of FINA look this way."

Charlie's business classes had landed him an internship that blended his fluent expertise in the German language with his degree in international finance.

The company he worked for was called the Federal Investment Network Associates (FINA). It was an international company headquartered in Hamburg. Charlie's division was one of the real estate arms. His division was tasked with the job of diversifying their portfolio and making significant acquisitions in Washington State, California, and British Columbia, Canada. They currently owned real estate in New York and Washington, D.C. so the west coast was a new venture for them.

And Charlie was sure part of their motivation to expand to the west coast had a lot to do with why they offered him the scholarship as compared to the other applicants.

"They are interested in buying a significant portion of the Meridian Tower in Seattle. The numbers they talk about? Suffice to say it's a long way from River's End," he told her on the phone recently. Her mind spun at all the figures she imagined he was dealing with. Trying to earn his master's and manage the internship, she knew Charlie had zero downtime. She did not want the two jobs to run him ragged but seeing him now, he looked it.

He seemed exhausted. His skin was always white, but now it was very pale. His freckles seemed brighter too, although his professional attire made him look like a young Robert Redford. He had a bit of scruff around his chin and neck that only enhanced the rest of his masculine look. He told her he rarely spent any time outside anymore and feared he was becoming a vampire.

They let each other go and held hands as they fell into step together. He picked up her bag at the luggage carousel and they left the airport.

Hamburg was huge. Leaving the airport, Cami's eyes glowed with awe as she gazed all around. "Do you mind if we leave tonight for a place I rented? Out of the city. I want this to be a real vacation and something special with you, so, surprise."

"But... all that..." she waved towards the city as they started to walk, and she wondered *towards where?* Charlie carried her duffel bag and she followed him, getting instantly confused by all the traffic and throngs of people. She was very unsure of where to go.

"Charlie, where are you going?"

"Train station. We'll take a shuttle over there."

Charlie acted like a local and looked like one. Of course, he could read the signs and knew what they meant, and she couldn't. When they were seated together, she caught glimpses of a large body of water and saw ornate buildings hugging it. Cruise ships and other large vessels were harbored. The new and old architecture seemed to blend perfectly.

"So you don't want to explore Hamburg together?"

"I do. But let's do it when we come back, okay? I'll show you everything. The port and the older district and anything you want to see. I just need to relax. A few days up north at this little resort town and then we'll come back, and I'll show you all around. Hamburg is where I work and rather ordinary. I really long to get away from it. I can't wait."

Excitement overcame her anxiety. What did she care where they went? It was all new to her. A foreign country. Another damn continent. She was clear across the Atlantic Ocean.

"Which waterway is that?" Cami inquired.

Charlie glanced over toward where she pointed. "Port of Hamburg, which is on the river Elbe, which empties into the North Sea. *Tor zur Welt.*"

She saw him smirk as he rattled off the words in what she assumed was a perfect local accent. "Which means what to the rest of us uneducated Americans?"

"Gateway to the world. It's the second largest port in Europe."

She shook her head. "I can't believe I'm in Europe. Everything feels so exotic. It's all new to me. So, where exactly are we going?"

"To a fantastic place that's right on the Baltic Sea. The guy I intern for took his wife there last year. It's called Timmendorfer Strand. He asked his friend to let us stay there for a ridiculous price. And it's right on the beach."

"The Baltic Sea? Why does every single thing you say sound so glamorous? And did you say beach?"

"Yeah, the Baltic Sea will remind you of the Pacific Ocean."

"Okay. How are we getting there?"

"By train."

"I've never been on a train before."

"Pretty common here, not like where we come from. We'll leave from the Hamburg *Hauptbahnhof*, or the main train station. We'll take it to Lubeck, stay two nights there and then move onto the beach. I think you'll love Lubeck. It's smaller than Hamburg and when I first saw it, all I could think of was showing it to you," he said, squeezing her closer to his side. Cami's heart swelled with joy. She was long beyond excited and magically entranced.

Lubeck was the quaintest town she could ever imagine. A hamlet comprised of red roofs and bluish-colored spires on the churches that glowed under the summer sun. Ignoring her jet lag, Cami wanted to melt when she saw their old-world, picturesque hotel. Charlie had everything prearranged. Cami succumbed to his warm kisses and, in a matter of brief moments, they fell into the bed, both of them eager to reunite after their long separation.

Cami instantly fell into a deep and much-needed sleep. When she woke up, she was hungry and thirsty. Charlie was feeling her upper body before her eyes fully opened and she smiled, stretching. She let him finish her off without ever reopening her eyes and his mouth remained planted securely on hers.

The next morning, however, Cami had different plans. "We must see Germany. We aren't in River's End anymore. Please."

He nodded and laughed. "Okay, a city tour is required."

Thank God for Charlie. Cami would have been hope-lessly lost and turned around in the old city. First, they went to the Holsten Gate, which was built in 1464 and part of the original fortification for the once medieval town. To Cami's American eyes, it was *old*. Super, crazy old.

The oldest thing she'd ever toured in Washington State was an unused military fort called Fort Spokane, that was first established in the late 1800s. However, there was very little she could explore since most of it was dismantled. Cami had never seen anything from the freaking *medieval times*. Her culturally deprived eyes stared at the gate. It looked like a castle with two round towers and an arched walkway underneath. It was brick and very gothic.

She loved seeing it and made Charlie stand at every

possible angle in front of it, so she could take pictures. She instantly sent them to AJ and Kate. She kept a running travelogue with her parents, as if she were trying to let them experience her trip with her. The regular roadway was split around the gate and cars zipped past. People just came and went, leading their regular, old lives, and Cami was rendered speechless as she gazed at the relics of ancient history.

To the left, she saw more brick buildings with deep burgundy rooftops. There were other streets that featured cream and white facades, and again, red, brown, and burgundy rooftops. The fronts of the homes were a pleasing array of square and angles, curves, and attractively tapered points. Many of them still used the old cobblestone streets and others were made of bricks. Some roads followed the canal that ran throughout the city.

Cami and Charlie took a walking bridge over it and stopped dead center to stare into the water. They looked up the river at the charming city that surrounded them. He put his arms around her, briefly trapping her against the iron guardrail. They stood there staring out, talking quietly, and exchanging frequent smiles. He turned, and they kept talking as they kissed and smooched until goofy smiles brightened their faces. "It's like that first summer when we were together, huh?"

"Kind of. Except, you know, we're in freaking Europe," she said, waving her hand around. "Sooo, nothing like River's End." She reached up and cupped his square chin in her hand, rubbing his smooth skin. "You've... *we've* come a long way, huh?"

"Yeah." He kissed her again. "*We* have. I have to tell you something, you've changed the most over this last separation."

"Must be the job."

"I think it's because you are finding yourself and getting

to know yourself at last."

She smiled and finally stepped away. "Lord, I hope so. Come on, there is so much still to see."

"And yet, I'd rather lie in a bed with you all day."

She rolled her eyes. "In that case, you should have come to River's End. You asked me to come to *Germany.* Become an international traveler. I'm not going to sleep. Not when I could explore and learn and grow and experience ancient history. I'm here to expand all my limited, narrow horizons. Now come help me do that."

Charlie let Cami tug him across the bridge and they explored some more. "Oh, look. Another one!"

Cami loved how every different alley or street they saw had interesting angles and views like storybook towns. From the cobblestone streets to the towering spires of churches on the horizon. Pointing straight up like great spears aiming at the blue sky and nearly matching the hues in the turquoise-silver rooftops, the scenery and angles of the old city seemed to purposely draw her in every different direction she turned.

There were several different doors she saw in one of the tour brochures from the bed and breakfast. They were so elaborate with vibrant colors and windows of circles. Some were arched, and some were square with little panes of stained glass and a framework of brick or iron supported them. "They even know how to make doors look more like artwork." She had Charlie take a picture of her in front of each unique one she found. "Can you imagine something like this in Brewster? Or at River's End? They are nothing like what we have."

They went to the *Heiligen Geist* Hospital, which Charlie translated for her: The Hospital of the Holy Spirit. It was built in 1260 and located right in the center of the town. She found the old building so ornate that it seemed like the exterior of any church or castle to Cami.

The churches were in a category all their own and she never imagined she'd be so eager to explore them. Learning that they were *centuries* old fascinated her. Walking around the huge and cavernous structures, Cami was shocked to see what they managed to build so long ago. The painted ceilings took her breath away. Ceremonial altars with huge, awe-inspiring arches and stained-glass windows that caught the light and reflected it downwards.

They visited St. Marien's Church where a cordoned display of broken church bells lay on the floor with wreaths around them. The haunting scene held some obvious significance. "What happened there?" she asked Charlie. When they explored the churches, Cami choked up and lost her voice. Talking in whispers, a sense of holiness, reverence, and history enhanced the places, imbuing them with a mystical aura.

"Let's see, the church was fire bombed on Palm Sunday in 1942. These bells fell and became imbedded in the church floor. They were left in place as a warning to future generations." Charlie was reading the information from a tourist book he had about Lubeck. All of it was written in German. "This church, which is over 700 years old, nearly burned down in 1942..." he continued.

"Wow." Cami could not think of anything more profound to say. She was in awe of her surroundings.

He nodded. "Yeah. Wow. Honestly? I've been past so many old churches in Hamburg and I've even been inside a couple of them, but I failed to 'get' it. The history and unique elegance of each of them was nothing like I am experiencing now, because I am exploring them with you."

She grinned at him and sensed he wanted to lean over and kiss her. Swiftly ducking away from him, Cami began shaking her head. "Charlie. We're in church. A very old, and very sacred, nearly burned down church. So that is inappropriate."

Gasping, Cami approached the altar and worship area. The ceiling went up and up with huge columns and windows and light. The cross hung from the rafters and seemed otherworldly. "Oh, my..." Cami wouldn't dare to utter *God* here. Her dad would have loved to have attended mass there. Perhaps she would have too, although church came into her life rather late. At the time, she did not appreciate it as much as AJ hoped she might. Here, however, Cami was moved by something she revered and saw as so much bigger than Charlie and her.

Holding hands, the couple wandered for hours, which turned into all day, stopping only to grab food and drink from the vendors they saw outside the different courtyards. They were sitting at the Rathous, a well-preserved courtyard that harkened back to the red brick of medieval times. Cami could envision women dressed in long dresses and fancy garb of centuries ago.

"It's so hard to believe nearly half this town burned, isn't it? They did an amazing job in restoring it to its original integrity and charm."

Cami glanced up and found him grinning at her. "What?" she replied, slightly perplexed at what he was smiling about.

"I had no idea what a tourist you were. And a lover of history. I wondered if you'd like it, but never thought you'd take to it this much."

"Are you kidding? I love it. This is gorgeous. I never in my whole life could have imagined what this would feel like. This place bubbles with so much history and culture. I thought it was exaggerated by Americans, but touching bricks that were laid in the early thirteenth century? I mean... I, Cami Reed, feel so lucky to be able to do such a thing. It's incredible." She all but spun around in joy as the sun set. Hues of glorious pink and blue and orange and yellow created a uniquely, almost holy, white light that streaked over the clear summer evening sky, silhouetting the city skyline in black. For one moment, the glorious riot of colors made Cami believe the universe was putting the show on simply for her benefit alone.

Charlie pulled her close and kissed her, nearly bending her backward over his arm in his exuberance. When he lifted his face from hers, he was grinning as he said, "It's a hundred percent better with you. I didn't feel like this before. Not until today."

She laughed and wrapped her arms around his neck, pulling herself up to kiss his nose. "Well, I'm here now and I intend to make this the trip of our lifetime."

"So do I." Charlie eagerly agreed with a grin.

They found a place that served local seafood and drank wine with their meal. Leaning over, Cami kept giggling and telling Charlie that they looked like such cultured citizens. As they finished their meal, she added, "There is still sooo much we could explore, Charlie. I mean, we could spend the whole week here. Never mind Hamburg and the Baltic Sea. I'd love to see East Germany too and visit at least a few war memorials."

Charlie nearly spat out his wine. "Cami? You mean you want to do all this in a week?"

"Okay, perhaps we can't do most of that. There's just so much we could do if we had more time."

"There is," Charlie agreed and nodded. "I've just never seen you like this, I mean, you're so into the history and the famous places marking it—"

"I never was before though. Not even for a day. Seeing this now makes me realize how much I don't know about it. I could start anywhere and enjoy spending hours just reading all about it and learning more. It just—"

"Inflamed your imagination?" Charlie interrupted with a smile. He leaned forward and took her hand in his. "I have to tell you something, it doesn't mean quite as much for me as it does for you. Shocking to both of us, since I always thought I had to see more of the world. But when I did, it felt... I don't know, just flat and dull and hard. Now I look at you, and your face is shining at seeing a new culture and country. That's how it's supposed to be. I think your appetite for life might turn out to be much bigger than you ever thought."

She blinked. "I—I don't know about that. You mean, you don't feel an urgent, crazy, overwhelming need to see and explore and read everything you possibly can around here... and over there... and...?"

"No, I actually don't. It would take more than just a few days to fit all of what you suggested in. I prefer to lie on the beach with you."

She blushed and squeezed his hand. "How about tomorrow afternoon?"

He nodded smiling with gentle amusement. "Tomorrow? After we explore the Thomas Mann Museum, you mean? Now that you read all about him and his contribution to literature and because he defied the Nazis..."

"Yes, after we explore his house-turned-museum. I think I might know how to get there, it's right near the *Marienkirche*."

"Listen to you. Using the German pronunciation of St. Marien's."

"I read it in the book. And I have to admit that I've heard Thomas Mann's name before but knew nothing about him or what he did. His life is so fascinating... maybe I should read some of the literature he wrote." She nearly flinched at her suggestion. Cami reading literature? On her own, and not because of English class? She flopped back in her chair. "I really don't sound like myself at all, do I?'

He shook his head. "No. But I actually love it. You're so turned on and so passionate about something new."

"Is that all you think about?" she laughed.

"I didn't mean like sex. You're getting high on life now. I've never witnessed anything like it before with you. Usually, you seem to struggle just to survive and feel safe. You have to grope your way through the days. I don't know, but this is almost unbelievable for me to witness."

She sipped her wine. He was right in describing exactly how her life had been. The polar opposite of how she felt here.

They explored a little more of Lubeck before taking a train and heading towards Timmendorfer Strand. They were walking towards Charlie's friend's place.

Cami gaped all over again with eyes as big as saucers as she took in all the quaint, old shops, and immaculate parks and boardwalk, and oh, yes! The beach. Blue water lapping against the light brown, pristine sand. There were rows of canopied basket chairs lining the shore. They were double-seated wicker with bright fabric seating and some had footrests that could be pulled out. Puzzled, her first inquiry was, "What the hell are all those?" Not just a few, but rows and rows, by the dozens. Maybe a hundred or more standing like soldiers on the beach cove.

"*Strandkorbs,*" Charlie replied, smiling. Cami scowled at him for his usual German answer and tapped her foot, waiting for the American version. "They are provided on nearly all the beachfronts and resorts located on the Baltic and North Sea areas. People rent them, and some families bring their own."

"Strange."

"Different preferences. Seems like a perfect idea to me."

"You mean, so that the freckled, red-headed, pasty-white-skinned man can hide from the harsh rays of the sun?"

"Exactly," he grinned.

Their small apartment was located on the second floor of a four-story villa. It was *ridiculously* beyond their affordable price range. Cami gulped at the high quality and obvious expense considering the location, the exterior, and the interior furnishings.

"Are you sure this is it?" she whispered to him as they stared inside from the front door.

Charlie glanced down at her bug-eyed expression as she looked around. He suddenly dropped all of his stuff and slid hers off her shoulder to the ground. He started laughing as he grabbed her around the waist. Shutting the front door with his foot, he kissed her senseless.

When he finally released her, he was still grinning. "What was that for?" Cami asked.

"You. You never expect anything special and say everything is always too fancy or too much. You were whispering it to me like a burglar or intruder who is waiting to be kicked out of the palace."

"Well, in any social hierarchy, I'm usually low woman on the totem pole."

He gripped her waist with his hands. "You embody the highest qualities of any person I know. Honestly, Cami, these people I work with here in this place have so much money to spend…" Shaking his head, he glanced around. "It's unfathomable. It makes my dad look like he has nothing. It seems like a lot to us, but this is actually considered low rent to them."

"You like living like this? Spending so much money on first class accommodations?"

"Actually, I do. I enjoy learning all the different lifestyles we never could have imagined at River's End. And don't forget, I rented this villa just for us."

She was lost for several moments. Placing his mouth on hers, Charlie watched her shut her eyes, lulled by the soft, deep tone of his caring voice. When they separated, they were both grinning like kids. "Let's explore."

"Yes, let's. Who knows what we might miss?" He grinned while quickly setting their luggage inside the bedroom. His wry tone obviously amused by her eagerness to see more of Germany rather than have sex on the big bed in their fancy villa. He'd have chosen to have sex all afternoon, but she was too excited to explore to stay inside.

They changed into beachwear and sandals. Cami gaped at the huge surf and empty beach under the endless glow of the sun. It was every bit as glorious as the architecture and charm of Lubeck. But so different in its grandeur.

They walked forever along the beach, holding hands and kissing every so often. They waded in the cold water, comparable to the Pacific Ocean beaches at this time of year, so it was not too surprising to them. The wind whipped around them and Cami's hair flew into her eyes. It churned the surf up even more into frothy whitecaps.

Walking along and holding hands, Cami suddenly stopped dead, and looked confused. She wrinkled her face and lifted one eyebrow as she glanced up at Charlie who was poised on the verge of laughing hysterically. "What the hell?" she muttered.

"Nude beach," he said answering her question before cracking up at her reaction. She punched him in the arm.

"You saw a sign."

"Yes."

"Oh, gross. NO WAY."

He grabbed her waist and tickled her. "Oh, c'mon, you prudish, modest American."

"Yes, yup, and forever so. Didn't you notice something?"

"Lots of genitalia?"

"Ooh, who's looking? No. Most of the people are old. Like senior citizen-old."

He laughed even louder. "You are so easy to shock and amaze." Charlie laughed intermittently as they wandered back. They stopped to wade some more. Eventually, they grew hungry and grabbed something called a *doner*, which Charlie insisted that Cami try. It was a lovely blend of seasoned meats, wrapped in a pita and filled with yummy vegetables. The flavor was unexpected and mouth-watering, and Cami was sold. They found a small market and took their groceries back to their villa. They prepared a lovely meal of shrimp and pasta along with more wine. Sitting on the small balcony, they watched the sun setting before the stars came out. They were barely tipsy before they eagerly collided in crazy frenetic heat on the bed.

The next day, they slept in, choosing to spend the entire day resting and soaking up the sun on the beach. Their only job was figuring out what to eat. They talked and laughed and kissed all day and it was so easy to love each other. They were totally in sync. Two more days were spent exactly like that. They explored parts of the small resort town but mostly enjoyed their leisure time on the beaches. Charlie's smile became his constant companion and the tired circles beneath his eyes started to fade. The stark pallor that first greeted her replaced his ordinary paleness. The sickly look from spending too much time indoors that she first perceived in him was long gone.

While browsing the shops, Cami commented how much she liked a certain black dress. Charlie urged her to buy it, promising they'd go out to dinner and celebrate in it. "I can't," Cami replied glumly.

"Consider it a souvenir. How often do you get to continent hop? Make the most of it, Cams."

Grinning, she finally relented. She was very unsure of the currency conversion and how many euros translated to one American dollar or whatever, but Charlie ignored her concern and shrugged it off. "Let's just pretend for once, it doesn't matter."

Cami tried it on, dressing in the bedroom after a long shower. She put on some perfume and makeup too, along with a subtle piece of jewelry, which was so unlike her. When she walked out to model it for Charlie, her small, toned body really made it seem like something special. She wore heels with it and maybe for the first time in her life, Cami felt elegant. Not something she believed she'd be someday, but here and now. She conformed to the different atmosphere, which seemed like a fairytale. She liked the change from who she really was and would always be. This was, after all, the vacation of a lifetime, so why not do that?

Charlie turned from the balcony where he stood perusing the view. He wore another suit and Cami's breath caught when she realized he looked like a man, not a gangly boy from Senior Prom. He grabbed her hand and tugged her closer. "You look stunningly beautiful, Cami."

"I think... dare I say it? I think I actually am stunning and beautiful. I really can feel it for the very first time in my entire life."

Charlie smiled and leaned down to softly and tenderly graze her lips with his. "You finally realize exactly how I see you."

She smiled and let his serious words fill her heart with joy. They left and strode the short distance to a small bistro with outdoor seating and lighting. Live music played, and the atmosphere was perfect and lovely. Cami could not do anything but smile. Charlie read and translated the entree choices to her and ordered for both of them. Cami liked to hear him speak in German although she had no idea what he said. She enjoyed his tone of voice and facial expressions.

They sat there for a long time, holding hands on the table top, enjoying glasses of wine, and almost giggling at themselves. They pretended to be a couple of sophisticated, cultured, international dining critics. When they finished eating, they walked towards the pier. It jutted out from the main part of the town center into the Baltic Sea. Street lights illuminated the path out there and they stopped three quarters of the way when they found a quiet spot all alone. They leaned against the railing, staring at the water and waves, as well as the stars overhead. She sighed as she squeezed closer to his lapel and shoulder. The air was pleasantly warm on her face and refreshing at the same time. "This moment could be the best I've ever felt in my entire life."

His hand was on her waist and he squeezed her. "I agree," he said as he leaned over and brushed his lips across her cheek. His kisses trailed towards her ear. "That's why, Cami, I want to ask you right now to marry me."

She blinked rapidly. His words entered her brain but didn't fully compute. Moments later, his proposal registered. Holding her hand in his, he slipped a ring on her finger. A gorgeous ring with a large diamond on it.

Her mouth dropped open as she stared at her hand, which he cradled in his... Her finger had a ring on it. Tilting her head upwards with her mouth still wide open, Charlie leaned down and pressed his lips on hers.

She shut her eyes, turning into his embrace and facing him. Her hands clutched his shoulders tightly. She felt dizzy, as if she could fall and slip away into the water. Or maybe she expected the world to tip her upside-down. Charlie proposed marriage to her? In Germany? In Europe? While on another continent? Was this really her life? Cami Reed, the homebody who never wanted to leave River's End, was really here now? Realizing her most wished for dream of her life? She felt like she belonged here too. Doing this with Charlie.

Lifting his head up, Charlie's gaze seemed uncertain. For the first time, Charlie seemed insecure and a little awkward. "Will you please marry me, Cami?"

Her mouth again dropped open. He gently lifted his finger to her chin and pushed it upwards to shut it. "You keep gaping at me. Does that mean you didn't guess anything like this would happen?"

She shook her head, whipping her hair back and forth.

His smile was crooked. "The resort? Beach? Dress? Dinner? You know… taking a vacation in a foreign country? You never even suspected I'd ask?"

Cami again shook her head to the negative.

"Wh-what is your answer then?"

Swallowing, Cami finally snapped herself out of her reverie and utter shock. She enthusiastically nodded in the affirmative.

"Yes?" he said to her response. She kept nodding as tears filled her eyes and fell down her face. She couldn't find the words to express herself. There were no words. No English words anyway, and if she'd known German, she was sure they couldn't describe how she felt either.

Charlie started to slowly smile, and his eyes glimmered with love and hope as he gripped her hands in his. "Cami? Are you going to speak?"

A million questions flashed across her mind. How? When? Where? But most of all: why? Why did he want to marry her? Was he sure about it? Shaking her head no, she launched herself against his chest and he caught her. Sweeping her feet off the deck of the pier, Charlie lifted her up and she cried and laughed. He joined her laughter as she kept her arms tightly wrapped around him while kissing her over and over.

Nothing else in the world mattered at that moment. How they got here and where they'd go from here didn't matter. The betrayals and past hurts, her childhood and his, none of it mattered at all. Her former desire to remain the same and live in the small town of River's End suddenly faded into the background.

She finally understood Charlie's need to seek something different and bigger than himself and River's End. In that continuum of time, and for just a moment, everything stopped except... them.

Now, only their love and relationship mattered. She was finally able to let it be. Cami had never lived in the present moment like this. At last, she could let something just be all that it was. She could experience it and feel it. And she could love and treasure it. It was something to believe in.

Charlie pried his lips and tongue from her mouth before he dropped her back onto her feet and straightened up.

"I had no idea how you'd react." His gaze studied her face, as if he were memorizing it for the first time.

"Is that why you seemed so stressed?"

He nodded. "Yes, and because I'm overly tired all the time. It's really hard to live and work here, Cami. I needed this vacation badly. Not just the break but being with you. Mostly, I needed you."

He rubbed her hand and touched the ring. "You know, it's considered normal for the intended to check out the ring after it's been given."

Cami nodded and grinned as she brought her hand up to the light. It was a square diamond in a platinum band. "How could you...?"

"Manage to live without you all this time? I don't know,

now that you're here," he replied in a heavy tone as his gaze stared at her harder.

"I was going to say, afford such a big, elegant ring? Thank you. But the issue has always been distance for us."

He sighed as he swung around to sit on a wooden bench near them. She moved closer and sat down too. He leaned forward, resting his elbows on his knees. "It hasn't been the same for me this time. I don't want us to ever be apart. I want..." He cleared his throat and took a deep breath. "I want you to stay here in Germany with me, only until I'm done. We could explore all of Hamburg and East Germany, then go down to Bavaria and Berlin. You could see all the things you'd ever want to see and we could do it together."

Her mouth fell open and she exclaimed, "Charlie. You can't be serious."

He turned towards her and took her hands in his. "I am. Deadly serious. Everyone else already knows about it. My dad and your dad. I already asked for their opinions and advice and my dad loaned me the money to buy your ring."

"You planned all of this?"

"Of course, I planned it. For half a year, at least. Since Christmas."

"But you have another year to remain here."

"Yes, I do. Another year I can't stand to live without you. I don't want to simply survive, Cami. I want to *live* it. It isn't like when I was in college, it's too long between visits. I'm afraid I can't do it again. I can't be apart from you. Not anymore."

"We can't get married just because you're afraid to be alone for a year."

"I don't mean that," he said calmly. "I want to get married now because I love you and we are both old enough and mature enough now. I want to live with you and see you every day of my life. Don't say no yet. Think about it. A year.

It's just a year. You and I could explore all kinds of other countries in Europe, and it'd be like traveling to Idaho or Oregon except we'd be in France or Spain. Think of it. I have to work, I know, but it will be worth it as long as we're together. They already offered me a paid position starting this fall..."

Standing up, Cami braced herself on the railing, needing more air and space. She was overwhelmed and rather shocked at Charlie's plan. It sounded more like a scheme she might have concocted in order to get Charlie to marry her... not Charlie doing it to her.

"I have so much responsibility now. Not only at the Shield Shelter but also the camp I helped formulate. I can't just stay here in Germany. I'll lose everything I worked so hard to build and... I loved it, Charlie. I found something that totally improved my life, something besides you and us. I am helping people. The ability to do that healed something inside me, and it made me better. I finally saw how right you were, after all these years. We were too young to have a baby."

Charlie stepped closer to her. "I want all those things too with you. Just later on. First, I want to marry you and embark on a journey together to explore the entire world. I want to see places that no one we know ever saw, and no one we know could imagine doing either. It's just for a year. And then we can go where ever we want. We can go home or somewhere else. Maybe FINA will put me on at their Seattle office, the one they are currently setting up. If I stay with them, I could make a lot of money. I have the bilingual skills and two degrees they require. I've already caught a few good errors that have been noticed."

Cami smiled up at him. "Are you saying they know how wonderful and smart Charlie Rydell of River's End is?"

He stared down at her, his head shaking. "You're the only

one I ever care about. If you see me as anything special, you have to realize this: you are what makes me feel and be wonderful."

"I don't want you to take care of me anymore."

"I don't want to take care of you. I do, however, want to be with you."

"I have too many other things to do. I have a job."

"It's only a year, Cami, not forever."

"You told me to find something that didn't involve you. Now you want me to move to a foreign country where I can't speak the language and have no job. You're asking me to be as reliant on you as a baby would be."

"I simply want you to live in a foreign country with me for one year and yes, it will require learning some language skills. But think of all the things you could do and read about and explore during the day. I doubt very much you'd ever get bored. Dad said Kianna suggested you could work on your plans for the camp from here… and if you choose to make it an annual thing, you'll be back there after this."

"Wait… *after this?* Are you saying I won't go home now?"

"You can go home if you want to. You can do whatever you choose. I just asked my dad and your parents for their honest opinions. Dad consulted with Kianna because he knew her. He also knew how seriously you take your responsibilities and commitments. So it's up to you now; you can do whatever you want or need to do."

"You've never needed me so much before."

"I've always needed you. But we weren't at the same place in our lives. Now, we're ready to be together all the time. For good," he said quietly. "And I think you assumed I had no problem handling our separations, but this one is the worst."

"What then?"

"What then… what?"

"What happens after you finish your final degree?"

"We decide what to do. FINA will probably offer me a full-time job, barring something stupid that I would do. They have branches all over the world, you know, so we might even be offered the chance to go live someplace else... or not."

"Or not? You mean that's now an option with you? Would you go home?"

He stepped closer. "I'll go wherever *we* decide. Not about what I decide anymore. I just had to prove to myself that I could leave River's End and make it on my own. Now I don't need to prove anything, I've done it, and I'd just like to live happily. With you. Or whatever version of that you prefer." He pressed his lips together. "I understand it if you think all this is happening too soon. We don't have to change anything yet, believe me. But if you like being here, maybe we could finally have a real adventure together. Maybe we could spend some time traveling the world... together."

"The world? Like..."

"FINA branches are all over the place: in Amsterdam, Sydney, London, New York, Paris. I mean, there would be plenty of choices for us."

"You want me to live in another country across the world and away from my parents, with you?"

"I just want to live with you wherever it winds up being. I would like to live in a few places, yes. Just you and me, like we've been on this vacation. I would love to spend a few years like this. And when we're closer to age thirty, I'd like to start a family with you. Perhaps the best place for us to do that would be back at home."

"I—I usually have some idea of where you are on things. But this? I am totally flummoxed. Unsure how to even react. Much less, to decide what I want. I mean, I found a wonderful job. Now you want me to go back to being unemployed?"

"If we go somewhere that is predominantly English speaking, and a lot of people in Hamburg speak English, by the way, you could probably find a job, if you wanted to."

"But living in Hamburg. For a whole year?"

"For a year. Actually, not even a full year."

"Let's say that I decided tonight to stay here with you, what then? Tell me your best-case fantasy."

He gripped her hands in his. "We'd stay here before going home to Hamburg. We'd start living and exploring there, spending all of my time off together. Then, assuming I successfully graduate with my master's, we return to River's End and get married. If that's where you want to be married, of course. Then we see what our options are and decide together from there."

"That's a lot of uncertainty."

"That's why I want to do it now. Before we have any kids. Before we settle in to raise a family. I fully intend to do that too, *someday*. But first, I'd like to experience life. I don't have any plan of where I want to travel next and what country I want to see, but I'd like to live outside the box for just a little while. Mostly, Cami, I want to do it with you."

"And if I can't?"

He nodded, and a gentle smile tugged his lips. "Then I suffer another year here alone, and when I finish up, I come home."

"To Seattle?"

"Seattle, River's End, wherever you are."

"You'd come back to River's End?"

"I would."

"And hate it?"

"No. I'd find a way to make it work. Maybe commuting or doing whatever. Look, I have no intention of yanking you away from a job you enjoy doing. But our circumstances are offering both of us this chance, one that I can't imagine ever having again. And naturally, I'd like to share it with you."

"But your real goal is to become some kind of international real estate buyer? Doing things I don't understand in foreign languages I can't understand?"

"Well, there's only one language you can't understand." He dropped his head down almost as if he were ashamed. "I'm pretty good at it, Cami. I like working with numbers and wheeling and dealing, yeah, I do like it."

"Just my luck to fall in love with the small-town boy who never had any small-town dreams or aspirations, isn't it?"

He shrugged. "No. You didn't. I was never the small-town boy, not even as a teen. Maybe a guy like that would have been better for you. Someone like Ben. You could be happy too, living like them now, neighbors with all our parents and right there at home with everyone. But I've never wanted that, not even a little bit. I want... *this*." He flapped his arm around as if to encompass the whole world. "The thing is: I want it with you. And only with you."

She closed her eyes. "I realize that. But what you describe is nothing I've ever dreamed about. So you have to let me think about it. I hate to ruin this moment. It's so magnificent. But I do need to think seriously about it."

"You can think about it for a year. Really. I just wanted you to know the offer was out there for you. Your choice. I wanted this to be special. Something much better than going up in the hills above the ranch or bending down on one knee alongside the river. And Cami, I do want to marry you, regardless of where and what we decide to do."

She smiled softly. "I will marry you, Charlie. And you made this moment magnificent." She wrapped her arms around him and he swung her off her feet in a slow circle. She laughed until their lips found each other, and they both smiled and kissed each other, right there in the middle of Europe.

No matter what happened, Cami could never forget how romantic it was. She'd also never make the mistake of thinking that anything about them was ordinary or small. Not when it came to Charlie. Or their relationship and perhaps more binding than anything else, their future.

CHARLIE WAITED years for both of them to be ready for what he knew Cami wanted out of their relationship. Stability, togetherness, and living together. Her former desire to get married and have a baby was a meager attempt to somehow make up for her ill-spent youth. She never had any of the luxuries that Charlie had. He knew that. He blamed himself for making her live in a way that was hard and scary for her, lasting for years, never realizing how much of a hardship it was for her.

Now, so close to finally merging their lives together in an adult and very real union, Charlie sought a way that allowed both of them to live however they wanted.

He understood why she might not choose to be with him or do what he wanted, but he still hoped to make it happen someday.

They left the pier, holding hands, grinning like little kids and stopping every so often to kiss and hug and smooch. When they finally reached their villa, they fell onto the bed, and Cami quickly began stripping Charlie and he undressed her while laughing, teasing, and enjoying the erotic fun of true love. When their bodies eventually joined, it was more fulfilling and hot than ever before.

Later into the night, they dozed off until Cami suddenly shook him. "Charlie?" she whispered.

"Yeah?" he mumbled. His voice was right in her ear as she wrapped up in his arms and cuddled closer.

She flopped over, turning flat on her back and turned her face up towards his. "Yes."

He was half asleep and he blinked his eyes a few times to wake up. "Yes? Yes, what?"

"Yes, I'll move to Europe with you and we can both explore it for several years. Yes, I'll go home and marry you too. Yes, I'll someday raise my kids with you, in whatever place *we* decide to live. I'm just saying yes. To all of it. Yes to spending our lives together from now on. Yes to sharing adventures and becoming different and unordinary. Yes to being adults, that are still free enough to enjoy this. Yes. Yes. To living our lives together. Yes, I'm agreeing to it all."

Charlie's breath remained in his lungs. Shaking his head as if to ward off a misty fog, he asked Cami, "Are you sure? What happened? What changed your mind? I thought you said you had to think about it?"

"I have thought about it. I need to go home though and make sure I have the Shield Shelter Horse Camp administration duties passed along. I need to help Kianna find someone who can cover me at the Everett Shield Shelter and I want to say goodbye to Sammy most of all, but to all the other kids who worked with me at the other camp. I want to go back there to work, if we decide to return to the area. And in the meantime, I have a good idea of someone who could take my place as camp coordinator."

"Who would that be?"

"Brianna."

Charlie's eyebrows rose almost to his hairline. "Brianna, as in Brianna Starr? Are you sure you're thinking clearly?"

Cami smiled and cupped his face as she smooched his lips. "Yes, of course I mean her. That Brianna. Brianna Starr. We spent a lot of time together over the last school year and she's intrigued, sympathetic, interested, and supportive of all the children. I have related a whole lot about this job to her since my time there. The individual kids' stories really touched her and affected her in ways that surprised me. I honestly think she'd be a good fit. She's the only one I would trust to honor the title of camp facilitator and the only one I would assign to it next year."

"I'm sorry you have to give up anything."

"Well, we've given up years of our time. I think this is worth it and that's why it's right."

He squeezed her closer to him. "I hope it lives up to every expectation. And if you say Brianna is the right person to cover for you, then I believe you. I know how much you care about that place and the kids who live there. So... one last goodbye?"

Smiling softly, Cami rumpled his hair as her gaze scanned his. "Do you have any idea how many goodbyes I haven't wanted to say, but did because of what you needed to do?"

His arms drew her closer. "I do. I finally and fully do. I also appreciate how hard it was for you. I can hardly stand it now."

"That's quite a startling change. But I need to do it right. Closing up loose ends, and not burning bridges that I intend to come back to. I could see us living in the Everett area someday. You could work in Seattle, and I could work with the Shield Shelter again. But I also see all the opportunities that are being offered to you right here and now. Surprisingly, this has awoken a passion in me to see new things and experience the world first hand. But I'd like to do it with you as a couple. You and me, Charlie, with no more separations, other than the mundane absences that work and training and other responsibilities might entail."

"That's exactly what I want. How long do you think you'll need?"

"The summer? I'll go home on the fourteenth as sched-uled and return here in six weeks."

"Six weeks?" he groaned as he nuzzled her neck.

"That's child's play for us, Charlie."

He nodded. "I know. You're right. About all of it, of course. I admire you for that. I just suddenly felt very needy."

She laughed and kissed him. "I've always felt needy. But now? I feel less need and more want. It makes all the difference."

He kissed her briefly.

She tilted her head and then ran her thumb over his bottom lip. "So... Just one more goodbye, and then I hope to never again separate from you."

"One more. And then, never again," he mimicked, smiling and looking deeply into her eyes. The relief was bittersweet to Charlie. He held her against him and spent hours just talk-ing, planning, dreaming, and imagining before Cami fell into an exhausted, deep sleep. Charlie, however, couldn't sleep. Slipping away from the bed, Charlie grabbed the phone and dialed the one person whom he knew would understand.

JACK RYDELL PICKED up the ringing phone after hurrying in from washing his hands. "Charlie?" he called over the line, more than excited to hear his son's voice.

"Hey, Dad. Am I interrupting anything?"

"Nah, Erin and I just came in from work and... that's not what matters. Tell me what's going on?"

Jack waited the long moment, his heart hammering in his chest. "Charlie?" he muttered almost breathless, his stomach twisting. What if, once again, the timing wasn't right for them?

"She said yes. Yes to everything, Dad. I can't really believe it. She definitely liked my marriage proposal although she was shocked. How could she not realize…? Anyway, I know how she had to struggle to believe how much I love her. But she said yes and promised to think about the rest of it."

"What changed?"

"Now she wants to stay here until I graduate and she's even open to getting a job here or who knows? Maybe we'll go to London or New York or just somewhere else." His breath faltered. "I don't think we'll be coming home, at least not permanently, for many years, dad."

Charlie's tone was hesitant, but Jack's smile was huge. Clashing emotions climbed up his throat. Leaning his head into his hand, Erin made a small sound of distress. He lifted his gaze to hers, shaking his head and smiling to tell her it wasn't bad news. It was good.

No, it was the best. The greatest news ever. "Charlie, I am so happy. I can't tell you how much I wanted this for you. You earned this. You always managed to succeed at anything you chose. I can't believe you, my son, have chosen to become an international financier."

"How did you always know that? Why didn't you ever try to make me do what the rest of the valley was doing? Doing the work that you, Ben, and even Ian, Joey and Shane were doing? How did you know I was so different and why did you let me be?"

Laughing with a choking sound, Jack remembered all the times he tried to support Charlie's quirks and differences. Jack was smart enough as a father to respect them. "Your intelligence was always higher than anyone else I ever knew. Your insatiable curiosity and thirst for knowledge told me you were meant for more than anything so ordinary as working here. I knew you were special and gifted and wonderfully different. I would have been content if you decided to settle down here and be like me or Ben or Ian. But

I just knew you were destined for so much more, Charlie Rydell. My extraordinary son."

"You'll be okay with us gone so long then?"

"I'll miss you like crazy. But your destiny isn't here. It never really was, Charlie. I always knew that deep down in my gut. I'm just grateful I got to raise you for a precious little while. But your destiny requires that you seek change and see the world. All I could ever want is to see you reaching your full potential."

"Do you think I'm taking Cami away from all that she needs?"

"How? Not if you two are starting the adventure of a lifetime. Look what she gains and what you both gain together."

He sniffed. "Thanks. I needed to hear that."

Jack let out a small laugh. "You, my overachieving son, rarely need to hear encouragement from me. But you have it regardless. You proposed to Cami on the Baltic Sea... yes, my son, you are no longer a local from River's End."

"Dad?"

"Yeah, Charlie?"

"River's End is still the best place to be from."

"Yes... *to be from.*"

Charlie chuckled. "You know what I mean. It's a good place to grow up and you were the best father ever. I couldn't have gotten where I am, and I now hope to go, not without your help and continued support and prodding. You never once insisted that I train the horses or help AJ in the barn or stay on the ranch. You always knew who I was and never required me to be anything I wasn't. Not even when I failed to go along with the rest of the ranch."

"You never failed anything to me."

"Yeah, maybe not to you. My father. Thank you, Dad. For everything."

Jack nodded, and tears filled his eyes as if Charlie could

see him nodding. He finally croaked out. "You are forever welcome. Talk to you soon."

"You too, Dad."

Erin was holding their baby girl, and she looked at Jack curiously. "Cami said yes. They are staying in Europe. They intend to spend a few years abroad and work somewhere else. Somewhere probably halfway across the world."

"I'm glad he'll have Cami at his side and they'll do it together. But are you okay, Jack?"

"I am. I'm just going to miss him, but also—"

"Also?"

"I'm just a rancher here. I could help Ben fulfill his dreams and follow his path, even when he so suddenly veered off. I knew I could always help Ben. But I stressed and doubted that I could do the same for Charlie. What he needed in life is the polar opposite of what I know about. Charlie needs the entire world. He was always just... different. Crazy different. And now he's going to seek his own path."

Erin smiled and stepped closer, brushing her hand through his hair. It sprung over his forehead and she repeated her caress in a tender gesture of care. "You doubted your parental skills as a father?"

He put his hand to the silky head of his sleeping toddler and leaned down to kiss her. "I did. I do. I always will. But I have one son living next door to me, and another living halfway across the world."

"And what about your daughter?"

"Maybe she'll end up somewhere in between. Whatever happens, she will always have you and me to help her find her dream, her path, and to fulfill her destiny. Whether she chooses to remain alongside this river beside us or reaches out for the stars like Charlie."

"And your love and pride for both your sons and their

chosen destinies shines in every interaction you have with them. And that, Jack Rydell, is your greatest gift to them, and what you can give to our child too."

Jack smiled as he stared out the window. A nagging sadness made his heart ache in knowing Charlie would be gone for such a long time. Even if he were not physically there with them, a soaring sensation lifted his heart in knowing that a piece of him managed to make its way across the world.

Destiny... Never the same for any two people and never a set course, but a zig-zagging path of trial and error, and more often than not, it is pure luck.

Jack's sons had finally fulfilled their destinies, just as he and Erin continued to live right where he always wanted to be. Beside Erin, Jack continued to expand his family's legacy and rescue more horses.

It was even better because of all the people who now loved him, be they at River's End or all the way across the ocean. They would always be together and connected, their destinies irretrievably entwined.

The Rydell name and legacy and even the ranch and resort were testament to that.

ABOUT THE AUTHOR

Leanne Davis has earned a business degree from Western Washington University. She worked for several years in the construction management field before turning full time to writing. She lives in the Seattle area with her husband and two children. When she isn't writing, she and her family enjoy camping trips to destinations all across Washington State, many of which become the settings for her novels.